A Note on the Author

MICHAEL PITRE is a graduate of Louisiana State University, where, as a double major in history and creative writing, he studied with Andrei Codrescu and Mark Jude Poirier. He joined the US Marines in 2002, deploying twice to Iraq and attaining the rank of Captain, before leaving the service in 2010 to get his MBA at Loyola. He lives in New Orleans. *Fives and Twenty-Fives* is his first novel.

D1078170

MICHAEL PITRE

FIVES AND TWENTY-FIVES

BLOOMSBURY

LONDON · OXFORD · NEW YORK · NEW DELHI · SYDNEY

Bloomsbury Paperbacks
An imprint of Bloomsbury Publishing Plc

50 Bedford Square
London
WC1B 3DP
UK

1385 Broadway
New York
NY 10018
USA

www.bloomsbury.com

BLOOMSBURY and the Diana logo are trademarks of Bloomsbury Publishing Plc

First published in Great Britain 2014
This paperback edition first published in 2015

British Library Cataloguing-in-Publication Data
A catalogue record for this book is available from the British Library.

ISBN: HB: 978-1-4088-5444-0
TPB: 978-1-4088-5445-7
PB: 978-1-4088-5446-4
ePub: 978-1-4088-5443-3

2 4 6 8 10 9 7 5 3 1

Printed and bound in Great Britain by CPI Group (UK) Ltd, Croydon CR0 4YY

To find out more about our authors and books visit www.bloomsbury.com.
Here you will find extracts, author interviews, details of forthcoming events
and the option to sign up for our newsletters.

For Stephen
For Shawn

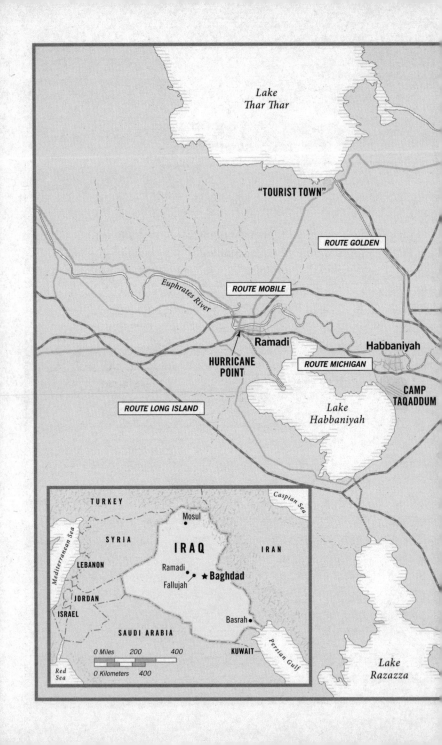

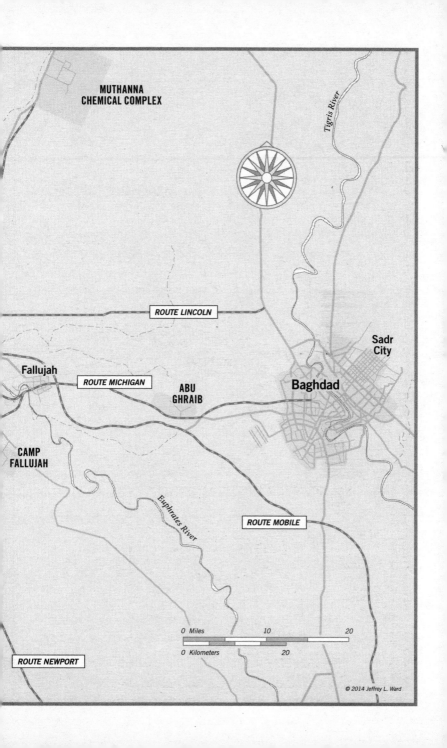

FIVES
AND
TWENTY-
FIVES

To: Secretary of the Navy
From: 1st Lt. P. E. Donovan, USMC

Via: Headquarters Marine Corps

I hereby resign my commission as an officer in the United States Marine Corps.

The Secretary of the Navy, acting on behalf of the President, may accept an officer's resignation subject to the needs of the Marine Corps, the completion of the officer's obligation, and the character of the officer's service.

I have fulfilled my obligation. I cannot imagine how the Marine Corps could still need or want me. And though the character of my service is a matter of debate, I ask that my resignation be accepted.

Respectfully submitted,
P. E. Donovan
First Lieutenant

THE MARINE I KNEW

I'm running through the desert. I know it by the sound of my breath.

Caustic air scours my lungs as I settle into a panting cadence opposite the rhythm of the rifle bouncing against my chest. My flak jacket doesn't quite fit. The straps float an inch off my shoulders, bringing thirty pounds of armor plate down hard against my spine each time a bootheel strikes hard-packed dirt. The Kevlar around my neck traps sweat and grime that froths into an abrasive paste. I feel patches of skin behind my ears start to rub away.

The afternoon sun washes out my vision; other senses compensate. Desiccated shrubs strewn with garbage bags and empty plastic bottles crunch under my boots. Farther up my body, the gear clipped to my webbing clatters like a tinker's cart. The tourniquet I always keep in easy reach of my left hand taps against my uniform blouse. Thirty-round magazines rattle in ammunition pouches around my waist. Thirty-round capacity, but never loaded with more than twenty-eight, I know. Save the spring. Prevent jams.

It all moves with me in a way so familiar, so exact, that for a moment I think this could only be real.

My eyes adjust and I see the convoy in front of me. Four Humvees and two seven-ton trucks. I understand suddenly, and with queasy certainty, why I'm running. I need to warn them about the pressure switch, hidden in a crack in the road. It's a length of surgical tubing stitched through with copper wire. The driver won't see it. They don't have a chance.

The lead Humvee rolls over the crack. The front tire collapses the tubing. Wires touch. Voltage from a hidden battery reaches a length of detonation cord wrapped around artillery shells, buried with jugs of gasoline and soap chips.

I wave my arms, a heartbeat before the whole nasty serpent shrieks to life, and fill my lungs to cry out.

And then, like always, I wake up.

I kick the sheets from my small mattress and search across the dim corners of my studio apartment. Thin bands of morning sun seep through the window blinds. I'm still tired. I consider going back to sleep, but the nine empty beer bottles on the kitchenette counter promise me I'll only twist and groan, searching for a position that might ease my headache without putting additional pressure on my bladder. Better to get up and face it.

It's a trade-off, drinking to fall asleep. I used to come out ahead in the bargain, but lately I've hit a point of diminishing returns. Three or four won't do the job anymore. Worse, I've taken to rich, hoppy craft brews that I supposed would make me feel better about the whole sad routine. No committed drunk would waste money on topflight beer, right? I'm a young gentleman. A distinguished veteran entitled to some relaxation during this brief, graduate-school interlude, after which I'll emerge fully formed into the business world, armed with a new vocabulary by which to describe the more intense flavors of these nice, heavy ales. The hangovers are more intense, too. A price to pay for the sake of my self-respect, certainly. And with self-respect in mind, I decide to punish myself with a long run.

The air carries an unfamiliar chill. It's the first morning of true winter in New Orleans. Dew clings to the cool grass of the St.

Charles neutral ground. I weave to avoid the green streetcars. The damage bleeds away, and pushing into a fourth mile, I feel good.

These morning runs once formed the cornerstone of a meticulous program meant to burn away that small, but persistent, gut of mine. The mark of weakness that made me stand out against the phalanx of impossibly lean lieutenants back in Quantico. I've abandoned that dream, and running is more enjoyable for it, a way to center my thoughts for the day ahead.

I think through my course assignments. Finance. Accounting. Marketing. Papers coming due at the end of the semester. Readings for class discussion and outlines to review for exams. I should find the time to call my mother and father, back home in Birmingham. And my sister in Mobile.

Wait. Do I have a social commitment tonight? Someone coming into town?

Zahn. Damn it. I told Zahn I would meet him out.

Zahn found my e-mail address a few months back. I'm not sure how. I've kept myself off the Internet as best I can, but out of nowhere he started sending me notes about coming to New Orleans for something. A wedding, I think. Rambling notes untouched by punctuation, all lowercase. Only a few years younger than me and it's like these kids speak a different language. I always thought they hated me, Zahn and the other corporals. I'm surprised he wants to see me.

I go home, shower, and spend the rest of my Saturday finishing term papers, idly thumbing through class notes while staring out my open window. The cold breeze feels good, and the idea of a beer resting on the windowsill grows to an urge.

I resist the temptation. A beer or two in the afternoon will only blunt the six I'll want before bed.

I've finished studying by the late afternoon. I imagined that business school would offer more of a challenge. Now I wish it weren't so easy. With more coursework, I might have a legitimate pretext for canceling on Zahn.

I spend a few hours crafting excuses. Evaluating the feasibility of various lies. But like an automaton, I pull into my boots at the appointed hour and dig through the pile of books next to my bed for something productive to read on the streetcar. My Advanced Finance text, heavy and intimidating, anchors a messy heap of notes and paperback case studies. Next to it, in a neatly organized stack, rests my ever-expanding sailboat research library.

John Vigor's *Twenty Small Sailboats to Take You Anywhere* sits atop the pile, catching my attention first. A compendium of Albergs and Bristols, Pearsons and Catalinas, all readily available for salvage in the marinas of America. A legion of boatyard derelicts just waiting for rescue, left behind by the downturn, or in the case of New Orleans, the storm.

It wouldn't take much work to bring a derelict back to life, or so I've read. Start with a fiberglass keel, punctured and scarred. Fill the divots with fairing compound and apply fresh topside paint above the waterline. Sand and oil the teak brightwork. Polish the brass. Mend the lines and refloat the hull. Stock provisions and hang new sails.

A resurrected sailboat can take you anywhere, and quietly.

I reach for Vigor's book, though I know it almost by heart at this point. But before closing my grip on the glossy cover, I take a moment to consider the tattered paperback behind it. It's a novel. Wedged, almost hidden, against the baseboard trim. I shake it loose from the stack and inspect its yellowing pages, the scarring left behind by its missing cover. Grains of sand slide out from between the pages.

It's Dodge's copy of *The Adventures of Huckleberry Finn*, complete with his insane brand of marginalia, half in Arabic and half in English.

Leaving sailboats behind, I slide the ragged, coverless orphan into my back pocket. I chastise myself, knowing it's something of a ploy. I'm hoping Zahn will notice it there, rolled up and dog-eared, and mention Dodge. It would give me a chance to talk about him. Who knows? Maybe Zahn's heard from the guy.

I walk to St. Charles Avenue and, after waiting for the streetcar in the cold, arrive at the bar thirty minutes late. It's one of those drop-ceiling places. Uptown, near campus. Pool tables and nasty fluorescent lights. It's cold. I pull the jacket tighter around my shoulders and push, with my hands in my pockets, through the thick, plastic sheeting that serves as a door.

Zahn's voice hits me all at once, like a belt to the face. It's how I remember him. Barking orders into a pack of young men. But I don't see him. Just young guys in suits, all huddled around a touch-screen trivia game on the bar. A shaggy giant shoves his way through the pack, unhemmed pants making an untidy mound of fabric around his shoes.

His wide frame towers over them, and he shouts, "There! There! The bottom's a different color!"

With a sinking heart, I realize—it's Zahn.

He paws at the screen with the thick, limp digits of an all-day drunk, light beer sloshing from the plastic cup in his other hand.

I walk over and tap him on the shoulder. He spins around, takes a moment to place me, then smiles and wraps me in a bear hug. My head settles in the middle of his chest. Beer spills down my back.

"Sir," he slurs softly.

"No," I mumble into his shirt. "Not anymore." And I realize, suddenly, how happy I am to see him.

The rest of his suit fits worse than the pants, like he borrowed it from his dad. He's gained weight and grown a beard. The Zahn I knew kept his blond hair close-cropped against his scalp. Now it's so long and knotted, it's hard to tell where the hair ends and the beard begins.

6

He's not wearing his wedding ring, or the dog tags to which he once kept his wedding ring taped. I search for the Marine I knew, behind the bad suit and the swollen face. I can't find him.

Zahn introduces me to his friends. High school buddies who haven't seen him in years, apparently. They've all just come from a rehearsal dinner, but I get the sense that Zahn's the only drunk one.

"I'm buying you a beer, sir," he says. "Whatcha drinking? I'm drinking beer. Let me go get two. Stay put, all right? Don't go no place."

He lumbers down the bar and leaves me with them. Salesmen playing the part of young gentlemen. They take turns keeping me occupied. Square up, one at a time, and launch volleys of firm handshakes. Practiced eye contact learned from their fathers. Glowing praise for the potential customer.

"Hey. Really great to meet you."

"Walter's been talking about you. Talking up a storm, man. You two and the war, you know?"

"Hey, it's really great that you came out to see him."

They step away in twos and threes to convene hushed, impromptu meetings, as if these councils of war are out of earshot. Or that their one-on-one, fraternity-rush routine has me too distracted to listen in. They aren't, and I'm not.

I hear them discussing Zahn. What to do about him.

It's killing their buzz, this depressive oaf in their midst. This almost-forgotten interloper who's hijacked their night. All these guys in their midtwenties with their nice suits. Zahn snuck his way in, and they don't know him anymore. I see it clearly. Zahn does not.

It dawns on me why they're being so affable. Why they're in such a hurry to make a friend of me, asking questions about my life, questions about business school, questions about New Orleans. They act genuinely interested, but always bring the conversation back to

Zahn, mentioning offhand "his problems," inching closer to the clinical with their language. Problems. Issues. Disorders.

They're manufacturing a bond, I see, for later in the night, when Zahn inevitably passes out or puts his hand through a window. One of his friends will take me aside and say, "Hey, man. You mind taking him home with you? We can't get him into the hotel like this."

I'm overcome by a wave of nausea and begin constructing an excuse to leave early and take Zahn, my old corporal, with me. Something that won't embarrass him. Something that makes sense. Anything to get him out of here.

Which is when a fight breaks out at the back of the bar.

A pint glass shatters against the cinder-block wall and a young voice shouts, "You wanna throw down, motherfucker?"

Immediately, I suspect Zahn, missing on his trip to the bar for over five minutes, has found trouble. I hustle over to the standoff with the rest. Five of them and five of us. But Zahn is nowhere to be seen.

I assess the situation. A Tulane undergraduate threw the pint glass, I gather, by way of response to a perceived slight from one of Zahn's meeker friends. The undergraduate has the collar popped on his ratty polo shirt and his baseball cap turned around. Brown hair falls loose from his hat, draping across his forehead just so.

He advances menacingly on Zahn's friend until the poor kid is backed up to the wall. Then he leans into the kid's face with arms extended, flexes glamour muscles big and useless from long hours at the Tulane gym, and smiles like he's been waiting all day for this.

I step closer, thinking maybe I can reason with the guy. Maybe he'll guess by my age and demeanor that I'm a graduate student. Maybe he's even seen me around campus. We're classmates, of a sort, and surely that's enough to sidestep a pointless bar fight. I put a hand on his shoulder, about to say something like "Hey, calm down, okay? We'll leave. No problem."

But before I can speak, he turns around and shoves me. Hard, with two hands firm to my upper chest. Happy for the escalation. He smiles, and I know he's going to have this.

So I set my back foot.

Then Zahn appears. Like a bowling ball striking a fresh set of pins, he pushes through the crowd and positions himself between me and Popped Collar.

Immediately sensing the situation has changed, Popped Collar moves to throw a punch. But Zahn steps inside and takes him by the wrist. Then, while Popped Collar tries to fix his feet, Zahn reaches around with his other hand and takes hold of his upper arm. With a quick pivot outside, Zahn locks Popped Collar's elbow and shoulder, bending him over at the waist. The poor bastard gasps. How embarrassing.

But that's just the opening salvo. Just a quick burst of pain to distract. With a palm firmly in the small of his target's back, Zahn applies the full weight of his frame as unnatural torque against the ligaments and connecting tissues of Popped Collar's shoulder, elbow, and wrist joints.

Popped Collar lets out a high-pitched groan, almost a whine, as new, more urgent pain shoots through his arm, this burst delivered without regard to gentlemen's rules. Zahn, controlling his target as he would a bicycle, walks Popped Collar into the corner and pins him there with a knee deep to the inner thigh.

"The difference between me and you," Zahn tells Popped Collar with a scary kind of calm, "is that I'm serious about killing you."

And I finally recognize him. The Marine I knew.

Popped Collar recognizes Zahn, too. A blood memory, a cold dread crawling up his spine, carries the realization that this is a predator.

I glance back at Zahn's friends, gamely keeping their poise. But they can't hide their constant, nearly imperceptible steps backward.

They're terrified, and it makes me smile. It's Zahn who's the grown man now. And his friends? Children wearing their dads' suits.

I take note of my pulse. It's steady. Hardly elevated at all. Most people, Zahn's friends for instance, would call this a fight. But I would never think to call it that.

We're in the wilderness. The place without rules. I discovered it on the day when I knew for the first time, really understood, that a stranger was trying to kill me and nothing would change his mind. No words to save me. No police to call. And in the end, nothing between me and the dead man in the ditch but the will I had to put him there, to break his body into wet pieces without taking the time to wonder, what happened? Where'd that spark go? That soul? An animal doesn't think about that. It doesn't cross his mind.

Popped Collar makes a move to get free, like he might still have some fight left in him, some pride. But Zahn just tightens his grip and puts more weight in his knee. Popped Collar winces.

"Listen to me," Zahn says softly. "I'm gonna let you stand up, now. And you're gonna walk straight out that front door without looking back at me."

Zahn wants to say more, I can tell. He wants to explain to Popped Collar how easy it would be to crush his windpipe. Zahn wants to teach, dispassionately, the method. How to step inside your target's stance and gouge for his eyeballs. How, while your target is in a panic trying to save his eyes, he'll leave his throat open. How to sweep the legs out from under your target while keeping a firm grip on his arm. How, while your target is defenseless on the ground, you can send the edge of your bootheel into his exposed throat, just so.

But Zahn's not a corporal anymore, and the man he's pinned in the corner isn't a junior Marine in need of instruction. So, Zahn keeps it simple. "I'll watch you die and not feel a thing," he says. "Understand? Stuff like this? It's fun for you. To me? It's nothing at all."

Zahn gives the words a moment to sink in before releasing his grip. As Popped Collar stands up, my fingertips tingle at the thought that this guy might be dumb enough to open his mouth. But he goes right for the door without saying a word. His friends hasten to follow him out, in an orderly fashion, as they say. Kindergartners headed outside for the fire drill, holding hands.

Zahn's friends leave, too, after a few quick excuses and good-byes. So Zahn and I go back to the bar, finishing our beers like nothing happened.

Then Zahn notices the book in my back pocket. I'd forgotten all about it. "Dodge give you that book, sir?" he asks with a smile. "Or did you steal it?"

"I'm not really sure," I say, feeling guilty at how reliably my ploy has worked. "I found it in my pack the day after he left. Either he left it there, or it accidentally got mixed in with my gear after Ramadi . . ." I swallow. Embarrassed by how offhand I use the word. As if Ramadi were an experience shared between the two of us. As if it weren't much worse for him.

"I read it as a kid," I say, before we can settle on the topic. "Just giving it another crack. He left some notes in here. Mostly in Arabic, but the ones in English, they're pretty funny." After a sip, I add, "Really, though. Quit it with the 'sir.'"

"You ever hear from him?"

"Who? Dodge?" I say, like the idea of finding him never occurred to me. "Never even knew his real name."

"Doc does, I think. You ever get in touch with him?"

Doc. Some of my guilt evaporates as the ploy backfires, and Zahn makes it clear that if I want to ask questions about Dodge, I'll have to discuss Doc Pleasant.

Clearly, Zahn hasn't forgotten. And why should he?

The bartender walks over before we can get into it, telling us we should leave.

We walk back to my apartment the long way, enjoying the cool of the night. We chat like normal friends, forgetting all the facts that should make that impossible.

At my apartment, Zahn sees just how I'm making out: a tattered old couch, a lonely chair, and a mattress wedged into a corner. It seems to set him at ease.

He starts by investigating my book piles. "I'm noticing a real pattern here, sir."

"Yeah? What's that?"

"This one set of books? All about the boats? Kept nice and neat. This other set? A clusterfuck abortion. I get the sense that you don't think much of advanced finance."

I go to the refrigerator and grab two beers. "Well, that's not exactly true. Finance isn't my favorite, but . . . I don't mind it. Always liked math."

"Why are you in school, anyway? Thought you finished with all that a while back?"

"Getting my master's. The G.I. Bill is too good to pass up." I open his beer for him. "How about you? Thinking of using your benefits?"

I regret the question instantly. We had a nice conversation going, with none of the rank-based tension that so often poisoned our Humvee, and I had to ruin it, jumping in like the chipper lieutenant of old, with sprightly, unsolicited advice.

But Zahn doesn't seem too worried about it. "Never really been the college type," he says, and we leave it at that.

We empty my fridge of beer, get ourselves really drunk. He sits on the couch while I lie faceup on the floor, and we stay up all night talking. We talk about everything. About Gunny Stout. About Doc Pleasant and Dodge.

We talk about the day Marceau started tap dancing. It began as combat satire, an attempt to blunt the tension of a mortar attack. With the alert siren wailing late one night, and the platoon scrambling into their body armor in advance of the impacts, Marceau cut a lane through the hut with a few self-stylized shim-sham moves, held his helmet against his chest like a chorus girl's top hat, and ended with a real windmill flourish. That became his trademark. And somehow, despite the dozen times I saw him do it, it was always surprising and hilarious. He even ordered a set of instructional DVDs to watch on his laptop during off-hours, earnestly devoting himself to the art and craft of tap.

Later, when we run out of funny stories, we talk about Gomez. Zahn says he went to see her in Dallas and met her sister.

When I first ask the question, I refer to her as Sergeant Gomez. But when he answers, he calls her Michelle. It's an admission on his part, as if I didn't already know. But it seems important to him, this confession. I wonder if it has anything to do with his missing wedding ring.

I don't press him on it.

"What about you?" I ask. "How have you been?"

He shrugs. "Divorced."

"I was about to ask. Sorry to hear that."

"And I have the headaches. The kind that put you on the floor. Useless, you know? Just . . . losing time. Hour after hour. Waking up places, not knowing how I got there."

"I know," I say, and somehow it's the truth.

"I won't say it's why I can't hold a job. Doesn't help, though. I've been to the VA, but the concussions aren't in my file. Not service related."

"Because you don't have a Purple Heart," I say, before he has to.

"Nope. Don't have that."

It's my fault, of course. When Zahn went down, we requested an urgent casualty evacuation, watched his temperature spike and his pulse slow subthirty. But it didn't count. He wasn't out for more than thirty seconds, and there weren't any holes, no blood. Just a concussion. So no Purple Heart. That was the rule back then. I didn't know it. I would've lied on the paperwork if I'd known.

"And I have the bad dreams," he continues.

"Yeah, I used to be like that." I sit up, roll my shoulders back, and present an image of confidence. Like when I was a lieutenant. It helps me lie. "I have dreams, still. But it's different now. A couple times a week, I'm in the sky over the big lake. Just watching. Marines at Taqaddum load up convoys. Men from Ramadi creep out in their taxicabs, nursing those old crates through the checkpoints, perfectly calm. All around Habbaniyah and Fallujah. Right under the plateau. Right under our noses with those wired-up shells in the trunk."

"Yeah," he sighs. "I know that one."

"Except lately I'm having a different one. I'm crossing the Atlantic in a sailboat. All alone. A storm's coming, a gnarly, black squall-line. But I'm not even nervous. I just rig the storm sails and the weather vane to keep the boat facing into the wind and strap myself to the rail. The storm grows and the waves crash over me, but I don't panic. I just let the wind take me, not scared at all."

"Huh," Zahn grunts, looking for the point.

"It just takes time," I lie. "First you're there. Then you're watching. Then, a little while after that, you're having different dreams entirely. Just takes time."

He gets up to grab the last two beers. "What about Doc Pleasant?" he asks again. "Ever hear from him? He might need to hear something like that."

"No. I mean, I know he lives down here. Louisiana, somewhere."

"You should find him. Check in."

"I'll think about it."

"Might be good for you, too, sir."

"Don't call me that."

From: Hospitalman Third Class Lester Pleasant
To: Commander, First Marine Expeditionary Force

Re: Charge Sheet

I have been advised by counsel that I am charged with violations of Article 121 of the Uniform Code of Military Justice, namely larceny and wrongful appropriation of government property.

I understand that I am subject to discharge from the service under other than honorable conditions. I understand that I am entitled to have my case heard by an administrative separation board.

I hereby waive my right to a hearing. I will accept the ruling of my commanding officer. I have no statement to make in my own defense.

LESTER PLEASANT

Marceau made coffee so thick and strong you could stand your spoon up in it. Said he learned to make coffee down in the basement of the Cedar Rapids First Methodist. His parents would bring him along when they set up for meetings and have him make the coffee. Something to do, I guess. Something to keep him busy.

Addicts like it strong, but little Marceau didn't know that. Just grew up thinking this was, like, normal. That coffee any thinner than tar wasn't worth shit.

The other Marines in the platoon hated it at first. Banned him from the coffee mess. But after a while, when those days without sleep started piling on? Sergeant Gomez put Marceau back on coffee detail. And naturally she chewed his ass a little bit. Like it was his idea in the first place to stop making coffee. Marceau didn't mind. Just smiled. Never seemed to get to him, that sort of thing.

Real coffee, like the kind Marceau used to make? It's the only reason I keep coming to these meetings. Sure, I haven't got much else going on these days. But real coffee? A goddamn good reason to come to meetings even if I did.

I take a three-swallow sip as a bearded roughneck goes up to get his one-month chip. Just came in from the Gulf, this guy. An hour off the crew boat, still wearing a blue jumpsuit smeared with muck from the bottom of the ocean. Didn't even stop at home to change his clothes or get a hot shower. We give the guy a round of applause, and he smiles like he just won something.

He wanted that chip so bad. Wanted it in his pocket before driving home past those highway bars. Places that would cash his check, no problem. I picture him jumping off that crew boat in a panic, throwing gravel as he peels away from the docks, running red lights all the way to the Houma First Baptist. A classic white-knuckle. Keeping a death grip on that chip, like it's a lifeline. Like it's real. But sooner or later, when he realizes that it's just a goddamn poker chip, he'll let go. Walk down to the bar, feel himself falling, and enjoy it.

The applause fades and the meeting ends.

The Baptists stand in a circle to say the Lord's Prayer.

The atheists gather over by the coffee to ask the universe, or whatever, for serenity.

I walk between them, out through the double glass doors and into the quiet parking lot.

Night turned cold since the meeting started. First cold night this winter. I jog to the truck with my hands down my pockets. The heater's been broke for years, and the window on the driver's side won't roll up all the way. I tore out the carpet so it won't stink when rain pools up on the floorboards. I never lock the door, just do a quick walk around before getting behind the wheel. Habit, I guess.

My trauma bag sits on the passenger seat. Another old habit. I got my scissors and gauze in there. A few rolls of tape. I got a real compression bandage, and a combat tourniquet, too. Made it myself. Tied a length of webbing around a wooden spoon handle and sewed on some Velcro. Works pretty good.

I got splints cut from old beadboard and a twelve-foot length of rope. I even got a packet of QuikClot. I stole that from the field hospital in Bahraia and smuggled it out through Kuwait when they sent me home. Reacts with the iron in your blood, this stuff. Cauterizes everything. Sprinkle it on a bad wound, then watch it catch fire. Smell it burning up.

I got it all stuffed in my old backpack from high school. One of those green JanSports. Fits okay. Wish I had more room, though. Wish I could organize it just right. I need a few more compartments. All I got is the big one for books and the little one for pens.

It's all covered in black marker. Things I scribbled on there back in the day. Band names, mostly. Dumb ones, too. Bands even Dodge liked. I even got Judas Priest on there. When I look at that now, I'm like, *Fuck Judas Priest*. And anyway, they're like cave paintings to me. Scribbled by some prehistoric dude with a torch, a charcoal nub, and some time on his hands.

Got almost everything I need in there, though. And tactically rigged, too. Straps and slides all secured with electrical tape. Nothing dangles. Nothing makes noise. But I still wish I had more compartments.

I leave the parking lot and turn south on the levee road. It's late and cold, but Dad's still out in the shed, probably. My blood gets up just thinking about it, and now I'll stew about it the whole ride home. Stupid.

It wasn't a coincidence, him starting in with that tractor nonsense right when I got home. Needed a distraction from my bullshit, and I don't blame him. But it's years now, and he's still trying to fix that thing. He's clumsy, too. He'll knock over a jack stand one night, grabbing for a wrench or something. He'll kick it, not watching where he puts his feet. You have to watch where you put your feet.

He ran away to that shed, and I went to my room and put my trauma bag together. Two boxers in their corners, waiting years for the bell. And this whole time I've been thinking about the fastest way out to that shed. Organizing my trauma bag, too. Making it perfect.

It helped me gather my thoughts, at first. Helped calm me down. I even took the trauma bag with me to my first job interview. An ambulance job. Thought I'd just walk in the front door and tell the receptionist, "Hey, I'm a corpsman just home from Iraq. Was a combat medic for the Marines over there. Seen everything. Gunshot wounds. Traumatic amputations. Everything. So should I just jump in the next ambulance going out and get started, or what?"

It wasn't so simple, of course. Besides the application, they wanted to see things. Military documents and whatnot. I went all hot and red, lied and told the lady I had all that stuff out in my truck. She looked at me, with this heavy backpack on my shoulder, and raised her eyebrows. Like, "What you got in there, then?"

I went out to my truck and punched the ceiling. Over and over, until my knuckles bled. Fucking idiot. Did I think they wouldn't ask?

So, I sat around for a few more months, until I ran out of money. Then I went back to work at the oil-change place. Same place I worked at in high school, same stuff I was doing before. All my high school friends are gone, years now. Finishing up college at Nicholls or working offshore. Some, like Landry and Paul, are just fucking around in New Orleans.

I've been up there to see them a few times, Landry and Paul. They still message me once in a while saying I should come for the weekend. Still trying to convince me to move out my dad's house. Landry messaged me just a few days ago. He and Paul are starting a new band, and he wants me to come see them play. Just the two of them, trying something new. There'll be girls at the gig, he says. College girls.

I get home a little faster than I should, driving too fast, turning off the highway and throwing gravel. Lights are on in the shed. Just like I knew they would be. Stupid.

I park my truck and carry my trauma bag up the front steps. The door squeals on its hinges and I think about the rusted jack stands holding that damn tractor up. Those threads are gonna give out one day, and that tractor is gonna fall over. I imagine Dad pinned under the axle with his leg all crushed and bleeding out. All that thick, red blood. Thick with oxygen not going where it's supposed to. Oxygen just soaking into the dirt.

Those spots where blood soaks in? Right into the dirt? Plants always grow there. I never knew that before. We'd convoy by the same places all the time, and all those places where I knew there'd been a lot of blood? Sure enough: green, healthy plants.

But Dad . . . he's always been clumsy. Knocked out my top-left incisor when I was twelve. We were working on my truck, the one that became mine anyway, and he spun around without looking and clocked me with an eight-pound wrench. Put a nice, big gap in the side of my smile. When I enlisted, it was like wearing a sign: LESTER PLEASANT: JOINED THE NAVY TO ESCAPE SOUTHERN POVERTY. I never thought of myself that way. Didn't even know my missing tooth was all that obvious. Navy sure keyed in on it, though.

The other sailors up at corpsman school—all those junior achievers?—they talked all about how the Navy would set them up for swank paramedic jobs back home. How they were only in it for the college money.

"College money," they'd say. "I'll do four years at the pharmacy handing out pills, then go to nursing school with that college money."

Then they'd look at me, like four years of my company was the price they'd have to pay. But goddamn if I didn't show them the minute I got my hands on a trauma kit. It was like I was born for it. They could see it, too. All those achievers. So could the instructors. None of them could lay a chest tube like me, rig a splint, or do a field tracheotomy. I aced all the written tests, too. A natural.

22

I made first in the class. So, at graduation they gave me my choice of duty station. I picked corpsman, First Marine Expeditionary Force. This one sailor, this girl from Ohio, actually laughed out loud during the ceremony. Like, "Why the hell would he choose the *Marines*?"

If I met her today? I'd tell her that in all my time with the Marines I never *once* heard the words "college money."

When I first got home, though, it felt like I'd gone back in time. Starting at the welcome-home party. So, are you going to college, now? Gonna use that college money?

Dad put that party together for me even after I asked him not to. I don't think he ever understood what "sent home" meant. He was just proud, I guess. Real proud.

Uncle Chuck and Aunt Linda let him have the party out at their camp on Bayou Teche. Hung a banner that said GOD BLESS AMERICA. You know that banner you get at Walmart? With the block letters and the flag? Uncle Chuck and Aunt Linda paid for everything. Invited a lot of people I didn't know. Everyone brought kids. All night, they jumped in and out of the pool, screaming. My god, they would not stop screaming.

My cousins all drove in from Baton Rouge, too. They were just starting college, then. They all gathered around and asked me the questions.

Kill anyone? What's it *like* to shoot a machine gun? Must've been hot in the desert, huh?

Then they started telling stories to each other, mostly about bars. Not even stories, really. Just who was there, how drunk they were. After a while, they started talking about what they'd do in Baton Rouge that night, so I wandered over to the ice chest to grab a Coke.

On the way, I heard Uncle Chuck say to my dad, "I don't understand what he means by 'general discharge.' I tell you what, if it ain't honorable, it's the other kind. Hell, in the Air Force, I got an honorable discharge just for three years sitting around Germany. Ain't hard."

And I can't say that I went blind, exactly. Because I saw things. But for a few minutes I was outside the world. I heard it, though. Like I had sat down at the kitchen table to listen while a couple of grown men in the living room beat the shit out of each other.

The world came back to me as we were grappling across the patio, each of us with the other in a headlock. I tasted my own blood and felt Uncle Chuck's blood smearing across my cheek from his busted lip. I heard the kids screaming again, but no splashing in the pool. My cousins, Uncle Chuck's sons, pulled us apart with him screaming at me and calling me a fucking psychopath, and both of us trying hard to break free and keep throwing punches.

I felt another hand, all rough and calloused, pressed against my forehead. It was my father.

"Please, Les," he whispered in my ear. "Okay? Please."

So I gave in. Went limp until my cousins let go of me. All the while, my dad kept a gentle pressure on my forehead. He walked me back away from the crowded patio, then tried to hug me. But I shrugged him off. As I walked away, I heard him apologizing to Uncle Chuck and Aunt Linda. They were lecturing him about how much they'd spent on putting the party together and how ungrateful I'd been acting even before the fight.

That was the end of the hero talk. The end of family holidays, too. I drove my truck down the levee and found a spot under some cypress trees by the river with no noise but the bugs, nothing on the ground but branches, and all the leaves exactly where the trees had put them.

After a few hours calming myself down, I went home and apologized to my dad. That's when I decided to stay in Houma with him. Ditched the idea of moving out and getting my own place.

Dad. He's gonna freeze out there in that shed. I walk to my bedroom window and feel cold air trickling in. Am I gonna have to drag him out of that shed by his collar?

I shake it off, all this frustration, and go back to my computer, where the message from Paul and Landry is still open on the screen. It's a Facebook invite from a new metal band they're calling Vermin Uprising. They have a show in New Orleans. Some bar called Siberia. Maybe they're just inviting everyone they know to this thing. But what the hell? I'll just drive up for the night and say hello. I click on the accept button, then drift around Facebook awhile. Looking at people I used to know from high school, all married with kids.

On a whim, I decide to look for Dodge. I use his real name at first—Kateb. But nothing comes back. So I do a search on Google for "Iraqi interpreter Dodge." Again, I get nothing.

He might have changed his name, which wouldn't have been a bad idea. Or maybe he's dead. I give up, close the laptop, and go back to the window to watch the lights in the shed, wondering when he'll finish up out there so I can go to sleep.

To: Mr. Kateb al-Hariri. Sousse, Tunisia
From: The U.S. Department of State

*The Bureau of Consular Affairs has been unable to verify that you
were ever employed as an interpreter by U.S. forces serving in
support of Operation Iraqi Freedom. Detailed records, made available by the Department of Defense, contain no mention of your
name, nor of the code name (Dodge) you claim you were issued. As a
result, your petition for special immigrant status has been denied.
You can appeal this ruling by submitting a new Form I-360, with
additional details, documents, and references for caseworker review.
The 2009 National Defense Authorization Act allows for the issuance
of up to 500 Special Immigrant Visas to Iraqi translators and interpreters who worked for the U.S. military, but demand for these visas
is expected to exceed the annual limit. Please consider applying for a
student visa instead.*

THESE BOYS, THESE MISSOURI BOYS

The Americans sent me this letter via the standard Tunisian post. Someone at the postal center, some secret policeman, opened the letter before the carrier brought it here to my flat. American symbols, eagles and olive branches, adorn the envelope. The secret policeman at the postal center probably copied the letter, made note of the address, and placed my name onto some list. What is worse, the fundamentalist gentlemen from downstairs, with their thick beards and scowls, watched me retrieve the post and now must wonder who the shy Iraqi kid is, in truth.

They are still trying to get me killed, the Americans.

I take the letter and the envelope down the dark hallway to the toilet, burn it there, and flush the ashes. I should think less on America and more on attending university here in Sousse. Their university is lovely, situated on the sea, its ancient, whitewashed edifices highlighted in blue. Truly, all the buildings here in Sousse are lovely, quite a few of them adorned with stylish filigree. It is no wonder the Europeans flock to this place with their cameras and their sunscreen, lie on the beach, and wait for me to bring them their drinks.

The whitewash makes me think of Tom Sawyer and his fence, and I am reminded, again, that I should think more on my thesis and less on the dream of America. My thesis is still the key to everything. I must remember the parts I lost in Baghdad, consider my new ideas. In this way, I should become a true scholar.

With the best of intentions, I open the thesis document on my computer and laugh. Because, of course, it is impossible. My thesis? It is all about America, man. The place I have never been. And in any case, it is pointless to attempt creative work when assailed by the noise of the riots. It is too loud even for thinking.

Outside, the university students throw bricks and scream the president's name. They chant for all young people to come out into the streets and join their revolution. They sing the Tunisian national anthem and "Tunisia Our Country," by that rapper El Général. They are not doing him any favors with that. President Ben Ali will have El Général arrested soon, I predict.

Now they are chanting for Ben Ali to join them in the streets, too. Thinking they can give him some justice. Foolishness.

Each night for this past week, the crowd has moved closer to the government center and the main square. Today, I overheard English tourists on the beach discussing whether they should leave, mentioning how the rioters in Tunis touched the iron gates of the presidential palace last night. Insanity. Riot police pushed them back and splashed the streets with a bit of blood. Soon President Ben Ali will send his army into the streets to relieve the police, and then the real bleeding will begin.

Through my window I see red police lights flashing in the smoke and tear gas. Nearer to our flat than it had been an hour before, this riot. Police chase the people down. They are coming my way, and the state intelligence service will be behind them carrying lists. Perhaps they carry a copy of that American letter. Perhaps they will find me and see that the name on my Syrian passport is different from the name on that letter.

My flatmates are out there. University gentlemen making time with the ladies and the cool kids. They had wanted me to come out with them tonight, but I declined. "Go have fun without me," I told them. "I had my adventures at home. Besides, I have to work in the morning. The English tourists on the beach need more drinks before they decide what to do."

I sit down at my computer and reopen my thesis. With fingers on the keys, I consider where to start and try to remember where I stopped. I think of Baghdad years ago, when I met Professor Al-Rawi for the first time to discuss *The Adventures of Huckleberry Finn*, his favorite book by his favorite American.

He awarded me the special task of reading it in the off-term, when the other students of English relaxed at home. Each day, I went to his office on the Karada campus and he explained to me things which I could not have possibly understood then.

Truly, I did not comprehend a single thing at first. How Mark Twain wrote. How these Americans spoke, so ignorant and rough. Why Americans today thought of this story of terribly behaved children as such high art.

"Kateb, you must understand the context," Professor Al-Rawi said. "What the American reader knew then, what Americans today do not remember, and what you certainly cannot understand. These were not just boys making silly plans in caves. These were boys growing up just in time for their war. Sitting there, making plans to start this robber's gang, this was quite humorous to Americans reading the book in the nineteenth century."

"But not the Americans of today?"

He lit a cigarette. "Humorous, yes. But for other reasons. You see, Americans today . . . forget. Ten years after these boys met to scheme in caves, their civil war fell upon them. These boys, these Missouri boys, they would have cut each other's throats in that war. And the sides they would pick? This was determined in their youth, you see."

We were silent for a moment while I considered this.

"Have you thought about Huck Finn cutting Tom Sawyer's throat?" he asked.

"No."

"You should, Kateb. You should think about that." Then he smiled, like he knew all along what would come for us.

A grenade goes off in the street. A stun grenade, I should think, from the exaggerated noise and the lack of shrapnel clicking off the cobblestones. Lethal grenades, I know, make only the noise that they must.

The riot turns a corner now and moves closer to me. Soon we will lose our electricity, and I have only this old desktop computer with no backup battery for emergencies. This makes writing treacherous, and I must save my work often. I stop, save my changes, and close the document. Then I think that while there is still some electricity remaining I should look at the Internet to pass time. I open a few windows of porno to distract, but this does not work.

Soon, I am searching for Pleasant's name, and the *mulasim*'s name, too. This is what the American letter told me I should do. Find Americans who would know me. Americans who would know that I am truthful, Americans who could write letters for me saying, "Kateb. Yes, I knew him. He served with us. A good man. He helped us."

I find Pleasant soon enough, right on Facebook. But the *mulasim*? He is nowhere, as though he is hiding.

I begin my note to Pleasant, "Old friend. Crazy-man Lester. This is Dodge." Then I close Facebook without sending.

Then, though I know I should not, that it is pointless and no good can come of it, I open the video clip of Mohamed Bouazizi, again. What started these riots. Burning himself in front of the Sidi Bouzid police station. I have watched it many times, now. We are the same age, almost. And he is skinny, like me. He cries and hits himself in the face. He throws paint thinner down his back, howling like a

31

wild thing. Then, when he lights his match, he is suddenly calm. Like he knows this will work. That the revolution will grow from this.

The foreign news, still sneaking through on the Internet, claims that Mohamed Bouazizi is still alive in hospital. I check on him several times each day, without good reason. I did not know him. I am not even Tunisian. Why should I care so much?

In any case, I still find it foolish, this chanting in the streets on his account. What do they think will happen? That President Ben Ali will leave because a young man selling fruit from a cart lights a match? That because the kids all have cameras on their mobile phones, President Ben Ali will not kill them with bullets and clubs?

An idea comes to me and I return to my thesis to put down one more thought, quickly, before I abandon work for the evening. I scan for the passage about Huck's guilt and make a new paragraph.

"Huck believes in the Widow Douglas," I begin. "Her opinions on right and wrong he considers as fact. He even accepts the Widow's assertion that he will go to Hell as a hard truth, with the simple caveat that he does not mind going to Hell so long as Tom joins him there. He wishes to do what is right for his friends on Earth, even when he knows it is wrong. His abiding desire to help his friend Jim, in particular, brings him dire feelings of guilt, as if he has betrayed the good Widow."

Just then, the electricity leaves our flat with a loud pop. The computer screen becomes black and I lose these words. But I am not upset. I have already changed my mind about them.

I sit in the darkness and listen to the chanting in the streets before getting up from my chair and moving to the window. Without heat now, I grope in darkness for my coat and put it on over my jumper. It is a nice coat, abandoned by some careless French tourist at the resort. The bosses allowed me to take it home once they realized that I owned so few winter clothes.

The crowd will come around the corner at any moment, and I wonder if my flatmates will appear with it. I wonder if I should go onto the streets if only to see this thing. This revolution.

Then I think of Lester, his picture on Facebook in my mind's eye, and I wonder if he will help me, if he even should. I wonder where Mulasim Donovan can be found, if not on Facebook. I write down a note in the dark. Universities. Newspapers. Places to look for him.

Professor Liebert:

As requested, please see the attached excerpt from my Official Military Personnel File, and the substantial leadership instruction (equivalent to over thirty semester hours) I received as an officer-in-training at Marine Corps Base Quantico. Again, I ask that you apply this instruction as a transfer credit so that I may be excused from Management 901: Leadership Dynamics and Business Ethics.

Respectfully,
Peter Donovan

LEADERSHIP DYNAMICS

The classroom has stadium-style seating with chairs built into tables. Concentric semicircles rise up from the podium on carpeted terraces. A wealthy alum, his name bolted to the door on a bronze plaque I've never read, paid for the renovation as part of Liebert's endowed professorship of business ethics and leadership.

The university designed this lecture room for modern, multimedia instruction, but never ran that idea by Liebert, apparently. He has thirty years of tenure, so no one can complain that he doesn't have an e-mail account and refuses to prepare PowerPoint presentations. Even the whiteboard annoys him. He laments constantly on the demise of chalk.

Liebert stalks up and down the terraces, hunched over with his hands clasped behind his back. Wild, gray hair shifts slightly from one side to the other as he glances at our laptop screens to make sure we're not checking our e-mail or streaming videos, while, at the podium, Paige Dufossat briefs the weekly case study. The semester is almost over. We'll submit our final papers in a few weeks, and I'll start my winter internship at Poydras Capital, a downtown investment firm.

I'm still savagely hungover from my night with Zahn. Knowing Liebert's habits by now, I've hidden *Twenty Small Sailboats to Take You Anywhere* inside the casebook. It's the only thing that keeps me from putting my head down on the table and passing out. I spend the class reviewing the dimensions and handling characteristics of the twenty-eight-foot, sloop-rigged Pearson Triton, in response to the line I have on a Katrina wreck at West End. The harbormaster might let me have it for free if I move it at my own expense.

I haven't read the case study, but glean from the sparing attention I give Paige's brief that it's about a fast-food chain expanding into the Chinese market. Now she moves to her conclusions, the moment when she can only fail. It's Liebert's practice to destroy any ideas that aren't his own. We all know it by now. She grasps the podium and, using only the muscles of her neck, throws her long, brown hair over each shoulder while bringing her gaze back to Professor Liebert.

"So, in my opinion," she says stoically, "the executive's lack of empathy for a foreign culture and his unwillingness to adapt to the Chinese mind-set led to these difficulties in supply-chain management, which in *turn* led to the stalled expansion effort."

She knows what's coming next. I can see it on her face. Or maybe it's just the default state of her delicate features that I mistake for fear. Her appearance doesn't exactly scream, "Ruthless business executive," like that of some of the other girls in our class. Most of her female classmates arrive on campus in heels and power suits, but Paige is more of a T-shirt-and-jeans type who eschews makeup. It works for her, allowing her pale blue eyes and her slight, upturned nose to stand out.

I can't recall offhand the eye color of any other classmate. Nor can I imagine any other classmate citing "lack of empathy" for a business failure. Paige can't expect Professor Liebert to respond favorably to any of this, which makes it an interesting choice. I wonder where she's going with it. I close the casebook and its clandestine rider, sitting up for the first time in an hour.

Liebert reaches the front of the room, places one hand on the podium, close enough to Paige's hand to make her uncomfortable, and says, with his back turned to the class, "Was it empathy that he lacked, Ms. Dufossat? It seems to me the executive had ample empathy. He recognized the feelings of his Chinese colleagues, certainly. He simply refused to accept their mediocre standards. Refused to conduct the affairs of his firm, of his employer, in that way. Is it empathetic, Ms. Dufossat, to acquiesce to mediocrity? Is it *leadership*?"

Paige knows not to answer. She purses her lips, taking a step back from the podium. But as Liebert moves to take her place, something in the curt nod Paige gives him catches my attention. I recognize it only vaguely, hidden behind those slender limbs and that button nose, as a compact "Fuck you."

"A leader would've changed the Chinese approach," Liebert says confidently. Stating the obvious and yet the essential. "A leader needs empathy, of course, to know the mind-set of his subordinates. But a good leader would use this knowledge to alter their mind-sets. Leadership, kiddo, is changing your subordinates so that they are better equipped, better motivated, to achieve the goals you set."

I groan involuntarily, fighting a wave of nausea. I reel my legs back under the chair, plant my elbows on the table, and bury my face in my hands. When I pick my head up, the whole class is looking at me.

"Thoughts, Mr. Donovan?" Liebert smiles.

"No, just a little sore," I lie. "I didn't mean to interrupt."

"Please, Mr. Donovan. I've been hoping to hear from you at some point in this semester. Given the extensive leadership experience I'm told you have."

"Really, it's not a big deal."

"Nonsense, Mr. Donovan. You're a veteran, correct? You were an officer in the . . . *which* branch of the service was it?"

"The Marine Corps."

"And you have experience overseas? In Iraq?"

"Yes." He knows all of this, and it's starting to piss me off. My classmates shift in their seats to get a better view, sensing, as do I, that this line of questioning will continue for the remainder of the session.

"And so we should assume that you needed the principles of leadership when relating to that foreign culture, correct?"

"Not really," I say with a shrug. "I had a gun."

But after a wave of bashful laughter from the class, Liebert keeps after me. "I sense you're a little reluctant to discuss this. So let me put it to you another way: You're using your veteran's benefits to pay tuition, correct?"

"Yes."

"Then, as taxpayers, I believe your classmates are entitled to the benefit of your experience, no?"

The laughter is more effusive now, as my classmates attempt to placate their professor. They're younger than me, fresh from undergraduate life and eager to share their experiences, interning here and traveling there. They couldn't possibly conceive of how badly I want to break Liebert's arm just now.

I consider walking silently from the room, going to the registrar, and withdrawing from the class. But that would only confirm me as the troubled veteran. It's my fault for writing a letter citing my military experience, I decide. Professor Liebert's smug grin is a just punishment.

My classmates are grinning, too. Empty vessels awaiting the master's touch. All except Paige Dufossat. She stands stock-still behind Liebert and watches me warily. Nervous, perhaps, that I might deflect Liebert's assault back onto her. Or maybe she's keeping faith, under the impression that we're a team now. Either way, she's mistaken.

These thoughts distract me for a moment, and I stumble back into the discussion a beat behind the action. "I'm sorry. Would you mind repeating the question?"

This time the class doesn't laugh.

Liebert steps away from the podium and gestures for Paige to take his place. "All right, then. Let's reframe. Ms. Dufossat asserts that empathy is required of a leader. From *your* experience as a veteran, as someone who's led men, soldiers, in wartime, would you agree with her?"

She stares me down, those blue eyes striking against her brown hair. Maybe she's right. Maybe we are a team in this.

"Well, first of all, I led men *and* women. Not just men. And we don't call ourselves soldiers in the Marines. Soldiers are what you call people in the Army. But in any case, yes: I agree with Paige. Empathy is a good quality for a leader to have. Maybe essential, even, though I'm not sure I'd want to go that far."

Paige's blue eyes narrow, and I notice a something like a smile spidering across her tight lips. Professor Liebert starts to speak again, but I'm no longer listening. I see his lips moving, but I'm elsewhere.

I'm listening to Gunny Stout give the mission brief, standing in my body armor on the hard dirt of the convoy staging area, just inside the wire at Taqaddum. Watching how the faces of Zahn and Marceau and Gomez and Pleasant brighten as he speaks to them, just as surely as they frown when I take over.

And then I'm back in a Quantico squad bay with a shaved head, desperately willing myself through to graduation and commissioning, having known from the first day, when the sergeant instructors herded us across the scalding parade deck, frothing like rabid dogs, that I was inadequate to the task. I'm muddling through, watching better men than me wash out or break their legs and receive medical disqualifications. I'm on the endurance course, bringing up the rear, staggering across that red clay in the brutal summer heat while the other candidates, the real leaders, the scholarship athletes and the presidents of their fraternities, muscle their way over the endless hills. I'm laboring under the weight of my pack and rifle, panting and frantically trying to catch up. Sweat pours down my face while the sergeant instructors run alongside me, screaming. "What's happening back *here*, Little One? Can't meet the standards, *runt*?"

Then I'm back at the beginning. Before Quantico. Back at college, with the on-campus recruiter, applying for Officer Candidates School. He tells me his quota is met for the year, and though I probably don't have a chance at getting past the selection board, he'll start my application package. Afterward, I call my father in hope that I might get a word of encouragement. But all I get is a grunt and an admonition to pack extra socks.

"Leaders must have a strong sense of the great responsibility of their office," I blurt out, interrupting Liebert. I must be yelling, barking it out like a drill instructor, because Liebert cuts off midsentence.

"Leaders must have a strong sense of the great responsibility of their office," I continue. "Because the resources they will expend in war are human lives."

After a moment, Liebert smiles. "Go on, Mr. Donovan."

"That's something you memorize at Officer Candidates School. And it's true. So true that I think my experience in the military might not apply here. Unless there's a line item on a balance sheet for human lives we haven't learned about yet. So, I was wrong. And I'm sorry I tried to get out of your class."

Paige's lips have loosened slightly, and she's looking at me with her head cocked to the side.

"Though Paige is right," I say. "When you truly lead people—which, for the record, I don't think I ever really *did*—you make them believe that you care. That you know how they feel. And often you do. But in a war, to empathize too much with the people who might die on account of the decisions you make . . ."

Professor Liebert and all my classmates stare at me until they understand that I'm finished.

"Well," Liebert snorts, "Mr. Donovan certainly has a point. And thank you, Ms. Dufossat, you may be seated. Now, moving on, the text for next week . . ."

He goes on for a little while, but I don't listen. I come to with the noise of books and backpacks signaling the end of the session. I stand, rub my eyes, and start gathering my things. It takes me a moment to notice Paige Dufossat sitting next to me. Her original seat was across the room, and I don't know what she's doing here.

She looks up at me with her fierce, strangely delicate face, as if someone carved that absurd little nose out of marble, and says, "Thanks, Pete."

"Sure," I say with a shrug. "No problem."

She touches the cover of my book. "You sail?"

"No," I say honestly. "Never set foot on a sailboat. Not in my whole life."

"Oh," she says, pushing her eyebrows together in confusion.

"See you next week," I say, turning my back on her. It's easier to turn my back on a pretty girl with Gunny Stout on my mind.

I walk out through the student lounge adjacent to the classrooms and grab my winter coat off the hook next to my in-box. A flat-screen television mounted above the couch plays footage from Tunisia. Police in the night. Riot gear, body armor, and the outline of weapons. Civilians stand in stark relief against flames. I look away.

Dad.

Got a few days off next week.

After work today I'll be headed up to New Orleans.

Probably won't see you before then.

Anything you need up there? Anything I can bring you back? I'll probably be sleeping on Landry's couch. Call you if anything changes.

Les.

THE RULE

I leave a note on the kitchen table for my dad and sneak out the front door quiet as I can. I tiptoe out to my truck before he wakes up. Walking barefoot over the cold, sharp gravel so as not to make noise. I put my boots on in the cab and bundle up with lined leather gloves, the old woolen watch cap pulled down tight over my brow. My overnight duffel gets thrown in the truck bed. The trauma bag gets put on the passenger seat next to me. I always bring it with me on long drives. Why not? A useful thing to have, depending.

I let the truck idle slow and quiet across the driveway, not even touching the accelerator till I turn onto the highway. I imagine the route up to New Orleans for later tonight. Picture all the roads and towns and intersections up ahead. Thorough and detailed like a convoy brief. Like how Gunny Stout gave the convoy brief. Before Lieutenant Donovan took it over, anyway.

Gunny Stout used to make Marines lift my trauma bag so they knew the weight of it, showing them that I *earned* my way. That I wasn't a goldbricker—not some nasty sailor doing a little combat tourism.

"Pack your own trash," Marines said. Earn your way.

No one packed their own trash like Gunny Stout.

"Five and twenty-five's the rule," he said. Gunny Stout had a lot of rules, but five and twenty-five, that was most important.

He was short, five-seven maybe, with sandy hair and freckles. Must have been almost forty, but in his body armor and sunglasses he looked like he could've been in grade school. The sunglasses hid the wrinkles around his eyes, and the flak jacket smashed the folds of middle age flat around his waist.

"At a halt, you stay in your vehicle and scan," he said. "You look around, five meters out from the wheels in every direction. Inside five meters, our armor plate is vulnerable to frag. Vulnerable to blast overpressure. A shock wave can rip the doors right off. You spot a wire, or two rocks stacked on top of each other, or a patch of disturbed dirt, you call it out. You spot a piece of trash that seems too heavy, you call it out. If it holds your attention for more than two seconds, you call it out."

I stood next to Gunny Stout when he gave the brief. He said it helped the Marines to see a corpsman next to the bomb tech. Everyone stood still when he talked. The only Marine allowed to move around during the convoy brief was Sergeant Gomez. She circled us like a sheepdog, making sure we all paid attention. Michelle Gomez, her full name. Found that out a long time later.

Sergeant Gomez owned that platoon. She and Corporal Zahn, the two of them. They ran it as a team. Not because she needed Zahn for anything. Gomez had motivation to spare. Marines a foot taller than her would flinch when she came up on them. Just her voice could break bones. Full and Texan.

She looked the part, too. Always kept her hair tied back and out of her eyes. Shiny, black hair smooth as a feather. If a strand or two fell down and tickled her cheek, she'd curse and step away to tie it right back. I watched her do it in the morning once, before reveille, behind the barracks hut when no one else was awake. She sat on the steps with her hair down, hands working it back into a bun. I couldn't help but stop to watch. She noticed me and narrowed her eyes, all mad. Like, what the fuck you looking at? Turn around. Get back to work, asshole.

Gunny Stout stopped talking as a cargo plane came in low over the lake, right on top of us. He never raised his voice, Gunny Stout. And he never looked at planes, even when all the other Marines did. Even Lieutenant Donovan and the other officers, standing off to the side while Gunny Stout gave the brief. They all looked up like it was the first plane they ever saw.

Lieutenant Donovan had brown hair, brown eyes, and real good teeth. Had a bit of weight on him, but was tall enough to wear it, just barely. A real southern college boy, the lieutenant. Like he was on his way to an outdoor jam band festival one day, took a wrong turn, and somehow ended up in the Marines. He sat on the hood of his Humvee, his flak jacket and helmet stacked next to him while Gunny Stout gave the brief. The rest of us, the enlisted? We showed up to the brief with our gear already *on*. Sergeant Gomez made sure of that. The lieutenant, though, he could take his time, I guess. Cross his arms and watch with gold bars on his collar. Happy to be called "sir." Happy to let Gunny Stout run the convoy. Happy to let Sergeant Gomez and Corporal Zahn run his platoon.

Gunny Stout didn't work for him, really. Lieutenant Donovan had the road-repair platoon, out filling potholes all day. Just that road repair had six vehicles and enough Marines to pull security while they did the work of patching the holes. It was tough work, too. Dirty and hot as hell in that body armor. But worse than that, those potholes always had another bomb under the rubble. And I do mean always.

So it made sense we roll with them. We only had the one vehicle, the bomb disposal team. Gunny Stout, Staff Sergeant Thompson, a driver, and me. We didn't even have a spare body to man the gun turret up top, though anyone could've jumped up there in a pinch.

We'd go first, check the hole, and clear whatever new bomb was put in there overnight. Then Lieutenant Donovan's guys, they'd come in behind us and get to work, filling the hole and patching it with concrete. First, they cut the jagged asphalt from around the edges to prep for aggregate. Then they carried those heavy bags of concrete over to a beat-up, old mixer. Just pouring down sweat inside that body armor. Had to watch for snipers, too. Never could stay in one place for too long or they'd take fire. Sergeant Gomez always nipping at their heels, telling them to hurry the hell up.

Gunny Stout kept going when the plane noise faded away. "When the vehicle commanders roger-up," he said, "clear inside five meters, then the dismount team executes the twenty-five-meter sweep, on my order." Gunny's voice got tight. Not loud, just *tight*. "Dismount team, eyes up."

Most Marines stared at the dirt during a convoy brief. Tucked their hands inside their body armor and rested their chin against the ballistic plate. But when Gunny Stout said, "Eyes up," they rolled their shoulders back and locked onto him. In unison, you know? Like one creature.

"When I say go, do not hesitate. Three seconds." He held up three fingers. "Every door open. Every door closed. All Marines working a tight search pattern in three seconds. It takes three seconds for a triggerman to initiate a device, and you can't let that happen while that armor seal is broken. Move with a purpose. No sidebar conversations. No laughing."

Sergeant Gomez explained it to me, once. How Marines managed to do everything in time, on a silent drill count. She smiled and said, "Oh, you mean that Snap, *Pop*?"

It was how they spoke. How they did every little thing: Snap, *Pop*.

Satisfied, Gunny Stout tapped his notes. "Right. Dismount leader, when you confirm no devices, no threats to dismounted

47

troops inside twenty-five meters, return your team to the vics. On my order, or as you were, on the lieutenant's order, we set security." He pointed to Lieutenant Donovan. "You all right with that, sir?"

Lieutenant Donovan looked up and smiled. "Sounds fine, Gunny." He crossed his arms and swung his dangled feet off the hood of the Humvee.

He had that Alabama gentleman's drawl, the lieutenant. I never could tell—was he even paying attention? Was he just relaxed? Lieutenant Donovan had a gunnery sergeant of his own. Gunny Dole. But that guy never went outside the wire. A fat pension-grubber on his last deployment. He'd wander around the company office talking about the promotion boards coming up. Talking about his retirement. Talking about his deployments to the Philippines in the nineties. How much *fun* they were. Not like *this* shit, he'd say.

Gunny Stout never talked about anything but the mission. He gave us a smile and looked around, studying us.

The turret gunners wore bandannas to keep the sweat out their eyes. Under her helmet, Gomez wore the sleeve of a green T-shirt stretched out over her hair. Corporal Zahn had grenade pouches on his flak to hold cans of Skoal. We all wore tan flight suits. Flame resistant, for a little extra protection.

Gunny Stout looked to Lieutenant Donovan. "You have anything to add, sir?"

"I do." He nodded. "Just one quick item." He jumped off his Humvee and strolled into the briefing circle, glancing over at the command building to make sure Major Leighton was watching from the steps before he addressed the platoon. "This isn't the best forum for this bit of gouge, I know. But the company commander wanted it passed to all Marines before noon today: He's fed up with the bathroom graffiti. He says he's over it. The stalls in comfort trailers get painted today, and we're due for new Porta-Johns tomorrow. So, it'll be a fresh slate. All graffiti removed. Then, starting tomorrow, if any drawings of penises or gossip about female Marines shows up in the bathrooms . . ." He paused and peeked over at Sergeant Gomez, kind of an embarrassed look on his face. "If the company commander sees anything like that, he'll have the first sergeant post a twenty-four-hour watch in the shitters with orders to check each stall as Marines come out."

Corporal Zahn closed his eyes and bit his lip. Probably trying like hell not to laugh.

Gunny Stout didn't miss a beat. "Good deal, sir. Thanks for the gouge. Anything else?"

"No, that about covers it." The lieutenant ambled back to the hood of his Humvee to put his flak jacket and helmet on.

Then, his voice low so the lieutenant couldn't hear, Gunny Stout said to us, "I'm running over to the shitters after we break. In fact, I'll give the whole platoon three minutes to do the same. You know that glistening, goddamn beautiful cock in the last stall on the right? I want a picture before it's gone forever. One of you miscreants is a regular Leonardo da Vinci of dicks, and I'd hate to see the evidence erased for all time. Fucking tragedy."

After a quiet laugh, Gunny Stout turned to me, put his hand on my shoulder, and said, "Doc Pleasant's in the second vehicle with me. Real quick, Doc, take us through the casualty plan."

And I stood there, in front of those Marines. Right there, nineteen years old. Big ears, red hair, and a missing tooth. Two dozen Marines listened to me as I told them all the different ways and everything I'd do to save their lives if the time came for it.

"You get hit, you follow the steps," I said. "Apply self-aid. Use your medical kit. Do what you can. Buddy aid comes next. Closest Marine to the casualty is responsible. Use the wounded Marine's medical kit on him. Save your medical kit for yourself. Make sure you got your tourniquet where you can get at it quick. Be able to apply your own tourniquet in under ten seconds. Bright red, frothing blood is arterial. Get a tourniquet on it. And if you go down, stay down and don't thrash. I'll get to you."

Then, like always, the convoy team huddled up in a big circle with Sergeant Gomez in the middle.

"Everybody touch somebody," she said.

We all bent at the waist and put our arms on each other's shoulders. Even Lieutenant Donovan. He couldn't just watch. Not for the deep breath.

Sergeant Gomez filled her lungs. So did we.

Then she let it out, loud and theatrical. So did we.

"That's right." She laughed. "Deep breath, no worries."

She passed it off to Corporal Zahn, who said a prayer, and we mounted up.

We drove across base to the entry control point and waited there for a big supply convoy to clear the gate. I sat in the backseat, next to Gunny Stout. I recognized Lieutenant Donovan's voice, all confident and clear on the radio, while he let movement control know that we were twenty-two packs in six vehicles headed to Saqliniah through downtown Fallujah. They cleared us through the gate, quick. Even moved us ahead of a few other convoys in the departure order. They did that for the route-clearance teams.

We made the left turn onto Route Long Island and picked up speed. The lead vehicle got out in front about two hundred meters. The other vehicles got their spacing, fifty meters apiece. We spread out in the desert and tightened up in the towns. Each vehicle kicked up a rooster tail of trash that came down like confetti on the vehicle behind it. Off the road, everything turned beige. It was hard to find the horizon with the desert blending into the buildings, blending into the smog.

We passed a few little, nameless towns on the road north to Fallujah. Two or three buildings deep on each side, filthy and falling down. The Iraqis lay plywood sheets down over the sewage so they could get in and out of their houses. Sometimes, through an open door, we'd see the courtyard of one of those little fortress homes, thick with green plants and flowers. We'd wonder aloud, between the sewage, the garbage fires, and the pretty green courtyards, just who the hell these people were.

Something else: Over there? In the Middle East? They line the side of the road with yellow and black curbstones. They do it on all the roads, even down a hundred miles of highway. I didn't know that before I went over there. You could look out the window, down at the curb, and tell how fast you were going by how quick it went between yellow and black. I guess that was the point of it.

The turret gunners waved red flags to warn off civilian traffic. The Iraqis, in their beat-up little trucks and twenty-year-old Japanese sedans, they all pulled off the road. They knew what the red flag meant. Meant we don't stop. Don't come near us. The gunners also kept ammo cans filled with flares strapped to the turrets. If a car ignored the flag and came within a hundred meters? Gunner would launch a flare. At fifty meters, they'd put two M16 rounds into the road right in front of the car. They loaded tracers for the first five rounds in every magazine so the Iraqis couldn't miss seeing the shots.

The kill line was twenty-five meters. A vehicle crossed twenty-five meters or accelerated into us at any point? The gunner spun the turret and fired for effect. Machine-gun rounds through the windshield and into the engine block until the vehicle came to a stop. Then the gunner would drop down into the crew compartment for better protection. A vehicle that accelerated into us was gonna be a vehicle bomb. Almost always.

I looked out though the front window and recognized Corporal Marceau, standing behind the gun in the turret of Lieutenant Donovan's Humvee. The other corporals acted hard to establish their place in the pecking order. Not Marceau. Everything amused that guy. Even his own stripes. Just as I focused in on him, I heard him come up on radio.

"Gomez, Zahn. This is Marceau. Roll freq to Convoy-Two."

Convoy-Two was a channel reserved unofficially for the NCOs. A place where they could pass radio traffic in private without worrying about the lieutenant listening in, or the gunny. I decided to eavesdrop and changed the channel on my radio.

"Listen," I heard Marceau say. "You two deserve to know that most of those penis murals are mine. And I'll be honest—I don't think I can quit cold turkey. Over."

Zahn and Gomez, in separate vehicles, both keyed their radios just to let Marceau hear them laughing.

Marceau kept going, deadpan. "So here's my compromise: I'll keep drawing penises, and you can go ahead and put me down as a volunteer for the overnight shitter watch. Out."

I smiled and rolled back to the main convoy channel.

As we moved through the battle spaces, little territories carved out on the map, Lieutenant Donovan radioed the unit that controlled the area ahead of us and requested passage through. When we got close to the bridge into Fallujah, he radioed the Amphibious Assault Battalion. They controlled the highway traffic through there. "Tracks," we called that battalion, because they spent all their time in floating tanks. Amphibious assault vehicles. *Tracks* for short. Always strange, you know? Seeing those floating tanks out in the desert.

Lieutenant Donovan asked to use Phase Line Fran, the highway that ran from the Euphrates River bridge straight through the center of town, to the highway cloverleaf on the eastern side. This was Main Street, Fallujah. An exposed, crowded route, but the fastest way to get to the track on Route Lincoln, disabled by an IED blast. Gunny Stout needed to get there fast to check for secondary devices. The track's commander had been up in the turret and got hurt bad. So, the officer running the command center knew exactly what Lieutenant Donovan was talking about. Cleared us for Phase Line Fran without much discussion.

The Marines on guard at the bridge waved us through, and Phase Line Fran opened up. Convoys in front of us pulled over and blocked the side streets. We accelerated in a tight little pack, six prey animals at a sprint. I sat in the backseat, driver-side, Gunny Stout across from me. Heat poured in through the turret hatch—so hot you could hardly open your eyes. It stank like diesel fuel, too. A drop of sweat rolled onto my lips, tasting of salt and soap. I licked all around just to get more of it. Anything to clear the diesel fuel and garbage out my mouth.

Arab chatter filled the streets around us. An imam making a speech from the mosque got louder as we passed, more pissed off. The buildings along Fran were all shot to pieces. Looking down an alley, I saw two guys in jogging pants and ratty T-shirts with rags tied around their mouths. Not their whole faces. Just their mouths. They started running.

I went for the intercom, but Gunny Stout saw it first and keyed his radio. "Actual, this is Hellbox. I got two guys, military age, running south down what looks like Route George. Also, up ahead on the left, two hundred meters, I got a red dump truck idling. Looks like two guys in the cab. Young guys. Can't see their hands. Over."

Gomez came up on the net. "Roger. I see it, too. Over."

Donovan joined in, sounding a little bored. "Roger, I see it. Your call, Gunny."

Gunny Stout glanced at his map, looked out at the dump truck, and frowned. He bit his lip and keyed his mic. "Push."

We rolled by the dump truck, the two guys in the cab watching us the whole way.

"Gunny?" I had to shout, almost.

He looked up from his map.

"Why are we pushing through?"

"Two guys in the truck." He shrugged. "Suicide bombers come one at a time."

We turned north at the cloverleaf and rolled about ten kilometers up to the intersection of Route Lincoln and Route Golden. We spotted the disabled track, charred black on one side, leaning hard to the right and half off the shoulder. The explosion had ripped off the tread and opened the turret. It wasn't smoking, though. Another track, undamaged, sat just outside the cordon farther down the road. Someone inside kept spinning the turret to scan the desert.

We popped out. Did our fives and twenty-fives.

Lieutenant Donovan waved to Gunny and me. He was right at the edge of the security zone, staring down at the blown track. He walked back and forth, kneeling every few seconds to get a look at the track from different angles.

Sergeant Gomez walked over to Donovan. They had some quiet words before she took off at a fast walk. She pointed to the security Marines, yelled for them to push out and get farther back.

The blown track had been second in line, so it wasn't a pressure switch that set off the bomb. Someone had let the first one pass, then triggered the device when the second track got in range. Someone had to be watching.

Lieutenant Donovan motioned for us to come forward. Me, Gunny Stout, and the other bomb tech, Staff Sergeant Thompson. They studied the road as we walked, looking inside every crack.

Gunny turned to me with a smile. "This looks good, Doc. Should be real quick."

"Okay, Gunny."

"You trust me, right?" He laughed to make sure I knew he didn't really mean it. That he would never, could never, ask for my approval.

But it didn't look good. You could tell right away, from how Gunny Stout and Staff Sergeant Thompson whispered. From how the blown track held Lieutenant Donovan's attention. When did that guy ever pay attention to anything?

It was the grenade launcher.

See, those tracks weren't really tanks. They were armored personnel carriers, had to be light enough to float. They had thin armor, and a turret-mounted, automatic grenade launcher instead of a cannon.

The explosion, it had ripped open the turret and the ammunition-storage box inside, scattering live grenades all around the desert like Easter eggs. No one had told us about the grenades before we rolled out. Complicated everything and had everybody spooked. Gunny Stout's equipment could sniff for explosive material, and it was registering off the charts. But was it because of the live grenades everywhere, or was a second bomb up ahead?

Gunny Stout and Staff Sergeant Thompson started poking around with the robot. Lieutenant Donovan and I leaned against the Humvee and watched them work. I had my trauma bag and backboard sitting on the hood, ready to go. Lieutenant Donovan had his radio handset pulled out through the window so he could answer when the company commander called looking for updates. Maybe since we were the only ones doing jack shit, he started chatting me up.

Where you from in Louisiana? Do you follow college football? Getting your mail, all right? Crazy, pointless stuff. I tried to ignore him. Finally, the radio squawked and he had someone else to talk to. It was Tracks, looking for an update.

"Roger. We're on-site. They're working with the robot now. No estimate on when they'll have it cleared . . . Roger, stand by. I'll have an update in five."

Gunny Stout walked over, shoulders tight. "Can't find any secondaries, sir."

"So you think it's clear?"

Gunny lifted his eyebrows, chewed his lip.

But the lieutenant needed an answer. "Push the track off the road and wait for recovery? Get that hole filled while we wait?"

"Yes, sir," Gunny said. "Sounds like a plan. But first we'll need to clean up these grenades."

Lieutenant Donovan whistled. "Do it with the robot?"

"No. I'll have to pick them up by hand. Each one. Pile them up and reduce."

Donovan winced. "Goddamn, Gunny. Are you sure?"

Gunny shrugged. "It has to happen, sir."

And that was it. No more discussion. Gunny Stout walked out into the blast zone, not even wearing his suit. He told the lieutenant he couldn't pick up so many grenades with that bulky suit on, and the lieutenant didn't argue with him. Just nodded and went back to walking the perimeter, reminding his Marines to cover their sectors.

But they couldn't stop watching Gunny. None of us had seen anything like it. He bent down to pick up live grenades, one at a time. All alone, a hundred meters away. One at a time and calm as could be.

No one said a word.

I had my backboard and kit ready to go, the closest man to him. The sun crawled up right on top of me, heated my helmet like a griddle. Sweat poured down my face and the wind pelted me with tiny grains of sand. I rolled my shoulders every few minutes to set the body armor a little higher and shifted from one foot to the other.

Gunny Stout used hand signals in the blast zone. Radios were no good. Could set off bombs. He scratched out a little hole in the sand for the grenades and waved to Thompson each time he put one in there. Three more grenades. Two more grenades. One more. He put the last grenade in the hole and then stood with two fists held over his head to show he was walking back to the secure area.

Behind me, someone exhaled and shouted, "Hell yeah!" Someone else started to clap. Sergeant Gomez got on them in a heartbeat, telling them to shut the fuck up.

Gunny Stout put both hands on his rifle. About halfway back, when I could see his face clear, he smiled and mouthed the words, "Trust me?"

I smiled back a moment too late. His face went stiff. He looked through me.

It took me a second to register the shots, but then I turned around and saw a red dump truck coming at the cordon from the south. Two young guys in the cab. Zahn was back there, already putting tracer rounds in the deck. I turned back to Gunny as he made a move, about to break into a jog. Then he was twenty feet in the air, twisting and coming apart, his rifle and boots spinning away from him.

That sound. That groan chasing a clap. It hit me a second later. The shock wave knocked me on my back and my helmet cracked against the pavement. Bits of dirt and gravel rained down on my face. I couldn't hear a thing.

I turned onto my stomach to look for him. Focused in on a shape in the center of the highway. I watched it roll over. I'm sure of it.

I made it to my knees and searched for my bag. Thompson, already on his feet, ran by me at a dead sprint. He made it about twenty meters before another device went off. It came from his left side in a sickly, gray puff.

I was still deaf, but I could tell it was smaller than the first one. Frag clipped Thompson's left leg and swept out his feet. He cartwheeled over. His left cheek hit the ground before the rest of him. He arched his back and reached for his leg.

Then he clinched his teeth and kept going, crawling toward Gunny.

I stood and found my bag. Still couldn't feel my legs. Could barely walk. I took a step toward the shape in the center of the highway. My hearing came back and I heard shouting at the rear of the convoy, and shots. I turned and saw Zahn putting rounds through the windshield of the dump truck. Painting the glass red. Cracks grew with each shot, till finally the dump truck rolled into the deep sand, its engine compartment spewing steam and hot motor oil.

I got my balance and took another step. The feeling came back to my hands and feet. I picked up a foot and took another step. Right as I felt like I had the coordination to start running, something hit me from behind and put me on the ground. Thought it was another bomb, at first. Then I felt a pair of arms wrapping around me.

"Stay down, Doc. Stay down."

It was Lieutenant Donovan.

"No. I'm going to get Gunny."

"Doc, he was dead before he hit the ground."

"No. I saw him roll over. I can get to him."

"Doc. You didn't see that. He didn't roll over."

I threw an elbow into his ribs. Tried to break his grip. Then I thrashed hard and managed to break free for a second, until he wrapped his elbow under my shoulder, put his palm on the back of my neck and forced me right into the ground. My cheek scraped against the black asphalt, hot as hell.

"Sir, let me up. Lemme go get him."

"It wasn't a grenade, Doc. Okay? They missed something. Secondaries all *over* the place."

I tried thrashing again, but hardly got my hips off the ground. He had me pinned with my arms out in front, palms flat. From under the rim of my helmet, I could just see the shape of him. I dug my nails into the pavement and burned my fingertips, trying to dig my way to Gunny.

"We get Staff Sergeant Thompson, Doc," Lieutenant Donovan said. "We get him back to the cordon."

"Fuck you."

"Listen."

"*Fuck* Thompson," I said. I really did.

"Doc. Look over to your right." Lieutenant Donovan got quiet. "The curb," he whispered.

I knew what it was the second I laid eyes on it. A black curb-stone, not set in concrete like the others. It was a different color black, too. More gray than black. And it looked new. No scuff marks.

"It's a daisy chain, Doc. A kill zone. They didn't see it. They were looking at the dirt. We get Staff Sergeant Thompson, now. Gunny stays where he is."

I stopped fighting. Closed my eyes and went limp. He eased his grip, stood, and picked me up by my body armor. "Watch your feet, all right? Slow, now."

But I didn't walk. I just stood there and looked at my feet. The lieutenant went and got Thompson while I stood there. I don't even know who came and pulled me back, but when they did, I saw the shape in the road with a dark sheen all around it. Ten minutes had gone by, at least.

That was the last time I saw his body. Later in the day, after the Marines had cleared the other bombs, Personnel Recovery Platoon came out to gather him up. Put all the pieces of him in a bag.

Battalion folded the bomb disposal team, sent Staff Sergeant Thompson home to learn how to walk again, and put me in Lieutenant Donovan's platoon.

As the Duke and Dauphine tie up the raft to work over another town, Jim complains about having to wait in the boat. He is concerned that he might be discovered. So, the Duke disguises Jim in a calico stage robe and blue face paint. He places a sign on Jim that reads, "Sick Arab—But harmless when not out of his head."

The idea that simple blue face paint could convince the town people that Jim was Arab, not African, is shocking to readers in the Arab world. The scene once again shows the author's contempt for his countrymen, and their ignorance of foreign cultures.

DODGE

As we are deprived of electricity for heat, the night's chill crawls into every corner of our flat. It has been an hour, at least, that we are without power. Quite a long while for a blackout. This makes me suspect it is intentional. That President Ben Ali has contrived to deny the city of welcoming streetlights. They are hoping to keep people indoors, and the protests small.

I laugh to myself, imagining Ben Ali at his desk in the palace, with comically large switches labeled PHONES, INTERNET, and ELECTRICITY, all set to OFF.

I have begun to think that my extravagant French coat was meant for a woman. It has strange frills and soft fabric on the sleeves which does not feel masculine. It keeps me warm, but not quite warm enough to avoid the occasional, distracting shiver. Because I do not have my computer with which to record new, important thoughts concerning Huck, I have taken to a notebook. I write by means of a small candle, but it flickers and throws light everywhere but the page. In frustration, I blow out the candle and go back to the window.

I detect a faint draft of tear gas sneaking through the rusted window frame. The crowds are close now. I hear their chanting more clearly and see flickers of light against the building walls and in alleyways. It is too early for sleep, and without power there is not much to do but listen.

Perhaps it is boredom which sends me to wander the streets and watch the crowds pass. Or perhaps it is more than a diversion. Perhaps it is a sensible precaution. If the secret police do come, what better place to hide than in the crowd? Better to be out there than in this flat, where the secret police know the Americans addressed a letter to one Kateb al-Hariri.

Locking our front door behind me, I feel my way along the walls of the dark hallway until I reach the stairs, then continue down each step with a toe outstretched.

Then I bump into our neighbor on the dark landing. One of the older, bearded men who watched me retrieve the post earlier in the day. My shoulder is buried in his chest, like he set his feet wide apart to occupy the maximum amount of space and force this collision. He must have heard me coming.

"Excuse me, uncle," I say, stepping back away from him, "I did not see you."

"Much pardon," he says, making no move to clear a path for me. "I hope I did not startle you. Remind me, nephew. Your name? Fadi, is it?"

An icy shudder, separate and distinct from the chill night air, radiates from my heart into the back of my throat.

"Yes," I manage. "My name is Fadi."

"Ah! Fadi. It is good to know your neighbors, yes? Especially in uncertain times like these?"

He lights a cigarette and I see his face clearly. Lines deeper than usual for a man of his age. Skin worn by rage, now still and creased with the deadly confidence of faith. He searched through the post and saw my letter from the Americans. I am sure of it.

I step delicately past him, over to the next set of steps. I work to appear calm. "Yes, uncle. Excuse me. I must go and find my flatmates."

"Of course. And peace be upon you, Fadi."

"And with you."

I hurry down the steps, wondering what name I will take the next time I flee, remembering the first.

The Americans still called me by my real name on the first night I lived with them at their Government Center, but said the word to me as if it were a lie.

"So . . . *Kateb*, is it?" an American would say that first night, gently nudging me to admit that I was a terrorist. Like it would be a fun secret to share between just us two.

Even after covering my face, stuffing me into their Humvee, and taking me away from my friends at the lake, they treated me as though it had been my idea to come hide on their base at Ramadi. My elaborate trick.

But in those first interrogations I showed that I was not a complete fool, so they brought me into a large room with a tiled floor and too many lights. Old Iraqi men sat on cots in the room too bright for sleep, staring at their feet. Marines guarded every door, but smiled as though we were guests.

The Americans kept us two days in Ramadi, herding the elderly men and me as old bedouins would their goats. To the dining tent for meals, three times daily. Back to the administration tent for paperwork. Again to the hot, wooden huts for interrogation. Always in the shadow of the concrete walls where no one from the town could see us.

Bremer walls, the Americans called those. The taller kind. Large at the bottom and thin at the top.

The Americans asked us all the same questions, always. Screening questions, they called them.

They asked me if I was Shiite or Sunni.

I told them that I did not know, and that this had troubled me my whole life. Very confusing.

They asked me who was my father.

I told them I was an orphan, which was how my sectarian confusion had begun.

They asked me how an orphan could have learned to speak English so well.

I told them the orphanage had a fine library.

They asked me how I expected them to believe such an obvious lie.

I shrugged.

They mused that I must have a fine family, indeed, risking so much in not revealing them. Moreover, they said I was obviously a privileged Sunni, raised in wealth by a father who was almost certainly a secular Baathist, and, unlike the Shiite rabble flocking to the new Iraqi Army, a man with whom the Americans could work. Just give us your father's name, they said. Don't be afraid. We can protect you, and your family.

I said nothing and sat perfectly still, expecting they would send me back to the lake and its consequences. Or perhaps to Abu Ghraib.

But I somehow passed these tests, because on the third morning they gave me an identification card, like the old men. Signed by an American, these cards, with our pictures and names. Treasure to the old men, but not me. I doubted them, still.

They put us on a truck after that, where the old men suffered. Their vests did not fit properly. The marines had dressed them one at a time like babies, pulled the vests around their distended bellies.

They laughingly asked, "Can you still breathe?"

They laughingly asked, "Too tight?"

Then they shoved the heavy armor plates in and laughed some more, asking, "How about now? Can you breathe now?"

Always laughing and smiling, the Americans.

But my vest fit well, skinny as I was, and I was the same age as the marines. When they spoke to me, they forgot themselves. Forgot where they were. They said things like, "Hey, man. Grab that helmet for me?"

"Hey, man," they said. Like we were all just school chums, like even in my own country I was some sort of exchange student.

It probably helped that I wore my Metallica T-shirt and old jeans. I kept the Mark Twain rolled up in my back pocket. Everywhere I went, every time they searched me, I had to flip through the pages to show it was just a book, not a way to hide things. Each time an American searched me, he would smile and ask, "You really *read* this book?"

No, I would say. Just for luck, man.

The old men wore their best business clothes, ancient stains showing through those well-ironed shirts. They wore leather shoes, rotting and stiff but brushed clean nonetheless. Wedding bands sat loose on their fingers.

These wedding bands caused me to smile and shake my head. Acting like Europeans, those old men. A myth they had come to believe about themselves in Saddam's time, before the wars and the bombs and the arrival of the Islamists had reminded them, truly, of who we were. A silly, desert people. A people whom Europeans viewed with amusement.

Under their poorly fitting helmets, the old men kept their sparse hair neatly combed. They scowled and smoothed their mustaches. With dignity, they thought. Academics and professionals. Men of skill. Men who had always mattered—and always known it.

We exited the American compound through a twisting gate and accelerated onto a bridge over the Euphrates River. Once we reached the highway, tucked between the other American trucks, we slowed to a reasonable speed.

Swaddled in their flak jackets, the old men squirmed. Worried that someone on the truck might recognize them, some infiltrator, they stared at their feet. The truck took a sharp turn and the old men leaned forward for balance. Their flak jackets drifted up and pinched the fat of their necks. Their helmets bounced and slipped over their eyes. We all chewed on dust blowing in from the road.

Sitting near the tailgate, I imagined pretty girls on either side of me. I leaned back and draped my arms over the bench, pretending to touch them. This helped me to remain calm. I knew what bombs did to these trucks. I had seen that bloody mess. The Americans, with all their guns, could not defend us from those bombs. They could not defend themselves. And who better than we Iraqis who rode willingly in the back of an American truck would our countrymen rather see turned to a bloody mess?

I tapped my foot, hummed to myself, and fidgeted as the drive wore on. Then I decided it was foolish, all of us taking pains to not look at each other. So I spoke to the ridiculous old men.

They would not let me, not at first. They turned away, cleared their throats, and looked at the sky. I became angry about this, so I sat up and shouted over the noise of the engine, *"Shaku maku! Assalamu alaikum!"*

The old men shifted in their seats.

I spread my arms wide and shouted in English, "What's up, my uncles?"

Nothing. I leaned back and sighed. "We are all doomed. Yes, my uncles? This is true? Should we be bored as well?"

Someone groaned, so I sat up once again.

"You agree, uncle? Yes? Then I say we introduce ourselves. I'll start. My name is Hans Blix. They sent me here to ask if any of you have any weapons of mass destruction. Maybe at home? Maybe in your garden? Even the smallest weapon of mass destruction would help." Funny, I thought.

The oldest man, the one with the mustache of pure gray, spoke. He stared straight ahead and asked in high Arabic, "Did you learn English from television?"

I smiled and answered in English, "Yes, uncle. Absolutely. You?"

"Maybe you'd like us to think that." The old man kept to his Arabic. "To me, you sound like a child of Mansour. Was it Baghdad University where you learned?"

"Why? Do you recognize me? Were you a professor?"

"I recognize men in the morgue. Until then we are strangers."

"Then what better time to introduce ourselves, uncle?"

Finally, the old man turned to face me. "These jokes, young man," he said in English. "These are the jokes of a bachelor. The jokes of a childless man. You should keep these jokes to yourself."

I nodded. "I understand, my uncle. Apologies." I put my hand over my heart. "I will think of some Saddam jokes. This is okay, now? Yes?"

No one laughed.

The convoy bounced around Lake Habbaniyah, vast and green. The long route around, too. We crept into the shadows of the Taqaddum plateau, the long-forbidden place where Saddam had kept his air base. We turned sharply at the dusty cliffs before drifting back to the river, the green fields, the palm trees, and the reeds.

Finally, the truck made a hard left onto a paved road, almost hidden, and we started up the maze of bluffs. The river fell away. The engine noise grew frantic and the tires slipped once before finding their grip on the road. A gate appeared and the flat mess of the old air base grew beyond it.

The eyes of the old men became wide. They were pulled to the edge of the bench and then to their feet, straining to see through the veil of dust and exhaust into the place where the great man had kept his fighter planes and bombs. Where friends of theirs had long ago been taken in the night and made to disappear. Where the Americans now lived, gazing down at the river and their spoils.

I kept to my seat and stared back over the tailgate to the river winding north, to the ribbons of green holding fast to the bank and to the dirt and the horizon besieged by it. Then the truck kicked, turned a corner, and the river was gone.

We stopped again for a young marine to come aboard the truck and check our new identification cards. Sweat poured down his pale face, but he did not bother with it. The green canvas of his chin strap soaked it up.

The old men offered their identification with both hands, thumbs and forefingers gripping the corners. They held the cards just below their faces and peered over like schoolboys, nodding and trying to smile like Americans. All teeth and no shame.

The marine put a gloved finger on each card while using his other hand to steady the rifle slung across his chest. The old men dug through the documents we had been given at Ramadi for something more to offer the young marine, even after he had passed them, satisfied.

I waited my turn and, as he approached, pulled the card from my hip pocket and held it over my head, slow and cool.

The marine tapped my card with one finger, put his hand over his heart, and said, *"Shukran."*

"That is right, man. My name is MCA, and I have a license to kill." I heard that once on a Beastie Boys album and had always thought it sounded cool. It made the young marine laugh, anyway.

The truck jumped into gear and idled through the gate. We passed a line of American trucks waiting to leave the way we came in. A dozen cargo trucks and several Humvees. Men, and a few stern women, leaned against them. Tan jumpsuits covered them head to foot. I watched them put on their hoods and helmets and seal themselves inside their armor, wondering what they were going out there to do. Kill someone? Someone I might know?

Our convoy broke apart. The escorts with the mounted machine guns sped away toward their own corner of the plateau. Our truck turned a corner and arrived in America. Men in desert camouflage strolled with rifles draped across their backs. Fat civilians in collared shirts and khaki pants pushed through the hot wind with their heads down.

We passed helicopters parked in neat rows behind razor wire and an empty field becoming a city as we watched. A heavy crane unloaded metal living quarters, five meters square, from a line of waiting flatbed trucks and arranged them into neat rows. Carried five to a truck, these boxes looked able to accommodate two beds, keeping the lucky Americans inside well cooled with individual air conditioners. Those Americans without nice, air-conditioned boxes lived in long, plywood huts with a dozen others.

A dump truck followed the crane with gravel, which foreign laborers, Pakistanis I imagined, raked into walkways while armed guards watched them from all around. The field hummed with generators, compressors, air movers.

A cargo plane took off. I smelled the exhaust, felt the heat of its engines, and missed the river.

Eventually, we came to a cluster of concrete bunkers, isolated behind their own wire and gate on the far side of the base. These deep bunkers were made for surviving bombs. An American in khaki pants and sunglasses opened the gate for us. Our truck stopped and the brakes exhaled. The old men ripped open their tight flak vests and gasped, their lungs for the first time in hours free to inflate fully.

The tailgate fell away and a man called out in Arabic, "Leave your flak jackets and helmets on the truck. They go back to Ramadi. You get new ones here."

I stripped off my gear and jumped to the ground, taking the six-foot drop like a boss, slapping the dirt. The Americans would teach me to say that—*like a boss*—and laugh when I said it inappropriately.

"Help each other from the truck," the man yelled. "If you need more help, wave to a marine."

I put my hands in my pockets and smelled the air. I stepped away from the truck, walked in tight circles, kicking dirt clods and small rocks as Americans crowded the tailgate to help the old men down.

"Don't wander. Line up here, in front of me. I need to check you in."

I searched the crowd for the voice, imagining an Arab in an ankle-length shirt. I assumed he would have an olive complexion, at least.

"Directly to my front! Have your identification ready!"

There I found him, with his expensive sunglasses and his marine's uniform. He looked just like an American, and not much older than me. He waved a clipboard over his head. But despite his uniform, I could tell instantly that he was not a marine. Dark hair spilled out from under his hat, and his trouser legs hung straight to his bootheels. Real marines would tuck the loose trouser fabric neatly away above their boots. And they always trimmed their hair very, very short.

I walked alone toward him while the old men shimmied over the tailgate on their bellies, looking for the courage to let go.

"Let me see your identification," the man said in English.

"Sure, man." I dropped my identification card onto his clipboard.

"Thank you." The man checked my name on his clipboard and put the card under the silver clip. He pulled a new card from his pocket. "This is your new identification." The card already had my picture. "I keep the old one. From now on, you only get your old identification when you go home on leave. No name on your new card. Just a number. This is for your safety and your family's. Now, go down those stairs."

The man pointed to the door of the nearest bunker.

I leaned in close and smiled. "Might I ask you a question, man?"

"Sure," he sighed. "Quickly, though."

"Where are you from?"

He shrugged. "That's not really something you ask around here. But, what the hell? America. Michigan."

"I'm sorry. I was not clear. I meant, you know, before then."

"Lebanon."

I laughed. Who was he trying to fool? The Americans? Believing Lebanon somehow sounded better than the truth?

"Okay, man." I said, walking to the bunker. "Try that on the ladies."

"What?"

"Syria—that's what you meant, right?" I reached the door and called over my shoulder. "When you get back to Damascus, though, tell that to the ladies. Lebanon! Invite them to the beach."

"Michigan," he said sternly.

"Yes, and I went to Jordan once. But I will always be from Baghdad."

The door opened to dark, steep stairs. I saw lights at the bottom and heard men laughing and speaking English. I dragged my hands along the walls and moved one step at a time while feeling for the steps' edge with my right foot. I reached the bottom, turned the corner into a bright room, and understood at once the original purpose of this bunker. It was not some dirty hole, meant for simple storage. It was a luxury place built by Saddam, so his officers could shelter themselves from American bombs in their customary grandeur. And now, in this new Iraq, Saddam's old adversaries had found it and made themselves quite comfortable.

"*Schlonak,*" an American exclaimed. "*Assalamu alaikum!*"

My vision returned fully, and I saw a civilian in cargo pants, boots, and a collared shirt with an embroidered corporate logo. I made special note that he did not wear a pistol. He was middle-aged but still in good shape, hands planted on his hips, his chest puffed out.

A marine about the same age stood behind him; an officer, I guessed, from the shiny metal on his collar. He smiled and waved, as well.

"Take a seat anywhere," the civilian said. He gestured to the plastic chairs, in neat rows on the marble floor.

"Okay." I shrugged. I put my hands in my pockets and considered my options. The curses and heavy breathing of the old men coming down the steps grew louder.

The officer spoke again. Just to me. To me alone. "Safe trip?"

"Yes. Fine."

Deep in the bunker, down the long hallway behind the Americans, a man shouted. Angry Arabic words exchanged in the dark.

"No worries," the civilian said, pointing down the hall with his thumb. "Just, it gets a little loud back there sometimes. Don't stress."

Out from the dark came an Arab man, older, fat, and mustached. He wore a marine's uniform, but like the man with the sunglasses and the clipboard upstairs, he was not a marine. He stormed past the officer and his friend.

"Liars." He hissed, "No more liars today. Going to smoke."

The officer laughed and patted the angry man on the shoulder. "You're a saint, Cadillac."

I remained still. Cadillac brushed against me on his way up the stairs.

The officer turned to me. "Please, please. *Min fadlak!* Relax."

I did as he asked.

And now, the old men came in, one at a time, breathing hard. When we were all seated, the civilian with the broad chest spoke. He greeted us in polite Arabic, as though he had practiced the one phrase all day. Then he switched back to English.

"First, let me compliment your bravery. Even for what we pay, it is understood that you are heroes for this." He stopped to look us each in the eye. "True Iraqi heroes. Also, let me say we know the dangers your families face. This is *why*, once you leave this bunker, you will not *use* your real names. Not to me. Not to Colonel Davis. Not to the marines you *work* with. We will provide each of you with a nom de guerre." He shook his head and frowned. "Sorry. A fake name, that is."

I looked around the room. The old men nodded as though they understood any of this.

"Okay." The civilian examined his notes. "We need to discuss classifications. At Government Center in Ramadi, you were all classified by the intake marines. Category one, two, or three. Category two and three have provisional security clearance, and the ability to translate as well as interpret." He looked down at his notes and frowned as if he somehow disagreed with his own words. "I say provisional, because clearances are usually given only to American citizens. But with your demonstrated abilities and loyalty you are, uh, granted provisional status."

The old men smiled.

"Okay, *so*; category two and three interpreters will live in this

74

bunker and work with intelligence personnel. Talking to detainees. Translating documents. You will never leave Camp Taqaddum unless you're being escorted home for personal leave." He asked the officer softly, "We got any category ones here?"

The officer nodded and held up one finger.

"Category one cannot be granted provisional clearance, for whatever reason. So, if you are category one, you will work with marines in the field. Going out on patrols. Living with them. All right, then? Everyone check the cards Frank gave you upstairs."

We all looked down.

"Any category ones?"

I saw it on my card, a big green digit in the corner. I raised my hand.

"Great. Go ahead and stand up. We'll need you to leave now. Just head back up those stairs and talk to Frank, okay? You'll get a brief later. The rest of this is just for the cleared interpreters."

The civilian smiled like he was my friend.

I stood, my knees a little weak, and found the old man with the gray mustache in the back row.

"Uncle," I said in Arabic, "enjoy your time here. I hope you ask many good questions."

"I look forward to making your acquaintance," he replied.

I walked across the room and up the stairs.

Behind me, I heard the civilian ask, "Okay, anyone hungry?"

Back on the surface, Frank, the man in the sunglasses, the man from Michigan, laughed. "Back so soon?"

"Category one."

"No kidding," he quipped as he turned pages on his clipboard. He stopped on a page with three long columns of words, most of them scratched out with pencil. "Let's see what we have left." He moved his pencil down the page until he found a name he liked.

"Dodge." He smiled. "From now on, your name is Dodge. Understand?"

"Fine." I did not know what it meant and did not ask.

He told me anyway. "A type of car. A good, dependable car." He waved for me to follow him over to a line of white Toyota trucks, brand-new.

"So. Dodge. You have anything? Personal items?"

"No. In Ramadi they told us to leave everything there."

"All right. Then first thing to do is set you up with gear. Here, this one." He pointed to the truck at the end of the row.

We got into the truck and Frank turned on the radio. I knew the station from Fallujah, and the voice of the singer. Gehan Rateb. The hot Egyptian television host. I thought of what the jihadis would do to the Fallujah disc jockey with the audacity to play her music, if they ever found him.

Frank turned the dial before I could ask if he liked Gehan or thought she was hot. He landed on a station with an American disc jockey. A woman.

"Welcome back to the Country Convoy, *with Specialist Kristy . . ."*

"We'll skip the supply warehouse and just drop you off with your unit," Frank said.

"We're broadcasting live from the Green Zone on Armed Forces Radio . . ."

"Engineer Support Company is top of the list for a terp, so you can start out with those guys. Maybe another unit down the line."

"Before we get back to that great country music, a quick rundown of Green Zone events . . ."

"You'll get uniforms, flak, helmet, hoods, sunglasses, and boots. Maybe a medical kit . . ."

"At thirteen hundred, we have yoga by the south pool . . ."

"No weapon, though. Terps don't get weapons."

"At fifteen hundred, we have water aerobics in the west pool . . ."

"Engineer Support Company gets outside the wire a lot. They fix things. Roads and pavement. They build checkpoints, too."

"At twenty hundred, we have the weekly movie by the north pool . . ."

"You'll go out with them and deal with civilians. Sometimes civilians get too close and the marines shoot up a car."

"The movie this week . . . Cast Away, starring Tom Hanks."

"Those guys over at Engineer Support shoot up a lot of cars by accident. You'll go and apologize for them. Got it?" Frank lit a cigarette and switched off the radio. "Also, you talk to the Iraqi Army for them. Regular *jundi*s mostly, but a few officers, too. So if you have politics, or family with politics, or family at all, or religion, or opinions, or anything . . . now you *don't*. Understand?"

We drove past the hospital and the dining hall. Massive, metal-framed tents covered in white vinyl, with generators and air conditioners off to the side.

"So, Dodge. Shiite or Sunni?"

I looked out the window, at the Americans waiting to get lunch. "Neither. I am a Jew."

Frank laughed. "Sure, me too. But seriously"—Frank slapped me on the knee—"hey, you listening?"

"Yes, I am listening, man."

"Don't tell them anything. Do not tell. Anyone. Anything. Got it? Last week, out with some grunts over by Fallujah, we found a house with fifteen heads in it. No shit. Fifteen fucking cut-off heads. My family live in Michigan, okay? And that's all anybody knows. They don't know my *name*. They don't know anything *about* me, and I'm an American, man." Frank pulled on his cigarette. "So. What's your name?"

"Dodge. My name is Dodge."

"Good."

We passed a sign reading WELCOME TO ENGINEER VILLAGE, WHERE SAFETY IS PARAMOUNT. SPEED LIMIT 5 MPH AT ALL TIMES.

Frank lifted his foot off the accelerator and the truck rolled past a field of armored vehicles, of a type I had never seen. Marines wearing tan, camouflage trousers and green T-shirts walked back and forth with ice chests, machine guns, and ammunition cans.

The truck glided to a halt next to a concrete building left over from Saddam's old Air Force. Faded paint over the door read in Arabic TAMMUZ AIRBASE, 14TH SQUADRON. I wondered if the Americans knew that. I wondered if anyone had ever asked.

A forest of radio antennas grew out from the flat roof. A sign out front, stenciled on rough plywood, read ENGINEER SUPPORT COMPANY. HOME OF THE FINEST. MAJOR R. E. LEIGHTON, COMMANDING.

Frank put the truck in park and tapped out his cigarette. "This is you, Dodge."

We got out and walked under the awning, up to a plywood door bolted to the wall. Bad carpentry, that door. "Ghetto rigged," as the Americans would teach me to say.

Frank knocked and a marine with a pistol on his hip answered. Young and tall. Blond. Well muscled. A river of cold air spilled out with him.

"Can I help you?"

"Yeah. Hey. I'm with intel support. Dropping off your new terp."

"He cleared?"

"Category one. So, he can live with you guys, but he's a no-go for secret spaces."

"Not coming in *here*, then." The lieutenant stepped outside, letting the ghetto-rigged door close behind him.

"Wait. Lieutenant Cobb. Sir." The voice came from inside. Then the door popped open again and another marine came out. Older and out of shape. Smiling like he was well practiced.

"Yeah, Gunny?"

"Road Repair Platoon's due for a terp, sir."

"How'd you come to that conclusion, Gunny?"

"Lieutenant Wong over at Bulk Fuel Platoon got the last terp. Before that, you guys over at Construction Platoon got the plasma-screen briefing board. I'm just saying, sir. You know—just trying to keep it fair for my lieutenant, is all."

"Fine. Take him over there. Clear it with Major Leighton when he gets back."

Now another voice approached, this one full of command. "I'm back. Make a hole." He walked by us, this Major Leighton, wide-shouldered and bald with a white scalp burnt red from the sun. He pushed through our little crowd and walked into the cold room. "The memorial service is over," the major said from inside. "Everyone should be back soon. Get this shit squared away."

The lieutenant and the fat gunnery sergeant marine stood up straight. "Aye, aye, sir," they said in unison.

Once Leighton was gone, the lieutenant turned to the fat gunnery sergeant. "Listen, Gunny. Do whatever you want. I have no time for this."

"Thank you, sir. Corporal Jones can handle my desk while I'm out."

"Yeah. I know he can." The lieutenant disappeared behind the plywood door, not even trying to hide his dislike for this out-of-shape marine, this smiling politician. I did not like him either.

"Hi, how are you? I'm Gunny Dole." He forced his hand into Frank's palm and shook it hard. Up and down like a whip. "Road Repair Platoon chief, senior enlisted. I spend most of my time here, though. Working with the operations section. Making sure everything goes smooth. Lieutenant Donovan and Sergeant Gomez pretty much got it handled over at the platoon. Not much need of me."

All that explanation, all those excuses, and we had only just met.

"So, who's this guy?" He pointed at me.

"Dodge," I answered before Frank had the chance. I put a hand on my chest. "A dependable car."

Gunny Dole slapped my shoulder. "I had a Dart myself, for about ten years! That was back in the day, though!" He laughed, by himself. "Here, follow me over to the platoon. Let's get you a cot."

We walked around the squat concrete building, out back to a dirt patch guarded on all sides by tall, earthen berms. The whole company, all those Americans, were tucked right up against the edge of the plateau. I wondered if they knew that everyone down by the river could see them, clearly, moving around up there.

They kept an area of dirt, about thirty meters square, empty and smooth for exercise and such. Plywood huts, long and skinny with doors on either end, were arranged around the empty square three deep on each side. They had room enough inside each for about twenty beds.

"Most of the company's over at the chapel," Gunny Dole said, and then stiffly, "Memorial service. We took a KIA last week."

"Sorry to hear that," Frank said. Clinical and detached, like he had tried before, many times, to say it well but had learned that there was no right way.

"Yeah." Gunny Dole put his hands in his pockets. "He was a good guy."

It was the first thing I heard him say that I believed.

Gunny Dole knocked on the door of a plywood hut in the back row, built closest to the berm at the edge of the plateau. When no one answered, he pushed it open. "Anyone home?" He turned on the lights.

"Here, Gunny." A young man sat on his bunk at the far end. He had been sitting in the dark.

"Hey, Doc. Not at the chapel?"

"Gear watch. Someone had to stay back."

"With the lights off ?"

"Fuckin' sauna in here."

"Okay." Gunny Dole looked puzzled, as if trying to work out how a single light would add any appreciable heat to the whole, long room. He shrugged. "Doc, this is Dodge. Dodge, this is Doc Pleasant. The platoon corpsman. Medical guy, I mean. He takes care of us."

I nodded to him. "Good afternoon."

He looked me up and down and frowned. A few years younger, but skinny and gangly like me. He had some unfortunate acne left in what appeared to be the final months of his teenagerhood. His thick, red hair was cut short on the sides. Not exactly the best look.

"This is the only bunk," the Doc said, pointing to the empty cot across from him, addressing Gunny Dole rather than me.

"Guess that settles it, then. Dodge, go grab your bunk. Doc, look after him for a bit. Get him set up with gear when the company makes it back from the chapel."

Then, Frank and Gunny Dole left the two of us alone.

The Doc did not get up. Did not say a word or even look to me. He just sat there and stared straight ahead.

So I walked over and sat down across from him on my new bed, deciding I would let this truculent Doc speak first, whenever he felt like it. It took several minutes.

"You Iraqi?" he eventually asked.

"Yes. From Baghdad."

"The fuck you know about Metallica, then?" He did not ask nicely.

"This?" I pointed to my shirt. "I go buy albums in Baghdad. We have a place there called Music Street. We have Metallica. AC/DC. All that."

He nodded and lay back with his head down on the cot. Sprawled out and limp.

"What about you, man? Do you like Metallica?"

"No," he said. "Used to. Been a while."

"Not anymore, then? Why not?"

He sighed. "Look, I'm supposed to watch you, but I kinda need a nap. So just . . . Just stay put."

And then he fell asleep. So I did the watching. When I grew bored, I took the Mark Twain from my back pocket and began to read, arriving by chance on the page where Sherburn admonishes his lynch mob, saying they will not pursue him in the daylight, and that "the average man don't like trouble and danger."

I suppressed a laugh, careful not to wake the Doc.

Soon, marines came shuffling back into the hut and sprawled out across their cots as well, with red eyes and rifles seeming heavier than usual for them.

My new friends.

After Action Report: Enemy Activity Trends

1. *Anti–Iraqi Forces burning vehicle tires on roads to loosen asphalt for placement of improvised explosive devices under road surface.*

2. *Anti–Iraqi Forces burying fuel accelerants, such as kerosene or diesel, with improvised explosive devices. Fuel is typically combined with soap chips, causing flame to adhere to exposed skin.*

3. *Anti–Iraqi Forces initiating complex attacks following improvised explosive device detonations. Typical complex attack includes rocket-propelled grenade salvo followed by small-arms fire directed at dismounted personnel. Enemy withdraws into civilian population quickly in order to avoid counterattack.*

Suggested Procedures:

1. *Continued adherence to the Five Cs. Confirm the presence of a device. Clear friendly forces to minimum safe distance. Cordon area to prevent enemy entrance. Control access. Check for secondary devices.*

2. *Travel with a vehicle interval of 75 to 100 meters in order to prevent enemy attack on multiple vehicles with a single device. Fives and twenty-fives remain essential.*

Respectfully submitted,

P. E. Donovan

ROUTE CLEARANCE

Paige leaves a note in my letterbox on the last day of finals. I see it waiting for me out of the corner of my eye while passing through the MBA student lounge.

"There's a group of us meeting at Molly's each Thursday night during the Christmas break," it reads. "Just a way to keep up good relations. You should come. I'm inviting you. Also, why don't you list your phone number or e-mail address in the student directory? And for that matter, why aren't you on Facebook? Are you a spy or something? Call me."

She includes her phone number at the bottom, with the postscript, "(My family and I are members at Southern Yacht Club. We've had a Catalina 36 since I was a little girl. So, if you feel like setting foot on an actual sailboat sometime . . .)"

I fold the note five times and tuck it into the back of my wallet.

On my streetcar ride home, bouncing along the St. Charles Avenue tracks, I imagine the sailboat Paige's family keeps at the yacht club—in pristine condition, I'll bet. Not like the wreck I saw this morning in the West End boneyard, up on blocks, and such a mess that the old harbormaster could hardly muster a nice word to say about it, despite his obvious desire to see it gone.

"Well, it would be . . . a real project" was about the best he could say for the battered hull with *Sentimental Journey* stenciled across its stern. "But, then, you're a young guy, right? No wife, no kids. Gonna take on a project like this, now'd be the time."

I ran my hand along the pitted gel coat. "How did these abrasions get here?"

"The Storm." He shrugged. "Surge ripped all the boats off their moorings in the municipal harbor, carried them across the street, and left them piled up in the parking lot when the water receded. *This* gal was lying on her port side at the bottom of the pile. Owner never came back for her."

After mentally stumbling through a selection of half-remembered nautical terms for an intelligent question to ask, I settled on, "Did you manage to save any of the standing rigging?"

He laughed. "You're joking right? All that's left's what you're looking at. But you'd want to start over with the rigging, anyway. Gut the interior, too, and rebuild from an empty hull. That's one thing about these old boats—the hulls are thick. They take a beating, and you can always rebuild."

If I don't get back to him by early January, he's having it chopped up and taken to a landfill. I'm just glad he didn't ask me about my sailing experience or renovation plans. He probably assumes I'm looking for a party barge to impress girls, and I'm happy to let him.

I get off the streetcar at Washington Avenue and start walking the last few blocks to my apartment. Ahead of me, a funeral procession blocks the way across Coliseum Street as the horse-drawn carriage makes a slow right turn through the Lafayette Cemetery gates. I wait on the corner and shiver while the band and the mourners pass. They have a strange system in this city. A jazz band leads the mourners from the church to the cemetery, playing sad songs along the way so everyone can get their hysterics out. Then, after they put the coffin in its tomb, they play upbeat music so everyone can dance their way back to the church.

It's free-form and wild, the opposite of a military funeral. But how would I know? It occurs to me with a start that I've never attended a military funeral. Never heard a twenty-one-gun salute or seen a widow take her folded flag. We had plenty of back-in-country memorial services, but it wasn't the same. We always botched it.

I think of Paige and her speech about empathy. She might've been onto something with that, and I find myself wishing I'd put up a better fight on her behalf. It's what Major Leighton missed on the day of Gunny Stout's memorial. Empathy.

He got up and gave a big speech about getting over it. Heads back in the game. And while that might've been the right message from a leadership point of view, it wasn't effective. It didn't put anyone's head back in the game.

No one knew the procedure before Gunny Stout died. He was the company's first, and we had to learn on the fly. We messed up the family notification message. We messed up his personal effects. We messed up everything.

For starters, we needed a new comment for the personnel status board. We couldn't just subtract one from the company's total strength, apparently. We had to keep him on the morning report until after mortuary affairs had prepped his remains for transport. But how to list him? Were we supposed to just scribble the word *Dead* on the board and put his name next to it? No one knew.

Finally, the admin chief walked over to the status board and made a new box: *Outbound Angels—1*.

It offended me. I assumed that the admin chief, a religious guy known to proselytize, had made it up and tried to sneak in a preachy remark. I went to have a word with him, but Cobb stopped me. He told me the admin chief took the words right from the personnel

manual. So I looked it up. Sure enough. *Outbound angels*. That's
what we called them officially.

I didn't like it. No one who saw that vinyl bag, limp like feed,
hefted into the helicopter would've thought to call it an angel. Even
Doc Pleasant, usually pretty good about gore, shut down. He skipped
the memorial service. There wasn't an angel in sight for Doc
Pleasant, and he was the type who'd look.

After the memorial service, the other lieutenants, Cobb, Wong,
and the rest of them, slapped me on the shoulder and talked tough.

"You made the call, man. Not easy. No shame."

"Nothing you could do. That's a lieutenant's job. Why we make
the big bucks."

"Drive on. New day, brother."

But underneath, I heard them asking, "Are you sure he died
instantly? Are you sure? Weren't you in charge? Where were you
when he walked out there? Why didn't you tell him no? Why didn't
you make him wear his bomb suit at least? Muscled by a gunny again,
weren't you. Talked out of your rank. Yeah. That figures, runt."

I imagined them at chow, the whole pack of lieutenants
mulling it over at social hour. Cobb, with his square jaw and broad
shoulders, leading the discussion. Softly posing the question to my
assembled peers: "Who'll run the platoon for him now?"

Even Gunny Dole attempted, for once, to step up. He ambled
over after the memorial service and asked, "Sir, can you use me
down at the platoon? Anything I can do?"

I took the opportunity to scold him. It was pointless, but satisfy-
ing. "Sure could, Gunny. In fact, I could really use you out on the road."

He winced and shook his head. "Yeah. I'm sorry, sir. Really
sorry. Medical says I can't go out on the road with the bum knee.
Wish I could. I hate missing it. Anyway, I need to run over to the
phone center real quick. My wife has a question about the

mortgage." He walked away, the glow of a twenty-year pension around him like an aura.

Major Leighton didn't bother with any of that. He called me into his office a day later and asked me straightaway, "How many potholes has your platoon cleared so far, Lieutenant Donovan?"

"One hundred and fifty-seven, sir."

"Out of those, how many have had an explosive device, in some stage of emplacement and arming, buried in the hole?"

"One hundred and fifty-seven, sir."

"So, it's safe to assume that your Marines will encounter these explosive devices again."

"Yes, sir."

"Well then, you need to get back on the road as soon as possible. Best thing for the platoon."

"Yes, sir."

"Given time to dwell on this, your Marines will lose all fighting spirit. They will lose the ability to face these devices. They will hesitate. They will spend hours at every hole, poking around endlessly with those damn robots. They will lose the initiative. They will surrender momentum to the enemy, who will find a new way to kill them. While your Marines are stalled by fear, cowering on the same patch of highway for hours, the enemy will have time to maneuver on you with small arms, machine guns, and rockets. Maybe even indirect fire."

"Yes, sir."

"The dangers out there are sort of like the ocean." He chuckled. "You'd never swim if you knew how many sharks there really were."

"Yes, sir." There wasn't much else I could say, staying within military decorum.

"So, we keep the momentum. Here's the mission." He rubbed his bald head, sending flakes of peeling, sunburned skin cascading onto the map. "Route Long Island, from the Newport intersection north, all the way to Hit."

He walked the length of his map table to trace the route. Red dots marked the site of every enemy attack in the previous six months. As he dragged his finger along a major highway over fifty miles of open desert, red dots slipped under his finger like braille. He smiled. "Every pothole wider than a meter across. You fill it, you mark it, you make it safe."

"Aye, aye, sir."

"Take the new terp along. What's his name? Dodge? Get him oriented."

"Aye, aye, sir."

"Oh, and one more thing. The bomb technicians are an attachment from now on. None of this split command business. No ambiguity. The bomb techs work for you, and that's it." He put his hands on his hips and nodded at me.

"Aye, aye, sir."

We used that naval phrase by tradition. The Marines. The infantry of the sea. But it wasn't just traditional. The words had meaning.

Aye, aye didn't just mean "Yes." It meant, "I understand the order. I will carry out the order." And I understood him perfectly. It was my responsibility, from that point on, not just for the pothole but for the bomb inside it, too.

We rolled the next morning, before curfew lifted and Iraqi trucks and donkey carts choked the streets solid. We took Route Michigan east toward Fallujah, turned south onto Route Long Island, and watched the city slip away on the far side of the river. It was still dark. Generator exhaust shimmered in the green sodium light above the mosques. The shops along Phase Line Fran were all sealed up with corrugated-metal sheets. The radios crackled as infantry patrols came on and off the net with sporadic reports of rifle fire.

We sped up in the empty desert just south of the river, reaching the intersection of Route Long Island and Route Newport, at the southern tip of Lake Habbaniyah, thirty minutes later.

We negotiated the dark intersection and turned north. Gomez came on the net a moment later and announced that a massive hole, three meters across and a meter deep, blocked the road ahead. We stopped and assumed a security posture, still fifty miles from Hit. A crater so soon after the intersection didn't bode well for the rest of the day.

We parked in the middle of the highway, straddled the white line, and stopped traffic in both directions while we waited for daylight. Zahn tapped the gas pedal every few minutes to keep the engine warm. I sat next to him and worked the radios. Marceau manned the turret, and Doc Pleasant sat in the backseat with Dodge.

Our empty seven-ton truck, running point, was the nearest vehicle to the crater. An empty truck always led the way, as we'd learned by then not to keep anything of value on the first vehicle. No one said it out loud, but the lead truck was a mine roller. Simple as that. A corporal always rode in the lead truck to reassure the junior Marine behind the wheel. The corporals took turns; Gomez kept a list.

Gomez was always second in the order of march, right behind the mine roller in a standard gun-truck, a security Humvee with a turret-mounted machine gun. A long-bed utility truck followed her with generators and compressors, jackhammers and asphalt saws, pallets of concrete in fifty-pound bags, and a ten-thousand-gallon water tank. I always rolled last in the order of march, in a four-vehicle section with three gun-trucks protecting the bomb-disposal vehicle.

We made sure the bomb-disposal vehicle looked just like the others, and we varied its place in line. It was an endless game of three-card monte with the enemy triggermen, for whom killing bomb-disposal technicians was a top priority. According to intelligence reports, killing an American bomb tech could make a triggerman rich, satisfy his desire for revenge, or bring him great rewards in heaven. Plenty of incentive, whatever his motivation.

Dodge sat in the backseat of the command Humvee, looking brand-new in his gear. His crisp flight suit still sported the sheen from its flame-resistant fabric treatment, and the folds on his flak had yet to accumulate a single grain of sand.

Pleasant reached across the seat to adjust Dodge's flak. "You look like a goddamn soup sandwich over here. We'll tape up all these slides when we get home. Seriously, you look like some kind of traveling Gypsy." Pleasant pulled hard on a strap to tighten the fit. "Too tight? Can you still breathe?"

"Yes, man." Dodge sighed. "I can breathe."

"Seriously, though—tell me if you can't. I can loosen it."

"No, it's good. Really, man. It's fine." Dodge nodded and put a hand over his heart.

Behind the wheel, Zahn spit into his dip bottle and asked, "Light enough, sir?"

"Give it five minutes."

"Yo, Zahn," Marceau called out from the turret. "Pass me a can of Copenhagen. I'm falling the fuck asleep."

Zahn scoffed. "I look like Santa Claus to you? Should've fucking thought about that before we rolled out."

I watched Marceau settle back behind his gun and sigh. He let his black hair, prematurely flecked with gray, grow a few centimeters longer than regulation, and had an oddly flattering gap in his front teeth.

Marceau had a genuinely charming emotional blind spot. Perception didn't much matter to him. He cared only for reality. As long as he knew he was doing his job, and keeping his friends safe, he was immune to peer pressure. Free to be a Marine without having to act like one. Free to make light of our national follies and remind us all that in the scope of wars that had come before, our war was silly. Worth a laugh or two.

I had Gomez assign him to my turret whenever possible. I was selfish like that.

I watched as daylight crept through the palm trees off to our right and draped Marceau's face in an orange sheen. The same sunbeam drifted in through the armored window and came to rest on my cheek. I keyed the radio when my skin began to prickle from the heat.

"This is Actual. Execute twenty-five-meter sweep, over."

I watched the passenger door of Gomez's Humvee pop open, fifty meters down the road. Gomez leaped out as though she'd been held inside by a spring, and after checking the safety, draped her rifle across her back by passing the sling under her arm and over her helmet. Fighting six hundred pounds of rough steel, she pressed her shoulder into the Humvee door. Sand boiled over the toes of her boots. The door bounced back twice. She took a breath, pushed again, and almost slipped to her knees before the latch finally caught.

Then she stood up straight and wrestled her flak jacket back into place. The weight of her ill-fitting body armor sat so far forward that she had to force herself not to slouch. The ballistic plates, six full magazines, and her radio all pulled straight down. She rolled her shoulders, came off her feet and set her heels, coaxed the tan monster into place, and took a long step onto the road. Marines swarmed around her, doing their twenty-fives.

I glanced over my shoulder to check on Doc Pleasant and Dodge, and caught Doc Pleasant watching Gomez, too.

He looked away and seemed to take a moment to try to conjure a valid reason for staring. "We jump out, too, sir?"

"No. Same rules. Corpsmen don't dismount until it's clear."

I looked over at Dodge, fidgeting with the straps on his helmet. "You, too, Dodge. Stay in the vehicle. And when we get out, stay close to me."

"I understand you, man." He nodded. "I will stay close."

Doc Pleasant elaborated helpfully, "See, we can't replace you. Me neither. I'm the only medic and you're the only terp. So, we wait. Okay?"

"Yes. Understood."

"No. Look at me. Repeat what I said."

"I speak English, man." Dodge's voice got testy. "And I heard you."

I jumped in to defend Doc and insisted, "Say it back to him, Dodge. It's how we do things."

"Fine. I stay in the vehicle. And when I get out, I stay next to the *mulasim.*"

"*Mulasim?*" I asked. "Is that how you say *lieutenant* in Arabic?"

"Yes."

"What's it mean exactly? Like, what's it translate to?"

"It means 'not necessary.'"

Zahn stifled a laugh. "For real?"

Marceau didn't even try. He let out a howl of laughter. "You got an extra set of bars down there, sir? Guess you should promote me on the spot!"

Dodge seemed puzzled by our reactions. "It means the same thing in English, does it not? Like the actual French word. Instead of the real guy, it means like a place-keeper. Yes?"

"Sure," I said. "Just not accustomed to, uh, hearing it put so plain."

Up ahead, Gomez reached for her radio. I heard her in my ear a moment later. "Copy, Actual. Twenty-fives complete. I'm en route."

"Copy all. Set security." I took my thumb off the transmit button and turned to Zahn. "Roll up. Get Marceau a good line of sight behind the water truck and I'll catch up."

I jumped out as the Humvee rolled forward slowly, stood still, and let Gomez come to me. She marched through the cordon judging the merits of our perimeter, our movable fortress. Like Napoleon, I thought, and in the same dimensions.

Our trucks and Humvees parked at angles sharp to the side of the road to give the turret gunners good, overlapping fields of fire. An ambush could come from anywhere. From the road behind us, and the Iraqi cars stranded at the intersection. From the long, sloping desert with its rocks and shrubs on either side. From snipers hiding in the twisted remains of abandoned cars and burned-out tanks, waiting for a shot at someone's face. From triggermen waiting in the little town on the horizon, talking about us in square houses painted two-tone brown and screwing up their courage for a coordinated attack. From the innocent-looking kids slipping in and out of the alleys, stepping through the shimmer, ducking behind cars and through metal gates into courtyards, always watching.

Civilian traffic was the primary concern. Because of our cordon, a gaggle of beat-up cargo trucks had stacked up behind us, while a line of cars, a half mile long and growing, idled in front of us. The Iraqis in the cars nearest us kept their hands where the Marines could see and spared only the occasional sideways glance through their windshields.

Marines stepped from the staged security vehicles and shouted at each other.

"Set up on the right! Off to the right!"

"Hey! Turret! That's your sector. Down the road. Farmhouse on the left. Flat roof, blue stripe."

"Where? The fuck you say?"

"Yeah. Off the road a little more. Leave room for the compressor. Mixer after that. Water bull after that."

Always, they made sure to clear a lane for Gomez, stepping aside when they heard the rifle bouncing against her armor plate. It had a cadence all its own, with steps too long for a body so small.

I saw Marceau headed for the front of the column. He'd passed off his turret to a junior Marine to help heft the heavy asphalt saw up front. He was stooped over as he passed by Gomez, sucking wind.

She stopped short and squared her shoulders on him, staring him down like a third-grade teacher. She looked through his sweat, ignored his dark eyes, and let him know that she expected more.

Marceau passed her, said something to the Marine next to him, and they both stood up straight.

Gomez kept walking. "Yeah," she yelled over her shoulder. "You fucking know it, too. On the clock."

Then she stood in front of me, unwittingly doing exactly the same thing. "Look good, sir?"

"No complaints."

"Then let's knock this fucker out." She pointed. "Too much traffic here. Too many buildings over there."

We walked together, weaving through the cordon to the edge of the standoff zone where the trucks idled with the repair equipment and waited for the bomb techs to declare the crater safe.

Gomez and I took a knee behind the rear fender of the lead seven-ton, and I saw the crater for the first time. It was a hundred meters away and difficult to assess with any detail through the flickering heat, but I found myself searching for some clue, some reason to hope that this pothole might be the first one without a buried artillery shell rigged to explode.

The two bomb techs, combat replacements fresh into country,

had no illusions. They started prepping a reducing charge in the cargo compartment of their Humvee, without waiting for word.

I turned to Gomez. "Who's next on the list?"

Gomez pulled out a list of names, laminated between two contact sheets to keep it from disintegrating in her sweat-soaked pocket. "Marceau," she said, plucking an alcohol pen from a gear loop on her flak jacket and drawing a line through his name. "Help me up, sir?"

"Sure."

I interlocked my fingers and Gomez stepped into my hands. I lifted her waist-level to the truck bed, where she put her forearms and palms on the steel decking and dragged up a knee. I let go as I felt the Marines in the truck take her weight.

She started her interrogation of the two privates in the truck bed before she was even upright. "You have it ready?" she barked.

"Yes, Sergeant."

"Yes, Sergeant."

"Yeah? The fuck you waiting for, then?"

"Yes, Sergeant."

"Aye, Sergeant."

She sat near the tailgate and took off her helmet. The sweatband on her radio headset kept her jet-black hair tight against her scalp, dripping with sweat. She peeled off the headset and let it hang from her flak for a moment, ran her fingers through her hair in a vain attempt to push out all the sweat.

When she took a rubber band from her wrist to tie the hair back into a tight bun at the top of her neck, the sleeves of her flight suit slid down to reveal her tattoos. A snake wound down her right forearm until a forked tongue sniffed at her wrist. On her left forearm, a flight of songbirds fled.

A voice called from above me, Doc Pleasant's. Dodge was standing next to him. I'd forgotten. "Corporal Zahn said we should come up here," Doc said almost bashfully. "Should we have waited in the vehicle?"

"No. No, you're fine. My fault. Sorry about that. Got caught up. Here—get down next to me."

They each took a knee.

"You calibrate it?" I heard Gomez ask from the bed of the truck.

The junior Marines answered quickly.

"Yes, Sergeant."

"Aye, Sergeant."

"Well," she mused. "We'll see. Switch that fucker on."

I turned to Dodge, drops of sweat cutting rivers across his face. "Getting the feel for this, yet?"

Dodge looked at me. "Of course. Fine."

"Hold up your rifle," Gomez called out, extending a pole toward the junior Marines with a metal disk on the end. She passed the disk in front of the rifle, up close, then a few feet back. The pair of headphones sitting on her lap sang, an urgent bleat to a low hum. She reeled it in. "Looks good to go."

I turned to Doc Pleasant. "You know what happens next? Where you're supposed to be?"

Doc looked at me, mouth open, while Dodge hung on every word and sucked wind like he'd just run a mile. He wasn't yet accustomed to the weight of his body armor, how it trapped heat against his chest and made every step strenuous.

"Immediate actions," I said. "Look at your immediate actions, Doc."

He reached into his cargo pocket and pulled out a laminated index card. He flipped it over twice, looking for the right set of procedures. Dodge watched over Doc's shoulder and tried to read along.

"We've done our fives and twenty-fives, right?" I coaxed. "Set the cordon?"

"Yes, sir."

"Corporal Marceau is about to head up," I hinted. "What'll he need?"

"Cover, sir?"

"He'll get that from the trucks and the dismounted Marines. What'll he need from you?"

Doc swallowed. "He'll need me to be ready, sir."

"Right. So, get ready."

Gomez jumped off the tailgate with the battery bag on her shoulder and the metal detector in her right hand. "Yo, Marceau!" she called out. "Corporal Marceau!"

Marceau approached with his rifle slung over his back. Someone had already told him.

Gomez hung the battery bag on his shoulder. "Here we go, meat-eater. You ready?"

"Yes, Sergeant."

"Okay, then. Let's rig this shit." She tried to sound excited and smiled for him, too. That was a rarity.

Marceau took off his helmet. Gomez clapped the headphones over his ears while he slipped his hand through the metal detector's arm brace and wrapped his fingers around the handle.

"Traffic sees the cordon and doesn't stop," she said. "Accelerates at you. What do you do?"

"I drop and prepare for overhead fire from the fifty."

"You get to the hole, and it's clear?"

"One hand up in a fist. I wait. The repair team rolls to me."

"And what if there's something in the hole. What then?"

"I turn around. I come back. Right arm out, parallel to the deck. Open palm."

"Do you run?"

Marceau was distracted, looking down the highway at the pothole.

She slapped him on the helmet. "Hey. Do you *run*?"

"No, Sergeant."

"All right then. Get it done."

And then Marceau started walking.

Gomez keyed her radio. "Scout's out."

The net went quiet. Gomez followed close behind Marceau until he passed the front fender, then took a knee when he stepped into the standoff zone. After he'd walked about ten meters, she cursed under her breath and reached for her radio. Stopping herself, she looked over her shoulder at me, waved, and whispered, "Sir. Sir. Doc." She raised her eyebrows and cocked her head at Marceau, fifty meters out and walking briskly with the metal detector out in front.

"Doc, get up there with Sergeant Gomez," I said.

He scrambled to his feet, dragging his medical bag and backboard behind him.

"I shouldn't have to call you up here, Doc," Gomez lectured him. "Shouldn't have to bother the sir, neither."

Then it was just me and Dodge. He dropped flat onto his ass and sat with his legs straight out, leaning back against the fender.

"Dodge. Not a good idea," I said. "Stay on one knee. Easier to get up and move."

"All right, man," he groaned as he picked himself up.

"Has anyone bothered explaining this to you yet? How this works?"

He shook his head and pushed the brand-new sunglasses back onto his face, the palms of his awkward, gloved hands maneuvering under the rim of his helmet.

"Okay—well, see, Marceau's up there to check if there's a bomb in the pothole. Right? Which there probably is. When we know for sure, we send up the robot with the clearing charge and . . . blow it up."

"And then?"

"Then we cut away the jagged edges, fill the hole with gravel, and patch over the top with concrete."

"What am I doing at this time?" Dodge asked.

"While they're working, I need you at the front of the column with the bullhorn telling the Iraqi drivers to be patient. Tell them we're doing this for their protection and that, you know, we'll be done in a minute. Oh, most important: tell them not to get close to us."

Dodge nodded. "Of course. Very simple. I can tell them that."

Marceau stopped at the edge of the hole and walked the perimeter twice while passing the metal detector slowly over the broken asphalt. Mindful of his feet on the jagged edges, he bent at the knee and tested for soft patches of asphalt, extending the magnet out over the hole.

"Yo, Zahn!" Gomez called out. Her thumb hovered over the transmit button. "Looks at least three feet deep, ten across. Think ten bags, two hundred gallons."

Just then, Marceau stopped moving. He reeled back his arm, stepped away from the hole, and held his right arm out, parallel to the deck with an open palm.

"Hole is hot," Gomez called out.

Corporals in charge of the various work details echoed her, instructing their Marines to stay put as the reducing charge came up.

Marceau started back, walking slowly but with purpose.

Dodge nudged me. "Is there a fucking bomb in that hole, man?"

"Yes, there is. Pretty much every time."

"And you send him out there? Every time?"

"They take turns," I said.

"Fuck."

"That's the job."

"Fuck, man."

I stood and pointed at the bomb techs. They nodded and sent the robot scurrying forward with the clearing charge.

Marceau made it out of the standoff zone and chucked the metal detector into the truck. I noticed how he tried to hide the violent shaking of his hands as he unleashed a bit of prepared choreography, quipping to Gomez, "Shuffle, hop, step. Heel change. Paradiddle."

Zahn walked over, handed him a can of Copehagen, and said, "I just shit my pants for you, asshole. You're fuckin' welcome."

The robot placed a small explosive in the hole, then came squealing back at top speed. After waiting a beat, the bomb techs called fire in the hole and the reducing charge went off with a loud thump. A sharp crack followed as the enemy explosives detonated. Artillery rounds, I could tell, from the shrapnel hissing into the desert, kicking up a thousand little dust plumes.

Only then did the enterprise truly come to life. The two security Humvees moved forward to bring the pothole inside the secured area. Ground guides walked the Humvees through the tight spaces between the seven-tons and the shoulder while the gunners braced themselves against the turrets. Generators and compressors coughed to life and ground their way up to a loud, steady whine. Marceau and his minions worked at the edges of the hole with their asphalt saws while Zahn pushed his lance corporals at the mixer to have cement to pour the moment the hole was ready for a patch.

I stood and pulled Dodge up by his flak. "Let's get up front."

Dodge tapped me on the shoulder and yelled in my ear to be heard over the din, "Do they need assistance?" He pointed to the Marines struggling in their full combat load to pass bags of concrete from the truck.

"No. They're fine. Stay with me."

"They look like they could do with some assistance. I can carry bags. The people in the cars ahead of us know what to do. They are experienced Iraqi drivers, I assure you. They do not need instructions."

I opened my mouth to answer, but chose not to yell over the noise of the saws. I just grabbed him by the shoulder and pulled him along.

At the front of the cordon, where the noise faded, I reached into the passenger seat of the lead Humvee and grabbed the bullhorn. I pointed emphatically to the line of cars idling a hundred meters down the road and handed the bullhorn to Dodge. "Like we talked about. Tell them we're here for their protection and we'll be done in a minute."

Dodge smiled when he saw the bullhorn, instantly forgetting all his earlier concerns. "Of course, *Mulasim*," he said, wiping his brow. "I will do this." He snatched the bullhorn and, walking toward the Humvee's front fender, pumped it in the air like a prize. Standing up straight, he put the microphone to his lips and called out in Arabic. It was like he'd been waiting all his life for this moment.

He leaned back and howled with his eyes closed. Every few sentences, he put the bullhorn down, gestured wildly at the Marines, and laughed. He walked from one side of the road to the other, low to the ground and bobbing his head like a duck. He put his hands in the small of his back and shimmied like Mick Jagger. Iraqis got out of their cars to watch, laughing with him.

I didn't have time and didn't care enough to admonish him. I walked back to the massive pothole where the Marines were already awash in dust, covered head to foot in a fine layer of concrete silt. Sweat seeped through their flight suits and mixed with the powder. A stiff mud, always drying in the sun faster than the sweat could get it wet, added to the weight of their combat load and got heavier as the day wore on.

The concrete bags came off the truck. Marines at the mixer poured wet cement into the hole. Batch after batch, the hole got smaller. But even with Gomez and Zahn urging them on, the pace slackened. I looked at my watch. We'd been sitting still too long. I could feel the desert getting closer, the town. Eyes were creeping in on us, I knew. Estimating ranges. Setting up mortars. Sighting in their sniper rifles. Every inch of that place, every grain of sand, wanted desperately to kill us.

Soon, the generators and compressors rumbled to a stop. Marines collapsed the mixer and began moving the unused bags of concrete back to the truck. Gomez and a few of her underlings concentrated on smoothing out the new patch.

In the silence, it occurred to me that something was missing. I didn't hear Dodge. I squinted through the shimmer and looked for him at the front of the cordon. Failing to find him there, I searched the faces of the Marines walking past me.

I found him a moment later, twenty feet away from me with a bag of concrete on his shoulder. Nearly buckling under the weight, he struggled not to fall over backward. Two Marines brushed past carrying concrete bags of their own, mistaking Dodge for a Marine and urging him on.

"Hey," I called out, "Dodge!"

He didn't hear me.

I walked over and grabbed his shoulder, taking some of the weight and helping him lower the bag to the ground. "This is not your job. I need you at the front of the cordon, okay? *That's* your job.

Do you understand?" I saw immediately, in his glassy eyes, that he didn't.

"Just insane. It's too hot. Too much." He was slurring and not even sweating as he had been before.

I called, "Corpsman, up! Heat casualty."

Doc jogged over and took a knee. "Motherfuckin' idiot." He opened his pack. "I tried to tell him, sir. I tried. You hear me, Dodge? Dumb as shit. Just relax, now. *Grown*-ups in charge."

"Did you see me, man?" Dodge asked. "Back onstage? Looking good, huh?"

"Sure were."

"I was like David Lee Roth up there. Singing to my people. 'California Girls'!"

"No kidding?" Doc Pleasant, preparing a fluid bag and tube, turned to me. "I need his core temp real quick, sir. He doesn't look too bad. Just a little dehydrated. Still have to check, though."

I left Doc to his work as Gomez walked over with the concrete stamp. "Ready for you, sir."

The stamp was a length of steel rebar twisted into the shape of a castle, the symbol of the engineers. They were ready for me to mark the wet concrete to show it was the Marines that filled this hole, not the bad guys.

The convoy began to fall back into the original order of march. Marines loaded into their trucks and the security Humvees continued their watch. Zahn pulled up next to the patch with the passenger door open so I could hop in quickly.

I pushed the stamp into the wet cement and handed it to Gomez. Then I knelt and, with the back of my pen, scribbled the date, the time, and our unit abbreviation. I wiped the pen on the leg of my flight suit before I jumped into the Humvee. It was the only visible spot of concrete on me.

Doc Pleasant had Dodge sitting up in the backseat with a bottle of water between his legs and a tube taped to his arm. He looked better.

"I know you feel like it's the right thing," I told him, closing the door behind me. "But . . . Just leave that stuff to the Marines, okay? They have a job, and so do you."

"Of course, *Mulasim*," he said with his eyes closed. "Next time I will be . . . far more sensible."

Doc Pleasant tapped Dodge on the knee. "He's good, sir. Just needed a little pick-me-up."

Dodge opened his eyes, turned to Doc Pleasant. "*Shukran*, Lester."

It was the first time I'd ever heard Doc's given name. Dodge knew the kid before I did.

Gomez called out on the radio, "Actual, we're up."

"Roger. Oscar Mike."

"Saw you dancing back there," Pleasant said to Dodge. "Pretty funny."

"You liked that, man? Next time you must do it with me."

"Where'd you learn that, anyway?"

"Baghdad."

Small-arms fire cracked overhead as we passed the town. Two weak bursts, lacking commitment. The ambush they'd spent thirty minutes planning came together a few minutes late. I called in the contact report and rolled through. We didn't even stop for it.

"First time you've been shot at, Dodge?" I asked.

"No, man. Like I said, Baghdad."

Crazy big show! At Siberia! This Friday! Featuring!

THE BLOOD ROYALE. Metal/punk crossover from Austin, TX. Members of Gutbucket, The Drunks, Dixie Witch, Transfixr, Mala Suerte, Sap, Suburban Terror Project, and Bukkake.

WINDHAND. Richmond, VA, female-fronted stoner/doom metal featuring members of The Might Could, Alabama Thunderpussy, and Facedowninshit.

VERMIN UPRISING. First performance. NOLA-based metal duo.

LIZZY

I park my truck a few blocks from the bar, thinking this has gotta be the wrong place. Down the side streets, I see Ninth Ward shotgun houses, all dark and boarded up. Worse, some of them ain't boarded up at all. Could be anybody living in there.

And forget about streetlights. It's a black hole. Any place you turn off St. Claude. But the sign above the door says clear as anything SIBERIA, in big, block letters. And the crowd of white kids, standing outside to smoke, confirms it.

I unbuckle my seat belt, grab the door handle, and stop myself, just to give the potholed street and the trash-strewn sidewalk a good, hard look. Litter. Just an eyesore, right? A quick glance should be all you need.

Look, a bag of chicken bones covered in flies.

Look, an empty forty-ounce beer bottle in a brown paper bag.

I shouldn't notice that the bag looks a little too heavy, or that for some reason the breeze doesn't make that empty beer bottle roll around. It shouldn't take all kinds of science and a full goddamn minute of my life every time I step out this truck.

But it does. I should just go home.

My heart speeds up a little bit as I get out, getting madder at myself with each passing second. I'm about to walk into a heavy-metal show packed with knuckleheads. Not the best idea. I lock my overnight duffel in the truck next to my trauma bag.

Dodge told me about how he and his friends used to put on punk-rock shows in Baghdad. Before the war.

After we made it back from the mission where Dodge went down as a heat casualty before we'd even patched the first hole, Sergeant Gomez put me in charge of watching him. Told me to sit with him in the barracks, next to the air conditioner, and make sure he got hydrated.

"Make this fucker push fluids," she said, still wearing her flight suit from the road, still covered in sweat and caked with muck. "And don't let me see him outside until after evening chow. You hear me? Not even to piss. He goes behind that poncho and pisses in bottles, the dumb motherfucker."

Dodge smiled up at her, sitting on his cot with a bottled water between his thighs. "Much thanks, my sergeant," he said, slurring a bit. "Most kind."

She scowled at him, like she was looking for a reason to take offense. But after a few tense seconds, and after she'd pushed some of that black hair behind her ear, she turned to me and snapped, "Doc, save this asshole's piss bottles. I want proof that he's pushed at least five liters before morning."

"Aye, aye, Sergeant," I said, my back straight until she'd finished storming out.

Dodge's eyes were wide like saucers when I finally sat down across from him. "Lester, truly, will she examine my urine tomorrow?"

I nodded. "Probably. Not much for exaggeration, that one."

"Astonishing, Lester. This is the first American woman I have met, and she does not disappoint."

I laughed, despite having to skip my chance at a shower on account of him. And I guess because he was still woozy, not quite on his game, he started talking about his life in Baghdad before the war. Nothing too coherent. Things he probably wasn't supposed to tell me.

"My father and brother hated my rock music, and my friends," he told me, "they always threatened to inform the state morality police of our performances."

"Why didn't they?"

"Because this would have been an embarrassment for them, you see. Important in government, my father and my brother. So to have the second son of Abu Muhammad singing American songs, dancing with girls at secret shows . . . this would not simply not do. So for my friends and I, this was some protection."

"What about your friends? How're they making out these days?"

"We were running," he said, more to himself than to me. "But I left them when I came here to work." Then he got quiet for a second. "I left them by the lake. They were okay. Yes. Safe."

"What about your dad and brother? They safe?"

But Dodge was already done talking, his face behind that book of his. I took the hint.

The doorman shivers in his thin coat, asks for five dollars, doesn't bother to card me. Just looks me up and down. Kind of suspicious. I still got my work clothes on. Boots and jeans. The blue, SPEEDEE OIL CHANGE shirt under my camouflage, duck-hunting jacket has my name on it. And I'm all smudged with dirt and engine grease. It's probably all over my face and hair, too. There wasn't time to shower or change before I drove up.

The doorman waves me inside, and as soon as I step through the clear plastic sheet that acts for a door, I see why I might have confused him. I'm not the usual type for this place.

In the dim lights and the cigarette smoke I see people who're dingy and dirty, not like me, in my work clothes, but dingy and dirty because they're working at it. The guys all got denim jackets with sewn-on patches, the dirtier, the more stained and trampled, the better. Each denim jacket tells a story. Every patch and every stain a battle. Like dress-blue uniforms with campaign ribbons. The stains are a measure of dedication. They tell everyone in the bar, without stooping to say it out loud, how they once saw Cannibal Corpse. How they stuck with it through the nineties and the sad grunge years and how they never cut their hair or stopped slam dancing and smashing barstools. Never gave in and took up what you might call productive behavior.

The girls, the few of them mixed in here and there—they're a different sort. All of them much younger than the guys, for one thing. I see a few serious metalheads, but mostly they're just hangers-on. Girls in that dangerous phase, you know? Attached to some terrible boyfriend in a band or hoping to be at night's end.

I see Landry and Paul onstage. But I stop myself from waving or calling out to them. They're the opening act and need all the metal cred they can muster for this. Some high school buddy waving like it's the goddamn battle of the bands won't help.

It's eleven thirty already and they're only just setting up. Still pretty early for these metal types, I guess. I find an empty corner in the back of the bar and wedge myself into it, almost without thinking. I can see the whole club from this spot. No one can sneak up behind me.

I cross my arms so anyone looking will know I ain't interested. Not my first time at one of these. Landry and Paul dragged me to plenty of metal shows back in high school, and I remember how the best way to muddy up those patches on your denim jacket was to start a fight, pull some guy down into the beer and grime of the club floor, then get yourself dragged through the gravel outside when the bouncer tosses the both of you.

Landry goes to the microphone. He shades his eyes and searches the crowd. Maybe he's looking for me, or maybe there's a girl he hasn't told me about. He's starting to grow a beer belly, stretching out the GWAR T-shirt he's had since puberty. Coming in a little early, that gut. He never was much for exercise. He slings his guitar and says, "Check, check," with that thick Cajun accent. Then, just in case anyone thinks he gives too much of a shit, he tosses out, "Check. Motherfucker, check," and shakes out his hair. It's an old-school mullet, but real close-cropped on the sides.

Paul gets behind the drums and rubs his shaved head. He's had it shaved like that since I've known him, only now it looks less like a choice and more like he's halfway to bald, for real. Getting thinner, too, as Landry puts on weight. Must burn off a bit of that beer weight behind the drums.

Paul counts it off and they launch into their first number.

The whole drive up, I was wondering how Landry and Paul could have a legit metal band with just a guitar, drums, and Landry on vocals. But even on the first riff, I hear their strategy. To make up for not having a buddy who plays bass, Landry has his old guitar plugged into a bass amp and Paul has an extra kick-drum going. They're not the first to think of it, obviously, but it's a good sound. Landry steps away from the microphone and smiles at Paul. They rock out for a few bars. Having fun, looks like. Paul grits his teeth and closes his eyes. It may not be the usual thing, what they're doing up there, but the metalheads start moving around a little bit. Like bubbles stuck to the bottom of a pot just before the water boils.

Then Landry goes to the microphone and ruins it.

Much as I love the guy, and he is a good friend, you can't ignore that Cajun accent. It just ain't metal. The crowd, with the denim jackets and long hair, stops vibrating almost as soon as he opens his mouth and moves away from the stage like someone took the heat off the pot. They go back to the bar for more beer, back to the walls to lean and wait for the headliners.

I'm liking it, though. Okay—maybe Landry doesn't know what he's doing, maybe it's accidental, but there's something to this.

Paul hits both kick drums hard. Landry pulls a dirty riff down the strings and keeps at those lyrics, whispering just to stay on pitch: "I'll show you where I'm from, I'll show you where we bleed."

In some crazy-ass way, that Cajun accent of his might even *help*, you know. Almost like he's doing one of those old, French fais-do-do songs. It's thick and mean and ugly, but there's a truth at the bottom of it, like he's up there onstage standing knee deep in swamp mud. I rock my head up and down a little, trying to get the rhythm of it. Trying to like it for the right reasons, if there are some. I blink and try to bring the stage back into focus. But the smoke and the bright lights sting my eyes so I squint and watch the dance floor instead.

It's empty out there save for one hazy figure. I squint harder and a little blonde thing comes into view. A regular Tinker Bell, wearing a ponytail and what looks like a yellow . . . She actually came into this joint in a fucking sundress? I blink again, thinking I'm imagining this. The cigarette haze parts a second later and I make her out properly.

She's staring at me. Has been this whole time. Her lips are bright red, smiling like she thinks I'm funny. Like she thinks I'm checking her out and it makes her want to laugh.

My cheeks burn. I look away. Embarrassed as hell.

Landry hits the last note of his second song, and realizing the crowd ain't going to applaud, he goes right on, "Next song, it's called 'My Maw Maw'll Kick Your Ass.'"

I look back at Tinker Bell, mostly making sure I didn't just imagine her. This sundressed Tinker Bell of a girl. Sure enough, there she is. Still looking at me, too. Only now, she's seen me look her over twice. Makes me want to jump out of my skin.

Just watch Landry, I tell myself. Show some damn discipline. Just keep your eyes on him until it's time to leave, then get some sleep on his couch, nice and soft.

I get Landry fixed solid in my line of sight, and everything else fades from view. Tinker Bell, the metalheads, the walls, and the smoke. All of it. Then I feel the elbow in my ribs. I jump back into the corner with a thud.

"Whoa. Hey, sorry . . . ," I hear her screaming above the music. Loud, but still clear and girlie. "Didn't mean to spook you there, guy!"

I look her up and down. She's got bangs like Bettie Page, only dyed crazy blonde. On her forearm, she has a tattoo that looks like a rubbing of cypress bark—BURY ME UNDER A TREE IN LOUISIANA, it reads. She's got dark eyes. Freckles. And she's still smiling at me.

"No. You didn't spook me. I'm just, you know, watching." I look away again. For all I know the conversation's over.

She elbows me again, harder. "You like this?"

"What? The music?"

"No, the shitty metal bar." She cocks her head to the side, like she's annoyed with me or something.

"Well, see, it's my buddies up there," I yell into her ear. I take a breath between each sentence so I can fight against the speakers. "So that's why I came. But, yeah, I *kinda* like it."

"Why? What's good about it?"

Landry breaks into a fast, almost-rockabilly verse. "Maw Maw benches two-fifty . . . ," he wails. "And *you* can go *fuck* yourself . . ." I wonder if this girl's quizzing me or something. Like it's some kind of magic trick, finding a way to enjoy this stuff.

"Look, it's not good or anything. I know that. I just like it. Bad in all the right places, I guess." I chuckle to myself, sure she's already done listening to me. "It's like they're growing up. You know? Not lying about nothing. Grown-up enough to admit they love their maw maw. That they're Cajuns from Houma who never seen Brooklyn."

I look down at her. She's still here. Still listening. Still smiling, too. She bites her lip and punches me in the chest. "Come buy me a drink."

"Yeah? Okay."

She turns and walks toward the bar. I stumble after her.

"I'm Lizzy," she calls out over her shoulder.

"Lester," I shout after her.

"Yeah, it's on your shirt."

At the bar, she orders a PBR. "I'll let you pay for this because they're only a dollar and I won't feel like a whore."

I fumble with my wallet and scramble like mad for something to say. "So . . . you like this music?"

"Sure." She smiles. "It's better than the shit coming up next. At least it's different."

"Why are you here, then? If what's coming up next is shit?"

She shrugs. "My classmates, I guess. You can't be an art student without a side venture in punk or metal. It's like . . . a requirement?" She takes a swig, then gleefully belches.

I get that it's my turn to say something, so I blurt out, "I like art."

"Oh!" She laughs. "How very civilized of you!"

Just then, as Landry and Paul go offstage, the crowd starts to sway in our direction. They've been waiting for the house stereo to come back on so they can slam dance to some proper shit. A barstool falls over. A mosh pit starts to form, and someone groans. It's all so forced and annoying. Mostly, though, I'm thinking of this girl, Lizzy, this little Tinker Bell, exposed and getting pushed against the bar by this mass of fat, sweaty men.

I look down. Sure enough, she's grimacing, trying to keep from getting pinned to the rail by this fat guy behind her. Quick, without thinking, I step in between her and the crowd and try to shield her a little. But the crowd's begun to swell and get serious about this mosh pit. I reach out and lock both arms against the bar with Lizzy inside up against my chest.

"You okay?" I ask.

"Yeah." But I can tell she's nervous. No more flip, college-girl edge to her voice, like before.

Another barstool crashes over, and I can tell by the way Lizzy crumples to one side that it must've landed on her foot. She's about to go on the floor, in her nice sundress. Down there with all that broken glass and all those angry boots.

I throw another elbow and then a knee to clear the area around me enough so I can bend over and pick this Lizzy chick up. She's on my shoulder and I'm headed toward the door, shoving fat guys out the way. I burst through the plastic sheet and onto the cold street, jogging down the sidewalk with this girl on my shoulder, one-handed. I reach into my pocket for the keys to my truck, open the door, and toss her gently up on the bench seat.

I reach for my medical bag, but realize all of a sudden that this is crazy behavior.

A cold sweat breaks out on my forehead. Is this girl gonna think I'm some crazy serial killer trying to kidnap her?

Then I hear her laughing. Goddamnit, I'm already in love.

"You're pretty forward, Lester."

I smile and put my fingers through my hair, embarrassed— but at the same time . . . not. "Sorry. Just seemed like you might've broke your foot." Then I laugh, too. "That was a little crazy, I know."

"Absolutely not. Most fun I've had all week. I can't even *remember* the last time a man spirited me away from danger."

"I got some tape in the bag. Lemme see if I can wrap that foot for you."

"Are you a paramedic or something?"

"Nope. Just a guy with a backpack full of gauze."

"A good man to know then."

I stare up at her. Can't take my eyes away. Wrap her foot entirely by feel.

Huck is taught by the Widow Douglas to ignore the past, and that not all deceased people have wisdom to share, even in the sacred texts: "After supper she got out her book and learned me about Moses and the Bulrushers, and I was in a sweat to find out all about him; but by and by she let it out that Moses had been dead a considerable long time; so then I didn't care no more about him, because I don't take no stock in dead people."

ALI, FROM SADR CITY

Arriving at the bottom of our building's front stairwell, I unlock the metal gate and find a place on the street where I can watch the angry faces pass. The crowd comes slowly around the corner with signs for President Ben Ali in Arabic, and, for the cameras, in English and French. Ben Ali must go, they say, though not always with such polite phrasing. I lean against the wall and search the crowd for my flatmates.

The crowd has begun to change, I see, growing to include more university students, fewer old people. These young men and women walk together, some even holding hands. No fear of the Islamists. Like Baghdad University just before the war. A hint of freedom. Do jihadis mix with this crowd? Rifles hidden under their clothes? Waiting for their time? When the police and the army start to kill these people, will it become like that day in Ramadi?

It is all I find when I search for the *mulasim*'s name, that day in Ramadi. An article from the American news that calls him a hero, and this is fine. Someone should be called a hero.

I think of Hani and can almost see his face in this crowd. Foolish, for two reasons: First, he is not here. Second, he would never protest, never march in the streets. There would be no profit in it, nor any sensible gain to be made. It was always Hani's peculiar fault, his good sense.

*

It was February when the university canceled the spring semester and Hani convinced me to flee Baghdad. It had become so regular by then, his demands that we flee the death squads and the fighting, the gunfire and the hidden bombs, that when I heard him sprinting down the corridor after curfew, it hardly distracted me from my book. I turned the page to the next adventure just as a new thought occurred, and I reached for my pen to make note of it.

Hani bounded into Professor Al-Rawi's office and collapsed at the foot of my cot, where I'd taken refuge since my father and brother left the city.

"They killed the tennis coach," he wheezed.

I did not look up. "Who?"

"The tennis coach."

"No, I mean who killed him?"

"Some guys in masks," Hani scoffed. "What kind of question is that?" He waved his hand in the air. Sadrists. Al Qaeda. Washed-up Baathists. The masked fog. Men with guns. It made no difference.

Hani had been gathering stories like this for weeks, and with the stories came the grim, new facts of Baghdad life. Headless bodies in the street. Each week, victims more absurdly innocent than the week before. Ice vendors beheaded for selling during the hours of prayer. Barbers tortured to death with nail guns for shaving beards.

Hani asked after every new militia. He learned when new Shia mullahs tried to outdo their rivals. When one started using pliers, another would say, "Pliers? Fuck pliers. I have this welding torch."

He learned when a former army officer created a volunteer brigade to protect our old neighborhood of Mansour, after concluding that the American soldiers using my father's abandoned villa as a patrol base could not, or would not, protect the vulnerable Sunni elite from the Shia death squads wearing police uniforms. That was when Hani stopped going home and came to live at the university like me. If he had gone home, to the empty house left behind when his parents became trapped in Jordan, he would have been expected to fight. And Hani was too sincere for war.

"They pulled him from the car and shot him in the head," he continued. "And they killed two players in the backseat, too."

"So, those were the shots I heard earlier?" I put the book aside and sat up on my cot. "Were they collaborators or something?"

"It was the shorts. The shorts they wear at practice."

"The fashion police!" I coughed, queasy at my own reflexive attempt at humor. "Did we know any of these guys?"

"I am not sure, Kateb. Have you been hanging around with the tennis team? Have you been harboring a secret ambition to play tennis professionally?"

"Fine. Be an asshole. I would simply like to know why you came running to tell me this. People get killed every day, Hani." I gestured at Dr. Al-Rawi's empty desk with the same flourish of theater that Hani seemed to enjoy, then lay back on my cot and opened my book.

"You want to know why I ran to tell you? Why I thought of you first?" Hani moved to my laundry pile in the corner. He dug around and came up with a T-shirt. "AC/DC." He threw the shirt between me and my book. He bent down and came up with two more. "Gwar. Though Gwar might be just their style, this one. Bad Religion? This is a real problem. One of these guys is bound to read English well enough. A number of interpretations, my friend, none of them good."

"You gave me that shirt for my birthday, for one thing. And for another, your English is shit."

"Kateb, they killed three guys for wearing shorts at tennis practice. What do you think they will do to you? Or *me*, since I will probably be standing next to you. Or Mundhir? Think about Mundhir!"

I laughed. "Mundhir can bloody well take care of himself. But you? Yes, you are probably fucked."

Just then, as if summoned, Mundhir poked his head around the door like a great hawk. Seventeen years old, with a size, a resting power, that entered the room even before his body. His face, sharp and still, more than hinted at the grown man's beard that would emerge if he neglected the stubble even a single day. This gave him an advantage. Was he a lazy Sunni neglecting the razor? Or was he a burgeoning Shia militiaman, a boy growing his first beard? Who could say?

"Mundhir!" I threw the book across the room. "We were just talking about you!"

Mundhir moved into the doorframe, filling it. "I did not hear. What were you saying?"

"Hani thinks I will be killed by the Islamists this week. Him, too. Maybe you, as well. What do you think?"

Mundhir shrugged. "Is this about your T-shirts?"

"Hani! You went to Mundhir behind my back? Shameful."

Hani stepped to Mundhir's side. "We have to leave, Kateb." Hani put his hand on Mundhir's shoulder, acting as if he spoke for both of them. "People know your father."

"Fuck my father." I stood, walked across the room, and grabbed a Coca-Cola from the windowsill. I drank it hot. "He worked for the Ministry of Agriculture, okay? He is not on any list."

"Have you heard from him? Or from your brother? Do they know the Americans are using your house?"

"What about *your* father, Hani? When was the last time you heard from him? Doing a lot of surgery in Amman, is he?"

"At least I know where he is. What kind of son are you?"

"I am the second son of an old man. And he is outside Fallujah, somewhere, as far as I know. Like everyone else."

In truth, I knew much more than this. I knew with some detail how my father and brother were spending their days outside Fallujah. I knew because they had asked, if not demanded, that I participate. Why I did not simply admit this to Hani, I cannot say. What cause did I have to feel such shame?

Unwittingly, Mundhir helped me change the subject. He stepped all the way through the door and walked over to Dr. Al-Rawi's desk. "My uncle says Ramadi is the next Fallujah, filling up with all the foreign jihadis who survived and escaped." He sat on the desk, feet still touching the floor. "This time next year the Americans will burn Ramadi down, just like they did Fallujah."

Hani furrowed his brow, as if searching Mundhir's face for intent. Then, satisfied that his big friend was not just making an offhand comment, Hani brightened. "Yes. Thank you, Mundhir. You are right. And this is why we must leave *now*, before it is too late. We leave now, okay? Before we run out of money and are trapped in the city. Before the Americans launch another offensive in Anbar and cut us off from the Jordan highway. Before a death squad takes an interest in the university and finds us living here. We will not survive that, Kateb. And you know it. So we leave, find your father, and get enough cash from him to complete the journey."

I rubbed my eyes. "Hani. Please tell me this is not your beach-resort plan again?"

"Yes. Yes, it *is*. Okay? This is phase one. Next, we go to Jordan, get more cash from *my* father, and then we go to Tunisia with it. And, yes, we open a bar on the beach."

"Every time I hear this it sounds dumber." I crumpled the can and tossed it on the pile in the corner. "Mundhir, you are the muscle in this arrangement. Your thoughts?"

Mundhir shrugged. "I go where you go."

"Then *I* will *go* to *sleep.*" I fell onto my cot and pulled a pillow over my face.

Hani kicked the frame. "Kateb, this is over. Mundhir has his uncle's taxi. Do you hear me? I am done arguing. Meet us downstairs at six tomorrow morning, if you like, or bloody well stay here."

Hani kicked my cot again and waited for me to reply. I did not indulge him.

Finally, after a moment's pause, Hani walked out. Mundhir followed him, leaving me the choice. I could remain in Professor Al-Rawi's office, hoping Baghdad might improve, pretending that I could safely remain in this little room forever.

Or I could follow Hani and Mundhir into the western desert, feign an honest search for my father, and subtly herd them away from Habbaniyah, where, tucked neatly between the twin Sunni strongholds of Fallujah and Ramadi, it was rumored the old generals and ministers had gathered.

I waited until the footsteps faded away, pulled the pillow tighter around my face, and spat an English word into the feathers. *"Fuck."*

The next morning, we packed small gym bags, leaving plenty of room. Easier to keep hidden, that way. No bulges. No obvious weight. Nothing to suggest we were going any farther than across town.

We each carried two sets of identification. Our university cards, with our full, Sunni names, and then the taxi licenses Mundhir's uncle made for us with Shia first names. We could expect checkpoints whichever route we took to leave the city, so it was important to have the right name.

Our old passports we kept hidden in the spare tire.

Meeting on the street before dawn, it was agreed that Mundhir, who could pass for a cabdriver, should drive. He looked older and had been raised by uncles who drove cabs. He knew their habits and could fake the right kind of disinterest. Just a cabdriver taking two rich kids on a long fare.

I took my spot in the front seat without putting the matter up for discussion. "We will try the Karada Road first," I told Mundhir. "If we cannot get through that way, we will jump over to Abi Nawas and try to cross the river farther north."

Hani took his place in the backseat. I looked at him in the rear-view mirror. He was hurt. Typical. "Sound good to you, Hani?" I asked.

"Fine."

"You have a better idea?"

"I was going to suggest we take the Abu Ghraib Expressway and sneak south of Fallujah."

I laughed. "I veto the Abu Ghraib Express on principle."

Mundhir looked at both of us in turn. "So . . . Karada, then?"

Hani waved his hand. "Fine. Karada."

I slapped Mundhir's big shoulder and smiled. "I feel better about this already."

We passed under the university gate and turned onto Karada Street. The sun came up. Curfew ended. We passed through the first checkpoint, manned by Americans from the Green Zone concerned only with guarding the bridge over the Tigris and protecting their little American city. Our Sunni cards got us through with no problem.

We weaved in between the parked trucks and overturned donkey carts, stores, and cafés bombed out or boarded up. Even the shops not targeted by militias were wrecked by gunfire and abandoned. Our taxi was the only car on the road.

We reached the Iraqi Army checkpoint at Amar Square, and, as planned, shoved the Sunni identification into our underwear.

The soldier on watch accepted our story that we owned the cab in partnership and were taking it to Dora for repairs. Hani and I did not speak much, and the squealing timing belt supported Mundhir's claim. But when the soldier asked to see the trunk, Hani shifted noticeably in his seat. The soldier, becoming suspicious now, told us to get out.

Off to the side, before we were separated, I bumped against Hani's shoulder and whispered in his ear, "The beach, Hani. Think about the beach."

The soldier poked around the trunk with the barrel of his rifle, slid underneath the car, tapped the gas tank, and kicked the tires. Another soldier kept his rifle aimed at Hani, Mundhir, and me as we stood with our hands interlocked behind our heads.

I sighed and tapped my foot, trying to look impatient. Not scared or nervous, just put out. Mundhir stood rock still, his face impassive as a sphinx's. Hani stared at the pavement and smiled.

Finding nothing, and confident we were merely cowards, the soldiers finally let us leave.

"Well done, men," I said. "Way to keep your heads." Then I laughed, not having intended the double meaning.

Mundhir now turned north onto Abi Nawas. Before long traffic on the river road slowed to a crawl and then stopped completely. We could not reach a bridge to take us west. Fearing we might be caught on the road past nightfall, we turned onto a side street, ever mindful that the farther east we traveled, the closer we got to the Shiite militias of Sadr City and the more certainly our Sunni names would get us killed.

We reached the expressway a little after noon and turned north toward Taji. We began the long crawl through the center of Baghdad, where turning off the highway anywhere meant checkpoints manned by government troops or Shia militiamen. The trip north took us deep into the afternoon. As dusk approached, we were committed to the Highway One bridge over the Tigris. Too far north to reach Ramadi before dark.

"We will need to find a place to camp," Hani said. "There is nothing up there. And I do not know where we can find petrol. The Abu Ghraib Expressway on the other hand . . ."

"If I admit you were right, Hani, will you feel better?" I rolled down the window and felt the cooling afternoon air on my face.

"No. But you can say it anyway."

Mundhir perked up. "There is a good road that runs west along the Grand Canal, past farms and little market towns. You can get petrol there. I drove it once with my uncle all the way to Lake Thar Thar."

"You see?" I exclaimed. "It has all worked out."

Hani fumed.

We reached the river, and, after waiting for an hour at the checkpoint, crossed the bridge. A lorry bomb some months earlier had reduced the eastbound span to one lane, with soldiers and highway patrolmen in blue shirts now directing cars around the charred blast hole one at a time.

To save petrol, we coasted down the back side in neutral. I looked south into the expanse of the city. Columns of smoke rose from Mansour, Dora, and Adhamiya.

I thought of Professor Al-Rawi, and the day I told him of my father's plan to flee west into Anbar. I would have to go with my father, I told my professor, not aware that I was crying, having only come to tell him that work on my thesis would have to be postponed. While I flailed about with my apologies to him, seeking to make myself understood, Professor Al-Rawi moved about his office silently. By the time my embarrassing speech had ended, his couch had become a bed. My bed. I did not return home that night.

I thought about the Baghdad University campuses near each column of smoke on the horizon and wondered which had seen death that day. How many students. How many professors. I said good-bye to my city.

Mundhir's road, the one he remembered from childhood, ran parallel to Saddam's Grand Canal. Saddam had commanded that the canal be constructed on a line exactly east-west and not one degree off. My father had talked about this absurd requirement while the canal was being dug and how very difficult it became as work progressed.

We passed dry farms. Homesteads the canal had promised to irrigate before the pumps rusted and the water grew putrid. Dusk fell into night, and for the first time Mundhir acknowledged the petrol gauge.

"We have to stop. Twenty kilometers left. Maybe."

"Then it is simple," I said. "We stop at a market or a house, whichever we see first, and ask if they will sell to us."

"Right," Hani snorted. "Simple."

"*Or* we park and wait for an American patrol. Let them think the car is a bomb and watch them blow it up. Which would you rather, Hani?"

Hani said nothing and merely waved his hand. His new favorite thing to do.

Mundhir stiffened in his seat. "Look." He gestured with his great chin.

Green sodium lights spilled into the road from a cluster of buildings on the left, half a kilometer ahead. At least one, a squat building with a fixed awning, looked like it had been a petrol station at some point in the recent past. A regular souk with all the commerce and danger three young men could want.

"This is it," I said. "Get ready."

"Shia or Sunni?" Mundhir asked.

I had not considered our identification since crossing the bridge. We were well west of Baghdad, firmly into Anbar Province. Still, we were far enough from Fallujah and Ramadi for doubt. Serious doubt. A run-down market could be a net. A place to catch Sunni fighters fleeing west. Or it could be a gateway manned by Sunni loyalists meant to keep Shia out of Anbar. Who could say?

"Sunni," I said quickly, because there was no good choice. We fumbled with our papers, hands diving into our underpants, as Mundhir coasted into the market and turned off the lights. There was no one walking, no signs of trade. But lights meant a generator. A generator meant petrol and possibly men willing to sell it.

"Who goes?" Mundhir asked.

"We all go," Hani answered. I was tempted to argue, just for the sake of it. Just to frustrate him. But I could not. He was right.

"Yes," I said. "We all go. On the count of three."

Mundhir stepped from the car and closed his door without waiting for the count.

"Or now," I said as Hani and I followed him.

"Hello?" Mundhir called out, fearless. "Are you selling petrol?"

"We have money," Hani echoed, his voice too high. A voice that sought to appease. I wanted to choke him.

I heard movement in a building nearby. Footsteps on broken glass. Men whispering to each other. Then the sound that made my stomach turn. A Kalashnikov bolt snapping rounds into a chamber. Then another, and another.

"We are not armed," I called out in a panic. "We only wish to buy petrol!"

Men emerged from the darkness carrying rifles. Men with new

beards. Shia men. Men of a militia looking to kill Sunni boys just like us.

I put up my hands. "Just looking to trade, cousins. Please."

A fat man with the thickest beard among them stepped forward and pointed his rifle at me. "Your papers, dog."

"We left them in the car." I said. "Apologies. We did not know this was a checkpoint, commander. Please, let me go and get them." I turned around and pointed at the car. Mundhir and Hani had their hands up, too. "Mundhir," I said, as calmly as I could, "go and get our papers." So calm. So innocent and harmless that it would not occur to me that I should not talk to my Shia friend.

Maybe, in the darkness of the car, he could sneak the Shia papers from his pants.

"Shut your filthy mouth. And you." The fat man pointed his rifle at Mundhir. "Remain still." The militia leader did not believe. He turned his rifle back to me. "You. Talker. Tell me where you are coming from and where you go."

Mundhir's face held a look of despair only I would recognize, his eyes grown a little wider, his shoulders uncharacteristically sloped. He neither moved nor spoke. Meanwhile, Hani shook with fear, his jaw hanging slack.

I heard a man laugh like a demon in the shadows. "Mansour, I bet. Rich Baathist kids."

So this was it, then. And we had only just started to run. All our plans snuffed out. I considered sprinting into the desert if only to receive a quick death from the bullets and thereby avoid the pliers, the nail guns. But with Mundhir and Hani standing there, I could not. I swallowed hard and resolved not to say another word.

Then I heard chickens, and the sound of cages bouncing on a rickety cart as it turned from the pavement onto the dirt.

"Ali?" an old man's voice called out.

Though I sensed he was speaking to me, I did not turn around.

"What are you *doing*?" he continued. "I told you come directly to my house on the lake. No stopping. Why did you stop here?" The old man walked up behind me and patted my back. "Foolish nephew," he spoke into my cheek. "And I'll bet you ran out of petrol, too."

The militia leader lowered his rifle. "You know these boys, Haji Fasil?"

"Yes, commander. This is my nephew, Ali. From Sadr City. He is coming to visit me on the lake. And these are his friends. Very convenient for us. Their car saves Abu Abdul and me the dark walk home. Still, foolish of you, Nephew."

I took a chance and lowered my arms. The man with the rifle did not object, so I took another chance and turned my head. I saw the old man for the first time. Shorter than me, with cheeks shaved close. He wore the clean white robes of a bedouin. An elder, judging from his checkered kaffiyeh, a man who had made the hajj. He planted a hand in the small of my back, speaking to me with the pressure of his palm. *Play along, boy*, he told me with his fingertips. *Save your life.*

"I am sorry, Uncle," I said. "So foolish. Yes, I ran out of petrol."

He smiled warmly and nodded.

Another old man, older and shorter with an unkempt beard, shuffled past us, carrying two live chickens, wings tightly bound. He handed the chickens to the militia leader, who slung his rifle over his shoulder to accept them.

"Thank you, Abu Abdul," the militia leader said to the old man in a loud, slow voice, raising the chickens up with one hand while placing the other hand over his heart in thanks.

The little man, Abu Abdul, grinned, bowed his head, waving his palms as if to say, *Take them, take them; you are my friend.* I understood from this Abu Abdul's silence, from his grin and the motion of his hands, that he could not speak. Just as surely, I understood from the militia leader's oddly abiding patience with Abu Abdul that he was simple, or at least widely considered so.

"We have your rice, as well," Haji Fasil said, removing his hand from my back and walking over to his cart. He took two corners of a rice sack. "Nephew"—he laughed—"what is wrong with you? Come here and help me."

I walked over to Haji Fasil's cart, floating. My legs had disappeared. I grabbed two corners of the heavy sack and lifted.

Abu Abdul walked over to Mundhir and hugged him, like he had known the great big youngster forever. Mundhir hugged back, game if stiff. Hani let his hands drop, but kept his mouth shut.

Haji Fasil pulled me along at the other end of the rice sack. We stopped at the militia leader's feet.

"Well," Haji Fasil asked, "where should we put this?"

"You can drop it there. Your nephew needs petrol?"

"Yes," I said as we dropped the rice. "Just enough to get to the lake." The words tumbled over my dry tongue. Haji Fasil took my hand, like an uncle would his nephew's.

"Five liters for the taxi," the militia leader shouted to one of his company.

"We will be back next week," Haji Fasil said cheerfully, pulling me by the hand toward our taxi. *Time to go*, he told me with his grip.

"Good. Next week then, God willing," the militia leader replied, stepping back into the shadows. Two of his men bounded over to take the rice.

Meanwhile, Abu Abdul dragged Mundhir by the arm and motioned for him to lift the pushcart. Mundhir lifted it easily and followed Abu Abdul around to the trunk. Mundhir gave me a pleading look with his eyes. Open the trunk. Hurry.

A militiaman with a jerrican casually poured the precious fuel into the tank, yawning.

I opened the driver's door and groped for the trunk release. Then, not knowing what to do next, I stepped in and closed the door behind me. I put my hands on the wheel.

The passenger door opened and Haji Fasil got in. "Home then, Nephew?"

I nodded while looking straight ahead.

"You remember the way—half a kilometer to the empty farmhouse and then a right turn on the dirt road."

Mundhir and Hani piled into the backseat, with tiny, old Abu Abdul peaking out from between them, looking amused. I studied his face in the rearview mirror. A thick, ugly scar ran from his right ear, down his neck and boiled to a stop just above his sternum. He had few teeth left.

I had only driven a few times before. I pressed the clutch and turned the key.

"Easy left foot," Mundhir said. "First gear is the most difficult."

A force occupied me. A champion race-car driver from Germany. A taxidriver from Dora. I sent dirt and gravel flying as we bounced onto the road, free and alive.

Haji Fasil wasted no time. "You boys are very stupid."

"Thank you," I said.

"Thank you. Thank you. Thank you," Hani echoed. The words carried from him like leaves on a stream.

"Just drive normal," Haji Fasil said.

"Thank God for you," Hani said, suddenly religious. "God bless you. May the peace of the Prophet be upon you." A good Muslim boy.

I glanced again into the rearview, wondering why Mundhir, always so polite, had remained quiet. It was because he was looking at Abu Abdul, trying to understand the old man's gestures. Abu Abdul patted Mundhir's cheek and opened his toothless mouth in a silent laugh. He poked at Mundhir's arms 'and, pantomiming a strongman, scrunched his face tight. Mundhir smiled.

"We can give you money, Haji," I said. "We have a little."

Haji Fasil chuckled. "No. It is not your money we wanted. Had they killed you, you see, they would have left that safe house. We would have lost a customer. So no need to thank us. Just good business."

"You sell them rice and chickens?"

"And cooking oil when we get it."

"To Sadrists?"

"Of course. And to Ansar al-Sunna. And to Al Qaeda. That little market changes hands quite often."

I remembered my Matthew Arnold and smiled. *Where ignorant armies clash by night.* Then I considered questions for a time before deciding on the simplest: "Who *are* you?"

"Turn here," Haji Fasil said suddenly. After I did, he sighed. "We are two old men whose families live elsewhere. We have a house on the lake. We fish. We sell. We rescue stupid children from the blade."

"Can we stay with you tonight?" Hani said, reaching up to the front with a fistful of dinar.

"Yes," Haji Fasil said. "You are welcome. But put your money away."

At their little farm by the lake, we arranged fallen eucalyptus logs around a fire pit and ate dinner by lantern light. Lamb, rice, and flat bread. We studied the stars as boys from hazy Baghdad are wont to do. We listened to the gentle lake waves lapping the shore just a few meters away on their little beach.

Abu Abdul pulled Mundhir by the arm and pointed to heavy things he wanted Mundhir to lift. Sometimes these things needed lifting. A valid farmer's purpose. Other times Abu Abdul just wanted to clap and admire his new friend's strength. After a time, he did not need to pull Mundhir's arm. They walked together, shoulders close.

Hani stomped about the grounds alone and reported back from the darkness every few minutes to ask after Haji Fasil's business. How much land did they have here? How many buildings? A well for water? A cistern? How close were they to the highway? Why did they bother to bring supplies to the markets? Why not make this place a market of their own?

Haji Fasil gave simple answers and feigned laziness.

He and I sat by the fire pit and waited for the others to tire.

"How did Abu Abdul lose his voice?" I asked.

"Cancer. Many years ago."

"Ah. I saw the scar."

"Yes."

Cancer had taken my mother, so I knew he was lying. But I decided not to dig for the truth.

Mundhir and Abu Abdul went into the little mud shack with a lantern and emerged with Mundhir carrying a big stack of rugs and blankets. We spread them on the beach and readied for sleep while the old men retired to the house.

"Look at this beach," Hani kept saying, the idea growing. "This could be great."

I fell asleep thinking of ways to dislodge an idea I knew would kill us all. I wanted to crush it before it had a chance to mature. But I drifted into a dream before my thoughts, my heavy club of persuasion, could take form to do battle with his.

It was the best night of sleep I can remember.

sir it was good to see you this weekend and hope it wont be the last time also im sorry about how shit went down in that bar and i hate that i embarrassed you like that and i want you to know that im working on that shit and also like i said you should get in touch with doc pleasant i asked around and he lives down by some place named houma about 40 mls south of you maybe get a cup of coffee with the guy sir might be good for you too

cpl zahn

CURE

Only a year older than me, the senior account manager already has a corner office on the twenty-fifth floor and a client list longer than my arm. I drop by late on Friday afternoon to tell him that I'm leaving and find him sprawled out across his leather sofa, half-asleep. Caught like a mischievous golden retriever, he scrambles to his feet and smoothes his tailored wool slacks, smiling.

"Bro," he says, "get in here. Gotta talk to you. Close the door. Sit down."

I close the door, and he slaps me on the back as he makes his way over to the desk. An e-mail catches his attention. He coughs and starts to read, clearly forgetting about me. I sit quietly, waiting for him to remember.

Everyone calls him Stall, my boss. I forget his real name. Something like Tradd Poche, or Duplessis Poche, or Tradd Duplessis-Poche. A name fermented and bottled on Prytania Street, aged three hundred years. Nothing even remotely like Stall. I didn't give it a second thought at first hearing, but after a week in the office one of the other account managers let slip that Stall is short for "Bro-sev Stalin." A nickname he picked up in college, I gather.

Raised at the Mardi Gras balls, taken as a legacy by his fraternity at Ole Miss, and destined for some grand, old mansion on the Avenue, my boss sits behind a mahogany desk and calls his father's friends for business. Soon, he'll be calling his fraternity brothers.

Yet, he seems frail to me, Stall. Like some inbred Hapsburg monarch. He's short, and his black hair sits limp and thin across his pale scalp. His acne scars look fresh, and his teeth, though perfectly aligned, stand out against his warped jaw as the obvious work of a high-priced repairman.

"Sullivan have you doing analytics all day?" he suddenly asks, looking up as if surprised to find me here after just a moment ago asking me in.

"Yes, Euro bonds, mostly."

Stall scoffs. "Bro, Sullivan's a wonk. Blow that shit off next time."

"Really?"

"Who's your mentor, bro? Huh? Who's the big-swinging dick around here?"

"You?" I answer, after hesitating just a moment to join in the reference.

"Damn right, bro!" He slaps his desk. "Here's what you gotta understand. What Sullivan doesn't *get*. You listening?"

"I am."

"So, they call this the wealth-management business, right? But really, it's the Wealthy People Management Business. It's not about the analytics. Fuck that shit. We bill as a percentage of total funds under management, not as a percentage of return on investment. About a trillion dollars got yanked from the market during the crash. But with confidence building now? There's about to be a mad dash by all those lizard brains to put that trillion dollars *back*. The business is about getting to that money *first*. Crunch analytics all day and you end up doing maybe half a percentage point better than a monkey picking a portfolio at random. It's about pressing *palms*, bro. Getting the funds under management. Money into the market. After that, the shit's on autopilot."

"Right, I understand. But, Stall, and please don't take this the wrong way, I'm from central Alabama, okay? I don't *know* wealthy people. My dad is a good high school football coach and a pretty bad farmer. Plus, I'm not great at pressing palms. Research, on the other hand . . . I don't mind it. I find it relaxing, honestly."

Stall leans back in his chair with his hands behind his head and grins. "You know why I volunteered to mentor you?" he says with an odd glow of satisfaction. "Over the holidays, even? After I had a list in front of me of, like, a hundred names?"

"No," I say honestly.

A serious look falls across Stall's face. "Because you're a war hero."

My cheeks burn and the hair stands up on my neck.

Stall doesn't appear to notice. "You know what wealthy people like? You know what impresses them more than *other* wealthy people? Fucking war heroes."

"Stall. Listen."

He interrupts, "The Hero of Profane Twenty-four? Didn't I read that on the Internet?"

"Profane Two-Four," I correct him instinctively.

"Was that not, like, the first thing that popped up when I googled your ass? You already have a major leg up and you don't even *know* it."

"That article got some things wrong." Then, trying to move the conversation onto another topic, I add with a fake laugh, "I sure haven't met any wealthy people because of it, I can tell you *that* right now."

Stall smiles. "Well, you're going to! Tonight, bro!" He stands and slips on a dark sports coat, clearly tailored to hide his sloping shoulders. Subtle gray stitching pops against his light pants and pale-blue shirt.

"Yeah, I sort of have . . . plans," I lie. Plans that involved going home to watch television, read about the heavy-weather handling qualities of the Pearson Triton, maybe drink a beer or six by myself, and fall asleep.

"So? Cancel them." He smiles. "You're working tonight, bro."

I throw out a few more lame excuses as we walk down the dark hall to the elevator, but before I know what's what, we're in his BMW convertible. It's cold out, but he keeps the top down as we speed through the central business district, turning without signaling, weaving and accelerating without cause, then cutting off a city bus to make a sudden right turn onto Tchoupitoulas. I get the odd sense he's trying to impress me with all the reckless driving.

We cross into the Garden District and snap to a violent stop at a red light. Stall sighs, annoyed by all these traffic rules, and lights a Dunhill cigarette from a wide, blue pack.

"Where are we going, again?" I ask.

"Called Cure. Brand-new place. Really cool. Real nice. Like a gourmet cocktail bar. They make specialty drinks with hand-cut ice cubes and, like, bitters and essence of orange from eyedroppers and shit."

"And—sorry—*who* are we meeting?"

"Just some friends from school."

"Ole Miss?"

He laughs. "High school, bro."

He parks on Freret Street, in front of a shuttered tuxedo-rental shop, just across the street from this Cure place. The tuxedo shop has obviously been closed since Katrina. The whole neighborhood still carries the faint scent of mold, of sun-dried debris. The bar is about the only sign of life for three blocks. Still, it's progress, a sign of serious investment. The owners, I can see, gutted the old brick storefront and rebuilt the bar from scratch. Warm, recessed lighting glows out through new plate-glass windows, and shelves of upscale liquor climb the walls behind the bar, up to a twenty-foot ceiling of pressed tin. I watch a bartender in a bow tie climb a ladder on wheels, like the kind you'd see in an elegant library, and grab one of the expensive bottles up top. There's a strangely etymological motif, too, I notice, with framed extracts from Victorian texts on long wires, and exotic beetles preserved in mid-dissection behind glass.

Someone's clearly betting big that this block is going to anchor a new kind of New Orleans neighborhood, like something you'd see in downtown Austin or San Diego. I imagine their spreadsheets littered with sunk costs and projections. Soon, all these gutted houses, from which dockworkers and truck drivers would have walked around the corner to rent tuxedos for their modest but venerable Mardi Gras balls, will be picked up for a song by young college graduates and renovated. Maybe they'll stay to raise families, these urban pioneers, but probably not.

I hear young voices coming down the street, laughing and carrying on. The group, a well-dressed contingent equally divided between guys and girls, turns the corner. Just the kind of folks the investors are banking on.

"*Look* at this motley crew," Stall bellows, jumping out of his convertible. A receiving line follows in which he shakes each guy's hand while giving a half hug and kisses each girl on the cheek while placing his hand ever so lightly on her upper arm.

I stand off to the side, hands shoved in my pockets.

Finished with his friends, Stall turns to me. "Everyone, this is my buddy Pete. My intern for the Christmas break, MBA candidate at Tulane. And did I mention? Iraq War hero."

I wave, try to smile, then stick the hand back into my coat pocket.

The pioneers are quiet for a moment, their eyes wide. One girl chuckles.

"Damn, hell of an introduction, Pete," the tallest guy says finally. He walks over, shakes my hand, and slaps my shoulder. The rest of them follow with faux kisses and firm handshakes. My head swims and I don't even catch half their names.

Stall whispers something private in my ear about "feeling good," but it's drowned out by chatter, everyone in the group suddenly in loud conversation with everyone else simultaneously, and I don't quite catch his full meaning.

I follow them all into the bar with Stall's hand on my back. He rubs my shoulder with the other hand. "Yeah, you're feeling good, bro."

It's louder inside. A modern remix of an eighties rap song pumps cleanly from the new speakers. Old-fashioned lightbulbs hang on cords running all the way up to the ceiling. The filaments glow in a deep, comforting orange without seeming to give off much useful light.

We weave through the crowd and grab a booth in the corner, girls on one side, guys on the other. Stall tucks himself in back, dead center, three-deep with wealthy people on either side of him. They're still talking feverishly about something, or someone, who's recently disappointed them. Stall officiates the discussion like a referee, calling foul on spurious opinions, ad hominem attacks, or less polite thrusts of rhetoric.

I take a seat on the end, grab a drinks menu. Nothing on the list looks even remotely familiar to me. The drinks all have names like the Start and Finish, the Thousand Blue Eyes, and the Art of Discussion. Under each is a dense paragraph detailing all the ingredients and how it's prepared. If only they had a familiar beer or bourbon. At this point, I'm just looking to get drunk.

I slap the menu closed and rub my forehead, lost and embarrassed. The guy next to me, Brown Hair and Tweed Jacket, elbows me deliberately. I come to, squinting through dim yet somehow aggressive lighting, to see that the table has gone quiet and everyone's looking at me.

An insistent female voice calls out from above. "Mr. Donovan?"

I tilt my head and see Paige Dufossat, wearing a white, button-down shirt and a blue bow tie. She has her arms folded behind her back, high and stiff, and her long brown hair is piled on top of her head in neat, casual braids.

"Oh. Paige. Hi," I stammer. "Sorry, I didn't hear you."

"Wait." Stall jumps into the conversation. "You guys *know* each other?" He gives another ruling: "Weird."

"We had a class together this semester," I say.

"Business Ethics," Paige adds.

The tall guy, Blond Hair and Red Shirt, snorts the word "Ethics" and laughs.

The girl sitting next to him, Straight Black Hair and Green Dress, pushes him playfully. "Stop it, Chance."

Paige touches me on the shoulder. "So, what can I bring you guys?"

"Wow—I don't know," I say. "Ask them first."

She starts with the girl on the other end of the booth, Curly Brown Hair and Thin Yellow Shirt, and takes the drink orders in rapid fire.

"Blue Note."

"Floridian."

"Pinot noir. I don't care which."

"Belgian Trappist. Whichever Kirk suggests."

"Bandito."

"Cuvée."

"Bulleit rye, neat."

And before I have time to blink she's back to me. "Pete?"

I throw up my hands.

She smiles. "Alabama, right? Why don't I just bring you three fingers of Maker's Mark."

I exhale. "Perfect. Thanks."

Paige strides back to the bar with purpose, but still manages to turn around and catch me watching her. I look away before I can take note of whether she's pleased by that or annoyed.

I look back at Stall, who's smiling slyly. "What's all that about, Pete?"

"I know her from class. Like she said."

"No—three fingers of Maker's Mark? What's the significance of that?"

"Bear Bryant's drink. She's, uh, having a little fun with me."

The guy to my left, Tweed Jacket, elbows me again. "You know these girls went to school with her, right?"

"High school," I say, as much to myself as anyone.

"Sacred Heart," Green Dress says, and addressing her friend across the table asks, "I even used to crew her dad's boat for the summer regattas. I mean, *why's* she working here, anyway?"

"Hold up," Stall whispers, eyebrows pointedly lifted.

The table goes quiet as Paige places a small glass of water by each of us, nods at Green Dress, and says, "Pete's into boats. You should ask him about it." She sneaks a smile in my direction and walks away without waiting for a response.

Once Paige is out of earshot, Green Dress turns to a visibly distressed friend across the table and exclaims, "What the fuck was *that*!"

"What?" I ask. "What'd she do?"

"Marigny was Paige's sorority sister, and she didn't even say hello to her." Then, to her date, Chance: "And meanwhile she's, like, totally flirting with Pete over here."

Maybe hoping to ease the tension, Red Polo Shirt says to me, "So, you sail Pete?"

"Sorry?"

"Paige said you're into boats. You race? I got a buddy who's always looking for crew."

"No. She's just messing with me. I'm just looking for a renovation project. You know, a lark, really."

"So you don't race?"

"No, but I'd like to get into cruising. Maybe work up to a solo, open-water passage someday." I cringe on the inside, hoping no one at the table calls my bluff and asks me a more detailed sailing question.

Red Polo chuckles. "A solo passage? That sounds miserable."

Stall senses an opportunity to push the conversation in a new direction. "That wouldn't be an issue for Pete. Like I told you, he's a war hero. Seriously. You can read about it."

"Which branch of the service?" Tweed Jacket asks.

"The Marine Corps," I say.

"What did you do?" Curly Brown Hair asks. "Were you like a Navy SEAL or something?"

"No, I was a combat engineer."

"So, what's that?" she asks. "Like, what'd you do all day? Engineer things?"

"Filled potholes, mainly."

Red Polo chuckles.

Stall jumps in. "But tell them about Ramadi. About the helicopter."

Just then, Paige comes back with the drink orders and distributes the glasses all around the table. Everyone's quiet again, and I make a point not to let Paige see my face.

I hear the girls whispering to each other as she walks away and grab for my Maker's Mark, a wide, low ball full almost to the brim with just a few rough-cut ice cubes submerged. I take a long pull. Three deep swallows that numb my throat, just right. I come back to find Curly Brown Hair still looking at me.

She waves her hand insistently. "So? Why were you bothering with potholes?"

"Bombs. Insurgents planted bombs in the road. Under the asphalt sometimes, but mostly off to the side. You saw this stuff on the news, right? Improvised explosive devices? IEDs?"

Nothing. No response from the table. Another long pull, and my drink's already half-gone.

"The bad guys would put bombs in the same places all the time," I continue. "Basically *re*seeding the *old* potholes. So our mission was to get rid of the bombs first, then patch. It was called route clearance, but really it was just road repair."

"And this was . . . a full-time job?" Chance asks with a perplexed smile.

"Six hundred and forty-seven potholes." Another big sip. A third of the glass left, now.

"And out of those, how many had a new bomb in the hole?" Chance asks.

"Six hundred forty-seven."

Chance whistles. "Goddamn, son," he murmurs, and laughs nervously.

Next to him, Green Dress looks at me with a soft, troubled face. Like she's somehow concerned for me. "So then, why did you keep doing it like that? It seems—I don't know—like people would . . . get hurt? Like, did the bombs ever go off ?"

"Sometimes. Not often. We were pretty good at staying safe. But, yes. Sometimes people did get hurt." I finish the drink. "Just how it had to be done." I push the empty glass away and let the bourbon slosh through my empty stomach, my guts like a cauldron.

"But *why*!?" the girl pleads, like a teenager who's just been grounded.

Something about her nasal, childish insistence activates the bourbon seeping into my tissues, and my mood abruptly shifts.

"Because, Stall," I say, snapping my eyes onto him, for some reason, and ignoring the girl, "it wasn't always the hole that you had to worry about. Sometimes, see, they'd leave a fake bomb to make you stop. Then, while you were looking at it, all scared, they'd come at you with machine guns and rockets. Then sometimes they'd put an artillery shell inside a dead dog. Because who wants to mess around with a dog carcass, stewing all day in the hot sun? Then, just as you're getting used to *that*, they'd leave a bunch of headless bodies in the desert for you to deal with. And sometimes those were bombs, too."

I reach out and take another sip. No competition for the floor at this point.

"One time, after one of our platoons filled this Iraqi family's cistern with clean water, the local Al Qaeda crew rolled up after dark, locked all twenty of them in the house. And I'm talking about three generations here. Grandmothers and grandfathers. Little kids. And they blew up the house. Everyone inside."

I notice that my drink is warm and tastes sweeter than Maker's Mark. It's Tweed Jacket's Bulleit rye neat, and I've grabbed it by mistake. I wonder why he's not saying anything to stop me, shrug, and continue.

"Yeah, that house bomb was nasty. Blast hole cut all the way into the street. While they were recovering the bodies, I took my platoon out to patch the hole. And believe it or not, there was a second bomb in that hole, too." I laugh to myself. No one joins me. "Pardon me for a minute."

I pull away from the table, stand, and walk away.

Behind me, I hear Stall pleading with his friends, "Look, I know. But seriously, do a search for *Profane Twenty-four*."

Paige notices me on my way to the outside smoking patio. She's working with savage concentration behind the bar, constructing three different drinks with the precision of a heart surgeon. She motions for me with her chin.

I stride over, placing a foot on the bottom rail.

"You know those assholes?" she asks curtly, rubbing a lime around the rim of a glass.

"No. Just that guy Stall. He's my boss for this internship. They're his friends."

"I know. Used to be my friends, too."

"Small town that way, huh?" I scratch the back of my neck and take a deep breath. "Guess your sorority sisters took offense at the deeply counterculture motives that led you to business school?"

Her smile is a fault line in granite. "I happen to be concentrating in nonprofits, or didn't you notice in ethics class?"

"Yeah, I didn't notice much in that class, honestly." I start searching the bottles behind her for something I might recognize.

Paige notices. "What? You already finish the first one? Christ, I poured you a triple."

"You sure did. Thanks. And, uh, yes, I did."

"Here." She turns for a glass and pours me another.

I take a sip and enjoy it so much I have to pause before setting the glass back down. I sneak another quick tug while Paige is looking at those busy hands of hers, letting the liquor touch every corner of my mouth before it slips down into my throat.

"So you're working down at One Shell Square?" she asks. "Figures. We've been wondering about you."

"Who?"

"Your classmates. We meet every Thursday at Molly's, or didn't you get my note? Everyone's been asking about you. They seem to think I should be the one who knows."

"Yeah? Well . . . tell everyone I say hello."

"You won't come and say hello yourself ?"

"I'm not real social."

"Except with douche bags like Stall?" She motions another bartender over to grab the tray of completed drinks. Little works of art, all of them.

"It's not exactly a social occasion. Stall's trying to introduce me to, you know, potential clients."

Paige laughs. "You mean suckers?"

"Sorry?"

"Derivatives? Securitized debt obligations? Euro bonds? Ponzi schemes, all. It's a sinking ship, Donovan. Even with the bailouts." She opens a bottle of water and takes a sip.

"Professor Cole seems to think the market's found its footing."

She shrugs. "We'll see. It's all just paper, anyway."

A memory suddenly takes hold in my mind, and I chuckle to myself. The smell of burning paper. The glow, the aggressive heat, the gnawing flames. I hear a chorus of laughter in my head, steeped in crazy, manic relief. How funny it was to live.

I close my eyes and rest my head on my hand.

Paige pokes me in the shoulder. "Donovan," she says, a bit of concern in her voice now, "are you . . . *laughing*?"

I look up at her, my goofy smile its own answer, as I trace with my eyes from her trim, little lips to the worry lines on her cheeks, all the way up to her button nose. Then I allow myself to take the rest in, too. Her slender neck, her narrow, defined shoulders, her fierce, lovely little frame—not caring anymore if she catches me.

"Smiley Pete Donovan," she says, smiling herself now. "What's so funny?"

"I ever tell you about the time I watched a million dollars burn?"

"No. But you can tell me now." She smiles and takes back my drink.

Hey, you. Lester. There's yogurt in the fridge. (Yogurt! So girly, right?) No coffee, but you did get to fuck me so I suggest you deal with it, son. I have a few slices of bread. Make toast? It would be dry toast, though, as I have literally nothing else. I'll be home from work in a few hours. Stick around?

NASR WAL SALAM

Smells like soccer practice in her little bedroom. Her sheets and pillows, I mean. Like fresh-cut grass in the afternoon. She roll around on the lawn before crawling into this bed, or what?

That's right. I remember now. We did roll around on the lawn for a little bit. Just after she grabbed me by the collar and pulled me out the truck. I was thinking I'd just drop her off and head over to Landry's place, but then out of nowhere we end up flopped all over the lawn like a couple damn teenagers.

Wait. Could this girl *be* a teenager? With parents in this house somewhere? And if not, whose house is this really? Is nobody paying the goddamn heating bill? Goddamn fifty-five degrees in here.

It was the kinda thing a crazy kid would do, rolling around on that lawn. What about the neighbors, I said, won't they hear? Can't they see? But this girl, Lizzy. She just giggled, bit my chest, and laughed at the way I gritted my teeth and tried to make like it didn't hurt when she knew it sure as hell did.

I remember the lawn, and I remember what we did in this room, too. What I don't remember is how we got in here. It was so damned fast. I roll over and try not to drown in this girl's wedding cake of a bed. It's midmorning, judging by the angle of the light coming through the cheap, metal blinds. Probably not past nine o'clock, though. Can't ever sleep that late, even when I really want to.

I sit up and listen for voices or the sound of someone moving around on the other side of that door. Can't hear nothing, so I'm willing to believe I'm alone in this house. A good thing, too, since my underwear are gone and my crotch is rough and sticky. Goddamn, I need to find my clothes.

This girl Lizzy's got laundry piled up on the floor so high I can roll onto my feet without bending my knees. It's hard to find my clothes, though, with hers lying all over the place. I pick through skirts and skinny black jeans, little dresses and undershirts. Nothing of mine.

Am I gonna have to crawl out this window? Sprint to my truck buck naked in the cold and grab the change of clothes from my overnight bag? What if someone already stole my bag, my truck sitting unlocked like it is? What then?

I'm starting to consider it seriously, then I spot my name on a piece of sketch paper, taped to the wall over the only corner she keeps clean.

"Lester," it says, a big arrow pointing down to an old architect's plotting table where all my clothes are folded, nice and neat. I pick my way across the floor, trying not to step on too many bras. All those clips and wires hurt my cold, bare feet.

Another note's sitting on top my underwear, like the one she left on the wall:

"These are very aggressive underpants, Lester. Did you get them in the military? Olive drab. Official but silky smooth too. They're like danger panties."

Goddamn adorable, this Lizzy. She's right, of course. Marine Corps silkies are a strange beast, like boxer shorts with a liner. They do feel odd at first. But now it's the only underwear that don't bother me, and since I gave up the dog tags, the last bit of my uniform still in daily rotation.

I shake the pair off the top of the pile and pull them on. Soft and dry. That's the advantage of the silkies. You can wear them for days if need be. Helps out on the road when you have to sit in the Humvee for hours, sweating and steaming. I pull on my jeans and undershirt and fall back across her bed, feeling a little more relaxed now. No one's gonna walk in on me naked. No roommates. Or parents, if I've messed up that bad.

That grass smell is all over me again. Beautiful.

The phone in my pocket vibrates. I take it out and see the voice message from Landry. I delete it without listening. He's probably looking to congratulate me. I could listen to it, but then I'd just feel worse. This girl Lizzy. She'll get to know me soon, so there's not a lot of time left in this. I'll just stick around until she comes home. Just to be polite.

Goddamn, that grass smell. What *is* that? What does this smell remind me of ? What am I trying to remember?

The grass down at Nasr Wal Salam. That's right. Thickest damn grass I ever saw.

We stopped there one day, on our way back from fixing ten miles of potholes. Everyone just exhausted and hoping to push through. But Major Leighton himself got on the radio and told Lieutenant Donovan to stop there and pick up some State Department reconstruction types. They had their own vehicle. Just needed an escort back up the river to Camp Fallujah.

The State Department types, they had grass down there in that little compound, a legit lawn out front of their command shack. A crazy thing to see in the middle of all that.

Lieutenant Donovan went inside to talk to them while Dodge and me leaned against the Humvee. Marceau, up in the turret, stood and took off his helmet. I stared at the lawn and even went so far as to get down on my knees and stick my nose in it. So damn sweet, that grass.

Dodge kicked me in the ass. "Crazy-man Lester. New things for you every day in this war, I see? If truly there is no grass in America?"

"This is a good lawn" was all I could say. "They really take care of this."

"They must be using bottled water," Marceau said, looking down from his turret.

"Really?" I asked.

"Yeah. The gray water around here, the kind they pull from the river and have us shower in? It's alkaline. Put water from the shower tanks on that grass and it'll shrivel up."

That got Dodge's attention. "How do you know so much about plants, James? Are you a farmboy?"

Marceau looked straight ahead. "Yeah. Kind of. Parents had a farm when I was a kid."

"Ah! Goats and cows. Corn and wheat," Dodge said. "This is why you are always waking so early? A farmboy habit of childhood?"

Marceau looked straight ahead. "Lost the farm a long time ago. Dad's a security guard, now. Mom's a substitute teacher." Then he dropped back into the Humvee to prep his gear, before anything else could be said about it.

I plucked a few blades of that grass and shoved them down in my pocket.

When Lieutenant Donovan came back, he had a look on his face like he was nervous about something. Not nervous about an ambush or a roadside bomb. Nervous like someone had just told him a funny secret by accident. Like now he knew something embarrassing about these guys he wasn't supposed to.

Two private-security guys with beards and expensive sunglasses came stumbling out behind him with a big transit case. They were big, these guys, yoked like bouncers, but even they were straining under the weight of that case. An armored Suburban came around from their vehicle lot and the security guys loaded the transit case in the back. Real quick, like they couldn't wait to wash their hands of the thing.

"Sergeant Gomez!" the lieutenant called out as he wiggled into his body armor. "Corporal Zahn!"

Zahn walked over slow and calm as ever, a nice slug of dip behind his lip. Gomez jogged, her back stiff and straight. So different, those two.

"Do a quick radio check with these guys," Lieutenant Donovan said to Zahn. "And make sure they have our freqs. If we lose track of these guys, it'll be bad."

Zahn chuckled. "Worse than usual, sir?"

"Yes." The lieutenant nodded, leaving it at that.

Zahn shrugged and walked off to coordinate with the civilians.

Sergeant Gomez stuck around. "Something I should know, sir? Before we get on the road?"

Lieutenant Donovan smiled like he wanted to tell her, but then just said, "No. Treat it like any other vic. We'll do a quick, rolling stop at Fallujah to drop these guys off and head home. Easy day."

We got settled in the Humvee, and the lieutenant said to Zahn, "Put the Suburban in front. Keep them sandwiched between us and Gomez."

"You gonna tell me what's in that truck, sir?" Zahn smirked as he worked the used-up wad of dip from behind his lip into the half-full spit bottle.

"Sure. A million dollars in cash for the sheikhs."

Dodge reacted first, laughing. "Yes, man! I *knew* it! You Americans are very clever, indeed!"

Zahn sat still, his eyes fixed on the lieutenant. "You serious, sir?"

"I am. These State Department guys are delivering it to the civil affairs guys in Fallujah, who are delivering it to the sheikhs west of Ramadi. Not enough local Sunnis joining the army, so the million dollars is a bribe to get their sons in uniform." The lieutenant buckled his helmet strap. "Get a comm check with Gomez."

Zahn keyed his radio and, speaking over the sound of Dodge's laughter, said, "Vic four is up."

"Thug life!" Dodge laughed.

The lieutenant turned around with his mouth open, like he wanted Dodge to shut up. But then he turned around like a father too busy to argue, or too honest to try.

Myself, I couldn't keep my eyes off the back doors of that Suburban. We left the compound, and desert filled the window on my armored door. The black and yellow curbstones blurred away into one color, and all I could think of was that million dollars. What'd that even *look* like? Would I get to see it before the Suburban drove off at Camp Fallujah? I thought about the stacks, like the kind you see in movies. How many stacks make a million dollars? I thought about what *one* of those stacks could do for my father. The new tractor he could finally get.

And then, in an instant, the Suburban disappeared in a big-ass fireball.

"Fuck, fuck, fuck," I heard myself whisper, as Zahn swerved to avoid the Suburban, skidding sideways off the highway and into the sand. As we passed, I could see that the explosion had only taken the back half. The security guys up front, in a separate armored compartment, looked unhurt.

"Yahtzee!" Marceau screamed, laughing over the hiss and crackle of the burning vehicle.

Lieutenant Donovan keyed his radio. "Vic four is up. Fives and twenty-fives."

The other vehicles checked in, calmly as he had. But the contractors in the Suburban—they were a little more hopped up, you know? Jumped up onto the net all screaming and cursing. Not what you're supposed to do. No injuries, at least. But no saving that truck.

Reaching for his can of Skoal, Zahn nudged the Humvee off the side of the road.

Dodge bumped me. "Lester, man. Check your window. Fives, Lester."

We checked around the Humvee while the dismounted team secured the road and the desert around us. When we didn't find any secondary devices, the lieutenant said, "Doc, go check them out. Make sure they're okay." He sounded kind of put out by the whole thing.

I took off down the road at a quick walk, cutting by Sergeant Gomez as she was pushing a security team farther out into the desert, getting ready for the bomb team on its way to do a postblast analysis.

The Suburban was in full inferno by this time. The security contractors sat on the curb looking like a couple of guys who knew they were about to get fired. But they were fine. Cuts and bruises only.

Lieutenant Donovan walked up behind me. "Is that case fire-proof?" he asked the lead contractor.

"Nope," the guy said from behind the beard and the fancy sunglasses—not even bothering to look up.

Just a few steps behind the lieutenant, Dodge was laughing his ass off. "This is even *more* gangster, man! It's like some rap video! Right? You Americans, you have money to burn!"

And then I started laughing, too. I stood up and looked at Dodge, laughing so hard tears ran down my cheeks.

Then, over my shoulder, damned if I didn't see the lieutenant laughing, too. But just for a second. He had to go back and radio Major Leighton. Guess the poor bastard had to compose himself for that.

Huck has difficulty abandoning friends, even when they pose an obvious danger to him. "Well," he says of the Duke and the Dauphine, "it's a rough gang, them two frauds, and I'm fixed so I got to travel with them a while longer, whether I want to or not. I druther not tell you why; and if you was to blow on them this town would get me out of their claws, and I'd be all right; but there'd be another that you don't know about who'd be in big trouble. Well, we got to save HIM, hain't we? Of course. Well, then, we won't blow on them."

TOURIST TOWN

My flatmates come screaming and chanting around the corner, waving flags and stomping feet. I fold *Huck Finn* into my back pocket and step into the middle of the sidewalk where they will notice me. It seems they have waited for the other university kids to pass in order to sweep up all the pretty girls who have fallen away from the protest for fear of the police.

It is a fine strategy. My flatmates comfort these girls and offer protection, telling them to meet at this building on the corner if anything goes wrong. We live here together in a spacious flat, they say. Follow us back here for safety.

They see me and call out. Our friend, they say. He is Iraqi and has seen much worse than this. And look. He is not afraid. Come with us, friend.

I join with them, but only so my flatmates are not embarrassed. They would not forgive me if I stayed away. We are pushed closer together by the growing mass of people, my flatmates and I, closer and closer together with these pretty girls. The crowd becomes louder and more serious in their chanting as we are pulled forward into the smell of riot gas and gunpowder. We march closer to the main square. Smoke drifts through the abandoned cars ahead of us, the overturned carts.

Our Iraqi friend speaks perfect English, my flatmates tell the pretty girls. He can talk to the Western journalists should we find any. You girls are too pretty to not go on television. He will find a reporter and speak in English for us. You girls will stand behind him and smile for the camera. This is the best way to fight Ben Ali. We will show to the world what pretty girls we have in Tunisia.

A few of the girls laugh, but most of them frown at this foolishness. They are smarter than my flatmates and seem to know better what awaits us in the square.

A pretty girl asks me if I fought the Americans before I left Iraq.

I tell her that I did not. That I am a coward, you see.

"You speak English," she says. "Did you speak English for them instead of fighting?"

"Sometimes. But most of the time just for myself. For business."

She turns away, disappointed.

Instantly, I find myself wishing I had told her a lie. Still, I do not blame this pretty girl for her disgust in me. I have disappointed many others before you, I think to myself.

I woke to waves lapping against the bank, opened my eyes, and looked east. I felt the morning sun on my face, listened to Abu Abdul's rooster, and felt good, for the first time in weeks, months even. Mundhir and Hani had left, and by the touch of their cool blankets I knew they had been awake for some time. I walked up the path to the mud farmhouse, smelling fire and a fresh pot of tea. Haji Fasil came outside with another pot, this one filled with rice.

"Good morning, Haji Fasil."

"Peace be with you, Kateb."

"And you, as well." I yawned, sat down on a fallen eucalyptus log, and warmed my hands by the fire. "I know you have a stove, Haji. Why this fire?"

"It seems the right time for it. I enjoy a fire. Spring is coming and this is most likely the last cool morning until next year." He handed me tea in a metal cup.

"Are you sure this is not just a show for the city boys? Are you not teaching us a lesson about our bedouin roots?"

"No, of course not." He wiped his hands on his long shirt. "Besides, I'm sure you do not need any lessons. You look like children of the Party, to me. Baathist fathers? Yes. I'm sure you boys spent each summer at an oasis outside Ramadi. Living in tents, shooting rabbits for sport. Perhaps, as a boy, you once shook the hand of Saddam? How exciting."

I did not answer. No need to discuss all that, not just yet. I stared out across the lake and waited for the air to thin. "Hani and Mundhir had gone before I woke this morning. Are they off somewhere with Abu Abdul?"

"Mundhir, yes. He walked down the peninsula with Abu Abdul to retrieve the fishing boat. Hani went into town with your car."

"Did he say what he was doing with it?"

"Yes. He is buying goods at the market. Trinkets to sell to the Americans as they pass by." Haji Fasil pulled a knife from under his shirt and began cutting basil on a stump.

I nodded slowly to hide my fury, trying to pretend that it had been our plan all along. "Ah. How much money did he take?"

"All of it, I presume. But this should not worry you. Rich boys can always get more money from their fathers. Yes? Where is your father, Kateb?"

I stood, brushed off my jeans, and ignored his question. "Thank you for the tea, Haji Fasil." I turned back toward the lake.

Haji Fasil stopped me. "Abu Abdul did not lose his tongue to cancer. You know this, yes?" He pointed the knife at me and raised his eyebrows.

I stopped, turned around. "Yes, I figured that." So, it was time to talk.

"We are from Halab."

I sat back down.

Haji Fasil continued chopping basil and spoke as if he were telling me the recipe for his rice. "After the first war with the Americans, Abu Abdul and I joined the uprising. Saddam's helicopters came and slaughtered us. We had families, then. Wives and children. All dead. I ran away. The Mukhabarat found Abu Abdul and cut out his tongue. I escaped."

I nodded and took a sip of my tea.

"You three boys were young children then."

"Yes."

"Living in Baghdad? Mansour, I suppose? Big houses? Gardens, fancy cars?"

"Yes," I whispered. "All of that. University, too."

"And now you are running away."

I nodded and pushed dirt around with my toe. "We . . . ," I began, like I, too, had a story to tell. "We are running away," I said simply.

"Oh, how it feels to run!" Haji Fasil diced faster. "I remember it." The knife became a blur. "But how will you run without money to fuel your car?" Haji Fasil stuck his knife in the stump and pushed the basil into the rice. "And if Hani cannot make a quick profit on these goods, quickly turn your dinar into dollars, I imagine you will be forced to sell your car. And I wonder what will become of it? After it is turned into a bomb, I mean. Driven into a checkpoint? Left by the side of the road? This all depends on the buyer, I suppose. You Sunnis are becoming more fond of martyr attacks. More like Sadrists all the time."

"I am not one of them," I said, the edge on my voice sharper than I had intended.

"You are not Sunni?" Haji Fasil took a step in my direction. "Do you think me stupid?"

"No, Haji Fasil. I am not a terrorist. I am a student. I do not care for any of this."

"Yes? And what do you study, child?"

"English."

"You fool." He went back to the fire and hung the pot over the low flames. "What does your Baathist father say about that? What does your mother think about a son who does not fight for the Party?"

"My mother died long ago. Cancer. Which is how I knew you were lying about Abu Abdul's scar. My father raised my older brother and me while working for the Ministry of Agriculture."

"Ah, the son of a simple farmer. How pleasant."

"An engineer. He designed the Grand Canal." I pointed to the stagnant ditch in the distance, leeching slowly from the depths of Lake Thar Thar.

"A rather poor engineer, then."

"He could never finish it. He could never procure the necessary pumps after the first war. The Americans would not allow it."

"Is that why you learned English? To help your father with the Americans?"

"No. My father wanted me to study English, yes. But only so I could go abroad for secondary school. My father still hoped, even after the first war, so I still learned. I grew quite fond of American books, and of their music, too."

"And your friends? Hani? Mundhir? What do they study?"

"Hani studies business. And Mundhir . . . Mundhir is not a student. We met him in Karada when we were finishing second-level school. Hani and I organized rock music shows in Baghdad for our university friends. Mundhir was our security."

Haji Fasil stirred his rice. "May God be merciful on all three of you. You are such fools for coming here." He went back to the stump and pulled out his knife.

I was tired of him, tired of his knife. Sick of the way it watched, like the third member of our conversation. I stood and took a step toward him. "Have you *seen* Baghdad lately, Haji? Do you think I left my garden and my bloody Mercedes to come here? I have not seen my father in a year, if you must know. I sleep in my dead professor's office. I work diligently at a thesis he will never read. This place?" I waved my arm over the beach and the lake. "This place, Haji Fasil, is paradise. Look, your family is dead and I am sorry. But I did not kill them. Mundhir and Hani did not kill them. You want Iraq? It is yours now. You can have it."

He took a step toward me and scowled. I did not move, but prepared myself.

Haji Fasil just smiled and patted my cheek. "Brave boy. Who wants Iraq? *I* want fish. Fish to serve over this rice. And they might have it." He pointed his knife out at the lake.

I turned around and saw the boat. A little *kitr* with a ratty triangular sail. Abu Abdul worked at the sheets while Mundhir rowed.

"We will have family breakfast, if God wills it."

And God did. Heaping bowls of delicious rice and fish. And toward the end of breakfast, Hani returned with the car. He came bouncing down the dirt path, wearing a wide grin. The shocks labored under the weight of the merchandise he had purchased. Boxes piled high on the backseat, and the trunk so full it would not latch. He had to tie it down with a length of twine.

I walked out to meet him, trying not to show my anger.

"So, you went shopping," I said to him through the open window of the driver's door.

"Wait until you see what I found," he said distractedly. "We will be rich."

"Did you not think to discuss this with Mundhir and me, first?"

"Discuss what?" Hani scoffed. "Turning our pitiful pile of dinar into something we can actually use? No. We need dollars for Jordan, and for the long term. This is necessary. And besides, you were sleeping."

"But what if we need to leave quickly, Hani? What if we need to keep moving west in a hurry?"

Hani looked puzzled. "But what about your father? He might be nearby, yes? Perhaps sheltering with old friends in Ramadi? Should we not try to find him the next few days?"

"Yes," I said, defeated. "Of course."

The matter settled for the moment, Hani insisted the first order of business, before unloading the car, was to clean the beach. Mundhir and I walked the twenty meters of beach and picked out shards of glass and bits of rotting wood while Haji Fasil and Abu Abdul cleaned fish and hung them in the smokehouse.

Hani moved about the grounds inspecting the little mud huts to see which were in usable condition. He quizzed Haji Fasil on business: What did customers pay for rice? Where did he get his rice in the first place? How did he create profits? I listened from my place under the eucalyptus tree and began to understand how Haji Fasil operated.

Haji Fasil was a middleman. That was his skill. His little farm was the neutral ground, and from it he could go anywhere, shuttle goods between enemies, blend with any faction. Kurds from the north with rice imported from Turkey sold to Haji Fasil at a discount because they were afraid to travel any farther south. Sunnis traveling from Ramadi with cooking oil imported from Jordan sold it to him at a discount because they were afraid to travel any farther east.

Shia traveling from Baiji with diesel from the refinery sold to him at a discount because they were afraid to travel any farther west.

On this sharp edge, Haji Fasil found a way to balance. He could be Sunni, Shia, or a Kurd on any given day. His arbitrage came on the premium of fear. That was his business, and why he had not turned his farm into a market. His profits depended on merchants who could not mingle for fear of decapitation. He took that risk for them.

Hani was impressed, but believed that Haji Fasil had forgotten one important customer: the Americans.

Only after Hani had laid out his goods in the afternoon did I fully understand. The farm was to serve as a branch franchise on behalf of several merchants from Dra Dijlia, selling soft drinks, pirated Hollywood DVDs, and assorted Iraqi souvenirs, all on consignment. At the end of a week, we would repay the suppliers, take our share of the profits in dollars, and decide whether to reinvest our earnings into additional inventories. After the first week, Hani hoped to be self-sufficient, with sustainable cash flows.

Mundhir unloaded the drinks from the trunk and put them into a fishing net that he lowered into the lake, so the cans could be kept somewhat cool. Just before dusk, Hani arranged the movies and souvenirs on display racks fashioned from old, broken chicken cages and staged the racks where they could be seen from the road.

Haji Fasil went about his work befuddled, yet sufficiently amused to let Hani continue. At dinner, he asked Hani how he intended to run his marketplace. "Americans have passed by here many times. They never stop."

"Yes, but now we have an advantage, Haji Fasil. Kateb speaks English."

I put down my rice. "Hani, we can travel up the river to Syria in three days, no problem. Or the Rutbah highway to Jordan, if need be. But we are wasting time here. Worse, we are risking our lives."

"Think of it as a test run for Tunisia. If we can attract Americans to this little beach resort, we will surely have no problems there."

"I never agreed to Tunisia either! Also, this is a beach resort, now? Last I checked it's five mud-brick houses on a shitty lake."

"Kateb! You'll offend our host."

Haji Fasil said, "No, he is right, Hani. This is not the Al Rasheed."

Mundhir returned from the boat with Abu Abdul close behind. "Abu Abdul has tarps. I can rinse off the fish guts tomorrow and rig them on poles for shade."

"You too, Mundhir?" I threw up my arms. "This is foolishness. If we do business with the Americans, we will die."

"Actually, I think you'll be fine," Haji Fasil offered. "This is a no-man's-land. We do what we like."

Hani smiled. "Do you hear that, Kateb? All we need now is a sign." With that, he produced a can of paint from behind the log. "For which, we need *you*."

For an hour, I refused. I went down to the water to read my book. Made notes for my thesis. Only when the sun went down and the moon rose over the lake did I go back to Hani, busy sorting through DVDs by the light of his lantern. "What do you want the sign to say?"

He smiled and retrieved a sheet of plywood, lowering the lantern for me. "I want it to be inviting. We need a name that says, 'There is no war here. This place is safe. Come and relax. Come and spend your money.'"

I got on my knees and dipped the brush in black paint. "You are insane."

"The Thar Thar Hotel and Casino, perhaps? Can you translate that?"

"That's what you want the sign to say?"

"Kateb. Kateb, my friend." He knelt with me and put his hand on my shoulder. "I want you to write what *you* think would work. Be a part of this! Participate, Kateb! This is our future!"

"All right, then. I have the perfect name."

"Wonderful, my friend." Hani kissed my cheek. "Wonderful."

I drew the English words in big, thick letters.

"What does it say?" Hani begged.

"Exactly what you wanted. The Americans will read it and feel safe. We will do a good business. Only make me a promise, Hani."

"Yes. Anything."

"This is temporary. One week. Two at the most."

"I promise, my friend."

I looked over Hani's shoulder and watched Mundhir hanging fishnets out to dry with Abu Abdul. Mundhir smiled at the old man and they walked together down the beach holding hands. I saw Haji Fasil counting rice sacks in his storage hut. I looked back at Hani and marked the look on his face.

They were having fun, meaning we would be stuck here, by the lake, for too many days. We were uncomfortably close to Habbaniyah and risked a passing encounter with someone, some merchant or former soldier, who knew my father and brother.

I went to the road and hung the sign on a pole Hani had secured in a pile of rocks:

TOURIST TOWN. STOP AND SPEND MONEY ON BULLSHIT.

Significant Incident Report: Criminal Act, murder and intimidation

While executing a road repair mission on Route Golden, an Engineer Support Company convoy, Hellbox Five-Six, was approached by three Iraqi nationals who claimed that soldiers of the Iraqi Army wearing civilian clothes had murdered several local merchants. Assisted by a coalition-employed interpreter, the Iraqi nationals led coalition forces to the bodies of five men in the vicinity of the Dra Dijlia Market. The bodies were found bound and blindfolded and appeared to have died from gunshot wounds to the back of the head. When asked by coalition forces how they knew the men had been murdered by members of the Iraqi Army, the locals claimed it was common knowledge in the area that Iraqi soldiers were members of a Shiite death squad. The bodies were turned over to the local Iraqi Highway Patrol, and coalition forces continued their mission.

Respectfully submitted,
P. E. Donovan

BIG BOY RULES OUT HERE

This might be the worst hangover I've ever had. It's like a straw
siphoning the moisture from behind my eyes, sucking it across
my brain and down my spine. Why did I drink so much whiskey?
And what did I say to Paige?

I grab my phone to check the time and see a text message from
a new contact labeled Empathy.

"What time are we meeting at West End? I'm excited to see
this boat. And, um, terrified for you. You have *no* idea what you're
getting into."

Good God. I told her about *Sentimental Journey*.

Her crack about Bear Bryant and his three fingers of Maker's
Mark had got me talking. She knew just what to say. Just how to get
me telling stories. This is a problem.

It's not smart for me to tell stories. Makes people uncomfortable. But with a few bourbons in me, everything takes on a gallows
humor and I just want to share, share, share. It's why I drink alone,
mostly. I don't have the discipline to drink around people and answer
their simple questions without saying something awful. Even the
memories that seem funny in my head come out sounding like the
summer vacation of a psychopath.

It's even worse, though, when I just sit there quietly and refuse
to discuss the war at all. People get the impression that I'm the
stereotypical brooding vet. That's why I always keep two or three

stories on deck, harmless and cute, to distract and move the conversation elsewhere. The million dollars burning on the side of the road is a real winner. Fred the Scorpion works well, too. That's Cobb's story, but I pretend it happened to me. I used to tell stories about Marceau, but had to stop; people asked too many questions about him.

Suddenly, I have a flash of recollection. A national championship ring. A pile of hay. Good Christ, did I tell Paige the story about the old man?

I remember pulling the Nomex hood away from my face and slowly working the fabric under my chin with a knuckle of my gloved hand. My fingers gripped a pen; the Humvee hit a bump and I double-clutched, barely catching it. I tried to wipe my face, but there was too much sweat. I was just pushing it around.

Up ahead of us, a goat herder in an ankle-length shirt flailed and slapped his thighs to urge his animals from the road. Zahn tapped the accelerator. Just a tap. Just enough to stoke the engine but not enough to spin the wheels. The sound of it reached the herder and he panicked. He jumped up and down, waved his staff, and beat his animals to move them from the road before the wild American ran them down.

Zahn spit into his dip bottle. "Real combat petting zoo out here, sir," he said, laconic as ever.

I had radio handsets wedged under the rim of my helmet, pressed against each ear, and secured to my chin strap so that the microphones floated in front of my lips. The thick cords twisted up to hooks above the windshield. Like ceremonial braids.

Up ahead, in the dusty traffic circle where men sold produce and bales of hay from donkey carts, I spotted an old man with a thick, gray beard and a black-checkered kaffiyeh standing next to his cart of alfalfa hay, having a heated argument with a customer.

The old man turned away from his customer and slapped his forehead in distress.

The fat, middle-aged customer clenched his fists, stomped his feet, and scowled so violently the hairs of his mustache seemed to plug his nostrils.

The old man wiped his brow and pushed his hand into the fat man's face. He pointed to his upturned palm and shouted.

I thought of my father and smiled. "Look at my sweat," I said to myself. "Look at it, here. You see that sweat? Not one dollar less. I'd sooner salt my fields. Not one dollar less."

Zahn perked up. "Say something over there, sir?"

"Yeah, just something my father used to say. Folks would roll by late in the afternoon, looking for bargain hay, and he'd go, 'Sooner salt my fields in sweat. Don't you try to muscle me. I played tight end for Coach Paul Bryant.'" I pointed to the old man. "This guy up here? The old guy in the head scarf ? Reminds me of him, a little bit."

The old man's features grew more animated out the windshield. He screamed and pointed to his ring finger.

I turned back to Zahn. "You *see* this ring? National champions, 1961!"

Zahn smiled, but only to keep his lieutenant happy. It was hard enough, his job. Guiding an awkward, top-heavy vehicle through a poorly designed traffic circle without losing speed—hard enough without having to indulge the idiotic musings of his college-boy lieutenant, skipping down memory lane. I understood.

All at once the men doing business in the traffic circle heard our engines above the din. We had four Humvees and two trucks that day, all with heavy guns mounted up top. The gunners waved red flags and shot flares, and the merchants fled like birds. Most moved away from the curb in a tight knot. A few, the bold ones, ran into the street to save their little Daihatsu bongo trucks.

But the old man with alfalfa for sale didn't move. A bongo truck careened through the booth next to his and bucked to a stop against a pile of sacks. The old man didn't even flinch. He just slapped his face and protested to the universe at large. The injustice of alfalfa prices. The idiocy of these terrible drivers. The imperial arrogance of the Americans.

I craned my neck to watch him as we rolled through the traffic circle and back into the desert, until the town faded behind us, before turning back to the horizon and searching through the smog and the shrubs festooned with garbage. A brown smudge stood out in the distance from inside the green ribbon hugging the river. I glanced at my map to make sure it was the right place, the *right* smudge.

I smiled, wiped my nose, and said to Zahn. "Hey, how about on the way back we buy some hay from that guy? Just to do it, huh? What do you think?" I turned to the backseat to face Dodge. "Can you barter for hay?"

Dodge looked up from his book, the one he was always reading, the one from which he'd removed the paperback cover to hide the title and avoid questions. "I haven't a clue, *Mulasim*. I've not once bought hay in my entire life."

"Hell, *I'll* do it," Doc Pleasant chimed in. "Teach me three words, Dodge. Seems like that's all you need. The rest is just yelling."

Then we heard the bomb.

Behind us.

I was looking right at Doc. I saw him flinch and grip his seat. The shock wave kicked me in the ass and pulled through my chest.

I dropped my pen, bending over out of instinct to get it. The radio cords grabbed me by the chin, like a rock in a slingshot, and sent my head bouncing back up. The pen skittered away over the floorboard.

Zahn squirmed in his seat and fixed his grip on the wheel. "*Fuck*. That fucker was big." He reached for the can of Skoal in his grenade pouch.

All at once, the convoy net built to a fuzzy brawl in my right ear, excited transmissions and shouts coming in from all six vehicles. The vehicle commanders, keying their handsets at the same time, all stepped on each other and reduced the net to a dull bleat.

In my other ear, an unknown radio operator in the combat outpost up ahead, the brown smudge in the window, continued speaking casually until the sound reached him a few seconds later. A low rumble came through the concrete walls of his operations center, into his radio, and back into my ear. A time traveler.

I unclipped the handset and tossed it away before I had to hear about the bomb again. The handset bounced off its hook like the telephone in my parents' kitchen when my father didn't want calls during dinner.

"You see that," I yelled up to Marceau in the turret, twisting in my seat to get a better angle. I waved at Zahn. "Speed up, speed up."

No sharp crack of an artillery round. No steel frag hissing by the turret. I could tell by the sound, full and deep, that powerful as the bomb had clearly been, it was probably homemade. A hot-water heater, maybe, packed with ammonium nitrate fertilizer soaked in diesel fuel. That was becoming more popular around that time. Slow, powerful blast waves that might not be capable of piercing armor, but could throw a Humvee into the air like a child's toy.

Dodge cursed loudly in Arabic and asked Doc in English, "Are you okay, man? Are you okay?"

Doc opened his eyes. "We're fine. Way behind us. We're fine." He didn't loosen his grip on the seat, though. And he kept on flinching.

The highway curved right and I saw the smoke in my side mirror. Inside the smoke, a cloud of gray debris rained down on the traffic circle. The attack had obviously been meant for us, and we'd been spared by a triggerman late on the switch or a bomb with a bad fuse.

After all six vehicles had reported up, I called out on the common net for the convoy to push through. The outpost up ahead had a quick-reaction force. Marines on twenty-four-hour standby with gunned-up security Humvees. They could take care of it. It wasn't our job. Push through.

I turned back to the horizon and watched the smudge become a thumbnail, growing slowly into an earthen berm with empty Hesco baskets stretched out on top, waiting for a front-end loader to come by and fill them with rocks and dirt. The canvas lining of the Hescos flapped against the steel-mesh frames in places, rotting away like clothes on a skeleton.

Zahn turned off the highway, down a steep embankment, and onto a dirt track. Ahead of us, five Nissan trucks with Iraqi flags painted on white doors lurched through the gate, an American Humvee belonging to the military adviser team following them like a determined sheepdog. The white Iraqi Army trucks swerved and jockeyed for position on the narrow road, all of them nosing violently into the soft sand at times before finding their place in line. Iraqi soldiers stood in the truck beds and braced themselves. They wore ill-fitting helmets and flak jackets over old-style, green camouflage uniforms. Their tan boots looked brand-new.

The American Humvee slowed down like they might be expecting a report from us. Zahn slowed down in response. But the

Humvee just rolled by with the turret gunner gesturing at the Iraqis, giving us a sarcastic shrug. "What more do you want?" he called out, hand over mouth. "We got them out the gate!" Then he settled back behind his gun.

"*That* was weird," said Zahn, having apparently caught the musing bug from his lieutenant.

We reached the gate, where an Iraqi soldier on watch waved us through before returning to where two more soldiers squatted in the shade with their helmets off. He dragged his rifle behind him like a child's blanket.

Zahn whistled, the musing bug having now taken a thorough hold. "They got a truck bomb in their future, they keep sitting around like that."

A young Marine from the adviser team, wearing running shoes and shorts, a rifle slung across his back, met us in the vehicle assembly area immediately inside the outpost and gestured for us to follow. I slid my armored window to the side and called out, "Clearing barrels? You have any? A berm where we can unload the machine guns?"

The kid shrugged, gestured to his loaded rifle. "Big boy rules out here."

A plywood sign hung on an empty Hesco behind him, with stenciled letters reading IRAQI ARMY ADVISORY TEAM SIX WELCOMES YOU TO COMBAT OUTPOST CHILI MAC ON THE BEAUTIFUL EUPHRATES RIVER. Near the bottom, a poorly drawn cowboy proclaimed in a dialogue bubble, "Can be combative."

Across an overgrown field, a dozen more white trucks idled in a courtyard flanked by several long, one-story barracks buildings. Iraqi soldiers squatted or shuffled around in their combat gear. Some tried to find shade by standing with their backs flat against a wall, barely managing to get their faces out of the sun. Iraqi officers walked the edges in green cotton uniforms reminiscent of Saddam's time, smoking cigarettes and talking on cell phones.

We followed the kid in running shorts and parked at a building in the far corner of the compound, across an empty field from the Iraqis. The convoy team stumbled out, stretched their backs, and ripped at the heavy Velcro on their body armor. Flak jackets swung open and wet heat trapped for hours against their chests burned away like scraps of onion paper to a flame. The Marines exulted in it.

I stepped from my Humvee and called out to Gomez, two vehicles ahead. "Clear these crew-serves." I pointed around at the turrets. "Do it now."

She nodded and started yelling at the vehicle commanders, "Unload and check those barrels! Right fucking now!"

I stripped off my gear and staged it on my seat. I pulled off my Nomex hood and rubbed the sweat from my hair, my fingers raking up grains of sand and little rocks along with it. As always, I left my rifle locked to the seat post.

Dodge leaned against his door and chatted with Doc. He kept his hood on, letting it cover his whole face. "These guys, Lester?" Dodge pointed to the Iraqi soldiers across the compound. "All these *jundis*? These Iraqi soldiers? They are pissed-off Shia dudes from Basra. Pissed-off dudes, Lester. If they can manage it, they will take me to the desert, make me feel some truly astonishing pain before cutting off my head."

"Why? What'd you do to them?"

"This is quite the long story, Lester. Just know that I will not remove my hood, nor my sunglasses. Not today."

Without breaking stride, I waved to Dodge. "You're inside with me. Doc, go see where Sergeant Gomez needs you."

I pushed through the plywood door with Dodge behind me and found a long, tiled hallway. Camouflage ponchos hung over the entrances to four side rooms, which I assumed were sleeping quarters for the adviser team. Their accommodations were Spartan, save for tables lining the hall and piled high with juice boxes, muffins in cellophane wrapping, and open care packages.

I heard voices from the end of the hall, in a dark room that seemed larger than all the sleeping quarters put together. The room overflowed with radio traffic, and I walked instinctively to the sound, taking note along the way of the high ceilings and the walls covered with fading murals.

"What is it?" I heard someone ask in the dark. "What have we got? Two civilian dead? Three?"

I stopped at the entrance to the room while, behind me, Dodge lingered at the muffin table. I leaned on the doorframe and watched a young captain speaking into a field telephone. Taller than me, maybe six feet, with thinning, brown hair and skinny arms. He had small shoulders and I imagined that a heavy pack would slip right off.

He called across the room to a radio operator, "How many?" Then, back into the phone, he said, "Three civilian dead, sir."

Sandbags covered small windows near the ceiling. A small amount of sunlight trickled in, but most of the room's light was provided by a fluorescent construction light hanging from a parachute cord, bathing the room in a sickly green.

Across from the young captain, three senior enlisted Marines stood around an older officer in a field chair. They crossed their arms and spoke quietly past each other.

"How many wounded he say?"

"Yeah, what's the story on that postblast response team?"

"On their way back now?"

I couldn't discern anyone's rank. Except for the captain, they all wore sandals, utility pants, and green T-shirts. Isolated from the prying eyes of the commanders in Taqaddum and Fallujah, military advisory teams tended to loosen their grooming standards. Who could blame them?

The captain saw me, hung up the phone, and walked over. "Hey, man. Sorry to keep you waiting. Big morning. So, you the resupply truck? Everybody good?"

"Yes, sir. We're all fine. Bomb was way behind us. We didn't even stop." Realizing instantly the potential shame of this admission, I added, "Got your air conditioners, too."

"Fucking *right*!" Then, to the man in the chair, he said, "You hear that, sir? Air conditioners."

The man held up his hand to let the captain know he was busy listening to the radio traffic.

"A little tense in here," the captain said, and I followed him out into the hall.

I pointed to Dodge, rooting through the muffins. "That's our terp, sir. I wasn't sure what it would look like out here so we brought him along."

The captain shrugged. "Never a bad idea." Then, with an odd sort of enthusiasm: "Shit, man, sorry. Drew Kelly." He offered his hand. "What's your name again?"

"Lieutenant Donovan." I shook his hand.

"No, I mean your first name."

"Oh. Pete, sir." No captain had ever asked me that.

"All right then, Pete. Let's see what we got here."

We left Dodge to his scavenging and walked outside to the truck stacked high with brown MRE cases, bottled water, and window-mounted air-conditioning units that looked like they'd been looted from a housing project.

"Know where these came from?" Captain Kelly asked.

"I think the supply officer said they came in from Jordan, sir."

"Yeah? Look like shit."

Before I could respond, we were interrupted by the sound of a hundred men screaming one word. Turning around, I saw that the Iraqi soldiers who'd been milling around their barracks were suddenly standing up, agitated, as they watched the three white trucks bouncing back through the gate, filled with men in civilian clothes tied up in the Iraqi style: Piled on each other; hands behind their backs; empty sandbags over their heads. The adviser team's Humvee followed at a distance, still playing sheepdog.

Captain Kelly laughed and said, "Just in time for the show, Pete."

Another, older voice came through the plywood door behind us. "So it's Dodge, then? Okay, Dodge, walk with me."

I turned around and saw the officer from the field chair, now wearing a blouse with the gold oak leaves of a major on his collar. He had a Mediterranean complexion, with thick, black hair graying at the temples. Tall as Captain Kelly but with broad shoulders that conveyed an older man's strength.

The major walked over. "Resupply?"

"Yes, sir. Lieutenant Donovan from Engineer—"

"Hey, Sal Franco. Good to meet you. Glad you brought your terp, too." He smiled like a salesman. "Mind if I borrow him a little while? I'm walking over to have a conversation with Colonel Hewrami. Like to have my own interpreter when I do that."

I stood quietly for a moment, confused. A major hardly needed my permission for anything.

"Our guy's still out in town with that mess," Franco continued. "Won't be back for a while, looks like."

"Oh. Well, yes. I mean, yes, sir. No problem." I spat out the words, caught entirely off-balance.

"Great, son. Appreciate it. Join me? Drew can handle things here."

Major Franco put on the sunglasses he had hanging by a lanyard around his neck and started walking. Dodge and I followed a half step behind him, with Dodge still wearing his hood.

Iraqi soldiers unloaded their trucks as we walked through the field. First, they ripped the sandbags off the heads of their prisoners, who, to a man, kept their mouths shut, looking down like they knew the drill. The soldiers let the older men among the prisoners step from the trucks, even helped some of them. But the younger guys were pushed callously, even violently, to the ground, lucky if they landed on their sides or their backs.

As we weaved through the crowd, Major Franco stared at his boots. A dust cloud grew as the Iraqi soldiers dragged men through the dirt and put them on their knees in rows of five. The faces of the prisoners bled, and most of them had bits of yellow shrub in their hair. Not one of them said a word.

Kneeling at the end of the first row, I saw, was the old man, the alfalfa man from the market. He rocked back and forth on his knees, tears running down to his chin, through his beard, and into the sand. He mouthed words to himself and shook his head.

Suddenly looking up, as if he sensed my gaze, he started whispering. I stopped walking and let him talk to me, my face telling him that I was listening. His voice trickled out like exhaust from a car on the verge of a stall.

"Min fadlak," he rasped. *"Min fadlak . . . Ada'tu tareeqi."*

He had blood in his hair and a gash above his beard in the thin, worn skin of his cheek. It was hard to imagine how that cut would ever heal, in skin so old. His voice ran out, but he kept mouthing the words. Until it was just one word, over and over. As he bowed his head, I imagined all the things he might want to tell me.

Help me. Let me go. Save my donkey. Save my alfalfa.

An Iraqi soldier walked over, put the tip of his rifle against the old man's chin and pushed his face away. The alfalfa man closed his eyes and sat still.

I started jogging and caught up with Major Franco as he reached the advisory team's Humvee, parked twenty meters away from the Iraqi soldiers and their prisoners. Major Franco leaned against the Humvee while his Marines stripped off their gear. The weary rancher with his sheepdogs, he sighed and put his hands in his pockets, looked out over the river, up at the sun, then back at the Iraqis.

I walked over to him, my mouth suddenly dry, licked my lips. "Sir?"

He looked at me and smiled. "Yes?"

"I just wanted to say, we didn't halt back there. Didn't secure that scene. But I saw that old man over there selling in the market just before the explosion. He might know something. Thought maybe we could get him out of those cuffs."

"Tough call. Tough call."

"I'm pretty sure they meant that bomb for my convoy. My vehicle, even. But I knew the adviser team had a quick-reaction force ready to go in here, so I just rolled through."

"That bomb killed an old man and his two granddaughters walking through the market. It's a pretty bad scene out there. Bad scene."

Franco's men moved around their Humvee, checking equipment. The kid in the turret leaned over his gun and gawked at the Iraqi soldiers unloading their trucks. He yelled into the crew compartment, laughing, "You *see* this shit, man?"

A chubby guy stepped out from the backseat. A corpsman; I could tell by the medical scissors tucked in the webbing of his flak. The blood on his trousers was still wet.

Franco put a hand on the corpsman's shoulder. "Hear you saw some pretty evil shit out there."

The corpsman shrugged and spoke with a Mexican accent. "Yes, sir. Not good, you know. Couldn't do nothing for them. Little girls and an old man. Pretty much dead before we got there, I think. And everyone on the street, they were just sorta looking around."

"So who're these guys?" Franco swept his arm over the prisoners, at least twenty of them now.

"These dudes?" the turret gunner answered before the corpsman, like a kid who'd seen a good movie and wanted to talk about it. "*Jundi*s just started rounding them up, sir." He laughed.

"Really?" Franco craned his neck to look at the gunner. He crossed his arms and frowned. "Huh."

"Yeah, they took everybody. It was awesome. Just throwing dudes in the truck."

I searched the crowd and found the alfalfa man sitting with his mouth open, a rope of saliva hanging from his lower lip.

Then I found Dodge. I'd lost track of him as we'd pushed through the field, but now he had an open water bottle in his right hand and was trying to give one of the prisoners a drink. An Iraqi soldier stood in his way, shaking his head, both hands on his rifle.

"Dodge!" I called out. "Get over here!"

He hesitated, not ready to give up the fight; then seeing no support coming from me, he put the cap back on the bottle and walked toward me, quaking with a rage all but imperceptible under his heavy gear.

Over Dodge's shoulder, I noticed how the platoon was also taking note of the prisoners baking in the sun. Zahn and Marceau stood out front, watching us with their arms crossed. Behind them, Marines scurried around gathering water bottles from the pallet meant for the adviser team, filling their packs and cargo pockets.

Pleasant stood next to Gomez like a greyhound in the starting box, ready to run into the field with his medical bag the moment Gomez opened the gate.

Probably wondering why I wasn't opening the gate for her.

I swallowed hard, turned to Franco, and pointed to the alfalfa man. "Sir? See this guy over here? This old guy? He looks injured from the explosion. Can't imagine he had anything to do with it."

"Yeah, they just arrested *all* those guys," the turret gunner said. "Anyone over like, twelve, got the flex cuffs!"

"We saw a number of men on the street when we passed through, sir," I tried again. "None of them tried to hide from us."

"Damn, got more coming in, too," said the turret gunner. "The *jundi*s put on their big boy pants this morning!"

"Sir, I've always found that, most of the time anyway, when they know about the bomb, they get off the street beforehand."

"Look at this guy over here! They sure fucked *him* up!"

"They didn't seem to be expecting it, sir," I finished, unsure of who I was even talking to anymore.

"And *that* guy's bleeding out his ear! *Look* at that shit." The kid in the turret said, smiling, like punctuation on my thought.

Franco gave a heavy sigh when he finally spoke, to no one in particular. "All in all, that's a pretty good day's work, I'd say. For the Iraqi Army, in any case. Pretty well organized." He turned and asked the men in the Humvee, "Anything else? Anything jump out at you?"

They shook their heads.

"All right then. Good work today, Marines." Then to Dodge and me: "Let's go see Colonel Hewrami. You guys like tea?"

"Sir, can I get my corpsman over here to help out with some of these guys? Like that guy there. He might have a broken collarbone, the way he's leaning over like that."

Franco put his hand on my shoulder. "I know it sounds crazy, Lieutenant. But it's really better to let the Iraqis deal with this. I'll make the suggestion, though. And thanks for offering. Good thought."

We walked toward the nearest Iraqi barracks as two more trucks came through the gate, beds piled high with bound and hooded men. As three empty trucks went back out, I tried to get a fix on where the alfalfa man knelt relative to the others so I could find him later.

Franco tapped my arm. "You see that little building over there by the river?" He pointed to a decaying shack with a corrugated-metal roof nearly rusted through. "That was a British Army officers' club during the First World War."

"Oh."

"Sure was. I found a few artifacts in that rubbish pile over there. Rank insignia, a few buttons. I found some pictures of what the club used to look like, too—on the Internet. Real classy. Might put together a little shadow box when I get home."

"That sounds interesting." I pushed the words out like rocks. My tongue, heavy and dry.

"I'm an adjutant by trade, but they tapped me to lead this team so I could get some command experience ahead of the lieutenant colonels' selection board next year."

"Oh."

"And listen, Lieutenant—as far as what the *jundi*s are doing out in that field? It's their country. They know it better than we do, right? We have to stay a little hands-off in this job."

"I understand, sir. But still, I do think we can help out some with medical stuff."

"Crazy out here, you know? I did some deployments in the nineties. Floats. Just floated around and made port calls. Looks like *those* days are over."

We approached an Iraqi officer on his cell phone. Taller than the other Iraqi men, slim and clean shaven with a full head of brown hair.

Franco held up his hand. "Fareeq Hewrami!" he called out to the man. *"Marhaba!"*

The Iraqi officer waved with the two fingers hugging his cigarette, but kept the phone to his ear and walked in small circles while we waited.

Franco turned to Dodge. "When he's off the phone, could you tell him I'd like to have some tea and talk about what happened out in town today?"

Dodge didn't reply. It was impossible to know, with the sunglasses and Nomex hood still hiding his eyes and face, but I felt certain he hadn't taken his eyes off me since I'd pulled him away from that thirsty prisoner.

Finally, Colonel Hewrami finished his call and dropped the cell phone down to his hip.

Dodge addressed the Iraqi colonel, speaking quickly while gesturing to Franco and me. Dodge finished and offered his hand for Hewrami to shake, an American habit he'd picked up from us.

Ignoring Dodge's hand, Hewrami pointed to Franco. He said a few words, waved the cigarette at his phone, then put a hand over his heart and walked away.

Dodge spoke softly behind his hood, almost to himself. "He says that he's sorry. He has to keep talking to his commander in Baghdad, and that we should kindly go to his office and watch television. Someone will bring us tea while we wait."

"All right, let's go have a seat," Franco said. "You like tea, Pete? They have great chai."

As we crossed the asphalt, I scanned the field again in a final effort to isolate the alfalfa man in the crowd. Only I couldn't. There were too many trucks now, and too many men on their knees.

Franco, Dodge, and I went into the barracks building and walked down a short hallway to Hewrami's office, guarded by a stern-looking Iraqi soldier. Franco led us through without acknowledging the man. A small television was mounted high on the wall, playing an American movie from the eighties that I'd never seen. The characters spoke in dubbed French, with Arabic subtitles running across the bottom of the screen. Major Franco flopped down in an overstuffed, leather armchair with a familiarity that made me think the seat was more or less reserved for him.

Hewrami had a window-mounted air conditioner with motorized vents drifting between the floor and the ceiling. The room must have been below seventy degrees. Dodge and I, installing ourselves on the couch, began to shiver in our damp flight suits. A framed tourist map hung behind Hewrami's desk with the word *Kurdistan* splashed across it in festive letters. The room smelled like soap. The walls were bright white. Recently scrubbed.

A small, shirtless Iraqi soldier in tight-fitting shorts emerged from a side room with tea to warm us while we waited. Franco took a sip and gestured at the framed map. "Colonel Hewrami is Kurdish, you know. Years of experience with the Peshmerga. Fought against Saddam."

"Oh."

"In fact," Franco said, chuckling, "he still gets two paychecks. One from the Kurdish government, and one from the Ministry of Defense in Baghdad. Pretty sweet gig."

I raised my eyebrows and nodded, pretending to enjoy my tea, though in truth I had trouble pushing the hot liquid over my swollen tongue.

Just then, Colonel Hewrami entered the room, a young Iraqi man in jeans and a soccer jersey following him. Neither acknowledged the three of us already sitting down. The young guy in the soccer jersey sat in a chair near the door and started watching the movie. Hewrami moved around his desk, stood by the high-back chair, and emptied his pockets. Phone. Keys. Cigarettes and a lighter. A small pistol. He sat down, lit a cigarette, and rubbed his forehead, pointed at Dodge, said a few words, then shifted his finger to Major Franco.

"The colonel wishes to thank you for the assistance rendered by your men today," Dodge mumbled behind his mask.

Franco's face lit up. "Well, tell him that's what we're here for! There's anything else he needs, just let me know. Also, Dodge, please ask about the men out in the dirt. Are they suspected of involvement with the bombing today?" Franco looked away nonchalantly, leaning back in his chair with hands behind his head as if the question was an afterthought. He was just curious.

Dodge translated for the major.

Hewrami made a dismissive gesture, spoke for a moment, and clicked his tongue.

"The colonel suspects that all of the men in town are terrorists," Dodge said. "And that today's bomb is simply more proof."

Then Hewrami became animated. Before Franco could answer, the colonel sat up in his chair and ranted loudly, turning away from the television and speaking directly to Franco with sharp words. Twice, he slapped his desk. Franco furrowed his brow and nodded gravely, as though he understood.

Dodge translated, "He says that tomorrow his soldiers will go out and walk through the town, taking money from all the businesses and merchants. They will give all this money to the family of the grandfather and the two little girls who were so tragically killed this day."

Franco took a deep breath. "Yeah, let me check with my boss before you go and do that? Maybe I can get some funds for the family from our civil *affairs* people, so you won't need to bother about that."

Dodge translated, and Hewrami scoffed. He leaned back in his chair and spoke calmly.

Dodge turned to Major Franco. "The colonel says the money is good but it is better for the people in town to know the terrorists cannot give them anything the new Iraqi Army cannot take away." Then, as if editorializing, Dodge added, "He wishes for them to be afraid."

Franco stared down at the floor a moment, as if searching for some rhetorical avenue forward. Then he sat up with a start and turned to me, the brightness in his face renewed. "Colonel Hewrami, I'm so sorry!" he exclaimed. "I've forgotten to introduce you to this young American officer, Lieutenant Donovan, who was just missed by that bomb. He's here to resupply us."

Hewrami looked at me while Dodge translated, said nothing, then looked back at the television.

But Franco wasn't finished. "Lieutenant Donovan told me earlier today this has been the most interesting day of his deployment so far." Franco reached out to put a hand on my shoulder but, unable to quite reach, turned his hand over to point my way instead. "He told me how honored he feels to be in the field with the new Iraqi Army."

Just then the young Iraqi in the soccer jersey, who'd been so quiet and still that I'd forgotten about him, let out a great laugh. "Is that right?" he said with an accent even more proper and British than Dodge's. "Well, bully for *you*, old boy."

Dodge's chest heaved and pushed out a breath, half cough, half growl. His hands shook.

Major Franco didn't seem to notice. "Go ahead, Dodge," he said excitedly. "Translate. Tell him."

I imagined the things Dodge might say in Arabic, knowing Major Franco and I wouldn't understand him, and made a snap decision before Dodge could speak.

"Sir," I said to Franco, "I need to get back to my trucks and supervise that off-load."

"Of course. Of course." Franco slapped his knees. "Colonel Hewrami, I'll go talk to my people and get back to you on where we stand with that situation out there. And I'll see you at dinner, I hope." Franco stood, cleared his throat, and smiled. Dodge and I stood, and Hewrami gave a brusque wave as we left his office.

We shuffled down the short hallway, schoolboys fresh from discipline at the hands of the principal, then stepped outside into the bright sun. I heard Iraqi voices and, when my eyes adjusted, found a throng of Iraqi soldiers crowding around us. They patted me on the back and posed next to me while their friends took pictures with disposable film cameras.

"I know that might have been a little disappointing, Lieutenant," Major Franco said as we pushed through, the last word hanging in the air as if he'd wanted to say something more.

We walked through the field, past bound and staged prisoners, toward the advisory team's headquarters on the other side. Iraqi soldiers busied themselves by picking up prisoners two at a time and leading them to their barracks. The sun was right on the top of us, tickling my scalp.

I scanned the rows of prisoners searching for the alfalfa man, but couldn't find him. He was gone. Just then, two white trucks come through the gate, empty, and I thought, maybe. Maybe they took him back. I imagined it, the alfalfa man being driven to his donkey cart in the backseat of a white truck, ranting like a wild man, with the good-natured Iraqi soldiers gently amused by him.

I broke into a jog and left Major Franco and Dodge behind me, starting to notice the dozens of empty water bottles littering the field.

I imagined Iraqi soldiers treating the alfalfa man's wounds.

I imagined the old man telling the soldiers, with gratitude, about a mysterious figure in a window overlooking the traffic circle, and how this mysterious figure had been playing with a cell phone in the moments before the blast.

I imagined Iraqi soldiers swarming the building, finding a cache of weapons and cell phones, cuffing the mysterious man and bringing him out to a cheering crowd.

I reached the open passenger door of my Humvee and unlocked my rifle. Putting on my vest and hood, I called out to the Marines still milling around. "Gear on!"

I smoothed my vest, waved for Dodge to hurry, and looked around for an empty patch of shrub and dirt where we wouldn't run the risk of crushing someone during the off-load. Gomez had the convoy ready to go, save for two young Marines still working to remove straps from the air conditioners and the pallets of chow and water on the cargo truck.

Across the field, Hewrami emerged from the barracks and began talking to another Iraqi officer. The officer slapped his palm with the back of this other hand and gestured at our vehicles, pointing furiously at the empty water bottles all around his prisoners.

Zahn stood at his door, resting his hand on the steering wheel. I sat down in the passenger seat and keyed my radio. "Gomez this is Actual. Do you see that open patch of dirt, between us and the prisoners?"

"Roger, Actual."

"Did you give those guys water?"

"Affirmative, Actual."

"See an old man with a gray beard? Cuts on his face?"

"Negative."

Zahn waved to the lance corporal driving the cargo truck and pointed to the empty patch of dirt. I latched the armored door behind me and held the convoy net to my ear, waiting for Gomez to give the order.

"Combat off-load, motherfuckers," she said.

Combat off-load, standard procedure under threat of an ambush, was used when the convoy needed to get back on the road, and fast. The platoon wouldn't have to explain itself, and I even found myself wishing that I'd been quick-witted enough to give the order personally. As usual, Gomez was way ahead of me.

"Nice." Zahn laughed, getting settled behind the wheel. "She's pissed now. Everyone look out for their ass." He craned his neck to watch her through the windshield. He kept his eyes on her, stomping around and waving her arms to direct the truck, a few seconds longer than necessary. He smiled with a satisfaction built of something more than just professional admiration. He could've watched her all day, I knew.

I wish I would've let him.

Instead I tapped him on the shoulder and said, "Zahn. We need to go. Get us lined up at that gate."

He nodded sheepishly, found his can of Skoal. "Aye, aye, sir."

As we pulled away, I watched in the side-view mirror as Gomez directed the cargo truck. It pulled forward and turned right. The driver lined-up his rear wheels and put the truck in reverse. He gunned the engine and gained speed for about five seconds before slamming on the brakes. The pallets slid off the tailgate, air conditioners first, followed by the chow and water. The air conditioners bounced off each other and settled into the sand with an alarming, metallic groan. Half the water bottles ripped open on the sharp corners, and a mud puddle began to grow at the base of the pile.

"Holy shit," Zahn said, choking back his laughter. "That was awesome."

Dodge laughed, too.

I turned around and saw that he'd taken off his hood.

Doc Pleasant handed him an open bottle of water.

I keyed my radio. "All vics. Oscar Mike."

And we rolled through the gate, into the desert, back through the little town. Women stood at a safe distance and watched the outpost for any sign of more white trucks.

A pile of alfalfa lay abandoned in the traffic circle, slowly giving itself to the wind. A small clump landed on the windshield and strands floated in through the open turret. It smelled like Alabama in September.

Findings of Fact:

Corpsman Pleasant had unsupervised access to the controlled-medications locker as a field medic assigned to Engineer Support Company. Following Corpsman Pleasant's transfer to Surgical / Shock Trauma Platoon, inventories taken of the controlled-medications locker showed significant discrepancies in stocks of Percocet, Vicodin, and Demerol. In his official statement, Lieutenant Donovan claims to have witnessed Corpsman Pleasant behaving erratically in the weeks before his transfer. Lieutenant Donovan further describes this behavior as consistent with opiate abuse.

A BOX WHERE I CAN KEEP THESE THINGS

Landry tells me I should be careful about Lizzy. "Seems a little fast, partner. All I'm saying. Living with this girl already? The first girl you've met in, what, five years?"

I shrug. "It's nothing like that. Just that my boss owns an oil-change place up here, too, and he says I can pick up with that branch, no problem. Lizzy's just letting me crash for a little while. Isn't it you always telling me to get out of Houma?"

"Sure, but, you know . . . I thought you'd be living *here* at first. With *us*."

Paul walks in from the kitchen with a beer and picks up his video-game controller. "Didn't that Lizzy girl just kick some other guy out?"

"What?" I ask before I can stop myself.

"Sebastian," Landry says. "I don't know if he was Lizzy's *boyfriend*, or whatever, but, yeah, he lived up in that house for a while."

"You'll probably meet him soon," Paul chimes in as he starts up his video game. "Lizzy's a real scenester. Knows everybody. Goes to every metal show. One of those art-student types. That run-down house she lives in? Her whole department's lived there, one time or another. I doubt she's even on the lease."

"But this guy Sebastian," I say, "who's he?"

I'm a little surprised by the chill I get at the thought of Lizzy and some other guy. Why should I care? I just met this girl.

"He's just . . . I don't know—a guy." Landry sighs, trying to be gentle with me. "I think he's more like her best friend, actually. He plays acoustic guitar in a few bands. Real pussy-ass folk-rock shit. Works at a coffee shop. I think he gets money from his parents. You know—that type." Landry stops, like he's got the idea that he isn't helping, and he's right.

"Fuck it," I say, standing up. "No worries. I'm just feeling this thing out."

I walk into the kitchen, my heart beating fast. The linoleum floor in here has soft patches that get deeper and more fucked-up as you approach the fridge. I'm surprised the fridge hasn't fallen through to the apartment below us, it's so weighed down by cheap beer. Old concert leaflets cover the door like fur, and the handle's stained black. I open the fridge and peer in at all the beer cans, packed tight like ammunition in a magazine.

Landry and Paul never offer to grab me a beer when they get up from the couch. But they don't ever make it feel awkward, either. They're real friends that way. I should treat them better.

I've never talked to them about the meetings, or why I got kicked out and sent home, but they know. And now I want a beer, more than I want Marceau's coffee. What'll they say if I go back to the living room with three cold ones? Will they confront me about it?

I close the fridge, step away, and march quickly across the tired linoleum until I reach the wooden creak of the hallway floor.

All of a sudden I'm calm. I take three slow steps and listen through the noise of Paul's video game to the sound of my boot-heels against that solid wood. It brings my heart rate down. I close my eyes and wrestle with my breathing.

It's the wood floors in my dad's house I'm missing. The way those boards creak when you walk across them, each board making the same sound every time. Like people talking. Familiar voices that might distract me from that arsenal of beers in the fridge.

But sometimes I'm trapped in my room while dad watches television, and I end up rummaging through old stuff. Old letters, old books. Eventually that old cigar box, from my uncle. Ordered from some specialty website. Cigars for military types. Shitty ones, too. Even Dodge thought so. Nasty, convenience-store things, slapped with military logos and sold at a big markup. My uncle had the box engraved LESTER "DOC" PLEASANT. Etched into the lid like he thought it was my special nickname, Doc. But Marines call *every* corpsman Doc. Even shitty corpsmen, guys who don't know what they're doing.

I keep that cigar box on my dresser at home and put stuff in there. Things I brought home. My dog tags. Different patches and things. My medals. A stack of memorial-service programs.

The programs are kept down at the bottom, buried. Down where I have to dig. The chaplain's assistant made a new program for each memorial service. They all look pretty much the same, though. He just changed the name and the picture. Maybe put a different quote from Scripture in there, depending.

It's good to have a box where I can keep these things. Pictures up top. Then medals. Then patches and stuff. Then memorial services. I put the memorial services in order. Gunny Stout first. Then Marceau.

Sniper got Marceau in Fallujah, that day on Phase Line Fran when we were coming back from delivering those air conditioners. We were rolling west through the city, later than usual. Too much traffic. That afternoon sun painting us. Marceau was in the turret of the lead Humvee. The lieutenant sent him up there at a security halt after we left the Iraqi Army post. Said we'd been hogging him, that it was the lead Humvee's turn to have the more experienced gunner.

Sniper snuck the bullet through a seam in his flak jacket. Right through his armpit and into his heart. Crazy shot. Everyone heard it, but no one knew Marceau'd got hit, strapped to the turret like he was.

Gomez came on the net and told everyone to push through to the bridge. Get clear of the city and establish a cordon. Get accountability there. Lieutenant didn't say nothing, so I guess he agreed.

The vehicle crew realized something was wrong at the security halt, from the way Marceau hung there, blood soaking down through his trousers. Corporal Watkins, the vehicle commander, yelled into his radio, which you're not supposed to do. Stepped on all the chatter, all the fives and twenty-fives talk.

"Corpsman up! Corpsman up!"

Dodge, I think, understood what was happening before any of us. The pitch of Watkins's voice, maybe. The way he couldn't control the volume of it. Dodge knew this wasn't no sprained ankle. He unstrapped himself from his seat and pulled off his headset.

Lieutenant Donovan tried to stop him. "Wait. Dodge, it's not secure." It was halfhearted, though. Like he couldn't even convince himself. Dodge didn't hear it, anyway. He was already sprinting down the highway toward Marceau's vehicle.

Lieutenant Donovan flipped to a page in his notebook and changed the frequency on his radio. "Sheriff, this is Hellbox Five-Six. Stand by for casualty evacuation nine line." He took his finger off the transmit button and said to Zahn, "Get up there. Go."

Zahn spat into his dip bottle and gunned the engine. "Fuck. Fuck. Fuck. Fuck."

Lieutenant Donovan turned in his seat. "Are you ready, Doc?"

I just nodded, my heart pounding up into my neck, tongue bouncing off the roof of my mouth like a basketball.

Zahn stopped short and I jumped out with my bag.

As I ran, I saw Dodge dead-lifting Marceau out the turret. Like a goddamn burly fireman, skinny, little Dodge. He slipped his arms inside Marceau's flak and hauled him up onto the roof of the Humvee. A crowd of Marines waited at the front bumper. Watkins and Gomez took him, lowered him to the pavement and opened his flak to look for the wound.

I ran over and yelled at them, "Stop! Stop! Leave his flak on!" I dropped to one knee and opened my bag. Everything was organized just right. I reached for the compression bandage. The ventilation bag. The morphine syringe. Didn't even have to look.

I heard Lieutenant Donovan on the radio behind me, calling in the nine line.

"Line one. Route Michigan approximate two hundred meters west of the Euphrates River Bridge. Grid follows . . ."

I took Marceau's pulse. Nothing. Dodge dropped to a knee next to me. I grabbed his hands and put them on Marceau's chest. "Push down. Like this. Keep doing it, every three seconds."

He nodded. "I understand, Lester."

Then I found the entry wound under his armpit.

I heard Lieutenant Donovan, still talking slow and calm into his radio. "Line three. Urgent surgical . . ."

The blood from Marceau's wound was just dribbling out. No heart to pump it. Torn to shreds by the bullet. I knew it from the first second I touched him. I looked up at Gomez and Watkins. They searched my face for a clue, so I said, "Go get my backboard."

They nodded and ran off, thinking they were helping.

"Line eight. Landing zone marked by smoke . . ."

Marceau was dead. His pupils were fixed and dilated. But I kept working on him. Can't tell you why I did it, even today. But I put a compression bandage on the seeping hole, strapped him to the backboard, and prepped him for transfer. Dodge kept on with the chest compressions, too. Working on a corpse while everyone watched and hoped. When the helicopter landed a few minutes later, Dodge and Gomez helped carry the backboard.

The flight medic took one look at Marceau and knew. I didn't even try bullshitting him. He gave me a real look—frustrated. Pissed, almost. And I knew why. Flying all the way out here and landing in a bad spot? For nothing. For a corpse. For my own little pretend-time fantasy. But the flight medic didn't rat me out to Gomez or Dodge. He just quietly took Marceau away, and the helicopter flew his body back to Taqaddum.

Gomez, Dodge, and I jogged back to the cordon where Zahn had the convoy team, everyone who wasn't on security kneeling in a circle. The Marines on security listened to us pray, "Protect our brother, O Lord," while they scanned the horizon, spun the heavy machine guns in their turrets, looked for targets. Looked for something to shoot at. They needed to shoot something so bad it made them crazy. All those weapons, all that ammo, all useless. Nothing to shoot at.

My medical bag was just as useless. Organized just right. Everything where I could get at it fast, and what did it matter? Nothing.

We got back to Taqaddum before dinner, but no one wanted to eat. Gomez kept the platoon around the barracks while Lieutenant Donovan and Gunny Dole went to the shock trauma tent.

We saw the two of them coming back from a long way off. Everyone else watched them for a clue about what I already knew. Soon they did, too.

"Now, we have to keep it in the family," Lieutenant Donovan said. "River City Condition One. No calls home. No e-mails. Let the notification officer get to his mother before she reads it in the town paper or sees it on the news."

Major Leighton, from the steps of the command building with his arms crossed, watched Lieutenant Donovan. Marines from the other platoons stopped what they were doing and listened, too.

"Nothing anyone could've done," Donovan said. "He died on the helicopter."

Did he make that up on purpose to protect me? Did he have any clue about the little show I'd put on with all those bandages on a corpse? Was he just choosing not to let on?

Right then, I remembered the morphine syringe in my cargo pocket. Never got around to using it on Marceau, but it was already listed as expended. I thought about throwing it away, tossing it out in the desert like trash. But I stopped myself. At first because I didn't want to litter, crazy as that sounds. Then, I thought someone might find it and get me in trouble.

Then I thought about all the useless guns. All the useless everything. I got the urge to put something to use. Any kind of use. So I walked over to the bathroom trailer. Word of what had happened was already flying around the company, and the Marine on duty from Bulk Fuel Platoon avoided my eyes, pretending like he was checking for toilet graffiti.

I locked myself in the stall farthest from the guard. A rabbit with an absurd penis was drawn in that stall. Marceau's standard character, scribbled in felt pen right above the toilet paper. The rabbit was laughing, tap-dancing, and shitting at the same time, with a bubble proclaiming, "I left a little present for you!"

I jabbed the syringe into my leg.

While I waited to feel something, I pulled the pen out my breast pocket and wrote, "James Marceau. 1986-2006."

Then, as I started to write "Gunnery Sergeant William Stout," a cloud of indifference swallowed me up, and I didn't even care to finish. I slipped the used syringe into my cargo pocket and floated back across the compound, back to my cot.

I felt better. I slept good, all night.

After some time in the wilderness, Huck begins to regress. "It was kind of lazy and jolly, laying off comfortable all day, smoking and fishing," he reflects. "Two months or more run along, and my clothes got to be all rags and dirt, and I didn't see how I'd ever got to like it so well at the widow's, where you had to wash, and eat on a plate, and comb up, and go to bed and get up regular, and be forever bothering over a book, and have old Miss Watson pecking at you all the time."

The Arab reader can relate. How easy it would be to cast away the twentieth century, with its cities and wars built on petro-wealth, and go back to our bedouin tents. Huck's regression, however, offers a cautionary tale.

ALL SMILES, ALL FRIENDSHIP

We circle around the main square in Sousse, my flatmates and I with these pretty girls. We scream for Ben Ali to come down from Tunis and face justice. We scream the name of Mohamed Bouazizi. We wave Tunisian flags and sing stupid songs.

I think of Lester, and how he stopped liking music, stopped making me listen to bands, after the business with Marceau. And how his bag, such a source of pride for him, became a mess as he began stealing pills.

With each time around the square, pushed by the chanting, marching crowd, I let myself drift farther away from my flatmates and their new girlfriends. They are all couples now, paired nicely with each other, and I will have no place in this when their protest becomes a party. Soon, I think. Soon I can slip away, and they will not notice. I can go home and make notes.

But the crowd stops quite suddenly after the fifth time around the square. A university student has found a bullhorn, like the kind the *mulasim* allowed me to use, and is standing on a balcony urging us to become organized. He tells us to block the entrances to the square so that Ben Ali's police will have to fight through with armor and make a scene for the Western news cameramen who are appearing, though choosing to remain inconspicuous and camouflaged by the crowd.

My flatmates grow excited with the work of this, and now I

cannot leave. They drag me along with their new girlfriends to help arrange city buses blocking one of the entrances of the square.

One of the girls, the prettiest one, grabs my arm and pulls me aside. A news camera is over there, she screams into my ear. I have to go speak English for the freedom movement. I have to tell the world our story and why we will win.

Always, I am speaking English on behalf of fools.

The day after I painted the sign, Hani sold his first Coca-Cola to the Americans. It was just a small convoy, those first Americans. Just four Humvees coming to see us. They were infantry marines, I know now. Not taking supplies anywhere or filling potholes. Grunts, they say. Marines who would venture out looking only for terrorists to fight. Freed from small matters, like taking food and water to their comrades or building checkpoints, they focused on this most warlike task.

Their convoy saw the sign and pulled off the road, swift and decisive. The infantry marines kicked up dust as they exited their vehicles, calling out sharp instructions to one another with their rifles up, suspecting some trick.

Hani was not afraid, and I admit that his new determination surprised me. He had a particular courage, unique to businessmen, that allowed him to feel safe walking out to the road with Coca-Cola under his arm. He smiled and waved for them to come forward. He kept smiling, even when they aimed their rifles at him.

Mundhir and Abu Abdul, Haji Fasil and me, we stayed back by the farmhouse. I told them to raise their hands. "They are going to search you," I said. "They will search the buildings, too. Anything they will not like, Haji?"

Haji Fasil put his hands behind his head and shrugged. "God willing, no. But I suppose we will find out."

Mundhir sighed, already bored. He stood close to Abu Abdul and made sure their feet were touching, always ready to step in front of the old man if need be.

A marine swatted Hani's Coca-Cola to the dirt. Another searched under his shirt and patted his jeans. Together, these two marines pushed Hani back to the farmhouse.

Hani kept smiling, even with his hands behind his head, acting always like a friend. All smiles, all friendship.

The other marines swarmed the farm like ghosts, and four of them emerged behind us to take control of our little fire ring. They approached us in a crouch, rifles tucked in their shoulders and eyes over their sights. They shouted in English and clipped Arabic.

"Hands! Hands! *La tetharek! Edeik! Edeik!* Don't move!"

We stood still while a marine slung his rifle across his back and pushed us down onto the log, one at a time with his heavy, gloved hands. When he had us all on our asses, he grabbed our fingers and interlocked them over the tops of our heads.

I peeked over at Mundhir, hoping he would not fight back on Abu Abdul's behalf. Thankfully, the marine was gentle with the old man and Mundhir complied.

The marines waited to see if we would move and possibly try to run away. I felt every rifle, every muzzle, aimed into my back. It made my skin burn and tickle. I could feel the bullet waiting in each barrel. Waiting for me to make a mistake. My heart pounded and my breath became shallow and hot.

The other marines led Hani around to each mud hut and watched him at the door. They waited for some reaction, I know now. For some hint of fear. They worried that maybe we had set traps, and they wanted Hani to know that he would die first, if so.

Finished with this search, they sat Hani down on the log next to us and called for their officer on the radio. The officer, a black man with arm muscles that showed through his uniform, approached with an interpreter at his side. The fat interpreter, a Kuwaiti judging by his accent and his expensive watch, smirked at us. He was younger than me even.

"Good morning, I am Lieutenant Pederson," the officer said in English. "Now look, sorry we have to search you like this. The anti-Iraqi forces in this area, the bad guys, they make it necessary. Need to ask you a few questions, though. Need to ask what you're doing here. Who are you. All that shit." He pointed to the interpreter.

"This guy? Pederson?" the interpreter said in Arabic. "He is going to fuck your whole world. Fuck you hard up the ass. Tell him where you have the weapons hidden. He's Fifty Cent's cousin. I'm not lying."

"Now, do you have any weapons here?" Pederson continued. "Any rifles? An RPG?" Pederson put the pretend weight of a rocket launcher on his shoulder. "It's fine if you have a rifle. One Kalashnikov per household." He laughed softly to himself. "I guess you could call this a household." He pointed to the Kuwaiti, who again spoke in Arabic for him.

"You *takfiri* know about Abu Ghraib? This will be worse. Tell Pederson where you keep the rockets or we will put you all in a naked pyramid right over there. Take pictures for the Internet. All over MySpace, tomorrow."

I wanted to stay quiet. Wanted all this to happen while I remained a simple witness. But Hani and Haji Fasil turned to me with their eyebrows high, expecting me to speak. They gave away the secret, so I spoke.

"Hello," I said in English, coughing and nodding to the lieutenant. "We can speak normally, if you wish. My English is quite good. First, I should tell you that there are no weapons here. I assure you. No rifles, even. This is just a farm. Also . . . it is a beach resort."

Pederson's eyebrows jumped.

"Yes, I probably speak English better than this Kuwaiti, too." I nodded to the interpreter. "And may I share something you should like to know? Your Kuwaiti is lying to you. He claims you are Fifty Cent's cousin. Remarkable if true, as Fifty Cent is quite good. A favorite of mine, personally. But regardless, this Kuwaiti lies to you. Most likely all the time."

The fat Kuwaiti turned to Pederson with his palms up and his mouth open.

"So, yes," I continued, "about this place. About us. We are simple merchants. We sell things for dollars, or for dinar if absolutely necessary, but dollars is what we prefer. We have Coca-Colas and other items of refreshment. We have Iraqi souvenirs, as well, for you to take home to America. This is not my business, to be honest. It is Hani's business. He is the one on the end who came out with the Coca-Cola earlier. He has poor English, however."

Pederson pointed a finger at us. "All right, go ahead and stand up. All y'all. Up."

I stood and put my hands in my pockets. The others slowly followed my lead. "Yes," I continued, "What does Fifty Cent say? 'Get rich or die trying'? This place, exactly."

Pederson rubbed his eyes and grabbed the fat Kuwaiti, seriously angry. He pointed to the Humvees with his other hand. Go away, he seemed to say. We're finished with you, not even giving the boy a chance to speak for himself.

After the fat Kuwaiti had waddled away in defeat, Hani and I walked Pederson around Tourist Town. Mundhir and Abu Abdul went back to the work of the farm. Haji Fasil stayed by the fire ring and sat quietly.

Pederson's marines spread out and kept watch. Hani smiled and showed the burly American officer his stock of head scarves, prayer beads, and old money with Saddam's face. All the while, I spoke English for him.

"Hani says you will not find items of this quality anywhere else outside of Baghdad," I told Pederson. And because I did not want him cheated, I said softly, "It is junk, however. No one wants these kaffiyeh, which is how Hani procured them at such small expense."

Pederson nodded. "I appreciate you telling me that. I do."

After the tour, Pederson went back to his Humvee and talked on his radio for a time. Hani and I went back to the fire ring and waited for him. When Pederson finished on the radio, he had a conversation with another marine. A sergeant, and his second-in-command it seemed. They both shook their heads and laughed.

"What is funny? Why are they laughing?" Hani asked.

"They think you are ridiculous," I said.

Pederson and his sergeant were still smiling when they came back. "We had to dig around for cash. We don't really carry money over here." Pederson handed Hani a wet twenty-dollar note. "We'll take the sodas. We'll come back for more later. Souvenirs and the like. But just sodas today."

Hani smiled and carried a few cases of Coca-Cola over to their Humvees.

Pederson pulled me aside. "I want to thank you personally. I never liked that guy. Never trusted him."

I shrugged. "There are bad people everywhere."

"We'll be back, you know. Often." He tipped his sunglasses to look me in the eye.

"Of course. You are welcome. Bring your swimming shorts."

He laughed, shook his head, and walked back to his Humvee.

Hani danced as the Americans drove away. He laughed and made me look at his first dollars. I congratulated him politely, but was not yet ready to admit that I had been wrong. I told him about Pederson's words. Back for more, and often. As Hani's smile grew, I began to wonder why Pederson had made such a point to look me in the eye.

The dust from the American Humvees had not settled before Hani's next customers arrived. A truck hauling diesel fuel from the Baiji refinery, south to Fallujah and Ramadi. An older man and his two sons, Sunnis probably, took a break and drank their sodas by the water while Abu Abdul flashed his friendly, toothless smile and brought them fried fish.

While waiting a few days for Pederson to return, Hani did a good business and created sufficient profits from his first inventory to give a generous share to Haji Fasil and Abu Abdul. He doubled his inventory with the next buy and still set aside a good sum for travel. Enough to get the three of us to Jordan and beyond, possibly.

But talk of leaving did not come, and I did not inquire. I feared it would necessitate talk of finding my father. If our departure seemed orderly, well planned, and safe, Hani would have insisted we at least attempt to find my family. He would have thought this a kindness for me. Better to wait for a gloomy moment in which a hasty exodus might seem justified. In any case, it seemed Hani might earn enough from his trade with the Americans to finance our travels, at least to Jordan, and quickly enough that we might not need my father.

In the mornings and the evenings, when we all gathered around the fire ring or at the beach, conversation went elsewhere. Weather, fishing, ideas for new inventory. Hani made plans for the future, though he did not dare to use this word.

Over those short weeks, we all took to the rhythm of life on the lake. Mundhir and Abu Abdul, silent and inseparable, rose at dawn to fish before the heat became too uncomfortable. Hani drove Haji

Fasil to the Dra Dijlia market each day around midmorning, and again at night, to do his old, dependable business. Militants of all stripes continued to buy from him. But in partnership with Hani, he began to see the possibility of expansion.

Maybe his own truck. Maybe a stall in the Ramadi Grand Souk.

For my part, I read in a chair by the lake and worked on my thesis. I had left my latest draft in Professor Al-Rawi's office for fear of checkpoints, but had enough in my memory to make notes, edits, and additions on bits of trash paper. I treated my time on the lake like a vacation. An academic retreat. I excused myself from farm labor with the rationale that I was the only true vacationer at Tourist Town. Important work all its own, keeping up that lie.

But then Pederson returned and was soon making an appearance each day, though the hour varied. My vacation activities were suspended during these visits, and for several hours I followed him around and spoke for him. The marines were less aggressive with each visit, but always made sure the highway was watched while their officer did his business with us.

Other potential customers, venturing down the highway in trucks and taxicabs, sped away at the sight of marines at Tourist Town, and I began to wonder how long before the men in the passing cars, all of them from Ansar al-Sunna or Jaish al-Mahdi or some other death squad, realized that the Americans were not searching or harassing us. How long before they reasoned that we were doing business with them and drinking tea like old friends? I knew we had until then to leave if we were to live. I would have to convince Hani.

To Hani's disappointment, Pederson did not always bring dollars. He sometimes brought Iraqi dinar, instead, crisp and new. Still, Pederson and his marines made up for this inconvenience with large buys of trinkets like kaffiyeh and prayer beads. Mostly, they wanted bootleg movies from Hong Kong cinemas. They bought all we had.

After business, Lieutenant Pederson always accepted tea and sat down with us to make light discussion. I interpreted for him, wanting to do well and hoping to be honest.

"Tell me, Hani," Pederson asked one day, after a long silence in the conversation, "seen any folks from out of town around here?"

I tried to appear bored, and not terrified, by this question. "Hani, he wants to know if we have seen any foreigners . . ."

Before I could warn him to watch his words, he answered happily, "Sure. Guys from Syria. Plenty of Syrians. And some Egyptians, too. Most are hauling fertilizer down to the farms. You have seen them, too, right, Kateb?"

Pederson had already heard the words, the English and Arabic pronunciations similar enough, and there remained no opportunity for me to lie.

"Syria and Egypt," I said. "He has seen gentlemen from Syria and Egypt."

Pederson took a sip and spoke directly to me. "What about you, Kateb? Seen any out of towners?"

"Sure. Nobody lives here except us. Everyone is from out of town."

Pederson smiled. "Right. Why don't we take a walk down to the lake, just you and me?"

I followed him down to the beach while Hani collected stacks of dinar from the marines in exchange for the bootleg movies I had labeled in English with black marker.

"This is a nice place, Kateb," Pederson began. "The only stop for miles. Everyone passes by, and I bet half of them stop."

"This was Hani's plan. And it is working for him. But when this place makes enough money, we are leaving."

Pederson frowned. "Leaving to go where? Back to Baghdad?"

"No. We will go to Jordan first, and from there we will travel most anywhere that grants us visas."

"Giving up on Iraq?" he asked, appearing confused.

"We lack good people. And without good people, we won't have a good country." I meant it, but Pederson smiled as though I had made a joke.

"Don't leave without telling me. And if you change your mind, come find me in Ramadi. We need good terps. Been meaning to give this to you." He handed me an envelope with papers, pulled from inside his body armor. "Hide this until you need it. But if you're interested, give it to the guard at Government Center. He'll let you in."

I slipped the envelope quickly into my pants before Hani or Mundhir could see. "*Shukran*. Most likely not. But thank you."

We walked back to the fire ring, where Hani counted his money. I could tell by his attention to the bills that he had not seen the envelope, and I decided to keep it secret.

"Pleasure as always." Pederson put his hand over his heart in thanks, as he had learned from us.

I shook his hand, firm like an American, and looked him in the eye.

When the Americans left, I asked Hani about his business.

"We need more movies," he said. "They buy them all. Nothing left for the truckers."

"Truckers buy those?"

"Of course. American action movies mostly."

I opened my mouth to say, "Ironic," but he had already walked away. Off to the strongbox where he hid his stack.

As he left, I noticed Haji Fasil in the doorway of the house and discerned at once, from the look on his face, that he knew of the envelope.

"Come inside for a moment, Kateb?"

"Certainly. I should like to have a nap."

Inside, I wasted no time. I simply pulled the envelope from my underwear and dropped it on the floor. "Papers to work for the Americans in Ramadi. Not money, in case you thought I might be cheating the group."

I walked past Haji Fasil into the room where I kept my book and notes, thinking the conversation over. But when I came back, I saw that he had scooped the envelope into his hands and was trying to lift a tile near the window under which he could hide it.

"No need for that, Haji," I said, confused. "We can just burn it."

Haji Fasil stood and pulled me by the shoulders, right into his face. "You need to keep these papers, Kateb!"

"Haji, I'm going to Jordan—"

"With soda money? Don't be a fool!"

I heard a car pull off the highway, the familiar sound of Iraqi customers who had waited for the marines to depart before they approached.

Haji Fasil dropped to his knees to finish the work of hiding the envelope and, when he rose to his feet, whispered, "You and Hani. You have different fates. You must know this."

I heard car doors close and Hani rush to greet our new guests. "No, Haji. I am afraid you are wrong. Hani is my brother. Mundhir might stay, and I would be happy for that, but Hani and I have plans and they do not include a knife to the throat in this desert."

Outside, I heard Hani call my name.

"Then go now," Haji Fasil said. "Leave him with me and I will take him south, to Ramadi possibly. He will do better without you here."

I looked to the dirty tile and considered the American papers hidden beneath it. "I'm not leaving him."

Growing insistent, Hani again called my name.

"I have to go see what Hani wants." I brushed past Haji Fasil and through the door.

As my eyes adjusted to the bright afternoon sun, I heard Hani say, "You have visitors, Kateb."

When my sight returned, I saw the old, black Mercedes from my driveway in Baghdad, and my father and my brother standing beside it.

After Action Report: Enemy Activity Trends

1. *Improvised explosive devices shifting from artillery shells to ammonium nitrate charges. Insurgents mix fertilizer with diesel fuel and pack the resulting explosive compound into plastic sacks. The devices have few metal components, making them difficult to detect.*

2. *New coalition jamming devices increasingly effective at defeating remote detonators. As a result, cellular phone and radio-based initiators increasingly rare.*

3. *Anti–Iraqi Forces shifting from remote detonation to victim-operated triggers. Insurgents construct pressure plates from two or more metallic leads, designed to compress under the weight of a coalition vehicle. Compression of metallic leads completes the circuit and allows voltage from a battery to activate denotation cord.*

4. *A washing machine timer often provides a circuit break between the trigger and the battery. This technique allows insurgents to plant a device and withdraw to a safe distance before the device is effectively armed.*

Respectfully submitted,
P. E. Donovan

A FAIR FIGHT

As planned, Paige meets me at the West End harbor on Saturday afternoon. I stand off to the side while she examines every inch of *Sentimental Journey*. She doesn't laugh out loud, as I feared she would at first sight of the wreck, but she stops short of encouraging me.

"I do love these old boats, though," she offers. "New boats don't have these lines, with the flying sterns and the low freeboard. Beautiful. But you should know that there's a reason. She won't be as fast or stable as a modern design."

"I've read all about that."

"Says the guy who's never been on a sailboat." Then a thought furrows her brow, and the pitch of her voice shoots up as she quips, "You know what?"

I follow her from the moldy scrabble of the municipal harbor, down the freshly scrubbed piers of Southern Yacht Club, to a blue-hulled Catalina named *Smile*.

"Dad used to be a real Beach Boys fan," she explains.

"Did they have a falling out?"

"No. I mean he was . . . He passed a few years ago." Before I can apologize or offer my condolences, she adds, "*Smile* isn't as well kept as it used to be. So don't take this as an example of how to keep yours when she's finished."

I take the hint and leave the subject of her father alone.

Paige tells me to sit still in a corner of the cockpit and not to touch anything. She hustles around the boat setting sail, with one word explanations for each activity like "Halyard," "Mainsheet," "Traveler," and "Tricky."

The late afternoon is overcast and cold, and the lake is gray and uninviting. We're the only boat leaving harbor. The rollers hit us as the bow rounds the navigation light at the head of the rock jetty, and the boat begins to pitch.

"You're not sailing, yet," Paige remarks over the noise of the exhaust. "That's just waves. Just so you know. We're still on the engine."

Huddled against the cold, with my chin in my chest and my hands in my coat pockets, I mumble, "Thanks for the tip."

I must look hurt, or simply wretched, because her eyebrows come together in an expression of guilt, and she offers me an olive branch.

"Here. Go up to the mast. When I tell you to start pulling that rope, the halyard, really put your back into it. It'll be heavy."

I nod in acknowledgment and step gingerly from the cockpit, one hand always on the boat.

"Now," she says, cutting the motor, "heave."

I pull down hard on the rope and hear the mainsail slugs squeal reluctantly through the dry groove in the mast. She wasn't kidding about the boat being outside its maintenance window. But the challenge grows on me, and five pulls later the mainsail is up. I cleat the halyard with a knot I know to be wildly wrong and make my way aft into the cockpit.

As I take my seat, Paige pulls the tiller toward her. The sail fills and stiffens as the bow comes around. *Smile* heels abruptly to one side and gathers headway. Paige helms us into the deep trough of a whitecap. The pit of my stomach delights when we break the crest.

I close my eyes and don't even bother with the fine sprays of brackish lake water pelting my face. Somehow, in my dreams, I've imagined this motion perfectly.

When I open my eyes and look up, Paige is grinning at me in a way that I don't recognize. She's released something, pulled some cotter pin that's held the muscles of her cheeks taut against the bone.

"You love this, don't you?" She beams.

"I do."

After about an hour, Paige lets me take the helm. The vibration of the wooden tiller against my palm sets my heart racing. We make laps up and down the lakefront, two hundred meters from shore. She talks constantly, explaining the exact purpose of every winch, line, and cheat. She walks me through the steps for executing efficient tacks and jibes.

When I turn too steeply into a jibe, she admonishes me with a smile to "Steer small. Seriously."

I give the rudder a sudden pull.

"Asshole. Steer *small*. You almost threw me overboard that time."

At dusk, I help her lower the sails and set the anchor.

We watch the moonrise. Pressed up against me for warmth, under a moldy blanket she retrieves from belowdecks, Paige tells me about a friend with a covered dockyard space I can probably lease on the cheap and use to work on *Sentimental Journey*. I take hold of her face and interrupt her midsentence with a kiss. Her body goes limp, and I exhale with complete deliverance as she kisses me back.

When nothing we do, no means of physical proximity we can conjure, will keep us warm, we go belowdecks. Eventually, reluctantly, we fall asleep.

In the morning, after motoring back into harbor and working to secure *Smile* at her moorings, I promise to meet her at Molly's on Thursday night for drinks with classmates.

"They have a special on High Life," she says. "Only a dollar."

"Just paper, right?" I say, spooling the bowline with newly acquired craft in my wrists.

Paige doesn't answer. She doesn't laugh. She puts on a serious, nurturing face as she waits for me on the pier. Showing me she's ready to hear more. More of that story about the burning money. More about the old man and his hay. More of anything else I'd like to tell her. She's ready to listen.

From nowhere, a terror rises inside me. The thought of responsibly drinking beers in public pushes me near to panic. I imagine standing next to her and smiling, our classmates asking me questions, and I yearn for the smallest, darkest room in the city where I can hide until I'm sure she's forgotten me. I fight it as we walk through the parking lot, back to our separate cars. But something has soured in me. I'm polite, kissing her good-bye as sincerely as I can, but I'm sure Paige notices it, too.

I sleepwalk through Sunday, and I go back to work on Monday morning. Stall isn't as friendly as he was on Friday afternoon, and he doesn't put up any fight when I tell him I'll be working on Sullivan's analytics all day. He feigns disappointment when I tell him I won't have time to grab lunch, like he'd wanted to cancel it himself but hadn't known how.

I leave Stall's office and shuffle down the hallway, to my cubicle in its windowless corner. The stack of research assignments sets me at ease. This much work is a gift, a reason to hide for the entire day, focus on these quiet tasks and not speak a word to anyone.

This much work might last into Thursday night, giving me a reason to break my promise to Paige. This much work might even follow me home from the office. When my mother sends me an e-mail asking why I never answer my phone, I can claim with a clear conscience that I've been too busy.

I sit at my desk, triaging Sullivan's research assignments, and try to convince myself that she'll expect me to stand her up. It won't surprise her, I tell myself, fighting the urge to smash my cell phone so I won't have to see her confused messages as the hours slip away on Thursday night.

I miss the phone center. The unreachability of it all. The line of people waiting to call home. The scratchy connection. The rough smell of industrial cleaner. All the good reasons to get off the phone whenever you needed it.

On my birthday, not long after Marceau died, I went to the phone center before evening chow. The guest worker, a skinny kid with shoulder-length, black hair, handed me an index card with a number on it. He gestured to the waiting area before settling back into his chair to watch a Philippine soap opera on his laptop.

I sat down and waited my turn to call home, sizing up the middle-aged national guardsman in my booth. I tried to judge from the look of him how long I'd have to wait. Skinny and hunched over in his Army uniform, he had gray hair and deep wrinkles in his face. He'd grown frail while other men his age had grown fat. I recognized him from his job at the chow hall, where he sat on a stool and made sure Marines washed their hands. That was his whole job. It was always strange seeing a forty-year-old private. It was strange having the National Guard here, at all.

I watched him arrange five calling cards on the desk and dial four times before he found a card that worked. When someone in America picked up, he leaned forward and spat, "Put the money back in the account." Blood boiled into his face, filling his wrinkles from the bottom up. "Put the money back in the account so I have something to live on when I get home."

He noticed me watching, and I looked away so as not to embarrass him.

"Put the money back in the account. Put the money back in the account. Put the money back in the account." Louder each time. Then this woman in America, whoever she was, went on the offensive. The guardsman reeled back in his chair and attempted to stifle her onslaught with a crisp "Sarah. Sarah. Sarah."

I looked over again, and the guardsman had the phone held away from his ear as she screamed. He closed his eyes, peaceful for a moment, then gave up. He slammed the handset down on the receiver, grabbed his rifle, and shuffled past me. No one in the tent seemed to notice or care.

I went to the empty desk, sat down, and pulled a calling card from my breast pocket. This gift from my sister, one thousand minutes, was sent with a demand that I call my parents at least once a week. I never managed that, but I made the effort on my birthday, at least.

I dialed and checked my watch while the line rang. I could never remember the time difference, Iraq to Alabama.

My mother answered before I finished the math, "Donovan residence."

"Hi, Mom. It's Pete."

"Oh—Pete!"

"I'm sorry, forgot to check. What time is it there?"

"Oh, it's about nine in the morning. A lovely one, too. So glad to hear from you! Happy birthday! Are you *having* a happy birthday?"

"I am. Thank you."

"Would you like to speak to your father, just right quick?"

"Yes, ma'am."

"Lemme run fetch him, then."

I heard her go out on the back porch and call his name. The screen door slammed, and I made a mental picture of the white trim and the black mesh. A green world beyond it. A cool breeze, birds, and insects buzzing in the pine trees. The screen door creaked open, a bootheel hit the kitchen floor, and I heard my mother say, "It's Pete. It's his birthday."

He picked up the phone. "Son?"

"Hello, Dad."

"Happy birthday."

"Thank you, sir."

"You do anything to celebrate, over there? A cake, or something like?"

"No, sir. Just another day, really." Marçeau's memorial service had been the day before. I didn't tell him. "What are you doing today?"

"Oh, not much. Working out in the yard. Trying to keep the kudzu vines from gobbling up the pine trees."

"How's that going?"

"Well, it's not exactly a fair fight, if you know what I mean. That kudzu just keeps coming." He sighed. "So, how are you? Doing good?"

"Yes, sir. Doing fine"

"Doing a good job? Working hard?"

"Yes, sir."

"Well that's the most important thing. That's a happy birthday, right there."

"Yes, sir."

"All right, then. Take care of yourself. Got to go work. Here's your mother." He handed the phone to her and I heard him cough on his way out the back door. Into the green. Into the breeze.

My mother didn't speak until the screen door bounced shut. "Do you need anything? Can we send you something?"

"No, ma'am. I'm about fine. On my way to grab dinner, actually. People waiting in line for the phone, too. So I should go."

"All right, then. Happy birthday, darling." She added in a soft voice, "Your father is worried sick, most days, you know."

"I know."

"And he can't wait for you to come home."

"I know."

"Love you. Be safe."

"Love you, too."

I hung up the phone, stood, and returned the index card at the counter as I pushed my way through the tent flap. The wind pelted my face with sand. Hot as a hair dryer, even at night. I walked across the tarmac, through rows of tents and plywood huts. I passed the gym and the store. I walked over to the mailbox and dropped in two letters. One to Marceau's father, the other one to his mother. Different addresses in different states.

"Your fiduciary responsibility," Major Leighton had called it. "You are required by law and custom to send his parents a letter. Anything else is at your discretion."

I walked across the unlit patch of hard dirt between the old tarmac and the chow hall while, on the flight line, the casualty-evacuation alarm wailed. In the few minutes it took me to reach the chow hall, two helicopters had made it airborne. They banked hard in the direction of Ramadi, low and fast. I tried to remember the tasking order for the night, and if the company had any convoys out near Ramadi.

I cleared my pistol at the entrance to the chow hall by pointing it into the clearing barrel and pulling the slide back to make sure it didn't have a round in the chamber. Every weapon was cleared before it entered the chow hall. I cleared my pistol twice while two national guardsmen watched. I put the weapon back on safe and holstered.

I moved through the chow line with my tray, and a guest worker from Bangladesh piled my plate high with mashed potatoes and Salisbury steak. Cobb and the other lieutenants sat at their usual table on the far side of the tent. I counted them. All there. No one from our company out near Ramadi, everyone safe.

A lieutenant I didn't recognize sat with them. A tall guy with broad shoulders and a carbine draped over his back—an infantry officer, from the look of him, and not working out of Taqaddum. The lieutenants at Taqaddum never carried rifles around the base. We locked our rifles in the operations center when we came in from the road and walked around with pistols, only.

I scanned the chow hall for another place to sit, an empty table where I could eat alone without looking like I'd meant to. Doc Pleasant and Dodge sat together, away from the rest of the platoon. Pleasant's dinner sat untouched in front of him, and I noticed for the first time how he'd lost weight, how his uniform hung loose on his shoulders. Dodge pointed at Doc's plate with a fork and began to take from it, perhaps thinking a foreign fork might encourage Doc to eat something. It worked. Doc brushed Dodge away with feigned aggravation and grudgingly took a bite.

I spotted Zahn and Gomez sequestered in a far corner, staring at their trays and attacking their dinners. They spoke in short bursts, nodding while they arranged the chow on their plates for maximum efficiency of consumption. It seemed like they were building the scene together, with purpose and shared understanding. It reinforced an image, for the junior Marines in the platoon, of a sergeant and her senior corporal, too busy, too focused on the work of war, to taste their food.

Under the table, I noticed their feet. She tapped the toe of his boot with her own and slowly pulled her foot away. He returned the gesture, all while they stared at their trays. I pretended not to notice and took the long way around to the lieutenants' table.

I sat down across from the new guy, the infantry lieutenant with the carbine, as the table burst into laughter.

Cobb held court. "I'm serious! They had the thing in a box under one of the cots."

"No fucking way, man." Wong, the Bulk Fuel Platoon commander, shook his head and tore open a dinner roll. "Hey. What's up, Donovan. You gotta hear this. Cobb—start again, man."

Cobb nodded to me. "Hey, Pete. Real quick, this is Brian Jagrschein." Cobb pointed to the infantry officer. "A buddy of mine from Quantico. Brian's with Charlie Three-Nine out in Ramadi."

I reached across the table, shook his hand, and said, "Pete Donovan. Nice to meet you. What brings you out this way?"

"Prisoner transfer. All wrapped up. Just letting my guys get some good chow before we head back." He made eye contact as he spoke, and I liked him immediately.

A female helicopter pilot sat on his right. I recognized her, and the call sign Moonbeam embossed on her flight-suit patch. She flew casualty-evacuation missions. She had a good reputation. A professional.

"Anyways, where was I?" Cobb recovered his thought. "Oh, right. So my platoon finds this scorpion down by the lake and they put it in an ammo can. They sneak it back into the company area and put it in a cardboard box. They throw some dirt in there, a few bits of shrub, and decide to keep it. It sort of becomes the platoon mascot . . ."

Just then, Moonbeam's radio, sitting on the table next to her tray, squawked to life. A garbled voice said something about clearing the landing zone at the hospital. Three casualties, urgent surgical, two minutes out and prepped for rapid transfer. She put a finger in her ear to block out Cobb's story as he pressed on.

"Then they go out and catch a bunch of camel spiders to fight the scorpion. Oh, and they name him, Fred. Right? Fred, the Egyptian death stalker. World's deadliest scorpion. I'm not kidding."

"Who is it?" Jagrschein whispered to Moonbeam as she strained to hear the radio traffic. "Which unit?"

She put the radio back on the table and turned the volume way down. She shook her head, not to say that she didn't know, but that it wasn't the time to ask.

"What those dumb-asses didn't know? Camel spiders are the natural prey of the Egyptian death stalker scorpion. So, I mean, it's not much of a fight, is it? More like a feeding. They drop in these big camel spiders and Fred the Scorpion just kills them in about five seconds and eats them whole. So, they're feeding this fucker, right? Constantly. And he's getting bigger. A *lot* bigger."

Jagrschein noticed me looking at my mashed potatoes, doing my best to ignore Cobb's story, and decided to chat me up. Maybe he wanted to keep his mind off the helicopter on its way to the hospital with those Marines. Maybe his Marines.

"So, Pete, you do outpost construction like Cobb over there?"

"No. I have the road-repair platoon. We fill potholes. Craters and stuff."

"Ever filled a crater in Ramadi?"

"Not yet. Fallujah, mostly. Habbaniyah and points north."

On the other side of the table, Wong stepped into Cobb's scorpion story. "Yeah, but tell them how you found it," he said eagerly. "Tell them how you walked in on them while they were feeding it."

Cobb smiled over at Wong. "Right! Thanks for reminding me. So, I go into the platoon's barracks to see if the corporals have their guys ready to roll in the morning, and I find the whole gang huddled around that cardboard box, cheering . . ."

Moonbeam's radio squawked again and she got up from the table, left her tray, and walked out in a hurry.

". . . and I'm like, 'The fuck is *this*? Do you know how deadly that scorpion is? Ever heard of neurotoxins?' Seriously, one sting and you're doing the funky chicken, foaming at the mouth. And here's the kicker: the nearest antivenom stocks are in fucking Germany . . ."

Jagrschein's eyes tracked Moonbeam as she left the chow hall, and he seemed to be debating whether to leave, too.

"So, Brian," I said, trying to distract him, "you operate out of Hurricane Point?"

He brought his eyes back to me. "That's right."

"Security patrols? Quick-reaction force?"

"Yeah. Well, sort of. I mean, we have our own mission, my platoon. Special tasking."

"Dude, did you lose your shit when you caught them?" Wong laughed hard.

Cobb shrugged. "No, I kept my cool. They stopped cheering when they saw me, though. That's for goddamn sure. I didn't say a word. I just walked out and went to see Gunny . . ."

"What kind of special tasking?" I asked Jagrschein. "Checkpoints? High-value targets?"

"Nah, nothing like that. We take the governor of Anbar Province to work every morning. Pick him up at his house, fight him into Government Center in the morning, and fight him home in the afternoon."

"Fight?"

"Yeah. It's a running gunfight. Every morning. Every afternoon."

". . . and I tell Gunny, 'Get that *fucking* scorpion out of this barracks. Kill it, release it, I don't care . . .'"

"Then why do it?" I asked. "Why not just tell him to bed down at Government Center?"

Jagrschein shrugged. "To keep up appearances, I guess. We do it at the same time every day. We change up the route a little bit, but otherwise it's a toe-to-toe fight. Whole city knows when he's coming and going. Brave guy, I'll give him that. He's the tenth governor in two years. The other nine were all assassinated."

". . . but Gunny tells me, 'Sir, we can't do that. They're attached to Fred the Scorpion. He's like a pet. We kill him, it'll crush morale . . .'"

"Whose choice is that?" I asked. "Going home every night? His choice? The regimental commander's?"

"His, I think. If someone was just telling him to do it, I'm sure he would've refused a long time ago. The Government Center offices? They're up high, so the bad guys have direct line of sight on the building from anywhere in the neighborhood. We put a flak and Kevlar on him, right over his coat and tie, and we drag him up the steps as fast as we can. Under fire, every time. It's a real bitch. All the spent brass on the steps? We're always slipping on the fuckers, trying to return fire."

". . . so we reach a compromise. I tell Gunny, 'Look, drown the little fucker in diesel to preserve his body, and we'll pack the corpse in epoxy. All right? Make a paperweight out of him, or something . . .'"

"We do foot patrols around Government Center during the day, just to keep the bad guys on their heels a little bit. Push them back enough so we can get out the gate in the afternoon without getting pounded by RPGs. Try to keep them from lining all the routes with IEDs. And those foot patrols, man? It's the real deal.

We do the whole patrol route at a dead sprint. Fire coming from everywhere."

". . . then, after three days floating around in the diesel, the Marines reach in with pliers and pick him up by his tail. They're about to drop him in the epoxy, and the fucker comes back to *life*! He wiggles out of the pliers and hits the ground running. Fred, the indestructible petro-scorpion! So, you know, somewhere on this base is the biggest scorpion in the whole world, and he's impervious to our weapons."

"That whole city. Ramadi," Jagrschein said, "it's ready to explode."

". . . Anyway, *that's* my scorpion story." Cobb looked up from his Salisbury steak, finding his table had drifted. Half the lieutenants were now listening to Jagrschein.

But Wong held true. "That's fucking hilarious, Cobb. You should write that down."

"Sorry for holding you up," I said to Jagrschein. "You probably want to go check on that dust-off bird."

"Yeah, I should do that."

He stood to leave. So did I.

"Nice talking to you, Pete," he said. "Look for me at Hurricane Point, if you make it out that way."

He turned for the door. I still had food on my plate, but I didn't care to sit back down and listen to Cobb and Wong. I didn't want to follow Jagrschein out either and have him thinking he had to keep talking to me. So I walked over to the dessert table with my tray and hunted around the slices of cake until I saw Jagrschein leave. Then I left, too.

I took a shortcut back to the company area, deciding to climb the berm and spend some time looking down at the river. I scrambled my way to the top and sat just as the full moon cleared the buildings behind me. The light painted the river and the flooded fields and shimmered in the exhaust of every generator in Habbaniyah.

I had a strange notion that I shouldn't let my birthday pass without at least a token commemoration. Not because I thought I'd earned it. It was more to do with the envelopes I'd dropped in the mailbox earlier. The pointless, empty words to Marceau's parents. I thought about the first leadership principle: *Know yourself and seek improvement.* Real OCS idiocy.

Then, as I searched for a place to start knowing myself, the barracks door creaked open below me, and someone muttered as he climbed the berm. I sat still as the climber slipped, planted a knee in the dirt, and cursed, "Fuck."

I recognized the voice—Dodge—but stayed quiet until he made it to the top and installed himself a few meters away from me with a book in his hands.

"Dodge?"

He flinched. "*Mulasim?* Fuck. You frightened me."

"Sorry. Didn't mean to."

"How long have you been sitting here, *Mulasim?*"

"Not long. A few minutes? You know you're not supposed to come up here, right?"

"Yes, I do know this." He smiled. "Are you aware of this?"

I smiled back. "Special occasion."

"Indeed?"

"It's my birthday."

"Well, then, happy birthday, *Mulasim.*" He put the book under his leg, mimed applause.

"How do you say 'happy birthday' in Arabic?"

"*Eid meelad sa'eed.*"

"I like that," I lied worthlessly. "I'll try to remember." We sat quietly for a moment and I sensed him wishing I'd leave. Suddenly not wanting to be alone, I forced him to keep talking to me. "What's with that book, anyway? Always meaning to ask you."

"This?" He pulled the book out from under his leg. "It is just something I study. Something I like."

"Can I see it?"

He hesitated. Then shrugged and extended the book my way. "Certainly."

I held the tattered title page up to the moonlight and read the faded words. "*Huck Finn?* Really?"

"Of course." Dodge kept his hand out, wanting the book back.

I flipped through the pages, thick with handwritten notes in both Arabic and English. "You really read this? I mean, this is hard for a lot of Americans."

"Of course. As I have said, I study it." He closed his hand a few times, growing more insistent, so I returned the book to him.

"Where did you learn to speak English? Been meaning to ask you that, too."

"School."

"College?"

He cringed. "I am told not to discuss that."

"Oh, that's right. Sorry." We sat quietly again until I found something else to talk about, some other reason to keep him there. "You and Doc Pleasant seem to get on well. I'm happy to see it."

"Yes?"

"Sure. You're both new to the platoon, still. And you know— good to have a buddy."

"Do you think so, *Mulasim?*"

I shrugged. "Sure."

"Because I have observed you somewhat, and you appear to have no friends at all." He waited for a moment for my reaction, then pressed on regardless. "Today is your birthday? And you come here alone?"

"True enough." I laughed. "I *do* have friends. Just . . . not around here."

"Not around here." Dodge nodded knowingly. "Yes. To have friends in this place is quite problematic."

I looked over at him, examining his face in the moonlight. His features, loose and easy with the platoon, here in the dark struck me as pitiless. He seemed to almost scowl, eyes fixed on the river.

"I'm not sure about all that." To show him that I wasn't clueless, I added, "Look, I know you can't be happy about . . . us. You know. Being here. But I hope we can be friends, anyway." What a jackass thing to say, I thought.

"Do you truly believe that I am upset about that, *Mulasim*? About the fate of Saddam?"

"What, then? Why can't we be friends?" I smiled and scooted over to nudge him, trying to keep it light.

"Because when you have friends, you have people."

"Sure. But that's a good thing, right?"

Dodge shook his head. "You misunderstand. People have enemies. *Other* people. People with a reason to cut off your head. All it takes is the one friend. Like you. If I am your friend, then all Americans are my people, and everyone else is my enemy. If I have friendship with a Kurd, then the Kurds are my people and I must fight the Sunni and the Shia." He waved the back of his hand at the river. "You cannot have friends, here. You cannot have people." Then he added with a sigh, "Only family."

I waited a moment before speaking. "You have family, Dodge?"

He sighed. "I have a father and a brother. That is all."

"Oh. Well, that's good, then."

"What of you, *Mulasim*? Do you have a family?"

I rubbed my hands together and nodded. "Sure. Sure. I have parents. A mom and a dad. They still live together. Still married." It occurred to me that this detail about my parents' intact marriage, always so essential when talking to Americans my age, might not be relatable to Dodge. My thoughts flashed back to the two envelopes. Marceau's mom and dad and their different addresses.

"My parents, they're teachers," I added. "My mom teaches French and my dad is the high school principal. He coaches the football team, too. American football, I mean. Not soccer."

"Brothers or sisters, as well?"

"One sister."

"Is she attractive?" Dodge asked with a smirk. "*This* might give me a reason to be your friend, if you are still so concerned."

"I suppose so." I laughed. "She's older than me. Of course, she's married. Pregnant with her first child, actually."

"You will be Uncle Mulasim soon, then?"

"Just Pete. Uncle Pete."

"Mulasim Uncle Pete."

"Even better. Leave it there. Unnecessary Uncle Pete. Nice."

We sat quietly again, for a full minute with nothing left to talk about.

Finally I said, "You know, anytime you need to go see your family, let me know. We can get you an escort."

"Thank you. *Shukran.* But that would not be possible."

"Don't want to see your father? Your brother?"

"I fear they do not want to see *me*." Dodge smiled.

"I doubt that."

"You should believe me, *Mulasim.*"

"All right, then. I'll take your word for it." I left it at that. I stood to leave. A good leader would let Dodge have the view. "Have a good night, then, Dodge." I dusted off my trousers. "Good talk."

"Eid meelad sa'eed."

I turned and began plunge-stepping in the loose dirt, sliding down the berm.

"Go and telephone your parents, *Mulasim*," Dodge called down to me.

"I hear that a lot."

"You must. Or else they will be disappointed." I saw him pull out his book.

I remember having a thought, just then. Something I wanted to share with Dodge on my birthday, but impossible at that distance.

It's us, I thought. *We'll* be disappointed. We'll remember this war as the last time we were disappointed by our parents.

I kept it to myself, letting him read in the moonlight.

Dad—

*Looks like I'll be staying up here for a little while longer. Mostly
cause the New Orleans shop needs an extra hand through the holidays. Might be a good opportunity, you know? Show I could run the
Houma shop by myself someday. I'll be staying with Landry and
looking for a temporary place here in the next few days. I'll drive
home on Christmas Eve and stay through Christmas morning. Grab
some clothes and things, but I got work again in New Orleans the
day after. Promise I'll call you.*

—Lester

TROUBLE IN RIVER CITY

Lizzy's folding my clothes on her bed, separating work clothes from regular clothes. Not that there's much difference. Three pairs of pants and six shirts. She hasn't bothered with any of her own clothes. Just added them back to the piles on the floor.

I'm leaning back against her pillows, feeling plain worthless. "You don't have to do that."

"It's no problem, dude." Not even taking her eyes off the television, she asks me, "Are you following this stuff in Tunisia?"

I look over her shoulder at the news footage. Smoke and bombs, police killing innocent-looking people in some Middle Eastern town. Not something I'd take an interest in, given the choice. "Not really. What about it?"

"Well, last week, some guy burned himself alive in front of a police station to protest government oppression. And now, everyone's out on the street. It seems like they might even get this dictator, Ali something, overthrown."

"Wow. Crazy."

"Totally. And what's crazy is that they were live-tweeting it and shit until the government shut down their Internet."

"Look at that," I say, watching the television over her shoulder. It's nighttime over there, and people in a traffic circle are setting up barricades. They're waving flags, chanting, and carrying on.

"So. Iraq," Lizzy says, easing softly into the question she's been wanting to ask for a few days. "When were you there?"

"'Round oh-six."

"And what you did over there, what you saw, does it affect the way you think about things? Like what's going down in Tunisia?"

"The way I feel about what? Riots?"

"No, dude. Fucking freedom. People fighting for their freedom."

I take a moment to try and think of something to say besides the truth, which is that I don't think much on it either way, and blurt out, "Well, I hope everyone comes out okay."

Lizzy smirks and goes back to the television for a second, with her forehead wrinkled all cute. She's confused, which is understandable, I guess, since I don't even know what I meant by that myself.

"You 'hope everyone comes out okay'?" she asks finally, like I said something stupid and didn't realize.

"Sure." I shrug. "I hate to see people getting hurt."

"Dude"—she laughs—"you were in a war."

I fumble around for words. "Well, I suppose you could call it that."

She laughs some more. "I'm sorry. I'm not trying to make fun, or anything. That's just not something I thought a veteran would say about this. I was thinking you'd be all like, 'Good for them. Fighting for their freedom. Rah, rah, rah!'"

Now I'm wishing I'd have said something better, more wise, because I'm stuck with this loser line about hoping no one gets hurt. I try to make myself believe it so the next thing I say might sound less stupid.

But Lizzy seems like she's already moved on. She turns back to the news and says, "I wonder how they turn off the Internet to a whole country?"

"They did it in Iraq, on a smaller scale. Not the Iraqis. The Marines, I mean."

Lizzy perks up. "Really?"

"Yeah. Whenever someone got hurt. They would turn off all the phones and all the Internet so no one could call or write home for a few days. They called it River City."

"What for?"

"You mean why did they call it that?"

"No, I get why they called it River City. I mean, why did they turn off the phones and the Internet?"

"Oh." I stop to think about the nicest way to say it. "Because they didn't want the family finding out from the newspaper or the neighbors, I guess."

"Finding out that someone got hurt? Would that make the news?"

I take a breath. "Yeah. Killed I mean. I didn't want to say it like that, but it was mostly for when people got killed."

"Oh. Sorry, Les. That sucks."

"It's fine. It happens."

I'm pissed at myself, now. For bringing it up. We're having a boring conversation, now. And she has to say boring stuff like, "That sucks." I figure I can say about five boring things to this girl before my time is up, and I was hoping this might last a little longer.

But then a question occurs to me. "Wait. What do you mean, 'I know why they called it River City'?"

"You don't?"

I shake my head.

"*The Music Man.* You know? The Broadway musical? There's a song called 'There's Trouble in River City.'" She folds the last of my laundry.

"You like Broadway musicals?"

"Tell any of my friends and I'll kill you." She throws a pair of underwear at my face, and I smile because despite everything

Landry's been telling me about her, this could last another week. Maybe all the way into the New Year.

I look over her shoulder, back at the news footage from Tunisia.

I think of Kateb. I bet he'd have something to teach me about this.

"Colonel Grangerford was a gentleman all over," Huck reflects. "And so was his family. He was well born, as the saying is, and that's worth as much in a man as it is in a horse, so the Widow Douglas said."

Huck understands there is no honor in a lucky birth. But he can't resist the charms of Colonel Grangerford, a well-born gentleman. The river drifts south, and while they are on the raft, Huck is happy to float. But when they go ashore, Huck craves strong leadership.

THE SECOND SON OF ABU MUHAMMAD

Bullets crack over our heads and the pretty girl next to me grips my arm with the force of a wrench.

"Not to worry," I shout to be heard above the din. "Those bullets? Just warnings. Merely to frighten us into going home."

She nods and starts to cry.

"Here," I shout. "Move against this wall."

The panicked crowd rushes behind us. If I can just hold this girl and keep her from running, maybe we will not be crushed to death.

I see my flatmates across the square. They hide behind a statue in the center and appear from their faces not to have expected gunplay. It is too much for them, and now of course they want to go home. I had wanted to stay there for a reason. Fools.

The girl asks me why I am so calm.

"Iraq, cousin. This is normal for us there."

I am thinking that in a moment there will be space to run away. The crowd will thin and we can escape back to the main avenue and move closer to our flat. But I see that after these first shots, no one is running. They are staying. And the police who fired these warning shots are growing confused. They had expected that we would flee. We have stayed through the tear gas. We have stayed through the warning shots. They have no options remaining, and I do not think they want to kill us.

The crowd begins to understand this and cheers the development.

Even this pretty girl. She jumps up and down while hugging me. "It will happen," she cries. "It *is* happening! Here!"

The crowd begins to celebrate, singing "Tunisia Our Country." This pretty girl puts her arm around my waist as she sings along, and we sway with them.

"Why are you not singing?" she asks after several verses.

"Because Tunisia is not my country, cousin," I say plainly. "I am just a visitor."

She frowns and looks away. Back to her people. Back to her singing.

Hani would do better with this pretty girl. He would know how to kiss her and would have done so by now, I am sure of it.

My father enjoyed Hani and would often say that he and I should have been born brothers. I always took this to mean that my father would have preferred Hani as his second son.

Hani returned my father's affection by apologizing on my behalf. We children of Saddam learned this trick very young. Supplication was love, and a confession wrapped inside a lie was flattery. When adventure kept us out late, when I missed dinner, or when we did not come home at all, Hani would show his love for my father by showering him with apologies, admissions, and lies disguised as plausible explanations.

"The respectful thing to do," he would say. "Your father is old and tired. Be decent enough to lie."

Late at night or early in the morning, he would come inside the dark house with me. There was never any point in sneaking, with the heavy front door and our footsteps echoing off the tile. My father would come out from his bedroom in his robe and slippers with his night hair carefully smoothed.

Hani would go to him and beg forgiveness, claiming difficulty with his studies and saying that I had volunteered to help.

My father understood these were lies, I am sure. He was never stupid, and he knew Hani as well as his own sons. But he valued my friendship with Hani. He valued Hani's optimism. I think he was proud I could command such loyalty from a friend.

He would send Hani away with a pat on the cheek, saying, "Let me have a word with Kateb."

But he never scolded me. He never struck me, even when I was a child and we were still mourning my mother. He would simply wander back to his room and ask softly where we had been. He would smile and gently tease me, worrying for my future. How, he would say, did I have such a lazy, mischievous son?

I never cared enough to apologize or to lie to my father, but Hani always sought to please. My father's dignity compelled Hani. My father was one of Saddam's old bureaucrats, upright and imperturbable. And we children raised with Saddam? Never quite free. Though our teenage years moved us to rebel, always the state brought us home again.

So, when my father and brother appeared at Tourist Town and stepped from the old Mercedes in slacks and fine shirts like nothing had changed, Hani followed his first instinct.

He went to the car and held my father's hand to his forehead. "Abu Muhammad, in the name of God, accept my apology."

My father smiled and cupped Hani's cheek. "In the name of God, I forgive you. You are a good boy, Hani. Peace be upon you."

Meanwhile, I stood in the farmhouse door, a guilty child afraid to approach.

"And look at Kateb! A grown man!"

My brother Muhammad stood behind Hani and grinned. The same grin from long ago, worn on days when our father had scolded me for sneaking treats. The satisfied grin of the firstborn, the oldest son from whom our father now derived his new wartime alias: the Father of Muhammad.

I remember, in that moment, wanting to show Muhammad that we were no longer children. That I was a man like him, not at all bothered by his satisfaction. Happy to invite my father and brother to drink tea around the fire pit. Happy to introduce them to my friends. I wanted all that gracious dignity.

Instead, when my father smiled and opened his arms for me, I went to him, wrapped my arms around him, and wept. I wept with happiness for seeing him alive and with regret for not having returned home from Professor Al-Rawi's office, all those months before. For being afraid to fight. I wept with guilt for not trying harder to find him. I wept like an orphan.

We lingered for a moment, my father comforting me with declarations of love. When I pulled away, I went to Muhammad. My brother held me close, messed my hair, and laughed. "You look like a woman with hair so long."

I reached over and tugged at his mustache. "And always a shopkeeper, you. Old so soon with this mustache?"

This was a joke from before the war, when I had teased him for joining Saddam's army. Muhammad had been an officer, a captain of the Republican Guard, but I made a point to refer to him as a shopkeeper. It had been funny, then. But with his army gone, the joke fell flat.

His embrace went stiff, and I will not say I did not know that it would.

Still, we walked hand in hand to the fire pit while Hani ran off to find Mundhir and Abu Abdul.

My father and brother sat across from me, puzzled, as they looked about at Hani's Tourist Town improvements. At first they were curious, but soon they were confused. The beach cabana had grown to include oil lamps and scattered, broken chairs. One of Pederson's marines had given Hani a length of little, plastic flags to hang on the awning, advertising an American beer.

"Hani told us about your little project when we found each other in the market," Muhammad said.

"Oh," I said, surprised Hani hadn't mentioned the meeting. "Do you like our little resort?"

"I suppose. It seems a fine place to stretch your legs. A safe place between Samarra and Ramadi is difficult to find."

Haji Fasil appeared in the farmhouse door, and my stomach tightened at the recollection of Pederson's envelope.

"Kateb. Nephew," Haji Fasil scolded, "will you not introduce me to your family?"

I stood. "Father, this is Haji Fasil. This is his farm. He saved our lives and sheltered us here, thanks be to God. He is my friend."

My father, on his feet before I finished speaking, went to Haji Fasil and kissed his cheeks. "Haji. God bless you. Thank you. Peace be upon you. Thank you."

Haji Fasil took my father's kisses, but offered nothing in return. No expression. Just the words "Praise God, it was his will," like a stone.

Haji Fasil went inside to make tea, and when he returned, we all sat around the fire pit.

"Your father lives close by, Kateb," Hani cooed. "In Habbaniyah."

Haji Fasil stirred at the mention of the town, knowing as he did the special quality of men, the Saddam loyalists, who could find accommodation there. "How did you come to live there?"

"Sheikh Hamza, whom I know from the construction of the Grand Canal. He provided the ministry with men for digging. He has given Muhammad and me the former home of an Air Force officer. But we are only there temporarily. Only until we return to Baghdad."

"When the Shia destroy themselves," Muhammad added flatly, then sipped his tea. "Do you know Sheikh Hamza, Haji Fasil?"

"No." He shrugged. Just a simple merchant, wearing his tattered bedouin robes like a shield. Haji Fasil had lived through many such conversations, I am sure.

"We will take Kateb with us, tonight," Muhammad said. "He should visit with his nephew." My brother kicked dirt at my feet. "Ibrahim asks for you, Kateb." He finished his tea in one long gulp. "I trust you can spare him, Haji Fasil?"

"Yes, yes." Haji Fasil waved his hand. "The business is Hani's. Kateb's only work is his studies."

"Good. We should leave, then. Evening checkpoints will begin soon." Muhammad stood and slipped his hands into his pockets.

My father placed his teacup carefully in the sand and stood as well. "Are you ready to leave, Kateb?"

They hung their shadows on me, like the old statues of Hero Saddam.

"Momentarily," I said, thinking of the envelope. "I just need to gather my things."

The envelope could keep me free and alive if the Americans happened upon us.

"No need for that, Brother." Muhammad smiled. "We can bring you back before you need a change of clothes."

With the matter thus settled, Hani and Haji Fasil said good-bye. I stood and followed my family to their Mercedes, my father and brother on either side of me like considerate guards.

Haji Fasil waved from the fire pit, quiet and polite as always.

My brother let the script die, turned to me, and said sternly, "Sit in the back."

I sank into the leather seat, and he closed the door behind me a little harder than necessary.

On the last day of Professor Al-Rawi's life, a full month after I had taken up residence in his office, he stayed with me late into the afternoon discussing my thesis.

"You seem overly concerned with the American understanding of authority," he said, lighting a cigarette. "You ask, 'From whence do the townspeople derive the authority to tar and feather the Duke and the Dauphine?' You ask, 'From whence do the Grangerfords gain the right to seek retribution against the Shepherdsons?' Tell me, Kateb, why does authority interest you so?"

I was flummoxed. After a moment of thought, I replied, "This is a story of rebellion, Professor. Rebellion must act against authority, yes? Is it not important to understand the authority against which Huck is rebelling?"

"Kateb, Kateb . . ." Professor Al-Rawi laughed. "In the end, Huck must learn two very important lessons. First, that civilization is an illusion. Second, that the only authority is one's conscience."

I nodded, as though I understood, but said nothing.

Professor Al-Rawi smiled. "Think about this, Kateb, and we will discuss tomorrow. I must return home now or risk the anger of my wife." He picked up his briefcase and added with a chuckle, "But perhaps you will not truly understand authority until you have a wife of your own."

I smiled back and wished him a good evening.

My brother dropped the car into gear and fought through the rutted path.

"You are lucky we found you, Kateb," my father said, smiling at me from the front seat. "Were you making trouble out here in the desert? Or just helping Hani study?"

"No," I said, "we left Baghdad, but we had to stop here for fuel. We discovered it was not safe to go on."

"Used your time to read, then?" my father asked. Then, to Muhammad: "Take the eastern route. I wish to see the state of the canal."

I rubbed my knees and made myself speak. "Such a joy to see my family well," I managed. "And after so long without word from you, I had begun to worry . . ."

"And these worries kept you in Baghdad?" Muhammad sighed. "I feel so loved."

"No," I stammered. "No, I tried to come home that night, but after speaking to my professor . . ." I trailed off, with no will to finish the thought.

My brother ignored me and returned to watching the road. This did not surprise me, but when my father sat quietly as well, a burning grief rose to my throat. I wished my father would demand answers from me. But he said nothing.

Muhammad turned the Mercedes east, onto the highway. The road ran close to the banks of the canal and the lake. Reeds and palms trees grew thick and bent over to the east with the spring wind. On the damp shores, desert shrubs flourished in a reluctant, dim shade of green.

All at once I missed Hani's stupid beach resort.

My father pointed to a low spot in the canal. "There," he said to Muhammad. "Like I told you. Pumps and a filtration system, powered by electric lines from Haditha. Built inside an operable lock, set in concrete with steel gates." He moved his hands like imaginary doors. His eyes became animated with the old dream, dead for so many years now, that he might finish his canal.

"Father . . . ," I said.

Muhammad opened the window and lit a cigarette. "I will talk to Sheikh Hamza and the American at this next *shura* and tell them that this is the project the Americans have wanted. A project for the television."

My father sighed. "The Americans will want government troops to guard the pumps."

"Troops from Baghdad," my brother said. "But we need not think poorly on that. Yes? Having those *takfiri* standing around in the sun? Exposed?"

My father nodded and rubbed his chin.

"Father . . . ," I said, louder.

He looked at me in the rearview mirror and smiled. "Do not worry. We have not forgotten you, Kateb. These matters require discussion while we can see the ground and make plans. You are welcome to join us."

"Americans, Kateb," my brother said. "We talk of Americans, and you know more of Americans than either of us."

My face burned. I opened my mouth, ready to say something, I did not know what. But the sounds would not come. I turned my eyes to the roadside, to the reeds and shrubs browning as we traveled farther south, away from the river.

"Kateb," my father said, turning around in his seat and looking confused. "Do you think we are angry with you?"

"Someone is angry. Sheikh Hamza, is it?"

"Kateb. My son." My father smiled with sincerity. "We are not angry with you. You deal with the Americans? So do we. Everyone does this."

Muhammad laughed and dropped his cigarette onto the road.

"But so few had the idea to sell them soda by the roadside. Well done, Brother."

My father frowned at Muhammad and continued, "Yes, Kateb. You have been successful, and we are proud of you. And now we will keep you safe, praise to God. This is why we came for you."

I crossed my arms and went back to watching the roadside. I felt my father's eyes on me. Willing me to talk. I had wanted this minutes earlier, and for years before. But that was before I knew where the words would take us.

"We will talk after dinner," my father added gently.

We drove the rest of the way to Habbaniyah in the quiet, save for an odd word from Muhammad on the condition of the road or the placement of a checkpoint, manned by American marines and Iraqi soldiers from the new army. These new soldiers were still learning their profession, Muhammad said. Still just thin teenagers from Basra, happy for money to send home. But they grew braver, more confident, all the time.

My brother gripped the wheel tighter each time he saw these soldiers, in ill-fitting uniforms discarded from old American supplies.

The sun had begun to fade as we reached Habbaniyah, and the checkpoints changed. Local police and young men in soccer jerseys appeared carrying Kalashnikovs, replacing the Americans and their Iraqi apprentices. These men seemed to know my father and Muhammad well. They let us through without questions. We passed from the highway onto the narrow roads of the town.

Trash marred the desert highways, as it had since the war began. But once we passed the checkpoints and entered the town, the streets became clean, like the old Iraq. Gravel spread through the market kept dust from clouding the merchants' booths. Traditional wares, like food and robes, sat in booths next to new necessities, air conditioners and mobile phones. Boards placed across gutters allowed pedestrians to avoid sewage, stepping from their shops and homes.

Signs of government. Signs of care, even.

Muhammad guided the car down a dirt road cutting between onetime officers' villas. High, yellow walls rose on either side of us, behind which sat identical houses made from poured concrete in the square, Soviet style. All but a few were abandoned and showed no signs of life. Dirt courtyards baked in the sun and dust blew through houses looted for metal window frames and pipes.

Muhammad approached a villa near the end of the street, and I saw green grass and dirty generator smoke through a small gap in the closed gate.

Two men appeared to push the gate open when Muhammad used his horn.

Muhammad drove slowly through the gate, and six men surrounded the car. Another three, wiping their hands on muddy clothes, appeared from around a corner to investigate our arrival. Still two more, with rifles almost hidden under long shirts, sat in chairs on either side of the front door.

They wore no beards and kept their mustaches smartly trimmed. Sunni men, both of them.

I saw my little nephew, Ibrahim, playing in the thin grass with a flat football. The boy I knew before the war was shy and always crying out for his mother. I noticed her, too. Nasim. Too smart and pretty for my brother, I'd always thought. From the kitchen window, she called for Ibrahim and waved for him to come inside with one hand while she worried about her head scarf with the other. She had never worn a hijab before the war. A university girl, Nasim. She had been studying to be a doctor.

Muhammad placed the car in park. A fat man came to my

window and opened my door. He smiled and reached over to unbuckle my seat belt.

I resisted him, out of instinct, and looked to my father for help.

"You have many new friends, Kateb," he said.

"The second son of Abu Muhammad," the fat man said. "You've come home, thanks to God." He smiled, like I mattered, like he wanted me to remember him.

"Hello," I managed with a weak smile.

I stepped from the car while the men swarmed all around us. They smiled and offered me welcome, then turned to my brother, ingratiating themselves. Sycophants hoping to be heard. When my father and brother started toward the house, the men melted away. I followed close behind, unsure of my place.

The three men in muddy clothes slipped back around the corner. It seemed they knew their place without question.

Ahead of me, my father whispered something to Muhammad.

My brother continued into the house, leaving my father and I alone in the yard.

My father reached out and took my hand. "You do amaze, my son. You have thrived without us. Nothing matters more than this. I am proud, Kateb. You should be proud, as well." He pulled me into an embrace. "Now, would you like to see?" he whispered.

I stepped back. "See what, Father?"

"How your father has become a businessman." He led me by the hand, around to the side yard where the workers had gone, and I understood that the generators did not power such luxuries as lights or air-conditioning for the villa. They powered industry, the backyard factory spread out in front of me.

"This is what your father does for money, now."

Cement mixers churned while rows of square molds waited for the wet mix. Two dirty men sat on low stools. One chipped away at the plaster encasing blocks fresh from the molds. The other man washed and painted them. Equal stacks of yellow and black stones sat behind him. The third man emerged from a shed in the back, pushing a cart piled high with more stones, still encased in plaster.

Focused on their task, or at least wishing to appear so, these men took note of my father without looking up to acknowledge him.

"Did you notice the highways on our way into town, Kateb?" my father asked. "And how clean the streets are kept?"

"I suppose. Better, at least."

"Sheikh Hamza is keen on this. Anbar should show these signs of improvement. He has the provincial governor pay him to replace the broken curbstones. He has men for this. We make the curbstones and sell to him."

"Ah, very clever." I remembered all the times my father took me to see the canal as a boy, and how he watched the construction work with such satisfaction. Honest work, unlike politics. Perhaps in this new Iraq he had left politics behind completely and become a simple businessman.

"Clever." He grinned. "Yes. So clever." He took my shoulder. "Let's go inside and see what Umm Ibrahim has cooked for us."

We left the men to their labor and entered the kitchen from the side door. Little Ibrahim latched onto my leg at once. "Uncle Kateb, are you home now?"

I picked him up and kissed his cheek. "Yes, I am home now."

"Good, because everyone here is too old to play with me."

Nasim walked over from the stove and pulled him away. "We must let Kateb rest before he can play with you." She held me in a long embrace. "So joyous to see you, Kateb. And safe."

"Wonderful to see you, as well. Cooking for all these men, Nasim?"

"Trying." She laughed and returned to the stove. "Breakfast and lunch for the workers during the day. Dinner for our little family when they leave." She carried Ibrahim to a mat in the corner of the kitchen, near the entrance to the sitting room, and placed a tray of bread and cheese in front of him.

I wondered about her dreams of medicine and how they had been traded for the role of cook and maid.

My father came in from the sitting room and stood behind her. He smelled the lamb roast and gave her a little smile. He walked over to the little mat and sat down with his grandson. He placed the boy on his lap and made a show of enjoying the flat bread in an attempt to trick his grandson into eating.

Ibrahim smiled and snatched the bread from his grandfather's hand.

I heard Muhammad debating with his colleagues in the next room. I moved to the doorframe near my father and Ibrahim. Feigning interest in their activity, I cast a sideways glance into the sitting room.

"Should we watch first or talk?" the fat man asked.

"Watch," Muhammad answered.

The stone floors squealed as the men pulled their chairs into a circle. The fat man retrieved a camcorder from his bag and played a video on its tiny screen as the other men leaned in close to watch.

The little speaker strained and squeaked. I recognized the sound of vehicles on a highway, of trucks stopping and men yelling. I heard the sound of breathing, too. The cameraman, a scared child by the sound of his whispering, told another child to remain quiet and stop moving.

"See there," the fat man said, "they all get out at the same time, using their radios to coordinate this."

"Yes," Muhammad answered.

"And there. They fan out. About three lengths of a truck."

"Hmm."

"But see, they are not fooled. They do not get their robot. It is too obvious. But if we can hide one here, out front, poorly enough that they spot it, well enough that they believe, we can put another bomb in the curbstone behind it. Right where they stop and get out."

"This is not new thinking," Muhammad said. "But, yes. True."

Down at my heels, sitting on my father's lap, Ibrahim finished his flat bread and looked around the kitchen for approval. First at my father, then at Nasim. She smiled and patted her leg, and Ibrahim sprang from my father's lap to run to her. She started a kettle boiling for tea.

My father stayed on the mat and watched his grandson play.

The sitting room hummed. The fat man spoke above the chorus. "You see how they send one man forward to check the old tire in the road? You see how they pull the trucks to the side farther down? We hit the man up front or we hit the trucks behind."

The other men whispered support, but only to one another. No one addressed the room at large.

My brother cleared his throat and they all stopped talking. "You should discuss that with your men. I am going for cigarettes." Muhammad saw me and smiled as he crossed the room. "There is a shopkeeper I must go see."

He stepped through the front door. One of the guards, a young man with a Kalashnikov slung inside his long shirt, hurried after him.

My father, still on the floor next to me, reached up for my hand.

The fat man took over the sitting room, the responsibility given to him by my brother's departure. He instructed his men, pointing at them in pairs.

"You two. Mark the attack site. Chalk on the curbstones. Use the old pattern."

My father's weight moved up my arm as he struggled to his feet with a fantastic groan. He pushed down hard on my shoulder and let his weight settle into his heels.

"You two"—the fat man pointed—"leave the new stones loose so the bombs and detonators slide in easily. The triggermen are not here. You won't know them." The fat man saw that my father and I were watching and listening. He stood and spoke to my father. "Abu Muhammad, we are ready. Should we leave now with the stones?"

"Yes," my father said. "They are outside. The workers will leave soon, too. You should leave with them, together."

The men pushed their chairs back to the corners of the room and filed out through the kitchen.

My father took my hand and led me to a window looking out onto the garden. We watched the men direct a flatbed truck through the gate, over to a spot where they could load a batch of curbstones.

"We have a problem, Kateb," my father said.

I said nothing as he let go of my hand.

"The Shia in the south want to give our country to the Iranians. The Sadrists in Baghdad kill men like us for spite. Out here in the desert, Saudi and Egyptian brats who joined Al Qaeda in a fit of boredom kill good men for nothing. The Americans and the Kurds kill us all."

The fat man directed his men to carry five specially marked curbstones to the open trunk of the Mercedes.

"We are the honorable resistance, Kateb. Ansar al-Sunna. The last Iraqis. We fight the jihadists who leave heads in the street. We assist the Shia with their blundering into chaos. And we bleed the Americans. Not because we hate them, mind you. Only because they are the invader. They must be driven out. The more they bleed, the sooner they go home."

The little convoy rolled through the gate, the flatbed truck followed by the Mercedes.

My father reached into his pocket and produced a stack of dinar. "Our next action is very near your beach house, Kateb." He handed the money to me. "God willing, the Americans will blame the Sadrists down the road. You will help us, yes?"

Memorandum for the record:

I first became aware of Corpsman Pleasant's erratic behavior on or about 25 June, when the platoon sergeant informed me that Corpsman Pleasant had withdrawn socially and, after returning from convoys and route clearance missions, would disappear into the barracks until dining hall hours. At meals, he ate very little and showed signs of significant weight loss.

Early in the deployment, Corpsman Pleasant earned a reputation for enthusiasm by seeking out Marines for specialized instruction in subjects beyond the scope of his duties.

However, by the end of June, Corpsman Pleasant became known more for his deteriorating morale and slovenly appearance.

Respectfully submitted,
P. E. Donovan

THE BRASS BUTTONS

"It's my car," I tell my mother. "It needs work that I can't afford right now. I don't think it can make the trip, how it is presently. And it's too late to buy plane tickets."

Of all the things I never thought I'd do, I'm lying to my mother so I won't have to go home for Christmas. I grit my teeth and hope she doesn't offer to pay for the flight.

She sighs, and for a moment I think she might be trying not to cry. I couldn't be more wrong. She comes back with her strong teacher's voice, asking, "Do you want to tell your father that? Or should I do it for you?"

I don't hesitate. "You can do that."

She gives me a moment's quiet to change my mind, a chance to grow up and tell the truth. When I don't, she says. "Well, merry Christmas, then. I love you."

"I love you, too." Guilt overtakes me. "I'm really sorry. I'll make it up to you guys."

She denies me the satisfaction, ending the conversation with a terse "I'll call you on Christmas morning so you can talk to your nephew. Try to answer."

The timed fluorescent lights click off in sequence across the cubicle floor as I return to the research assignment on my desk. The knowledge that I'm alone in the office sets me at ease. But the relief is short-lived. My cell phone, sitting on a stack of files, announces with a rattle that I have a message from Empathy: "?"

I type out a quick response: "Sorry. Busy at work. Call you soon," and my stomach twists as I hit send.

I return to the assignment in front of me, finding solace in how proficient I've become at this stuff. My speed is growing into an office legend. A machine, Sullivan calls me. No matter how many files he drops on me in a day, he always finds solid reports waiting on his desk the following morning. I think he's taking bets with the partners behind my back, searching for a limit to how much I can take.

I suspect Major Leighton played me similarly, placing bets with the officers at regiment. There's no limit to the number of potholes my company can fill. My Marines are supermen. There's nothing they can't do.

Major Leighton heard about the mission from some friends at regiment. Majors in command of other, more glamorous companies. They told him about a platoon on dismounted patrol in the abandoned employee-housing development near the Muthanna Chemical Complex. The grunts had been looking for weapons caches, instead finding an open pit stacked neatly with steel drums, sealed and left to molder in the sun. Someone had left in a hurry, before covering the pit with dirt.

Regiment had dispatched a chemical team to investigate, and the colonels must've held their breath thinking maybe they'd found the goods. The almost-forgotten reason we'd made the trip. Whispers flew up the chain, all the way to Baghdad with the best kind of bad news.

But, after testing residue on the drums, the chemical warfare team came back with nothing special. Just an assortment of common, industrial products. Caustic acids and pellets of concentrated pesticides. Dangerous and problematic, for sure. But nothing of interest to Baghdad, so the strategic, theater-level assets en route to assist turned around. The chemical-disposal teams. The civilian experts. They all went back to the Green Zone and left regiment to deal with the drums alone.

The drums couldn't stay. Over time, the steel would corrode. The contents would seep into the groundwater and eventually into the river. Or the bad guys would get hold of the stuff and put the chemicals to some clever use to make us hurt.

Regiment couldn't decide who had responsibility for hazardous chemical disposal, so Major Leighton volunteered his company. Supermen. Engineer Support doing a job no one else could, or would.

He announced the mission a day later, in the daily operations briefing: "This is what we came here to do. We enable our trigger-pullers. Because of the work we do, the grunts are able to fight the terrorists without distraction. This is a mission tailor-made for us."

His staff sat silent and still. The lieutenants kept their eyes on their notes. The gunnery sergeants, less intimidated, looked at each other with arms crossed in disapproval. But we all avoided eye contact with Major Leighton. No one wanted the mission.

"We have the State Department lined up to support, fortunately," Major Leighton continued, calmly rubbing his bald head. "A project officer from the provincial reconstruction office will meet us at the site with trucks and local nationals to haul away the drums. All we have to do is secure the scene, remove the sealed drums from the pit, and transfer possession."

The room didn't budge, even with this rare offer of encouragement.

"So that's why Road Repair Platoon has this one," he said finally. "Good rolling stock, familiar with the area of operations, and best prepared."

My mouth went dry, and I looked up from my notebook as Major Leighton raised his eyebrows and nodded at me. I couldn't look at him, so I focused on his sunburned head, his hairy knuckles, and the sunglasses hanging around his neck.

"Aye, aye, sir," I said.

Cobb, sitting next to me, held my arm in the air like I'd just won a boxing match. The staff acknowledged Cobb's mock support with nervous laughter, and I tried to smile.

After the operations briefing, I went to tell Gomez and Zahn. I made Gunny Dole come with me, and he ranted nonstop on our way to the platoon barracks.

"Unbelievable. Complete bullshit," he huffed. "Absolutely not in our lane. Not our responsibility. This is just crazy, sir. You have to talk to him about this."

"And say what, Gunny? Tell him the whole platoon has bad knees?"

He cursed under his breath. "Not our fucking job. I remember one time, in the Philippines. Must've been around '95. The company commander wanted the Marines to cut their liberty short to go out to help this village with their sewage problem. And the lieutenant said no way. He threatened to request mast. That was a long deployment, too. Must've been—"

"Gunny, shut up."

He fumed off to the side with his arms crossed as we approached Gomez and Zahn, waiting in the shade behind the barracks for details of the day's mission. I gave it to them straight. There was no way to spin it, and no sense in trying to soften the hard facts.

"We don't have a procedure for this sort of thing," I told them. "No instruction book. So, we use the procedures we *do* have. We treat it like a chemical attack. We break out the gas masks and wear charcoal-lined suits and rubber gloves. We work in shifts."

Zahn pulled a can of dip from his pocket and shoved a thick wad under his lip. He shuffled his feet and looked at the dirt.

Gomez pursed her lips, refusing to look at me.

"It'll be hot in those suits, no question," I continued. "So, we draw extra ice from supply. We make sure Doc Pleasant has plenty of fluid bags. We make a rotation and we stick to it. Twenty minutes in the suits, maximum. No heat casualties. And we stick to the decontamination procedures."

"What time do we roll out, sir?" Gomez asked with eyes on her notebook and her pen at the ready.

"Tomorrow morning early. Muster a zero two hundred. I want us on the site and working before dawn. Maybe we can knock this thing out before the afternoon heat."

"Okay." She sighed and added a lax "Sir."

I rubbed my sweaty palms on my trousers. "Listen. Both of you. Look at me."

Zahn and Gomez looked up.

"This is a tough one, no question. But there's no sense fighting it. And no sense pouting in front of the Marines. It'll just make it worse for them."

"Speaking of, is Gunny coming out with us, sir?" Zahn asked. "Taking a turn with a suit and mask?"

I glanced over my shoulder to gauge how Gunny Dole had taken the slight, but he hadn't heard it. He was already halfway across the expanse of dirt, on his way to the Internet café.

"No," I said, "Gunny can't make it."

Zahn shook his head and laughed under his breath.

I didn't admonish him. There would've been no point. "Questions?"

They had none, so I dismissed them to prepare the platoon. They would hardly have an hour to sleep, I knew.

I went to the supply section and drew my chemical suit before going back to my room and writing out the mission order in alcohol pen on my laminated template. I fell asleep with my socks on.

My wristwatch alarm woke me at midnight. I dressed with my red-lens flashlight, not wanting to ruin my night vision. I laced my boots, zipped my flight suit, and struggled into my flak jacket. I walked through the operations center on my way out of the darkened compound. Sweat rolled down my neck and cheeks and pooled at the base of my neck. The armor plate held it there.

Cobb had the overnight watch, and he smiled over his coffee mug. A laptop played a movie on the desk behind him. He reached around to pause it. "You out?"

"Shortly. Five vehicles, twenty-two packs." I went to the weapons rack in the corner and unlocked my rifle.

Cobb made a note of our numbers. "All right, buddy. Have fun." He put his finger on the space bar, ready to get back to his movie.

I stood behind his chair and looked over his shoulder at the watch logs and screens. "Anything happening?" The blue force-tracker screen, a map of Anbar Province overlaid with icons representing friendly units, showed a logistics convoy of civilian-operated trucks en route from Jordan, a few snap vehicle checkpoints, but not much else.

Cobb confirmed it. "No. It's pretty quiet."

I slung the rifle over my back. "I'll radio from the gate." As I walked out, I heard Cobb get back to his movie.

A scrum of red flashlights led me to our staging area. I heard engines warming and Marines cursing in the darkness. Two Marines brushed past me with an ice chest, and I heard them talking as they hefted it into the cargo compartment of their Humvee.

"Is he serious about these fucking suits?" one of them said.

His partner gave a mumbled reply, too soft to make out the words or the identity of the speaker.

"Gomez sounded pissed. I know this wasn't her idea," he continued. "Five bucks says we don't see him in one of those fucking suits."

I stood there, just another bulky shape with a rifle, and listened to things they wouldn't say about me if they knew I could hear. They shuffled past me again, on their way back to the supply yard.

"He'll give it the college-boy try, I bet. Maybe put on a suit right at the end to help with the last barrel, you know? Make a show of his leadership principles. OCS motherfucker."

My face burned and I backed away into the darkness, hoping they wouldn't bump into me. After about twenty yards, I turned around and approached the staging area from a new angle, calling loudly for Gomez and Zahn to make my presence known. The chatter of Marines fell away when they heard me, but they continued their work.

Gomez and Zahn jogged over and stood close to my face. Gomez gave me the report. All present. Chemical suits for everyone. Extra ice. Extra water. All vehicles fueled and ready. I went over to Gomez's vehicle and sat on the hood while she and Zahn gathered the convoy team.

I read the mission order word for word by the red glow of my flashlight—a straight-ahead brief without encouragement or bravado. I gave them the route and the order of march. I listed our immediate actions on near ambush, far ambush, improvised explosive device, and disabled vehicle. I gave them our radio frequencies and the call signs of supporting units.

I didn't let Doc Pleasant speak. I gave the corpsman's brief for him: "Push water. As much fluid as you can manage."

I asked for questions, then passed it to Sergeant Gomez before going to my vehicle, settling in my seat, and loading my radios with frequencies and crypto.

I heard a snore. It was Dodge, asleep in the backseat. He'd missed the brief.

Doc Pleasant slid into the seat next to Dodge and punched him in the shoulder. "Dodge, wake the fuck up."

Dodge came to with a snort. "I am awake. Awake."

Pleasant sighed. "You even know what the fuck we're doing?"

"Of course. We are going to some place in the desert where I will speak in Arabic to some Iraqi dudes. You gentlemen will move barrels full of bad shit while sweating and cursing. Everybody will be pissed off, all day." He closed his eyes, crossed his arms, and went back to sleep.

I let him. He had the mission about right.

The convoy rolled through the gate and fell into line. Our route took us through Fallujah. We cleared the city and took the northbound ramp at the cloverleaf. The interchange spat us out onto an empty, four-lane highway, which by some strange miracle was well lit by functional streetlights. The highway took us north into the desert.

No other convoys or civilian traffic crowded the road, so we used both lanes. We straddled the white line and stayed as far from the curb as possible.

Four times, Gomez halted the convoy to investigate suspicious piles of dirt or trash. We did our full fives and twenty-fives each time. We varied our speed and spacing. We made ourselves a hard target.

Even with all the time spent on precautions and security halts, we reached the prearranged rendezvous point before dawn. A grid coordinate, given by the State Department's Provincial

Reconstruction Office in Ramadi, took us to a dirt track leading northwest into the waste. We halted there, set the vehicles in a protective formation fifty meters off the road, and waited for the State Department to show.

Six hours passed.

The sun came up and the temperature climbed. The skin of our Humvees grew too hot to touch with bare hands. Civilian traffic filled the highway, with trucks hauling fuel south, beat-up bongo trucks taking piles of scavenged junk toward the city markets, and taxis with prying eyes rolling by our static and vulnerable perimeter. The rendezvous point placed us near a known intersection. Anyone with a mortar tube and a few airburst rounds could easily have judged the distance. The longer we stayed, the more nervous I became.

Gomez grew worried, as well. She never stood still. She moved around the perimeter constantly and snapped at Marines when they looked less than alert.

I sat by my radios and monitored the nets, but nothing came through on the frequencies given to us by the State Department. Meanwhile, the company net crackled with demands from the operation center that we stay put and wait.

At first, in the darkness, Cobb's easy voice came through the handset. When Wong replaced him on watch as the sun came up, I could hear how he grinned, amused by my frustration. I could even hear the company staff distracting him as they came through the operations center for morning coffee.

I made a nuisance of myself, asking for an update every five minutes. Eventually, Major Leighton's voice came through the handset.

"This is Hellbox-*Six*," he barked, all emphasis on the last syllable, the number that identified him as the commander. I could imagine how he'd snatched the radio away from Wong. "Remain in place. Regiment confirms supporting elements en route. Make no further requests to displace from your current position. Over."

I'd been told, insofar as radio etiquette allowed, to shut up and wait. I hung the handset on its hook, left Dodge and Doc Pleasant to watch the vehicle, and walked the perimeter.

I tried to look calm, relaxed, and unaffected. How would a guy like Cobb handle this? My Marines, in turrets or behind armored doors, acknowledged me with sweaty nods and hard stares. I tried to smile and nod back, the unwilling muscles in my cheeks twisting the gesture into something unnatural, grotesque.

The Marines took turns sealing themselves inside their vehicles to fill empty water bottles with urine. Regiment had directed no public urination as a perceived concession to Islamic culture. I checked the growing pile of urine bottles in the middle of the perimeter for signs of color. It heartened me to see that the Marines were at least hydrated. The liters and liters of piss showed not a hint of orange.

Still, I imagined how the Marines would look in the afternoon heat, in full chemical masks and suits, and how quickly they'd lose it all.

I went back to my vehicle, sat by the radios, and listened to Doc Pleasant and Dodge argue about music. Doc Pleasant lounged in his seat and let his feet dangle out the open door. His medical bag sat well out of reach. Mud caked the zippers. He hadn't opened it in a week.

"C-Murder is the real deal," he said, pushing the toe of his boot around in the dirt. "A true criminal."

"C-Murder is a dirty south poser, Lester," Dodge replied. "Those No Limit guys talk only of cars and girls. Concerned with their money, unlike the legit gangsters on the West Coast."

"You're half-right. But C-Murder also said, 'Nigga owe me some money. Bitch, I want it in blood.' And he meant it."

Dodge considered this. "C-Murder really said that?"

"He did. And he's a murderer. Convicted, I mean. Killed some dudes up there in New Orleans."

Dodge chuckled. "Sounds like Iraq. Blood as important as money."

I joined the conversation. "You're from Louisiana, aren't you, Doc?"

He looked out at the horizon and nodded. "Yes, sir."

"Close to New Orleans?"

"No, sir. Not really. South and west. Cajun country."

"Go to the city much?" I asked.

"Only to get fucked-up." He twitched and swatted at the fly on his forehead. "New Orleans will get you. Fucked. *Up*." He grinned, spacey and satisfied, bloodshot eyes shut just a beat too long.

I walked over and tapped his knee. "Why don't you take a walk, Doc." I smiled. "Walk the perimeter. Make sure everyone keeps pushing water."

He opened his eyes and stared at me for a moment.

"Give it a shot." I pretended not to notice his defiance. "Stretch your legs."

He stood and shouldered his medical bag, brushing subtly against me as he walked away.

I went back to my seat and, in the rearview, saw Dodge reading his book. I interrupted, "How's he doing lately? Doc, I mean."

Dodge looked up. "Why are you asking me, *Mulasim*?"

"I get it. You're not *friends*. But you do talk a lot. So . . . how's he doing?"

"I should say that Lester is doing nearly as well as you, *Mulasim*." Dodge turned the page.

Just then, Zahn yelled something from across the perimeter, something about vehicles approaching. I ran over to get the report.

I saw the dust cloud first, about a mile down the highway. Four armored Suburbans emerging from the haze followed by two older Mercedes flatbed trucks. They sped down the center line in a tight knot. Flares flew from the back windows of the Suburbans at regular intervals, whether civilian vehicles blocked their path or not. The lead escort driver made an effort to intimidate. He changed course a few times and charged down bongo trucks and taxis that didn't get far enough off the road.

"Security contractors?" Zahn asked.

"Looks that way," I said. "That's how State travels from what I understand."

I jogged back to my radios thinking maybe the Suburbans would come up on the net to identify themselves, but the net gave nothing but a soft hiss. I called out for Gomez, and she jogged a few paces toward me to stand just within earshot. "That's the friendly element we've been waiting for," I said. "They're not up on the net, but let them approach."

She frowned and jogged back to the perimeter. "Listen up!" she yelled. "*No* escalation of force on these fucking Suburbans. Hear me? Friendlies!"

Even with the warning from Gomez, every Marine winced as the Suburbans came charging through our cordon at high speed. They turned down the dirt road and, with the Iraqi trucks following, came to a halt twenty meters from us. They kept their engines running.

The Suburbans' doors flew open and men in khaki pants and black polo shirts jumped out. They brandished expensive-looking assault rifles and submachine guns bristling with optics and rail-mounted flashlights. They looked over their sights through new

Oakley sunglasses. They didn't wear helmets, but some of them wore hats. One guy had his hair cropped into a tight Mohawk. They moved like they'd learned it from the movies, sweeping their muzzles around the desert, aiming at nothing in particular but scowling with suspicion.

The contractors relaxed one at a time and rose up from their crouched poses like early man. A guy with a sidearm strapped to his thigh who looked like he was in charge walked over to me. An earpiece ran down through his beard, into the checkered head scarf he wore around his neck. It connected to a radio strapped to his comfortable-looking body armor.

"Dude, you the guy?" he asked in a Southern California lilt.

"I think so."

"Marine lieutenant? We're supposed to meet you here? I'm Doug. Let's go meet the brass buttons."

"What?"

"The brass buttons, dude. You know? The client? State Department guy?"

Doug turned and started back toward his Suburban. I stood there for a moment, then awkwardly chased after him. I called over my shoulder to Gomez, "Get them ready to move."

She nodded and set the Marines to work breaking down the perimeter.

Doug led me to the second Suburban in line and opened the backseat, driver-side door. "Mr. Moss? I've got the guy here."

I felt the ice-cold air-conditioning from three feet away. It poured from the vehicle, over my helmet, and settled on the back of my neck. Despite my growing frustration with everything this Suburban represented, I couldn't help but love the sensation of cold, first-world air.

My eyes adjusted to the dark interior and I saw a tiny,

twentysomething kid with a pleasant smile. Blond hair peeked out from under his big helmet. He wore dress slacks, tucked sloppily into spotless combat boots, and a blue blazer under his body armor. I noticed the decorative brass buttons on the cuff and the binder open on his lap.

"Hi. I'm Mr. Moss," he said in an upper-class Texas accent, without the slightest hesitation in bestowing on himself the honorific *mister*, despite his youth. He reached out to shake my hand, but made no move to get out of the vehicle or even unbuckle his seat belt.

"Lieutenant Donovan." I shook, my gloved hand soaked through with sweat.

Mr. Moss wiped his palm on his trousers. "Great. Here's how this'll work. You'll follow us to the pool. Your Marines will get the barrels onto these trucks, and our Iraqi friend will have the chemicals driven to his compound. Questions?" He grinned.

"Wait. Iraqis? And what's this about a pool?"

"Right. We're losing daylight. And air-conditioning, too. Let's get a move on." He reached out and pulled his door shut.

Doug tapped me on the shoulder. "We'll lead you there. It's not far."

Before I could ask why they were so late, why they hadn't contacted us on the radio, or who the hell he was, Doug had turned and set out for the front seat of his Suburban.

I went back to where Gomez and Zahn had our vehicles assembled in the original order of march. They leaned against the hood of my Humvee, waiting.

"What's the plan, sir?" Gomez asked.

"We follow them." I shrugged.

"Those Blackwater assholes give you their radio freq?" she asked.

Zahn jumped in. "Wouldn't matter anyway. They can't hear you over the sound of how awesome they are." He elbowed her and smiled.

"No freqs," I said. "They didn't seem interested."

Zahn laughed. "No shit, sir. I asked one of those assholes how he got his job, and the guy said he was working as a bouncer in San Diego. Some British guy slipped him a card. I don't think they even know how to use those MP5s. Fucking playtime for these guys."

"Then let's get it done quick," I said.

The driver of the lead Suburban honked his horn.

"Fuck this," Gomez huffed. "Let's just follow them."

We set out along the bumpy dirt road, and Dodge spoke to me from the backseat. "Did they tell you who is driving those trucks, *Mulasim*? Those Iraqi guys?"

"No. Why?"

"Ansar al-Sunna. I am certain of it."

"How do you know?" I set my hand against the dash and braced myself against the bumps while turning to face Dodge.

"You do know that this is not my first profession, *Mulasim*? I used to make business and sell to people around here. Those Iraqi gentlemen are Ansar al-Sunna."

I nodded. "I'll bring that up to the State Department guy. Thanks."

"Sure man." Dodge waved his hand. "They will probably get all those barrels anyway. Ansar al-Sunna runs this place."

The dirt road curved around a low bluff, and a walled subdivision, like something out of the American Southwest complete with stucco tract housing and culs-de-sac, appeared in the windshield. I blinked twice to make sure I wasn't imagining it.

"Well, that's different," Zahn muttered, ending our stunned, collective silence.

I turned back to Dodge for his opinion, and he shrugged. "The scientists who once worked on Saddam's gas lived here. That is why it is hidden far off the highway, and with only a dirt road."

The details of the subdivision became clear. I took note of the abandoned guard shack at the entrance, and the empty houses, all with smashed windows and missing doors. Looters had found the place long ago and had left nothing of value behind. Still, as we hit the bump that took us from the dirt track onto the smooth asphalt of the wide street, I couldn't help feeling as if I were on my way to see a friend in Alabama. The sensation deepened when the Suburbans ahead of us wagon-wheeled into a loose perimeter at the end of a cul-de-sac and the Iraqi trucks parked in adjacent driveways.

Gomez came up on the net and told the convoy to halt. We did our fives and twenty-fives, complete with the odd step of peeking through the broken tract-house windows for possible snipers, while the security contractors watched half-curious and half-amused. I jumped out and told Zahn to follow me.

Doug met us halfway. "The barrels are in the empty swimming pool behind this house. Follow me."

"Wait," I said. "What's all this about a swimming pool? We were told to expect an open pit."

Doug shrugged and turned for the nearest driveway. We followed him until he stopped at a side gate. "My contract won't let me go any farther." He assumed a tactical stance with his submachine gun as Zahn and I walked by, as though he planned to make up for this contractual inability to follow us by bravely guarding the entrance to the backyard.

The gate opened to a stone walkway running alongside the American-style house, spurring the sensation that Zahn and I were the first to arrive at a birthday pool party. Again, I tried to shake off the feeling of familiarity and remind myself that I was in a war.

The reminder became unnecessary a moment later. We turned a corner into the pool area, and the smell of chemicals punched us in the face. We coughed and winced. Thick tears ran down my face, immediately distinguishable from the plentiful sweat already there.

Zahn choked. "Fuck, sir. Fu—Christ—mother*fuck*," He turned around and went to his knees, unable to go any closer.

"Stay here." I coughed.

I covered my nose and mouth with my Nomex hood and shuffled to the edge. Peering gingerly over, I saw about a dozen barrels, once painted white but now slowly turning an oxidized-red shade. A mysterious white powder had eaten holes in the steel, seeped free, and coated the bottom of the pool in a fine talc. I heard chemicals reacting with each other from the heat of the afternoon sun as a catalyst. White powder ate into pink pellets and spat out green, oozing crystals. A shimmer hung over the pool, unnatural and thick. It attacked my eyes.

I staggered away from the edge and found Zahn on his knees, desperately trying to get his breath. I dragged him to his feet by the fabric of his flight suit, coaxed him down the stone walkway, past Doug, and guided him to a seat on the bumper of our vehicle. The steady flow of tears rolled over rising welts on his cheeks.

I called for Doc Pleasant, who scampered over without his bag, mouth agape.

"Doc, wash out his eyes. Try to . . . try something."

Doc nodded and reached for his bag, cursed, and ran back to get it.

Through my clouded vision, I could see the Marines on security standing against a backdrop of houses not dissimilar from the ones in which they might have grown up, and they appeared to me as the children they had been just a few years earlier. I pictured them passing footballs in the street. Walking up to front doors wearing tuxedos, carrying flowers for their homecoming dates. I even let myself picture the impossibility of Gomez coming to the door in a dress, accepting her corsage.

I blinked the tears free, and they were Marines again, with eyes wide and jaws slack at the sight of the solid and impervious Zahn, broken by the mere smell of the chemicals in that backyard pool.

Gomez ran over, fell to her knees in front of Zahn, and looked up into his face. "What's up, buddy?" she pleaded. "You good?" She tried to touch his face, but Zahn batted her hand away.

"Get *back*," he wheezed. "Further back, damn it. In case the wind shifts."

She nodded. "Walter. Walter. Look at me. Good. Okay, now. Lean back. Let Doc wash out your eyes." She turned to face me. "Sir—"

"Yeah. Get them back,"

"Sir. Your *face*."

I touched my face and felt the rising blisters. "Just get them back."

I found Dodge standing behind Gomez. "Dodge. With me."

He followed me toward the Suburbans staged at the end of the cul-de-sac, whispering, "*Mulasim*, you cannot do this."

"The State Department might have the local Iraqis here," I said. "I'll need you to talk to them."

"*Mulasim.*"

"I heard you."

Doug, having apparently surrendered his position at the gate, smiled and asked, "Ready to get going, dude?"

"No. I need to talk to Mr. Moss."

"Sure thing."

We followed him back to the Suburban. He opened the door,

and again cold air spilled out, this time pooling around my boots, thick as slush.

Again, Mr. Moss made no move to get out. "So, how long you think this will take?" He looked at his binder, then his watch.

"Mr. Moss, this is not the situation we were briefed to expect. We are not equipped for this."

He put on his sunglasses. "Well, that's disappointing."

"Listen. My Marines will not go into that pool, even with chemical suits and masks. Those are not sealed drums. We cannot properly decontaminate in these conditions."

Mr. Moss laughed. "Well then, that's more than disappointing. It means you've wasted my time. And you've endangered our lives by making us travel these highways. There will be a conversation with the colonel about this."

"Do what you have to, kid."

"I'll have to mention you by name. Lieutenant . . . what is it now?"

"Go fuck yourself." A surprising rage grew inside me. I worked to put it away.

Doug whistled and stepped aside.

Dodge took a step closer and put his shoulder into my back.

Mr. Moss closed his binder. "Okay, Lieutenant Go-Fuck-Yourself. Why do you think I agreed to come out here? Why do you think the Provincial Reconstruction Office took an interest?"

"Honestly, I don't care."

"Because this is an opportunity to win the war, just a little. To show the Iraqis that we are here to help. To show them what Americans are all about. Hard work." He pointed to the Iraqi trucks and the men squatting impatiently in the dirt by the tailgates. "These gentlemen will be offended. Worse, our Iraqi friends will be insulted that they're not getting these recovered barrels today, as promised."

Dodge snorted and laughed under his breath.

"Who is this?" Mr. Moss demanded.

"He's my terp. And he tells me that your Iraqi friends are Ansar al-Sunna."

Mr. Moss finally exploded. "How the fuck would he know that?" he yelled.

"I live here," Dodge replied, before suddenly, and conspicuously, taking the weight of his shoulder out of my back and stepping away. Something had spooked him, but with Mr. Moss's eyes locked on me I didn't have time to investigate why.

"So that's it?" Mr. Moss asked.

"Yes. That's it."

Mr. Moss yelled out for his man. "Doug? Bring Muhammad over here." He pulled his door shut and sealed himself inside the cold, armored cocoon without another word.

"Dodge, let's . . ." I turned around and found he'd already started back toward our Humvee, with the Nomex hood pulled over his face and sunglasses on to hide his eyes. He looked down and steered a wide course to avoid Doug and the young, well-dressed Iraqi man he was escorting toward the Suburban.

As I jogged to catch up, Doug called out to me, "Not winning the war today, dude?"

"Not today."

"Good deal." He laughed. "Means I'll get a new contract. Get to pay off the beach house thirty years early."

I started to look away, but something made me stop. Something about the young Iraqi man, Muhammad, walking with Doug. His familiar features. The way he squinted with interest and confusion at Dodge's back. He noticed me and our eyes met.

He nodded gravely and I nodded back, unsure why. The Suburban door opened again, and I watched as he entered into an animated discussion with Mr. Moss.

Dodge was already in his seat and eager to leave when I made it back to the Humvee. Zahn sat in the driver's seat with his helmet off and a bottle of water between his knees, looking like he'd been beaten up. Gomez stood by his open door with her hand on his knee.

"Sir?" she asked almost sheepishly.

"It's no good. We're leaving."

She cracked half a grin, not the full smile she reserved for Zahn. "For real, sir?"

"Yes. We're Oscar Mike in three minutes."

She turned and ran, screaming, "Button up! Vehicle commanders, get your reports ready!"

I settled into my seat and examined Zahn. The blisters had receded on his cheeks under a sheen of ointment, and his eyes had begun to dry out. "You good to drive?"

"I am, sir. But, you . . . Sir, you need to look at yourself."

Right then, and for the first time since I'd stumbled away from the pool, I felt the pain. As if hungry creatures, microscopic and clawed, had filled expanding cracks in the skin around my eyes and were digging their way into my sinuses. I winced and checked my face in the rearview mirror. Weeping blisters grew in concentric rings around my eyes. Horrifyingly symmetrical and moving relentlessly south.

Doc Pleasant leaned over my seat with a tin of salve. He'd had to dump the contents of his medical bag in the backseat to find it. "Rub this under your eyes, sir."

I did as he told me, and the relief made me gasp involuntarily. I closed my eyes, leaned my head back, and spread the ointment with quivering fingers. The stuff of luxury. My face felt suddenly cold, even in the stifling Humvee. I took deep breaths and sighed.

When I opened my eyes, both Doc Pleasant and Zahn were smiling at me.

"Good job, sir." Zahn reached out his gloved hand and slapped my knee.

Gomez came up on the radio. "All vics. Oscar Mike."

I frowned at Zahn. "Just go."

Zahn steered us out of the subdivision, back into the ruts and pits of the dirt road. Dodge pulled down his hood, took off his sunglasses, and showed his face, pale and dry.

"You good, Dodge?" I asked.

"About as well as you, *Mulasim*." He swallowed hard like he might vomit.

From: Road Repair Platoon Commander, Engineer Support Company
To: Hospitalman Lester Pleasant

You are counseled on this date regarding the following deficiencies:

Failure to adequately prepare for missions.

Failure to arrive on time for mission briefs.

Unprofessional personal appearance.

Unprofessional behavior toward superiors.

You are directed to take immediate corrective action. Assistance is available through your chain of command. Failure to take corrective action will result in adverse judicial or administrative action, including but not limited to administrative separation.

OVERPRESSURE

Christmas at home had a strange feel to it, and I wasn't expecting that. These last few years, since I messed up things with the relatives, it's been just Dad and me eating takeout for Christmas dinner, exchanging a gift or two, and watching college football. And that was good enough.

But this year, after I'd left Lizzy's place and driven home, I felt like a stranger in the old house. Like I'd violated some trust by leaving him alone down there and now the house had it in for me.

The floorboards groaned when I walked down the hallway with the framed pictures of my grandmother, my dad, all my aunts, uncles, and cousins. They smiled at me from the walls, and the groans started to feel like them talking. Asking me who I thought I was, leaving him down here without someone watching. You really think you can keep things straight out there with that punk-rock girl and her friends?

It seemed like wherever my dad went, the house leaned to follow him. When he walked out to the porch and let the screen door bounce shut, I felt the house tilt in his direction and the awnings settle over him like palmettos. When he walked into the dining room, my grandmother's crystal china in the old hutch rattled off a tune. More than once, I felt him standing outside my bedroom door thinking about whether to knock.

I gave him a pocketknife on Christmas morning, and he handed me a hundred dollars.

"Thought you might need cash, right now. For a lease, or things like that."

"Thanks for this, but I'm still not sure if the New Orleans thing is permanent. I'll probably see you in a few days."

That was Christmas morning. It's New Year's Eve now, and I haven't called him since I drove away with my truck all loaded up.

I stashed all my stuff at Landry's, so Lizzy wouldn't see it. I don't want her getting spooked by the sight of my things, ready to move in some place, and have her start wondering if I'm reading too much into this. Her friends are all back in town, and I'm not sure how much she needs my company anymore.

But then Lizzy invited me over to her house in the middle of the day, and now, after we've fooled around a bunch, she's asking me to come out with her and her friends to watch the fireworks. "Are you sure you won't go? Do you worry about my friends? Because you shouldn't. They really like you."

She rubs up against me under the sheets. Like she feels bad for mentioning Sebastian. Like she thinks rubbing on me that way will fix it. It won't, but I don't mind so much.

"I'd really rather not. I'm still pretty tired from work, plus it'll be crowded down there on the levee. Not sure I'm in the mood for all that."

She sighs, disappointed. "Okay . . ."

"Sorry," I whisper.

And the air in my nostrils gets hot. It's the shame burning me up. Here I am, keeping this girl from what she wants. Keeping her from seeing her friends. And I won't even tell her why. Won't tell her the truth, anyway.

She should just go by herself. I open my mouth to tell her so, but stop. I'm selfish. I want more of this. I like her chest brushing up against me. Her lacy bra scratching my side each time she takes a long, slow breath. I could do this forever.

But outside the knuckleheads have already started in with their fireworks. The noise of it boils up from everywhere. Cracks and whistles in flurries all across the neighborhood. Black Cats and bottle rockets cooking off in bursts.

It sounds like the machine-gun range, when we would park the two Humvees up on the berm so the gunners could practice. They didn't let me shoot or nothing. I just stood off to the side with my medical bag in case someone got burned by hot brass flying out the guns.

Zahn ran that show. He'd walk around behind the Humvees during the shoot, and when the gunners squeezed off a burst he thought was too long, or when both guns fired at the same time, he'd yell, "Talking guns! Talking guns, damn it!"

Later, out on the road, he explained what he meant by that: "Making sure they only fire one gun at a time. Saves the barrels. A short burst, twelve to fifteen rounds. Then you let the barrel rest. The other gun takes over, then back and forth. Sustained fire without stripping the rifling or overheating the weapon."

Back when he used to talk crisp and clear. Before the knock he took to the head slowed him down.

The fireworks outside get thicker, more intense. It's feeding on itself, this amateur hour before the big show, and starting to sound less like a controlled machine-gun range, and more like something worse.

But it's just parents in folding chairs, I tell myself. Letting their kids go crazy with the cheap fireworks that their dad drove over the parish line to get. Teenagers trying to show their girlfriends how they're brave. Holding on a little too long after they light the fuse. Laughing while the girls run away angry.

A bottle rocket flies by Lizzy's bedroom window. A bright, white flash like an airburst mortar. No pretty lights, nothing. All smoke and noise. Who could enjoy this?

Lizzy, I guess. She sits up and squeals. All giggles, this girl. Excited for the fireworks in a way that I must've been as a kid but don't remember anymore. Her eyes get round and she waves me over to the window to see. Her smile. It's different than normal. She can't control it. I look at her lacy, white bra while she's distracted and want it back up against me. So I shimmy over to the windowsill with my legs under the covers.

I can't see anything. Just blue smoke drifting down the street from over the top of the neighbor's roof and from around the blind corners at the intersection. I'm glad I can't smell it, yet. That sulfur smell, empty as death. A string of Black Cats cooks off somewhere and Lizzy's face lights up again. She smiles and tackles me, squirming like a goddamn puppy.

Another bottle rocket screams down the street, right past the window, and Lizzy cranes her neck again to look. She doesn't see me wince, and I'm glad for that.

We cuddle for a few minutes more, with me keeping my hands outside her little pajama pants. Staying a few inches back from her so she can't feel my heart pounding. Her hair dangles in my face and I try to bury myself in it, thinking the smell will calm me down. So clean, her hair. Like it's never had a single drop of sweat roll through it. I breathe it deep, and my heart slows a bit. Things get comfortable. We start spooning and I wonder if maybe she'll just fall asleep. She must be tired from working all last night. If Lizzy goes to sleep for an hour or two, I can put on her nice headphones and turn up the music real loud. I can wait it out while all the yahoos finish blowing shit up. Then maybe go out after the fireworks are done, just after midnight and in time for all the romantic New Year's Eve shit.

But she sighs. "You sure you don't want to go meet my friends down by the river?"

It's not really a question, I know.

I pull her closer. "Just a little while longer."

My breath pushes a blond curl down her cheek. She pushes it back behind her ear. Right into my face. Right where I can smell it.

She rolls over to look at me. "Please. Please, Les?" She smiles at me sweet, and there's nothing I can say. Nothing at all. I'll do anything she wants. Anything to keep her smiling.

"All right. The fireworks just for a bit? Then maybe that party Landry told me about?"

"Yes. Fireworks, just for a bit."

We take her car down Elysian Fields. The traffic thins out as we pass Rampart. Must be everyone is already up on the levee, what with only a few minutes left before they start the big show. Lizzy finds an illegal parking place and jumps out before I can argue with her.

I chase her down through the French Quarter, past the Old Mint. It seems like the whole city is gathering up on the levee. Families carry chairs and blankets to lay out on the grass between the railroad tracks and the walking path. Young people carry open twelve-packs of beer under their arms and hand out cans to friends as they pass. Lizzy takes me by the hand and pulls me through the throng. She's smiling. So excited.

With the sun down, it finally feels like winter. Might even drop below freezing tonight.

Still, my palms sweat and I keep losing my grip on Lizzy's hand. She slips away into the crowd and I hustle to keep up. I already feel panicked, but Lizzy doesn't seem to notice.

When I catch her, she smiles and kisses me on the cheek. "Come on! It's almost time!"

We cross the tracks onto the levee and find Lizzy's friends with their spot all staked out, blankets weighed down by bags of fireworks and cases of cheap beer. I see Sebastian first, lighting a sparkler, then opening a beer. He's tall and skinny, wearing tight black jeans to match his hair. Lizzy runs over and gives him a hug. He holds the sparkler way over his head and puts the other arm around her. I walk up from behind, through the nasty sparkler smoke.

Sebastian sees me and keeps his arm around Lizzy a second or two longer than I appreciate. Then he frees his arm and shakes my hand. "Hey, man. Glad you came down."

"Yeah," I say, "wouldn't miss it."

A couple of Lizzy's friends from the art program whose names I can't remember, the redhead with the big fish tattoo down her arm and the fat brunette with the crew cut, fumble through their arsenal of fireworks. Even from a distance I can tell that they're hammered drunk. They find what they're looking for and clap.

"I think they're about to start," Sebastian says to Lizzy. "They've got the barge in place. Should be any second."

A family is on a blanket next to the drunk girls. Three little kids. The drunk girls light the fuse anyway. One of those whizzing, flash-bang numbers. It cracks into the air over the family, throwing sparks. The nasty thing spins, right over our heads, wailing like crazy, and the little kids duck under their dad's arms.

"Hey!" I snap, taking a step at the drunk girls. "What the fuck!"

They look at me baffled. Everywhere, the smoke from their idiot fireworks reeking like a sulfur pit. Like hell.

"Look what you're doing! Fucking kids right here! Dumb fucking *assholes*!"

I move toward them as the first big fireworks kick off from the barge. The show starts with red starbursts just above the water, meaning to impress. I see the flash, feel the concussive thump in my chest, and hear the crack of the report in a tight sequence. Just how I remember it—

When it hit, I was looking at Zahn in the rearview, not out at the road like I should've been. He was looking at me because of the dumb question I'd asked him. Then I felt the kick, the overpressure, coming in through the gunner's hatch.

Not until the vehicle stopped rolling did I hear Lieutenant Donovan telling everyone to stay strapped in for a second, just to be sure we weren't still moving. Then I heard the machine gun rounds cracking overhead. A complex attack. A prestaged ambush. First they hit you with the bomb, then they engage with small arms while you try to get out.

The Humvee was already on fire. Smoke poured in from the engine compartment, forward of the armor plates. I heard loose machine-gun rounds falling out from the wrecked turret where the gunner had been standing, ready to cook off and bounce steel frag all over the crew compartment. We couldn't stay in the truck. I went to work on my seat belt.

Dodge got himself free before I did. "Lester man, come on. Out this way." He grabbed me by the arm and pulled me toward his door.

Wasn't until we were outside that I thought about the gunner. Where the fuck did he *go*? Did the Humvee crush him after the blast threw him out? And what about Zahn? Was he dead?

Lieutenant Donovan grabbed me by the shoulder and pushed me down into a ditch. He'd pulled Zahn out by the straps on his flak jacket. "Take him. He's out cold. Take him."

I nodded as Lieutenant Donovan ran off, talking calmly to Gomez on his radio. Then I was in a ditch, Sergeant Zahn's head in my lap while the firefight grew around us. I unbuckled Zahn's helmet and felt around inside for blood. I smelled the smoke in his hair and watched him open his eyes.

I smell the smoke in Lizzy's hair as she puts her shoulder into me and pushes me away from her friends. She yells at me over the sound of the fireworks, flashing and thumping in the sky all around. Faster and faster.

"Stop it, Les. You're screaming. *Stop* it!"

Sebastian's here, too, standing between me and the drunk girls. They're all looking at me, sneering.

I look down at Lizzy, and her smile is gone. I've ruined it for her.

"I'm sorry." I turn and walk off into the French Quarter, looking for a bar she'd never go to, the smell of her hair still with me.

Crazy-man Lester. This is Dodge. Remember me? Actually, my name is Fadi now. I had to change this due to certain dangers. Truly, it has been a long time, and I did not say good-bye to you when I left. For this I am very sorry. Things became dangerous for me after Ramadi. Many people would have soon known me, and I had to leave quickly.

I am in Tunisia, now. Things are difficult here, as well, and so I want to come to America. Can you help me? The American government needs a letter saying that I worked for the marines in Iraq. When the telephones work again, I will find a way to contact you, if you can give me a number to dial.

THE TRIGGERMEN

I send this note to Lester and turn off my computer monitor. I am embarrassed, but it must be done. We need contacts in America, and I am the only one in the flat who can achieve this. The only one with names.

Ben Ali is working to block access to the Internet, and our methods to defeat his firewalls work only in short bursts. Messages must be short. It is still New Year's Eve in America, and Lester needs to be out kissing girls, I should think. I might not hear from him for some time.

Here in Tunisia, there have been girls to kiss but neither celebrations nor music. Only serious kisses that carry our fears. After that first protest in the square, those first real bullets, and the bodies left in the streets, my flatmates finally came to understand. And now I think I like them better. Before the first protest, they wanted only an excuse to party. But when the police showed them death, they did not run and quit as I had expected. They grew committed.

Now they are making plans for the next protest and hosting this new committee of university students in our flat. They make calls to people in France and America using satellite phones stolen from the police. They make hacker friends across the sea who show us the tricks to defeat Ben Ali's shuttering of the Internet.

And they talk more and more about sending me to speak in English for the cameras. They do not even ask me. They just say this. A weapon, they say to each other. His polished English is a weapon. We must use him.

I wonder if Hani would laugh at this. Kateb the weapon. Much truth in that.

My brother, Muhammad, dropped me at the lake in the morning, while Hani, Mundhir, Haji Fasil, and Abu Abdul were only just stirring. After my brother had gone, I produced the stack of dinar I'd managed to hide in my trousers and took Hani behind the farmhouse.

"Hani, look at this money. My father gave this to me last night. We can leave now, Hani."

Hani's eyes grew wide and he began to count. "At least half must go to Haji Fasil," he mumbled. Then he shook his head unhappily. "But it is not dollars. We need dollars if we are to cross into Jordan or Syria. Dinar will not help us."

"We can find a way to change them to dollars along the way," I said, trying not to sound desperate.

"But what better place will we find than this for changing money? Pederson is coming back today. You can ask him for help with this, yes? Maybe at Government Center in Ramadi they would have dollars for us?"

I grew cold. It began on my palms, spread up my arms and down my legs. "Pederson is coming back today?"

"Yes. Of course," Hani said without concern. "He came back here yesterday, after you had left with your father and brother. He said he would be using our beach cabana to meet with soldiers of the new army and others. Merchants and sheikhs. Like a *shura*, I think."

"When?" I grabbed him by the shoulders as I asked this.

"Very soon. Morning, he said. Why do you ask?" Hani furrowed his brow, puzzled.

I left him and ran around to the front of the farmhouse, where I found Haji Fasil smoking and drinking tea.

"Haji," I began, out of breath. "You and Abu Abdul must leave."

"Why?" he asked, as calmly as Hani but not so stupid. "Are your brother and father on their way to kill us?"

"No, but the Americans are coming back today . . ."

"Yes, I know. Men passed by here late last night. I saw them planting the bombs, Kateb."

"Where?!"

"On the highway. Two bombs. One north and one south. I think they plan to trap the Americans with the bombs, and then attack with bullets and rockets from across the desert." Haji waved his hand about the air, as if we were discussing a football strategy. "I saw the men early this morning. Placing their machine guns in the dark. Hiding their cars in the desert. Preparing for a quick escape, if God wills it."

I became angry with him for sitting so calmly, for smoking his cigarette and drinking his tea. "Then why do you stay? Run away! Go to Ramadi or Fallujah and come back when it is safe."

"Because, Kateb," he sighed, "if we are not here, the Americans will know that there is a trap. They will pass quickly, and men like your father will be disappointed that they could not kill them as planned. They will blame me, Kateb. And finally they will kill me." He lit another cigarette. "No. No, you see, the thing to do is stay. Let these things happen as God wills and try to survive the bullets when they come. Let some Americans die if they must, let them kill your brother and his people if they can, and we live until tomorrow, Kateb."

In that moment, as Haji Fasil finished his tea, I heard the American engines. Pederson and his men were coming from the north. I went to the dirt path stemming off the highway and saw them in their Humvees, getting closer. I wondered where the bombs were hidden.

"Hmm. A little early," Haji Fasil considered as he stepped back to his spot in the shade.

I watched Hani venture out to wave and greet them, with not the slightest notion of the danger. Senseless as a rock, Hani.

"Where are Mundhir and Abu Abdul?" I asked Haji Fasil.

"Fishing." He sat with his back against the wall of his farmhouse, putting out his cigarette. "They will be safe on the water, God willing."

Pederson's marines parked their Humvees and searched around for bombs and dangers, as usual. But with far less concern than the day we first met. They had grown to trust us. Grown to enjoy Tourist Town in a way close to how Hani had intended.

Pederson came walking toward me on a direct line. "We missed you when we came back yesterday, Kateb." He shook my hand, smiling behind his helmet and sunglasses. "We had an Iraqi Army terp with us, but he wasn't as good as you."

I swallowed. "Of course. I was required to make a quick trip yesterday afternoon. I am back now, however."

"Glad to see it, glad to see it." Pederson motioned for me to walk with him to the fire pit. "So, today we have a little sit-down with your neighbors to see if we can make things safer around here. I appreciate you helping with that."

I heard more engines. This time from the south. Rough engines, without good American parts. It was the new Iraqi Army coming to talk.

Pederson sat down on a log, looked up, and smiled. "Good deal. Right on time."

I could feel the bombs that would kill them in their flimsy pickup trucks. Curbstones, which I had seen the day before in my father's backyard factory, waiting for them with artillery shells hidden inside.

"Tell them to stop," I heard myself say.

"What?"

"Tell them there is a bomb on the road, but do not cry out or become excited. There are people watching us."

He calmly nodded his head. Knowing. He put the radio to his lips. "Break. Break. This is Actual. We have intel on an imminent ambush. Raise that adviser team and tell them to halt. Push security west, over."

Then he sat still and looked at me, sweating and breathing hard but hiding his fear admirably.

"One bomb to the north for you. And a bomb to the south for the jundis."

"And then what, Kateb?"

"Bullets. From the desert."

He nodded, like this was all no problem. "Okay, then."

I looked down at my feet and shivered.

"You're doing the right thing here. We can handle this for you."

I believed him. As he stood and walked away to prepare his men to fight, I believed in the American with such confidence. Because he liked me. And I thought, for those few minutes only, that we could all escape. That when the fight was over, the Americans would take us somewhere safe.

Even when the bombs inside the curbstones exploded, one and then the other, while I dropped into the sand to protect my face, I believed for a few minutes more. Hiding behind the fallen tree and listening to the bullets snap over my head, I believed that everyone was going to live until the next day. Mundhir and Abu Abdul, safe on the water, would find a place to go and fish every day. Hani and Haji Fasil, pulled to the ground for cover by some dedicated marine, would be kept safe by American courage until they could go to Ramadi and open their own shop in the Grand Souk. Even when the weight of a knee fell into my back and pushed me deeper into the sand, I believed. Not until I felt the American tightening plastic cuffs onto my wrists did I begin to doubt.

They pulled me to my feet and I understood, for the first time, how good my father and brother had become at their war. The marines gave me a tour as they hauled me toward their Humvees.

I saw the Iraqi army truck to the south, smoking and ruined, with the dead pieces of men all around it.

I saw Haji Fasil's limp figure in a pile near the farmhouse, a jagged hole in his forehead and a splay of blood and gore against the wall behind him. Who had fired the bullet that killed him? An American? A *jundi*? My brother? Who could say?

I saw Hani scrambling to get away from the marines who wanted to cuff him like they had cuffed me. He wanted to reach Mundhir, who was swimming away from the stricken *kitr*, returned from its morning fishing excursion a few minutes too soon. I saw Hani break free and reach Mundhir in time to help him drag ashore Abu Abdul's broken corpse.

They put me in a vehicle with Pederson, who told his marines to remove the cuffs. "Get those off him, right now," he screamed, before turning back to me, suddenly gentle again. "Sorry there, bud. We put the cuffs to guard against the chance that someone is still watching. We're waiting for a postblast team, and then we're bringing you back to Government Center for a debrief with our intel guys . . ."

I stopped listening to him then. I watched from my window as Mundhir cradled Hani's head in his powerful hands and smoothed our friend's hair as they both wept.

"Of course," I said to Pederson. "Take me wherever. I do not care."

I acknowledge this nonpunitive letter of caution.

Though not directed at a military superior, and therefore not governed by the Uniform Code of Military Justice, my disrespectful remarks toward a member of the U.S. Foreign Service brought discredit on the Marine Corps and the United States naval service. My actions showed a lack of judgment and were unbecoming of a gentleman and officer of Marines.

This letter, though nonpunitive in nature, will nonetheless be taken as a corrective measure. I will exercise greater care in the performance of my duties, both in garrison and in combat.

Respectfully submitted,
P. E. Donovan

UNBECOMING

I hail a cab on St. Charles Avenue at eleven thirty on New Year's Eve and ask the driver to take me to the French Quarter. He's justifiably annoyed, but eventually agrees. I've decided on a whim to drift into Molly's on the off chance that I'll find Paige there. Without the courage to call her, it's the best I can do.

The crowds become impassable when the cab reaches Canal Street, so I throw the driver a big tip to compensate for leaving him stuck without a ready fare or an easy way out. Molly's is on the far side of the Quarter, almost to Esplanade. It's a mile to walk, down streets packed with drunks, meandering en masse toward the river in an effort to catch the last of the fireworks.

I pass through Jackson Square as the fireworks reach their crescendo, and trudging through the crowd with my hands in my pockets, I try not to notice the couples gliding off into dark corners.

A sense of embarrassment catches me off guard, as I become suddenly aware that I'm underdressed in my jeans and boots. Everywhere I look, young revelers are dressed to the nines. Women brave the cold night in their shiny party dresses by cozying up to men in slacks and high-collared sweaters. I bow my head and try to hide inside my canvas bomber jacket. I worry about running into a classmate, alone as I am on New Year's Eve, lacking the self-respect to even dress for the occasion.

I miss Paige in a way I didn't expect. I feel the urge to call her, but at midnight on New Year's Eve? After I've stood her up five days running? I can't. It would be worse than desperate. It would be desperately selfish.

Even if Paige isn't working, even if she happens to be at Molly's, it's hard to imagine how she'd have an interest in seeing me. Maybe I'm looking for Paige so she can tell me to my face that I'm an idiot. I need to grow up, and a midnight phone call isn't the place to start. I should bear things for what they are. I should take responsibility.

The brass buttons had hurried back to Ramadi to spread the story of our dustup. He must have told anyone who would listen because it became the talk of the Ramadi chow hall that night. The lieutenant with the nerve to tell off a diplomat. A decidedly junior diplomat, but still. All the regimental staff officers had a good laugh, I'm sure. But not the commander.

We pulled into the marshaling yard just after dark and I stood aside while Gomez and Zahn supervised the breakdown of the convoy and the cleaning of the vehicles. They pushed the Marines to hurry so they could get some chow before the dinner line closed.

Cobb, in the marshaling yard to prep his platoon for an overnight construction mission, pulled me aside. He'd been on watch in the operations center when Major Leighton got the late-afternoon call. Because I hadn't reached Taqaddum in time to warn him, Major Leighton was blindsided. Regiment learned about the dustup before he did, which was unforgivable. I'd made it look like he couldn't control his lieutenants or even stay up-to-date on their antics.

My stomach dropped. I imagined him bursting into the company offices in the morning, wheezing fury and letting it spill over the plywood walls so everyone in the company could know how incompetent and clueless I'd made him look. I decided that hiding from him wouldn't help me. I wanted to get it over with first thing, so I went over to the operations center and volunteered to take Gunny Dole's overnight watch shift. Gunny Dole smiled, thanked me, and hustled out before I had time to change my mind.

I didn't even bother to shower or change out of my stinking flight suit. The overnight shift would keep me awake, as would the quickly healing but still painful blisters under my eyes. I'd stand up from the watch officer's chair around six o'clock the next morning, set myself by his office door, and present myself for a dressing-down as he came in from breakfast.

I collapsed into the watch officer's rolling chair and pulled myself up to the desk, drawing a line in the logbook and writing in block letters, "I, Second Lieutenant P. E. Donovan, have relieved the watch. I have nothing significant to report at this time."

The sergeants stood, looking confused by my filthy uniform and wafting stench. They took turns briefing me. Intelligence. Movement control. Logistics tasking. They each issued a crisp, well-prepared update on the operational picture.

Most of our convoys went out at night. The watch officer represented the company while Major Leighton slept, responsible for all vehicles and personnel on the road, and ready at any time to update higher headquarters on the company's current operations.

The sergeants finished briefing me and returned to their routine. They'd been forced by Gunny Dole's empty uniform to run the overnight shift on their own and had consequently developed a tight system. Information packaged in clipped speech moved around the room in choreographed bursts. I didn't have much to contribute, so I leaned back in the tall chair and listened to the hum.

Computer screens, scattered at watch stations around the room, burned out my night vision. I rubbed my eyes, avoiding the sore patches where the blisters had been, and blinked away the spots. Printed banners came into focus. Over the intelligence desk, a banner read WHAT DO I KNOW? WHO NEEDS TO KNOW IT? HAVE I TOLD THEM? And over the door: COMPLACENCY KILLS.

Field telephones with ringers more grinding and caustic than any in the civilian world rattled folding tables against stone floors. Sketchy rumors of enemy activity flowed through the intelligence clerk to the movement-control sergeant, who used the information to alter convoy routes over the radio. Notations appeared in grease pencil on the laminated wall map.

A stack of radios, mounted to a table in the corner, squealed with transmissions from convoys and dismounted patrols moving under cover of night. Reports of small-arms fire and suspicious vehicles came through the speakers in snippets, breathy and rushed. A lance corporal from the communications section struggled to write it all down on yellow slips. Each slip had a box for the date and time, the sender's call sign, and the message description.

The lance corporal sweated over the details. The kid didn't understand friction, yet. How chaos in the field distorted everything. How it made every message irrelevant before it ever went out over the air. Still, he tried to understand it all. He massaged scratchy transmissions into coherent, if contradictory, exchanges and meekly offered me a stack of yellow slips every hour or so.

I'd thank him and give each message a glance, but only because he had worked so hard. The real story always came through the computer. We had a chat room set up on the classified network. Watch officers from around the battle space used it to coordinate operations in real time. The watch officer in Ramadi, a nameless major responsible for all of western Iraq, demanded status updates at random intervals. He used the same, easily overlooked message each time: "MNF-W_Watch Officer: All stations, update status." He did it that way, subtly, to ensure that the junior watch officers didn't fall asleep. If a subordinate station didn't reply inside thirty seconds with a curt "NSTR"— nothing significant to report—the next grinding ring on the tactical line would be an unpleasant, accusative call from regimental headquarters in Ramadi.

On the other side of the desk, a blue force-tracker terminal showed convoys and dismounted patrols as icons moving along the highways, or stationary at intersections. When a blue force tracker somewhere outside the wire reported an IED attack or a snap vehicle checkpoint, the terminal gave a beep and the icon flashed.

I selected the icon representing Cobb's platoon and checked how long he'd been sitting still. He and his Marines had set a cordon at an intersection north of Fallujah and were working through the night to build a vehicle checkpoint for the Iraqi Army. They arranged Hesco baskets in defensive positions on either side of the road and used front-end loaders to fill them with dirt. They set steel traffic barriers in the asphalt and strung them with razor wire.

When finished, the barriers would force approaching cars and trucks into slow, serpentine turns, making it harder to charge the checkpoint with a vehicle bomb. But until then, Cobb's platoon was a target, ripening with each passing hour they remained stationary.

Three times, Cobb's Marines sent up flares to warn off traffic. Kinetic events, like flares and escalations of force, triggered official reports to regimental headquarters, due within an hour of the event. So, each time it happened, Cobb called on the satellite phone to walk me through the sequence of events. The type of car. The provocative behavior. We called the assembled details "the word picture."

Most on-scene commanders used the radio to pass reports, but Cobb liked the satellite phone. It made him feel like a world traveler, a young adventurer. On the radio, he would have to speak in short bursts while the whole battle space listened in. Cobb didn't have the patience for that. He liked to tell stories and infuse each narrative with stock characters and surprise endings. Somehow, he always managed to make the story about himself.

Cobb's Marines finished their work around five o'clock, and their blue force-tracker icon started moving half an hour later, just as the watch shift changed. Wong took my chair and made a note in the logbook. The outgoing shift briefed him as they'd briefed me the night before.

Properly relieved, the sergeants shuffled off to the chow hall, but I spent thirty minutes sitting next to Wong. When it became palpably awkward, I ambled to the back of the room and hung around Major Leighton's office door.

The adrenaline of the watch drained away. My legs and eyelids went soft and I struggled to stay alert. I stopped myself from leaning against the plywood wall, afraid I might fall asleep standing up. My cheeks felt rough, and it occurred to me that I hadn't shaved in two days. The flaw in my plan came into focus. Not only had I humiliated him in front of the entire command, I now had the gall to appear before him unshaven while wearing a soiled uniform. I wanted to run, shower, and shave and come back in half an hour looking refreshed. But Major Leighton stepped into the operations center before I had a chance. He looked anxious and distracted, clutching his coffee mug and classified briefing folder.

I summoned my nerve and stood up straight.

He stopped midstride and raised his eyebrows, looking puzzled as to why a lieutenant would stand at attention by his office door at six in the morning. He waited for me to say something.

I searched his face for clues, having failed to anticipate this turn of events. I'd imagined the moment many times and prepared for a dozen unpleasant scenarios, but never planned to initiate my own reprimand. Finally, Major Leighton's face showed some recognition, like the memory of a root canal. He closed his eyes, pulled a slow, sour breath through his gritted teeth, and pointed at his office.

I followed him and came to attention six inches in front of his desk.

He didn't raise his voice or lose his temper. He just glanced at a typed document, formatted in flawless naval correspondence, and pushed it across his desk. "Sign it."

"Aye, aye, sir." I leaned forward at modified parade rest, bent over with one hand tucked in the small of my back, and signed it without reading. I knew what it said.

"There were better ways to handle that, Lieutenant."

"Yes, sir." I dropped the pen and stood up straight. Back to the position of attention. Eyes forward.

"You embarrassed us. You embarrassed me. The Marines in this company? They work hard. You took the spotlight from them and put it on yourself."

"Yes, sir."

"Worse than that, you showed a lack of bearing. No emotional discipline. And I'll be honest, Pete. It makes me question your leadership." He looked me up and down. "It also doesn't help that you look like shit."

"Yes, sir."

He stood, planted his hands on his desk, and leaned in close. "Would you like to defend yourself, Lieutenant?"

"No, sir." I smelled scrambled eggs on his breath. "No excuse."

"Good. Do better next time."

"Aye, sir."

"Dismissed." He sat down and opened his laptop to a website about sports.

"Dismissed. Aye, aye, sir." Even though he'd stopped paying attention, I made sure to leave his office in the proper way. I took a long step backward and came to the position of attention before finishing the ceremony with a proper "Good morning, sir."

I turned on my left heel with a crisp drill movement and marched smartly to the door. A water bottle filled with sand hung on a length of parachute cord. It acted as a counterweight and closed the door behind me.

Wong smirked, "Have a good one, Donovan." In the corner of my eye, I caught him smiling and dialing the satellite phone. Probably reaching out to Cobb to see what time he wanted to get breakfast.

Outside, under the awning, I leaned against the concrete wall and looked east into the sunrise, sickened at the thought of a night gone by without sleep. I worked to catch my breath and slow my heart. Three hauls of morning air, boiling and laced with exhaust, did the job.

I pulled the soft cover against my scalp and walked across the compound with the brim low on my forehead. The taste of hot guts stewed up into my mouth. I kept my eyes on my feet, hoping to avoid passing conversations with other lieutenants, or with Gunny Dole, refreshed and just back from an extralong breakfast.

Even looking at my feet, I stumbled. My toes caught the dirt with every third step. I worked my eyelids in an effort to get some moisture going. The gallon of coffee I'd needed over the course of the night, combined with the strain caused by dim computer screens, made my eyeballs feel like sponges wrung out in bleach. Letter of caution or not, I needed a few hours of sleep. I didn't deserve it, but I needed it.

I staggered toward my room, steering a listless course through the rows of enlisted barracks, sculpting in my mind the moment I'd fall face-first onto my cot.

A voice stopped me. Gomez at her most stern, lecturing a Marine somewhere in the maze of long, wooden huts. She was lacing into him, whoever he was. But then a laugh rose up and I peeked around the corner to investigate, expecting some sort of criminal, group hazing. Instead, I found my whole platoon up early and smiling.

"Look, the object is to wrap the horseshoe around the post," Doc Pleasant said to Dodge.

The rest of the platoon lounged on the barracks steps or leaned against plywood walls. They'd stripped down to their green T-shirts, folded their blouses and arranged them in three neat rows next to their stacked rifles. Obviously, the junior Marines had assembled expecting a morning formation run, but had found Gomez with another idea.

"Unless you can get a leaner," Doc Pleasant continued. "That's the most points."

"I understand, then. How do I get a leaner?" Dodge considered the weight of the horseshoe in his hand.

"Just practice, man." Pleasant handed a horseshoe to Gomez. "Will you show him, Sergeant?"

"What am I? Fucking schoolteacher over here? I look like Mary Poppins to you?"

The platoon laughed, either because she'd referenced some inside joke, or because her Mary Poppins crack had made no sense at all. I couldn't tell.

Gomez rocked the horseshoe back and forth, keeping her arm straight, her knees bent. "Easy does it, Dodge. Straight wrist. Arch that fucker in there."

She let go with too much force. The horseshoe flew well over the post and hit the plywood barracks next to me. I ducked and let it bounce over my head.

The platoon, suddenly aware of my presence, let out a collective gasp as they saw how close Sergeant Gomez had come to hitting me. In a stupor, which the Marines seemed to mistake for calm detachment, I went to the horseshoe and picked it up.

Gomez jogged over and took it from me. "Sir. Sorry, sir. Didn't see you, sir. Sorry."

Behind her, the Marines laughed hesitantly. She turned around and scowled at them.

"It's all right," I said. "Where did this come from?"

"The horseshoe set, sir? Doc's father shipped it over. Pulled the shit right out his lawn."

"And this is morning PT for you guys?"

Her face flushed bright red as she took the offhand remark as criticism, her platoon commander calling her soft.

"No, sir. Just some fun. Real quick. Then I'm gonna run them till they puke. Promise, sir." She smiled nervously.

"Well, don't do that. We don't need heat casualties inside the wire. We get enough of that on the road."

"No, sir. Course not. Just meant . . ." She stammered to a halt.

Without meaning to, I'd tied her in a knot. I never understood how I could make her nervous. How she ever viewed me with anything other than amused derision. An outsider, observing the platoon without context, would have no problem spotting its leader.

"It's fine," I said, balancing the horseshoe in my palm. "Just curious." Behind her, the platoon began to fidget. "Mind if I take a throw?"

She brightened. "Sure, sir. Course."

I walked to the spot where Dodge and Pleasant stood. "Whose turn am I taking here?"

"Me? I suppose?" Dodge looked at Doc Pleasant and shrugged.

Pleasant nodded. "Him against me, sir."

"So I'm Dodge's proxy then?" I smiled, light-headed and loopy. "Good deal for him. Alabama's been taking it to Louisiana as far back as Bear Bryant."

The southerners in the platoon understood and laughed, except for Doc Pleasant.

"Cold, sir," he said. "Cold."

I reeled back my arm and gave the horseshoe a few practice swings before closing my eyes and letting go. It wasn't technique, closing my eyes. And it wasn't some strange attempt to show my Zen mastery of horseshoes. I was just so tired, it couldn't be helped.

My eyes stayed closed until a soft thump and a metallic clang let me know that the horseshoe had reached its target. I opened my eyes slowly to the sound of cheers. The horseshoe leaned perfectly against the post.

A big hand landed firmly on my back. It was Zahn. "Damn, sir. You do this a lot back home?"

"No. First time."

Dodge laughed and feigned punching Doc Pleasant in the ribs. "Behold me, Lester. I am master of the horseshoe game."

"The fuck you talking about?" Doc Pleasant shot back. "It was the sir's throw."

"The *mulasim* was my proxy. Do you not remember?"

Doc Pleasant shrugged Dodge off. "Back up. My turn."

The platoon showered Doc with jeers and whistles as he pushed them aside to make room for his comically wide stance. He scowled and took his practice swings. The Marines kept the pressure on, gleefully unaccustomed to the sight of their meek corpsman so riled up. Even Gomez played along. She didn't join in, but she didn't stop it either. She just stood off to the side, arms crossed and smiling.

The heckling seemed to work. Doc's face flushed bright red, and he couldn't get comfortable in his stance. He tried in vain to find a grip he liked. He switched his feet and decided a two-handed tossing motion worked better. Each time he altered his approach, the jeers and laughter grew louder.

I watched Doc's face as genuine anger replaced the worry lines and grimaces. It crawled into his cheeks and out to his limbs. The beast in him. Something I hadn't seen before. I looked to the Marines to see if they'd noticed it, too. They hadn't. The intensity of the banter only grew, the Marines thinking it all in good fun.

Doc clinched his jaw and narrowed his eyes, alone in the moment. The more he delayed, the more seriously he seemed to take this throw, and the deeper the platoon sank into hysterics.

The jeers became more cutting.

"Doc Pleasant! Captain of the Olympic horseshoe team!"

"The fuck you doing, Doc? Yoga?"

"If you don't throw that thing in three fucking seconds, I'm taking it. You forfeit."

Through the haze of fatigue, I found a grin spreading across my face. I worked to remove it, tightening my cheeks and pursing my lips, trying to regain my officer's composure. My bearing, as Major Leighton had called it. But the grin would not be tamed. The muscles of my face succumbed to it, driven back by a force I was too addled to resist.

It was happiness, I realized. I couldn't remember the last time I'd been happy. The platoon, my Marines, had welcomed me. For the first time, invited me to join. In that moment, listening to them laugh and jeer, not standing apart from them or banished to my Humvee, I smiled.

Doc Pleasant made his throw. The platoon's laughter stalled, and a collective, anticipatory howl rose up as the horseshoe sailed toward the post. He missed it badly, and the jeers erupted again. No longer making any attempt to hide my participation, I smiled and clapped as Zahn walked over to jokingly pat Doc Pleasant on the shoulder.

Doc bristled. He brushed Zahn's hand away violently and turned on his heel in an attempt to shove him. But Zahn stepped back before Doc could connect and watched as he stumbled awkwardly forward.

Doc recovered his balance and snarled a sincere "Fuck you!" in Zahn's direction.

Zahn threw up his palms in defense. "Whoa, whoa. It's fucking horseshoes, Doc!"

The mood of the platoon turned. The laughs evaporated into cries of protest. They'd been having fun a moment before, a genuinely fine morning ruined by Doc's nonsense, and several Marines moved to break up the nascent fight.

Gomez got there first. Zahn shook his head with confusion while Gomez wrapped her arms around Doc's waist and put a shoulder into his chest. She dug her toes into the dirt and pushed him back. Dodge wanted to step in, too, but he saw something in the demeanor of Gomez and Zahn that told him it was a Marine thing. And he wasn't a Marine. He backed away and slipped his hands into his pockets.

Different elements within the platoon, sensing that morning PT had ended, began drifting back to their folded blouses and stacked rifles. They dressed and walked away without waiting for formal permission, hoping to get breakfast before the chow hall closed the line.

Zahn whispered in my ear, "Sir, you should probably go. We'll square this away."

"Right," I murmured. "Right. Of course. Thanks, Corporal."

Zahn was protecting the platoon, ensuring that I didn't witness something that would make me obligated to bring Doc Pleasant up on charges. And possibly even culpable if I didn't.

I walked away, expecting at any moment to hear Gomez's sharp voice lacing into Pleasant with threats of formal charges and extra duty. But all I heard was Pleasant's deepening stream of invective. Cursing her. Cursing Zahn. Telling the whole world to fuck off. I snuck a glance over my shoulder and saw that she'd sat him down on the barracks steps. She kept a hand on his shoulder while Zahn knelt and looked into his face, both of them trying to understand what had gone wrong.

I glanced in the other direction and saw Dodge choosing a path to avoid both me and the pack of Marines headed to the chow hall. He was walking with his head down, toward the nice spot on the berm overlooking the river, alone.

Half a block from Molly's, weaving through the packed sidewalk and feeling brutally sober, I wonder if Dodge has found his way into something like a home or met anyone he can consider a friend. That's what he always needed, I think. More than money. More than safety, even.

I walk into Molly's, elbow my way through the thinning crowd of drunk revelers, and, through sheer determination, manage to get a beer and a shot of Jameson from the little blonde behind the bar. I take the shot with half the beer and start to numb down. I feel instantly better, and much less interested in an ass-chewing from Paige. Still, I scan the bar to see if she's here.

And for a moment I think I'm hallucinating. But I look again and find there's no denying it.

It's Lester Pleasant, by himself at the end of the bar, looking drunk enough to fall off his stool.

hey lester its Zahn and im living at home back here in missouri and i thought you should know that the lieutenant is living in new orleans now and i saw him a while ago and he seems good i know you live close by there so if your ever up that way maybe say hello to him write me back and ill send you his number and stuff if you want it

ESCALATIONS OF FORCE

This guy keeps talking at me and calling me Doc.

"Sit up, Doc. Wake up."

When he's not talking at me, he's talking to this little, blonde bartender. This girl I've been hitting on. He tells her it's okay. That he'll take care of this. That he knows this guy, and he'll get him out of here.

I don't know which guy he's talking about, but he has his hand on my shoulder and I don't like that. Don't like it one bit. I shrug him off, about to get pissed and swing. But before I can, he locks up my arm and carries me off into the street where all these assholes are singing about people they used to know.

"Let's get you a cup of coffee."

"I don't need any fucking coffee, sir. Get fucked, sir," I say, not sure why I'm calling him sir. My feet won't push off the sidewalk the way they should, so I drag my toes and let this guy carry me, like Lieutenant Donovan pulling me around the day Zahn got beaned. "An asshole. Just like Lieutenant Donovan."

"Who?"

"You. You. The asshole."

"I guess that's fair." He puts me down on a bench while the singing reaches a high note. This guy takes a seat next to me, and I start to understand where I am. It's that little square with the fountain, right next to the French Market, where all the tourists buy their feather boas and shit.

"One more time, Doc. It's Lieutenant Donovan. It's Pete, I mean. It's me."

"Yeah . . . Zahn told me about you." I hear for the first time how bad I'm slurring these words. "Zahn told me the lieutenant was around here somewhere. Fuck that asshole."

And now this guy starts laughing, and I think maybe I'm sobering up, but that can't be because I'm still seeing the lieutenant sitting here next to me.

"I am an asshole. This is true."

"Sir?" I poke him in the face.

He pushes my finger aside. "Yes, but don't call me that. I went through the same thing with Zahn. Just skip it, okay? Call me Pete."

I reach out again, and when he swats my finger away like a fly, I come back to the world. There's no reunion or nothing. No hugging or any great-to-see-you bullshit. Or maybe there was earlier in the bar when I was too drunk to realize it, but for now it's right back to work.

He takes me over to this diner he knows, around the corner. I'm still staggering drunk. Doing better, but still leaning on him every now and again. The poison is on its way out, though. That's made certain enough when I puke into a gutter. The lieutenant hustles me away, worried the cops might put me in lockup for the night if they see.

He sets me down at the counter and starts ordering food. He makes me drink water, like we're back in the desert and he's making us hydrate. I tell him so. "You gonna check the color of my piss, too, sir?"

"Don't call me that."

Next, it's a plate full of french fries. These fries taste so good, I just want to tell everybody. I start raising my voice about it. The lieutenant keeps putting his hand over my mouth, trying to shut me up. I guess he thinks we're about to get kicked out of here, too. He might be right, but I can't tell.

It starts working. The coffee, the water, the fries, and the talking. And pretty soon I'm sober enough to understand that this is crazy. Running into the lieutenant in a random bar on New Year's Eve? He thinks so, too.

"Were you really out alone on New Year's Eve?" I ask him.

"I was. Were you?"

"No. I was with a girl for some of it."

He doesn't push me for details. "I was thinking about Dodge. Five seconds before I walked in there."

"That a fact, sir?"

"It is. I was wondering what ever happened to him. Where he ended up."

"You know his real name is Kateb, right, sir?"

"No. First I'm hearing it. And stop calling me that. Please."

"Okay, sorry." I put a finger over my lips and shush myself.

"What else do you know about him?"

"Well, I knew he liked shitty metal bands. But then, you knew that, too. He never shut up about that. Also, before he came to work for us, he'd been hanging out at some lake with his friends from school. Trying to leave Iraq and open a beachfront bar someplace. Didn't work out for some reason."

The lieutenant laughs. "He would've been good at that."

"And I knew something went wrong for him. Real bad, right after our Humvee got hit, remember? While Zahn was at medical? Just before Ramadi."

"Yeah? What was that?"

"It was one of those escalations of force. Out on Route Michigan, you know? Someone from the construction platoon shot up this old taxicab when it got too close. One of those Baghdad taxis, you know? That's why they got suspicious. It was out too far west of the city to make good sense. Anyways, they brought the two guys from the taxi back to Taqaddum. One of them got airlifted up to Al Asad, right away, and I heard that he died a short time later. The other guy, a real big dude, he got patched up at the shock trauma center and brought over to the company headquarters."

"Why did they bring him over to us?"

"Because Major Leighton had to give him money. The civil affairs people showed up with this stack of Iraqi money. It was our mistake and we owed the guy, they told us. Major Leighton came and got me and Dodge. He wanted Dodge to translate for him, and for me to check on the guy. Make sure he was well enough to travel, since Lieutenant Cobb's platoon was about to take him over to Habbaniyah and hand him over to the Iraqi police.

"That whole episode shook Dodge up pretty bad. This young Iraqi, a real burly guy about Dodge's age, was sitting in the truck all bandaged up. And Dodge was talking to him in Arabic, trying to give him all this money and saying a lot more than what Major Leighton was asking him to interpret. But the big guy . . . he wouldn't budge. He wouldn't say nothing. He wouldn't even take the money. He just kept staring at Dodge with these fucking dagger eyes. And eventually Dodge just lost it, just started throwing money at him. Like, begging him to take it. But nothing doing. Big guy didn't say a word. They had to haul Dodge away from the truck, eventually."

I start feeling bad, like I'm talking too much, and going on too long like drunks do.

But the lieutenant doesn't seem put off at all. He's listening close. "Did Dodge know this guy or something?"

"Not sure. He went straight over to the intel guys in that bunker by the flight line after that. Took a week off for leave.

Remember? Then, when he came back, we were back on the road before I had a chance to ask him anything. And then Ramadi . . ." I trail off, thinking he might not want me talking any more about that.

"Ramadi," he says, picking up my train of thought. "And Gomez. And then a few weeks later, I had you brought up on charges."

I nod my head. "Yes, sir."

"I'm sorry, Doc."

"Wasn't your fault." I mean it.

Through all his travels and adventures, and in spite of many moments of sadness and defeat, Huck will always shun pity. Even the Widow Douglas, for whom Huck has obvious affection, is brushed aside when she tries to pity him.

"The widow she cried over me," Huck remembers. "And called me a poor lost lamb, and she called me a lot of other names, too, but she never meant no harm by it."

FADI AL BAQUII

My flatmates spend all day making calls on the satellite phone in preparation for the next rally. They talk to journalists in France and America and tell me that tomorrow, at the rally in front of Sousse Government Center, the cameras will be there. Western journalists will come to ask questions and I will speak in English on behalf of the student committee.

I tell them the last time I spoke English for a job it went badly for everyone.

They laugh like I am making a joke for them. We love our brave Fadi, they seem to say. We love his jokes and how he tries to make us brave like him.

Then they ask me to write a letter for the cause. A press release to the American media, announcing the founding of our little chapter of the revolution.

I refuse at first. How will I even release such a letter, when it is time? The Internet works for us more and more seldom now. Ben Ali will shutter it firmly in a matter of days. Surely, before he sends the Army into the streets.

My flatmates, the committee members, say that I should use what Internet we have left to obtain telephone numbers. In this way, we might be able to use the satellite telephone to call a friend in America, perhaps the one with whom I am exchanging those Facebook notes.

"Get his phone number, yes? He can listen to the letter as you read it. Then he can write it down and send it to the media."

Why would Lester do this for me? My flatmates labor under the misconception that fighting together necessarily makes men friends.

I should tell them about the passport of a Syrian from Michigan named Fadi al Baquii, left carelessly in a desk drawer. I should tell them about Taqaddum.

The Americans in the bunker paid me my wages in dollars. An astonishing sum, handled with indifference by these unknowingly rich men. Enough money to take me all the way to Jordan, or farther if I was economical. Then they told me to enjoy my visit with family. Enjoy your holiday, they said. Come back safe.

I signed the checkout sheet on the clipboard, placed the clipboard back on the desk, and took the long stairs up from the bunker. A patrol took me to Habbaniyah and set me free inside the police station. Come back in five days for a return escort, the sergeant, a stranger, told me.

When the Americans left, I told the Iraqi policemen a lie. I said the Americans wanted me to sleep there in the police station and to patrol with them as a sort of training for me, and way to gather intelligence about the neighborhood. I made myself sound important, and how would they know otherwise? The Americans only ever spoke to me in English.

For three days, I traveled with the policemen through town. Always, I looked down the dirt road where my father and brother lived in their borrowed villa. I looked for a time when few would be home. No militiamen or workers. Only my family.

And I asked them about a big guy, shot by the Americans and

brought to the police station a week previous. What had become of him? Were his wounds healing? Where was he taken when he left here?

"Oh, him?" The police chief smiled. "Big Mundhir? Abu Muhammad took him to the house down the road. He will be fine there. Abu Muhammad is a good man."

I nodded as though this news were of no great concern to me.

On the evening of the fourth day, I tied a cloth around my face to hide, snuck from the police station, and ran through a field protected by army checkpoints. The rat lines, the Americans called this path. A place where men who worked in the American base could run under the protection of machine guns in their guard towers and perhaps make it to their homes and families without the militias seeing who they were.

I ran with a big group leaving their work and reached the wall of my father's home with the sunset. I walked around to the gate like a stranger, listening always for talking, but hearing nothing. No voices. No generators. No air conditioners or televisions. Against the will of my pounding heart, I climbed the gate.

My father's house was dark, and the old Mercedes was gone. In the quiet, I heard soft crying, a woman sobbing. I snuck across the courtyard, with its silly lawn, and moved to the window of the kitchen where the sobbing became something I understood. A voice I knew. It was Nasim, my brother's wife, crying alone on the floor of the kitchen.

She had a rifle across her lap, and she reached for it when she heard the crunch of my feet on the dying grass.

"Wait. Nasim." I entered the kitchen. "Just me. Just Kateb."

She stood and took me into her arms. Her wet cheek settled on my neck.

"Where is my father? Where are Muhammad and Ibrahim?"

"I do not know," she sobbed. "They left last night. Ibrahim was sick."

"What?"

"He developed a fever in the night. Vomiting next, then diarrhea. Cholera, Kateb. *Cholera*. It was after curfew, so Muhammad and your father argued, screamed at one another. Your father wanted to wait until sunrise, saying it was too dangerous to travel at night with the checkpoints. But Muhammad insisted that they leave right away. So they put Ibrahim in the car and left to take him to the Fallujah hospital. They have not come back."

"But where are all the men who guard the house?" I gasped.

"Sheikh Hamza took them a week ago. He needed them all to guard himself, he said. With all the foreigners making threats on his life." She paused. "I thought you knew? Isn't that why you sent your friend? Mundhir?"

"Yes," I lied. "Of course. Where is he now?"

"The roof." She started to calm. "Watching for headlights. Perhaps the sheikh's men coming back to protect us. Perhaps not."

I held her cheeks and told her it would be fine, that my father and brother were both smart and that they would bring Ibrahim home, soon. Then I left her in the kitchen and felt my way through the dark house, up the steps to the flat roof. Near the edge, I saw Mundhir's back in the moonlight. He did not move, but he knew I was there. He must have heard the whole conversation with Nasim, the way voices carried at night.

"Hani is dead?" he asked without turning his head.

"Yes. The Americans told me after they took you away." I approached him in the darkness, moving slowly. He had something sitting across his lap, and I thought it could be another rifle. "How did my father find you and Hani?"

"Find us?"

"Yes, how did he know you and Hani had been shot? How did he know the Americans had taken you to the Habbaniyah police station?"

I went to my hands and knees and crawled up to the edge with him. I saw that the object on his lap was not a rifle, but rather my father's old cricket bat.

"Kateb," he sighed, "he came for us the day you disappeared with the Americans. Why do you think Hani and I were on the road in that old taxi? We worked for him. Muhammad was behind us with the devices, and Hani and I were ahead of the triggermen in the scout vehicle." Then, with a stoic tone, he added, "We did our job."

I sat still and quiet, wanting to ask.

Mundhir was kind and did not make me. "I have not told him about you."

"Thank you."

"He thinks you are in Abu Ghraib because of the way we saw you taken away with your hands bound. He goes to the Americans in Fallujah once every week to look for you. But they insist that you are not on their lists. He thinks you are rotting in that place."

"Is it good work, with my father and brother?" I asked, wishing to change the subject. "More fun than working at our rock-and-roll shows?" I thought this might make him look at me finally. A good memory.

But he continued staring out across the town and the highway with its few headlights. "Hani enjoyed it more than I do. He liked your father."

"Does my father know what happened to Hani?"

"Yes."

"Then might I ask you another question?"

"Of course."

"What are you doing with that cricket bat?"

"I'm considering killing you with it." And after a moment, he added, "You preferred for Haji Fasil and Abu Abdul to die? And now Hani? You enjoy watching Americans live on?"

"No, Mundhir . . ."

"Your brother told me the plan for that day on the lake. It would have worked, and only Americans would have died. We would have been safe."

"My brother is lying to you."

Mundhir wrapped his right hand tighter around the cricket bat. "I was up here when Ibrahim . . . when he became sick. Did Nasim tell you? I realized it, the first of anyone. We sleep on the roof when the generators run out of fuel and it becomes too hot in the house. Sheikh Hamza has abandoned us and taken the petrol with him. But we still have the curbstones, and people still pay for them. In fact, the Mercedes had five hollow curbstones in the trunk. Prepped and ready for delivery in the daylight. After I carried Ibrahim down to the car, in the panic to leave we forgot about them. All of us. Your father and brother drove off, taking Ibrahim to Fallujah with five hollow curbstones in the trunk."

I swallowed. "How many checkpoints between here and the hospital?"

"At least ten." Mundhir shrugged. "And the trunk would be searched at each."

"How sick was Ibrahim? If the Americans have him? If they took him to the hospital?"

"You will never know, Kateb." Mundhir finally turned to look at me.

I stood and put my hands in my pockets.

"If I see your father again, I will tell him you were here. Just so he knows you are free. And then nothing else."

335

"I understand."

"Leave and never come back. Now. Or I'll kill you on this roof-top, so soft that Nasim won't hear it." I opened my mouth to apologize, but felt Mundhir pressing the edge of the cricket bat up into my ribs. "Never another word. Go."

I admired the view for a moment before turning to leave, the river twisting north into desert with the moon lighting its path.

Doc—

Here's a key. Stay as long as you like, help yourself to a shower and whatever else you need. But think about going after that girl, if only to apologize. I won't have cowards under my roof.

—Lieutenant Donovan

RETURNED TO DUTY

In the early afternoon, I walk softly down the stairs and out to my car, leaving Lester Pleasant asleep on my ratty couch. The New Orleans weather is shifting, and it's suddenly too warm for a coat. This doesn't feel like New Year's Day.

Following the advice of Gomez's sister, I'll take the interstate west to Baton Rouge, north to Shreveport, then west again all the way to Dallas. I'll need to sleep at a rest stop along the way, but it's the quickest route.

She was more open to the idea of a visit than I thought she'd be, Gomez's sister. Even with the phone call coming on the morning of New Year's Day.

"Of *course*! Michelle loves visitors," she assured me over the scratchy connection.

"That's good to hear," I said, trying to sound upbeat.

"We'll see you tomorrow, then?"

"Yes. See you then."

I settle behind the wheel and look at my phone on the pretense of checking the directions, but drift back to the note from Paige. After getting Doc home from the French Quarter, up my stairs, and comfortably arranged on the couch, I'd sent her the message:

"Can I call you?"

She'd responded instantly, wide-awake at three in the morning, with a curt "You can do whatever you need, Pete."

I examine the words again, as if it's possible to glean some insight from their pixels that I can't gain from their meaning.

I can do whatever I need? Does that constitute a good-bye? Is she trying to spare me the bother of what she expects will be a conciliatory breakup call? I doubt it, but for a reason I can't quite pin down. Perhaps it's optimism, but I let myself believe that the words are meant as strange encouragement.

"You can do whatever you need, Pete," I imagine her saying softly.

I start the car and make a right turn toward the interstate.

"You can do whatever you need, Pete."

Zahn went to the field hospital after our Humvee burned and spent the better part of his time there by himself, in a cold, dark room. Standard treatment for concussions, the Navy doctors told us. Give him a few days to shake it off, and he'll be fine.

Gomez and I went to retrieve him on the afternoon of the third day, borrowing a beat-up Toyota truck from the company motor pool. Doc tagged along so he could requisition a few items from medical, but Gomez and I went into the hospital tent alone so as not to overwhelm Zahn.

"Meet us by the truck when you're finished at supply," Gomez told Doc.

But Doc couldn't help but offer timid medical advice as we walked inside. "Sir. Sergeant. Make sure his eyes aren't dilated in the dark, sir."

"Will do, Doc," I replied.

"And his pulse, sir. Make sure it ain't elevated. Or slow. I wasn't too sure of the reading I took on him in the field, but it seemed kinda slow. We just gotta make sure it's back to normal, sir."

"I'll take a look. Thanks," I said over my shoulder.

"And one more thing—"

"We got this, Doc," Gomez cut him off. "Go take care of your shit. Meet us in ten."

"Aye, Sergeant," he said, deflated.

"We gotta get that little shit a puppy or something," Gomez grumbled to herself.

Inside, a young Navy nurse in camouflage utilities handed me Zahn's returned-to-duty chit and directed us through the maze of connected tents to the makeshift concussion ward near the back of the complex. This austere, vinyl cave had twenty green cots, neatly arranged in the dim light. A large, quiet fan oscillated cool air from one side of the tent to the other.

Zahn was the only patient. He lounged on a random cot, wearing running shorts, a green T-shirt, and sandals. Next to him sat a day's worth of empty boxed meals, neatly stacked and waiting for a member of the hospital staff to come by with a garbage bag.

"Corporal Zahn," I called out, moving with Gomez to the side of his cot. "Paperwork just came through. The docs cleared it. Returned to duty, effective now."

"Great. Sir," he said slowly, "it'll be good to get back to work, you know." He closed his eyes, as though we hadn't fully roused him from a nap.

Gomez chimed in, dropping a light duffel bag at his feet, "Brought you a fresh uniform and boots, killer. And this . . ." She slapped an extra rifle slung on her shoulder. "Been carrying it around for you, and that fucking sucked. So here . . ."

In a single, fluid motion, she lifted the rifle off her shoulder and brought it to port arms, pulled the changing handle to the rear, locked the bolt in place, and looked inside the receiver.

Confirming the absence of a chambered round, she said, "Clear," and held the rifle out for Zahn with one hand.

Zahn opened his eyes and looked up at the weapon, unsure, for a moment, of just what he was supposed to do. Then, as a surge of recognition shot across his face, he jumped upright, swung his feet over the side of the cot, and grabbed the rifle with both hands. But his elbows gave way as Gomez let him take the weight. The weapon came to rest on Zahn's thighs, cradled in his limp arms.

I took half a step forward, instinctually moving to keep the weapon from slipping out of Zahn's lap and falling to the floor. But Gomez put a palm against my chest, stopping me.

"Corporal," she said softly. "Clear your fucking weapon."

Zahn shook his head and mumbled, "Sorry, Michelle. I just . . . it's too . . ."

"The fuck you just call me, Corporal?" Gomez snapped. "It's *Sergeant*. And that rifle, the one with the bolt locked to the rear waiting for you to clear it, that rifle sure as shit ain't *too* anything. You heard me? That weapon weighs eight pounds. Same as a gallon of milk, Devil Dog. Pick that motherfucker up. Look inside the receiver. Make sure there's no round in the chamber, and say 'Clear' when you send the bolt home."

Without looking up, Zahn took a deep breath and carefully maneuvered his hand under the stock.

"Do it now, Corporal," Gomez snapped. "Don't have all fucking day here."

She kept her palm against my chest and increased the pressure until I took a full step back. I stole a glance at her face and took note of the tears welling in her eyes.

Zahn wrapped his fingers around the stock and slipped his other hand under the barrel. Leaning back as much as lifting, he managed to bring the receiver to eye level.

"Clear," he said, louder than necessary, hitting the release with the meat of his palm so the bolt snapped into place. With newfound energy, he popped to his feet and slung the weapon over his shoulder. "Sorry, sir. Just wasn't quite woken up yet."

Zahn smiled and turned to Gomez, about to make some joke, I could tell from his smirk. About to assure her that everything was okay, back to normal.

But she wouldn't meet his eyes. Without a word, she turned on her heel and marched smartly from the tent.

I stepped into her place. "It's all right. Get dressed, and we'll see you out front."

"Aye, sir," he mumbled, his enthusiasm fading with each stride she took away from him, the spark gone as quickly as it had arrived.

I left Zahn alone and chased after Gomez, dodging medical personnel as I scrambled through the maze of tents. I pushed through the vinyl curtain that led into the sunlight and felt her voice cutting through the glare as my vision struggled to adjust.

"What the fuck is wrong with you, sir?" she growled from somewhere behind me.

"Sergeant?" I asked, wheeling around to find her sheltering in the shadow between two tents. Moving toward her, I understood why. She didn't want her still-swollen eyes seen by a passing stranger, despite how gamely she'd recovered her composure.

"What the fuck is wrong with you, sir?" she repeated, louder, daring me to confront her. Hoping a bystander might hear her cursing at an officer, forcing me to do something about it.

"Sergeant, keep your voice down," I pleaded as I stepped into the shadow with her. "I don't know what you mean."

"Why aren't you kicking in the doctor's door, sir? Why aren't you telling them that Zahn needs a fucking CAT scan? Why the fuck are you letting him return to duty so soon? Why the fuck aren't you writing him up for a Purple Heart!?"

"Sergeant, it's not my decision—"

"Then what the fuck good are you?!" she spat. "Why the fuck are you here?"

I fumbled for an answer, mouth open, before offering a lame "I'm here to lead Marines, Sergeant."

"Then it's time to fucking start, sir," she said matter-of-factly.

"Sergeant—"

She cut me off with a punch to the shoulder. "Sir," she said, leaning in closer. "It's your platoon. You don't gotta explain shit to me. Just get it done."

"Sergeant . . . ," I began again, wanting to tell her that she was right. Wanting to tell her that I knew what I had to do. Wanting to thank her. Wanting to apologize. But in the end, I said nothing.

In the silence, she repeated softly, "Just get it done, sir."

I nodded my head, and Gomez stepped by me. She brushed against my shoulder as she left, walking the long way back to the company compound, shoulders back, all confidence, alone.

Doc Pleasant entered my field of vision as I watched her go. He stood by our truck with a confused look on his face. The trauma bag hung low on his shoulders and was filthy. Not only did mud cake the fabric, but the supplies he'd drawn from the hospital, the gauze pads, bandages, and alcohol wipes, poked through the zippers, so haphazard a job he'd done of stuffing them inside.

He stared at me with glassy eyes and a wry smile. He gestured at Gomez with his chin, his mouth open and a question seemingly stuck at the back of his throat.

I felt the urge to charge him, to tackle and choke him. The anger curled my fists, but Doc didn't seem to notice. He persisted with his slack-jawed smile, and any sense of obligation, of debt, owed to my corpsman melted away as I pushed back through the vinyl flaps and into the hospital tent.

Inside, the first doctor I found was a Navy commander. Tall, with gray hair longer than regulation, he reminded me of the first doctor I'd visited as a child. He looked busy, so I stood in front of him and blocked his path.

"Sir, can I speak to you for a minute about Corporal Zahn?"

"I'm sorry, who?"

"My corporal, sir. He's here with a concussion."

"Ah, yes. Zahn. He's fine. Returned to duty. Anything else, Lieutenant? We have a helicopter coming in."

"One more look, sir. That's all I'm—"

"Lieutenant, your corporal is just fine. And if that's all . . ."

He moved to get around me, but I blocked his way. "No, sir. There's one more thing." The next words spilled out of me, as though I had no part in choosing them. "I think I need an audit of my corpsman's controlled medications."

The doctor frowned, taken aback. "Really?"

"Yes, sir. I think someone needs to come take a look."

He nodded gravely. "Engineer Support Company, is it? Thanks for letting me know." He walked toward the emergency receiving area. "I'll make a note and get back to you as soon as I can."

The investigating officer arrived two weeks later.

After Ramadi.

Dodge. So you're okay? That's good news. Whatever you need, I'll do my best to get it to you. But you should know that I might not be the best reference. You had already left by this time, but I got kicked out of the military. I'm doing better now, but that stuff doesn't go away. I know someone who might be a better choice.

AN INTERPRETATION

I lift my fingers off the keyboard and give it some thought. Last time I saw Kateb and the lieutenant together, they were trying to kill each other. Zahn and I had to separate them.

I stand and walk over to the window. The apartment's one, single window. Kinda strange that the lieutenant lives in such a sad, small place. I always thought that college boys had it different, somehow. Otherwise, what's the point? But here he is, like he's trying to fit his whole world into a lifeboat.

But shabby and cramped as it is, there's a nice feeling to this room. He takes care, you know? Keeps it spotless and uncluttered, except for that pile of books next to his desk. Who knows what's going on with *that*. With everything else so squared away, the mess he makes of his book pile seems intentional.

I go to the fridge, taking up the lieutenant's offer that I help myself. There, I find where he keeps those fine, college-boy tastes. His fridge is just as filled with beer as Paul and Landry's, only the lieutenant's beer looks a hell of a lot more expensive.

My hangover's starting to ease up. Still bad enough that as punishment I let myself gaze on all that expensive beer, lined up in neat, pretty rows. Maybe I'll finally make the connection, you know? Nothing to go to a meeting over, just so long as I remember how this feels.

My phone buzzes with a message from Lizzy, driving home the point: "So . . . *that* was weird. But whatev. Call me sometime, guy."

I read it, feel nothing, and go back to the lieutenant's computer to finish my e-mail: "I don't know how satellite phones work. But here's a number you can call." I pause to find that note the lieutenant had left, his number on the back.

Dodge had just come back from visiting his family, and the lieutenant had just come back from the hospital with Zahn, and for some reason Dodge and the lieutenant were both real moody for about a week.

Dodge wouldn't even talk to me, not that I'd have minded or even noticed. My stash had grown real complex by then. Real powerful.

Our next mission back out on the road, Major Leighton sent us into Ramadi.

The lieutenant tried to fight it, I know, because he came out from the operations center fuming mad to give us the order. He was so pissed, so furious crazy, Lieutenants Cobb and Wong came out to watch like they thought it was some fucking stand-up comedy show.

When we left Taqaddum and got out on the road, I found out why.

"Michigan's blocked," the lieutenant said to Zahn. "This secondary route we're taking, it has some serious issues."

"How's that, sir?" Zahn asked, spitting into his bottle.

"It's too narrow as we turn north into the city, for one thing. And there's a bridge I'm not crazy about. This curve looks too sharp for the long-bed seven-ton." The lieutenant traced it on the map with his finger. "Major Leighton wouldn't listen. If one of our trucks tips over and blocks that bridge, there'll be no way into Ramadi from the east. Worse, it'll block Hurricane Point, so they'll have no way to get a quick-reaction force into downtown if they need it."

"Anything you want me to do about this, sir?" Zahn asked.

"No, goddamnit," the lieutenant spat. "I just want you to be cognizant, Corporal. Show some goddamn situational awareness." It was the only time I ever heard him curse at Zahn like that.

Zahn shrugged it off. "Roger, sir." He'd heard worse, I guess.

But then Dodge mumbled something under his breath, and Donovan jumped on him. "What was that, Dodge? What did you say? If you have a comment, I suggest you speak up."

"Poor Americans, is what I said. I was pitying you, for having to make due with our narrow Iraqi bridges. Too ghetto-rigged for you? What? Didn't bring your own? You can land on the moon but you can't build a simple bridge?"

"Fuck you," Donovan said without hesitating. "And shut the fuck up. Don't open your mouth again unless I ask you to."

"Fuck me? Fuck me? Fuck *you*!"

"What did I just say!"

Zahn stepped in, shy about telling his lieutenant what to do, but needing to control his vehicle somehow. "Gentlemen. Take a breath. Watch your sectors. Please."

They went back to their corners and fretted, but the air in the Humvee had soured. There wasn't much time to think about it, though. Because pretty soon we were coming up on the bridge that had the lieutenant so worried.

He got on the radio. "Gomez. Tell your guys to be real careful with this turn."

Then, like he'd jinxed it, the long-bed seven-ton that was two vehicles in front of us bottomed out. Sparks flew from its undercarriage, and like in a slow-motion bad dream, the truck tipped over and came to rest on the bridge's guardrail.

Gomez jumped out from the Humvee in front of us with two other Marines and ran up to make sure no one had been crushed. Both guys crawled out, just fine. But there was no way to move the truck. The bridge was completely blocked.

Lieutenant Donovan buried his head in his hands. "Fuck. We need a recovery vehicle for this."

"Orders, sir?" Zahn asked softly.

"I don't fucking *know*, Zahn!" the lieutenant screamed. "All right? Fuck! Get security pushed out! Show some initiative! Do something without my having to tell you!"

Dodge, in the backseat with me, laughed.

Donovan looked like he could kill. Like he was *about* to. "Something funny, asshole?"

"Yes. Funny is an interpretation, surely. But interpretation is what you pay me for, right?"

"Get the fuck out." the lieutenant said, catching himself as he unbuckled. "Get the fuck out of the vehicle, Dodge."

"Sure, man! Just a free Iraqi, going for a walk on a highway in his own country."

A flight of two helicopters, Marine attack birds from the squadron in Taqaddum, came in low over top of us. I saw them through the turret and heard them on the radio when the noise of their rotors passed.

The radio squawked, "Hellbox Five-Six, this is Profane Two-Four. Please advise on your situation. Do you require casevac?"

They were hailing our convoy by its call sign and asking for the status of our truck, sprawled out on its side at the entrance to the bridge. They wanted to know if we had any injuries from the wreck.

"Sir," I said. "Sir, I think that helicopter's calling you."

349

But the lieutenant was still in Dodge's face, not listening to anyone. "Come on, jackass. Say that shit again."

"Say *what*, *Mulasim*?" Dodge jeered. "That you are incompetent? That you should go home now? Maybe fuck your own country?"

This was about to get real ugly. I unstrapped myself, left the vehicle, and grabbed Dodge around his chest. Zahn did the same thing with the lieutenant and we held them apart for a moment, best we could.

But they were still screaming at each other. Still calling each other every kind of bad name, until the helicopters came over top of us again, drowning out their voices.

One of the pilots hovered, turned back like he wanted to get another look at the shitshow we'd created on that bridge, then accelerated away out over downtown Ramadi.

I watched the helicopter the whole way, until that missile, with its white-smoke trail, came streaking up from somewhere in the city and set it on fire.

THE HERO OF PROFANE TWO-FOUR

From: Commander, Multi-National Forces West

To: Investigating officer

Subject: Command investigation into the loss of Profane Two-Four

---

1. This letter appoints you, per chapter two of reference (a), to inquire into the facts and circumstances surrounding the loss, due to enemy action, of coalition helicopter call-sign Profane Two-Four, which occurred near Ramadi, Iraq.

2. Investigate the circumstances of the enemy attack, which resulted in the loss of the aircraft, and two (2) Marines killed in action.

3. Investigate any fault, neglect, or responsibility therefore, and recommend appropriate administrative or disciplinary action. Report your findings of fact, opinions, and recommendations in letter form within two weeks of receipt of this order, unless an extension of time is granted.

From: Investigating officer

To: Commander, Multi-National Forces West

Subject: Preliminary statement, command investigation into the loss of Profane 24

Encl:

(1) Serious Incident Report, dated 31 August
(2) Transcription of interview with Corporal Walter Zahn
(1) Transcription of interview with "Dodge," coalition-employed local national
(4) Transcription of interview with Hospitalman Lester Pleasant
(5) Personnel Casualty Report, case of Sergeant Michelle Gomez
(1) Bronze Star recommendation, case of Second Lieutenant Peter Donovan

Command Investigation, Enclosure 1:

Serious Incident Report, re: enemy attack on Profane 24

Combat Air Patrol, call sign Profane 24, attacked by surface-to-air missile. One AH-1 attack helicopter destroyed. Two (2) friendly killed in action.

Major (Name Withheld), casualty identification number ED431, killed in action. Captain (Name Withheld), casualty identification number ED561, killed in action.

Marine Light Attack Helicopter Squadron 435.

1455 ZULU.

Grid unknown at this time. Ramadi.

Approximately 1500 meters north of Tigris Bridge.

Immediate search and rescue mission initiated, tactical recovery of aircraft and personnel. Units from Engineer Support

Company, uninvolved with the initial crash, set security and recovered remains of friendly killed in action.

Remains of friendly killed in action returned to Camp Taqaddum for disposition.

No further remarks.

Command Investigation, Enclosure 2:

Transcription of interview with Corporal Walter Zahn

IO: Did you see the missile impact the helicopter?

Cpl Zahn: Yes, sir.

IO: What were you doing at the time?

Cpl Zahn: I was breaking up a fight, sir.

IO: Who was fighting?

Cpl Zahn: Our terp and the lieutenant, sir.

IO: Why?

Cpl Zahn: Sir, all due respect . . . (inaudible) . . . They had a disagreement about a traffic accident, sir.

IO: What happened after you witnessed the helicopter crash?

Cpl Zahn: Well, they stopped arguing. All four of us were stunned for a second, watching it go down. Then the lieutenant grabbed me by the flak jacket and pointed to this bare patch of desert off the side of the highway. He told me to take a few Marines over there and set security. Like we would need it for a landing zone.

IO: And did you?

Cpl Zahn: Yes, sir. I did. I went running out there with Sergeant Gomez and a few others. The next time I saw the lieutenant he was running over with Doc Pleasant, and the Huey was landing.

IO: And you boarded the helicopter?

Cpl Zahn: Yes, sir. The lieutenant, the terp, Doc Pleasant, Sergeant Gomez, and myself.

```
Command Investigation, Enclosure 3:
Transcription of interview with "Dodge," coalition-employed local
national
```

IO: Why did Lieutenant Donovan take you?

"Dodge": Did you ask him, man?

IO: Yes, but I'd like to hear your recollection.

"Dodge": He said he might need me because the helicopter wreck was in this sort of neighborhood. Like in a garden of a big house. He said he might need me to talk to the family in the house.

IO: When you reached the site of the crash, did you talk to the occupants?

"Dodge": Yes.

IO: What did you tell them?

"Dodge": I told them to run.

IO: With the house emptied, what further tasking did you receive?

"Dodge": They gave me a gun.

IO: And did you fire the weapon?

"Dodge": (inaudible)

IO: I didn't hear you. Could you say that again?

"Dodge": Yes. I fired the weapon.

Command Investigation, Enclosure 4:

Transcription of interview with Hospitalman Lester Pleasant

IO: Where were you when Sergeant Gomez was hit?

HM Pleasant: She was standing up, returning fire over the wall. I was on the ground with the lieutenant, trying to work on the wound to his face while he talked on the radio.

IO: Again, where were you?

HM Pleasant: Just underneath her, sir. Like I say, I felt her weight on me, is all. She just slumped over and fell onto my back. There was so much fire, so many rounds going by and cracking against that wall, I didn't hear the shot that got to her. I thought she'd lost her footing and slipped. So, I asked if she was okay. But then I felt her blood on my neck. You know? Running down into my flak jacket.

IO: What did you do?

HM Pleasant: After I knew she was hit?

IO: Yes.

HM Pleasant: I set her down next to the lieutenant. I saw that she'd taken a round to the head, so I kept the helmet on her and started compressions. I didn't look up, sir. Just kept up with the compressions, trying to bring her around. Didn't hear the fire taper off. Didn't hear the helicopter land, either. Didn't hear nothing until the flight medic pulled me off her.

```
Command Investigation, Enclosure 5:
Personnel Casualty Report, case of Sergeant Michelle Gomez
Immediate to Commandant Marine Corps, Washington, DC
Info others as appropriate
Classified
```

---

1. Sgt/Michelle/Luz/Gomez/-

2. USMC, active duty combat injury

3. Gunshot wound to the head

4. 1815/Ramadi, Iraq

5. Penetration of the skull by .762 caliber rifle round resulting in the loss of up to 40% of patient's brain matter. Immediate aid, rendered by combat medical personnel on-site, sustained respiration and circulation until patient could be evacuated to field resuscitation unit. Stabilization at surgical shock trauma hospital followed, with follow-on evacuation to Germany and CONUS. Patient retains very little cognitive function and voluntary muscle control. Will require lifelong care and full disability.

6. Prior to deployment, said named Marine requested official notification go to next of kin, Denise Gomez, sister, Dallas, Texas.

Command Investigation, Enclosure 6:

Bronze Star Medal, with Combat Distinguishing Device, case of Second
Lieutenant Donovan

For heroism in combat during Operation Iraqi Freedom. While
leading a combat logistics patrol through Ramadi, Lieutenant
Donovan and the Marines under his command observed an enemy
surface-to-air missile attack on a coalition helicopter engaged in
airborne over-watch of his convoy's position near the Euphrates
River Bridge. Fatally damaged, the helicopter crashed into a
nearby, residential section of the city. Recognizing that the quick
reaction force dispatched from Hurricane Point would be at least
an hour away, Lieutenant Donovan knew that his platoon was the
only coalition unit in a position to affect rescue of the downed
pilots. Without hesitation, Lieutenant Donovan radioed the second
helicopter in the over-watch flight and created a field expedient
landing zone. When the surviving helicopter of the Profane
Two-Four flight landed, Lieutenant Donovan coordinated with the
pilots and crew chief, volunteering to insert on the crash site with a
small team in order to mount a last-ditch defense, holding the
crash site long enough for reinforcements to arrive. Without
waiting for approval from higher command, Lieutenant Donovan
boarded the UH-1 Huey with two other Marines, a Navy corpsman, and an Iraqi-national interpreter. Lieutenant Donovan
surveyed the wreckage of the downed helicopter from the air and
inserted as close to the crash site as the Huey could safely land. His
ad hoc fire team encountered organized enemy opposition at once
as they moved to secure the aircraft wreckage and pilots. After
fighting their way to the crash site through coordinated small-
arms fire, Lieutenant Donovan and his Marines set security while
their corpsman and their Iraqi interpreter extracted the pilots

from the helicopter wreckage. Finding that both pilots had died on impact, Lieutenant Donovan deployed his team on the courtyard walls of the home where the wrecked helicopter had come to rest and committed to defend the helicopter wreckage and the remains of his fellow Marines at all costs. Over the next two hours, Lieutenant Donovan led his Marines in a gallant defense of the crash site. While a sustained enemy assault materialized on all sides, Lieutenant Donovan and his Marines ably held their position even as their ammunition began to run low. The enemy, sensing a chance to kill or capture a small, isolated group of Americans, committed all his resources to the attack. Hasty barricades of burning tires and wrecked cars, as well as ambushes and improvised explosive devices, blocked the Marines fighting through the city to relieve him. Lieutenant Donovan's leadership and courage under fire enabled his Marines to hold the crash site. He directed numerous strafing runs against enemy positions, and though wounded by bullet fragments from an enemy sniper round impacting near him, he remained actively engaged in the defense of the site until reinforcements arrived. Lieutenant Donovan's courage, initiative, perseverance, and total dedication to duty reflected a great credit upon himself, the Marine Corps, and were in keeping with the highest traditions of the Marine Corps and the United States Naval Service.

You are hereby detached for terminal leave for a period of twenty-one (21) days. You are directed and required to remain in contact with your parent command until that time, and a hard copy of your DD214 will be sent to your home of record in Birmingham, Alabama. Report to Personnel Administration Center, Camp Pendleton, California, no later than 2359, 30 October, for processing.

A GENTLEMAN STANDS

Denise Gomez has a room in the back of her small house with a special bed, and equipment to make sure her sister doesn't choke.

"The VA sends a physical therapist over once a week," Denise tells me. "Michelle is a tough girl, but you already know that. She's making good progress, too. Real good progress." Denise touches the hair on her sister's forehead. "I can tell she's real glad to see you. She brightened right up the minute you walked through the door. Just so happy to see her old lieutenant. Isn't that right, Sis?"

I smile and nod. "I'm really glad to see her, too. Both of you. You've been great hosts."

I arrived in the midmorning after driving most of the night and catching a few hours of sleep in my car. Denise greeted me with a cup of coffee and a hug. I was bracing myself for some level of blame or hatred, but it was nothing like that. This woman is all love. The hospitality didn't ebb as we walked back to Michelle's room. She even spared me the requisite speech about Michelle's condition, and the admonitions to prepare myself.

The first thing I noticed was Michelle's hair. I'd never seen it out of its tight bun, and the length of it shocked me.

Denise laughed. "Bet you never knew she was so girlie."

I noticed the tattoos on Michelle's forearms, next. The songbirds and the snakes chasing after them had withered and faded with her atrophied arms and no longer seemed to belong to her.

After a couple of hours, it felt as though I'd submerged myself into the quiet of this house. We sit and talk while Denise paints Michelle's fingernails and rubs her feet. It seems, at times, like she's looking at me and managing to focus. The spark of recognition I'd allowed myself to hope for, that never comes. But neither does the shadow of pain and despair that I'd feared. She moans from time to time when she wants her position shifted, and when Denise turns her, Michelle's long, black hair falls away to reveal a dent in her forehead where the skull is missing.

"I should be going," I finally say to Denise as the sun sets. "Long drive."

"Well, it was so nice to have you!" she says, getting up to hug me. With her arms wrapped around my neck she whispers, "You are always so welcome here. You know that, right?"

"I know," I try to say, but swallow the words when I realize I can't speak without embarrassing both of us.

When Denise releases me, I walk to Gomez's bed and take her hand. She doesn't move. "Sergeant," I say, with as level a voice as I can manage, before I turn to leave.

I drive around the corner, and about a mile down the road, before I put the car in park and let myself go. I want no possibility of Denise Gomez seeing me do this. Though I have no right, I rest my head on the steering wheel for what must be an hour. It's fully dark by the time I manage to compose myself.

They gave me a medal for valor.

Major Leighton pinned it on my chest when the company returned home to Camp Pendleton. After the ceremony in his office, Major Leighton gave me the floor and asked that I make some brief remarks. I thanked everyone for being there. I thanked my fellow lieutenants Cobb and Wong for their support through the long deployment. I thanked the major for his faith in me. I didn't say a word about Gomez, and neither did anyone else.

My separation orders were processed a week later, so soon after the battalion arrived home that I didn't even bother to retrieve my things from the storage unit where they'd spent the better part of a year. I just filled out the paperwork to have the boxes shipped directly to my home of record in Birmingham and accepted the invitation to sleep on Cobb's floor.

Things changed with Cobb, Wong, and the rest the lieutenants after Ramadi. They were different around me. Deferent almost, which I never understood. Cobb, in particular. Or maybe I imagined it. Maybe it was me. Maybe I was different.

I felt like it would've been rude to decline Cobb's offer. For a week, we stayed up late, watched movies and bad television, and didn't say much to each other. We didn't become friends and knew we never would, but I could hardly remember what I disliked about the guy.

On my last night of active duty, Cobb drove me to the San Diego airport to catch my flight home to Alabama. I had no plans for my month of terminal leave, beyond an uninterrupted week of sleep on my sister's couch.

As I stepped from Cobb's jeep with a duffel over my shoulder, he reached over to shake my hand and wish me well. "Glad you were around. Good luck, Pete."

Unprepared for his sincerity, I muttered something incoherent before recovering my wits and offering a curt "Thanks. You, too."

A flood of nostalgia swallowed me up as his taillights passed out of sight, and I realized with a start that my last true moments as a Marine had slipped away. I was alone, quite suddenly, with just the stories. The truth had driven off with Cobb.

Inside the terminal, I checked the departures board. My flight stood out in ominous red. Canceled, along with a dozen others. The woman at the ticket counter couldn't help me. Some sort of bad weather in Chicago had backed up connections west of the Rockies. None of the airlines had an available seat on a flight to Birmingham, or anywhere else, until morning.

Everything I owned was already in transit. Worse, I hadn't taken the time to replace the phone I'd deactivated before deployment. Not wanting to bother Cobb or invite another heartfelt good-bye, I had my ticket transferred to a morning flight, and I entered the concourse to find a secluded spot where I could stretch out and sleep. But I owed my sister, and maybe my parents, a phone call. So, I wandered over to the USO.

The airport USO was principally used as a gathering spot during pickup periods, when Marine recruits from around the country arrived in the middle of the night for boot-camp induction. Mercifully, the Recruit Depot was between cycles, and I had the small alcove to myself. An old man sat behind the volunteer desk, his arms crossed and his chin resting against his chest. He wore a Marine Corps ball cap and looked old enough for Korea.

Wondering if he was asleep, I approached him softly, my head down and tilted to the side.

"Need some help, young man?" he asked, wide-awake and perfectly still.

"Oh. Sorry for sneaking up on you, sir," I said, taken off guard. "Just wondering if there's a phone I could use?"

"Over here." He nodded, stood up, and gestured for me to follow as he shuffled on short legs over to a table piled high with beat-up cell phones. They looked donated. He grabbed one and stared up at me, apparently waiting for a number.

"Sir, I can dial the phone myself. I'm just looking to make a quick call."

He shook his head. "No, no. You have to mash a special code. Better let me."

"One second." I dropped my bag, unable to remember my sister's phone number offhand. I knew I had it in an address book at the bottom of my duffel, but I didn't want to dump the whole thing and root through my underwear in the middle of the USO to find it. My parents' home phone number, the first I'd ever memorized, came to the front of my mind.

"Dial area code two zero five . . ." I watched his odd, stubby fingers at work.

"Okay. Two zero five . . . and?"

"You know what, sir"—I picked up my duffel—"I really appreciate it, but on second thought I'd rather not disturb them."

"Your folks?"

"Yes, sir. It's a few hours later there."

"You sure? Bet your mother wants to hear from you."

"I'm sure. But I appreciate your help, sir." I turned to leave.

He stopped me. "Where you coming from?"

"Pendleton."

"Not what I mean," he said with a knowing grin. "Where you coming home from?"

"Iraq." After a moment's hesitation I added, "Recently returned from Iraq, sir," in an attempt to make it sound routine. Nothing out of the ordinary.

"Well then, welcome back."

He offered me his hand and I shook it, realizing for the first time why I'd noticed his stubby fingers. They weren't just odd; they were absent. Save for his thumbs, most of his fingers were missing beyond the first knuckle.

He caught me looking down at them. "Chosin Reservoir. A hundred thousand screaming Chinese couldn't touch me, but that cold, boy . . ." He chuckled and shook his head. "That cold was one mean bitch. Ate my fingers right up. Lucky to have what I kept. I'm Tippet, by the way."

"Oh. Pleasure to meet you. Peter."

"Well. All right then, Peter," he said with an air of inevitability. "Let's go get us a beer."

He waved his arm toward the sports bar across the way and indicated that I should follow as he ambled out into the concourse.

I scrambled after him, trying to decline. "I appreciate it, sir. But really, no thanks. I'll just find a patch of carpet where I can rack out for the night."

"Well, that's horseshit," he said simply. "You're drinking a beer with me, Peter. I got an ugly wife at home and it's quitting time."

"Again. Sir. I appreciate it." But then I realized that we were already at the bar. Tippet had covered the distance with surprising speed using his awkward but determined shuffle.

He called out to a waiter and pointed at the nearest tap with the nub of his index finger. "Two of these, Mark," he said, hardly taking note of the brand he'd selected.

I surrendered. "Just one beer, sir."

Tippet laughed. "Call me sir one more time and you'll eat your teeth."

"Okay. Thank you, Tippet. Just one, though."

"You're a lieutenant, right?"

"Until a few hours ago, yes. How'd you guess?"

"Not a guess. You got the stink on you, son. Hard to miss. More important, though, is that the lieutenant doesn't skip out after the first round. You got the next one. So that's two, at least."

We found an empty four-top in the corner and sat down as our first beers arrived. A pint glass for me and a mug for Tippet. He slipped his mitt inside the handle and locked his thumb around the top, well-practiced.

"To our Corps," he said, lifting the glass.

"To our Corps." I let the first sip dance across my lips. The alcohol bit into my tongue. Beer tasted so much better than I remembered.

We completed the first round inside of five minutes, and much to Tippet's approval I ordered a second round without hesitation.

"Sure aren't putting up much of a fight, are you, Lieutenant?" He laughed.

"First beer in a while. Might as well enjoy it, right?"

"Damn straight. You've earned it."

The second round arrived in the same configuration. A pint glass for me and a mug for Tippet. I watched him wrap his truncated fingers around the glass, and I knew for certain that I hadn't earned a goddamn thing. But by the end of the third round, I didn't care. The beer in front of me had ceased to be about what I'd earned, or what I deserved. It was about the weight of my eyelids, the numbness in my legs, and how it was all starting to feel so much better.

"You got a young lady waiting for you, Lieutenant?" Tippet asked as we each finished our fifth.

"Not presently." I searched for feeling in my cheeks.

"Hell! Let's get you one." Tippet stood and disappeared into the suddenly crowded bar. I didn't follow him, but it didn't matter. He returned to our table when I was already halfway into my sixth, flanked by two young women.

They were tall brunettes, both about my age, and each with a glass of white wine in hand. They wore heels, perfectly pressed slacks, and silk blouses. They smiled, apparently taken in by Tippet's charm, and they looked down at me showing what seemed like a fifty-foot wall of white teeth.

"This is the young man I was telling you about. This is my friend Pete, just home from Iraq. And, boy, wouldn't a few minutes of your company cheer him right up."

"Oh, wow," one of them said, pressing her wineglass against her cheek.

"That is really just so amazing," the other said. "Thank you for your service." She held out her hand in a strange way. I wasn't sure whether she wanted me to kiss it or shake it. In my growing stupor, I pulled her hand toward me and pressed it against my forehead.

"Ha! Hey now, Pete." She laughed. "Had a few?"

"A gentleman stands," I heard Tippet say in a stern tone. "A gentleman stands, Lieutenant."

I let go of the brunette's hand and pulled myself up, out of what had become an impossibly comfortable chair.

The brunettes introduced themselves, but I couldn't process their names. They reminded me of girls I'd known in college. Perfect and put together. They'd both be married any minute, and the conversation we were about to have would become a story at cocktail parties. They'd stand next to their husbands and tell the story of the Iraq vet they once met. How he was drunk beyond belief in the airport.

The nausea crept into my mouth. My tongue swelled, and the brunettes laughed at something Tippet said.

"I'm sorry." I pushed between them, dragging my duffel by its strap. "I'm sorry."

I searched for some place, in lieu of a bathroom, where I could throw up without attracting too much attention. A trash can. A janitor's cart. The nausea abated slightly as I careened through the concourse, and it occurred to me that I might just need some air.

The concourse exit materialized in front of me. Beyond it, I knew, was a door to the outside, to the cool San Diego night, and to the ocean air wafting from the bay across the street.

I doubled my pace, kept a straight line, and managed to leave the terminal without vomiting. I crossed the street and moved toward the smell of ocean air until I found a empty bench next to the bay. The world spun out of control, and I passed out with my head resting on my duffel.

I woke as the sun rose and rolled over to find a bay full of sailboats. A few were on their way out to sea, showing all canvas and heeling slightly with a westerly wind. Free.

A gentleman stands, I thought.

Sitting in my car, on the side of a Dallas cul-de-sac, I think about my father. We could talk about nothing at all and I'd be grateful for it. We could talk about football. He could tell me how many bales he cut from the fields. Square bales or round bales. I could play with my nephew and give my brother-in-law a firm handshake.

I don't deserve all that, but I want to. And I certainly don't deserve Paige, but I take out my phone and dial her anyway.

She answers on the first ring.

Zahn—Thanks for the heads-up about the lieutenant. I checked in on him and he seems fine. He's an idiot, of course . . . But he's good to go.

So it's okay that I come visit? What if I feel like staying for a while? I need a change in scenery, if you got a place for me. —Doc

FLOORBOARDS

I stayed at the lieutenant's place for about a week. I lost my job, but no harm done. I got enough money saved to live without a problem for about six months, I think.

The lieutenant talked to me about his visit with Sergeant Gomez and her sister, and he kept apologizing. I told him to stop. Then he asked if I had a way to get in touch with Dodge, and I lied. Told him I had no idea.

Dodge's gone dark, anyway. He hasn't replied in a week and seems less and less interested in catching up. He doesn't even mention his visa anymore. Just news from Tunisia. I can't follow everything he's talking about, but I still liked hearing from him.

The lieutenant also told me about some of Zahn's troubles. Like he was telling me about a Marine in the platoon with bad foot rot, and implying I should go take a look. Maybe offer some antifungal cream and give a quick class on the importance of changing your socks. Like he thinks I'm his corpsman again, or like he wants me to be.

Then he introduced me to this pretty college girl I think he's dating, and she seemed nice. I used my truck to help them move this wreck of an old sailboat into a covered workspace near the harbor. She reminded me of Gomez a little bit, with her hair tied back in braids and covered with a red bandanna. While we maneuvered the sailboat into place, she offered me all kinds of advice about Lizzy.

Said I ought to drop in on her just to clear the air. The lieutenant said the same thing. But I told them it would have to wait. Some other time. I had to get back down to Houma to see my dad.

I'm in my bedroom now, packing. It's a haul up to Missouri to see Zahn, and there's no coming back if I forget something, so I'm making sure I have everything I need for a long visit. My dad's out in the hallway, right outside my door. I can feel him there, thinking about whether to knock. He's pulling out all the air, just by standing there. The room is shrinking. I feel the door straining at the hinges, ready to break into a thousand splinters.

He walks away, and the floorboards talk about it as he passes.

He goes out to the porch, and as the screen door bounces shut, I feel the house tilt in his direction. This is a house full of gossiping ghosts and I'm fucking tired of it.

He walks out across the lawn, out to the shed to work on his tractor. It's too cold for that nonsense, too late at night, and for some reason I finally have it in mind to tell him so. So I march outside. I'm halfway to the shed before I notice the trauma bag in my right hand.

I drop the bag, leave it where it is, and wander over to the oak tree to have a quiet sit. The lights are on in the shed, and I listen to my dad work. A little after midnight he comes out, wipes his hands on his pants, and starts toward the house. He stops when he sees me and squints to make sure. He waves, stiff and awkward, before walking up and standing over me with his hands on his hips and his dark eyebrows furrowed. He doesn't say anything.

"Wanted to make sure you were okay," I tell him after a minute.

"I'm fine, Les." He sits down and puts his hand on my shoulder. He inhales deep and holds it, like he's gonna say something. But he doesn't. He just lets it out and sits there with me.

"He stayed on the ground for six hours, Dad," I say after a while. "He laid there, and no one could get to him. They had to call in another team and use line charges to clear a lane twenty meters wide. Bombs everywhere."

After a while, sitting there in the quiet, I tell him the rest.

"Stout. He rolled over. Everyone says I imagined it, but I saw it. He was probably conscious. Knowing it was bad, but thinking I was on my way, even. Thinking he might pass out for a minute, but that I'd get there. Put tourniquets on his arms and legs. He died thinking he'd wake up in Germany. But he didn't. Just bled to death, right there on that hot fucking asphalt, too. Not even in the dirt. Just a stain."

That's all I tell him. We sit there for a while longer, and the whole time he has his hand on my shoulder. He doesn't ask me any questions. He doesn't say a word.

But Huck cannot go home. He has grown to prefer freedom to what is right. "I reckon I got to light out for the Territory ahead of the rest," he says, "because Aunt Sally she's going to adopt me and sivilize me, and I can't stand it. I been there before."

FEW PEOPLE ARE SO LUCKY

"**O**ur revolution is your revolution!" I shout this into the camera. "We must all come home to this!"

Behind me, my flatmates and their new girlfriends cheer for me each time I raise my voice, even when they do not know what I am saying. Will it never stop, this absurd trust in me?

"Look behind me at all of these people," I tell the camera. "They have all made the decision to die in these streets with their friends and countrymen before they spend one more night in houses, alone and scared."

The light is too bright. I cannot see who is behind the camera filming me. An English journalist was asking me questions before, but I think he has gone. Or maybe he is letting me talk without interruption. Foolish of him, if so.

"Do you understand what started all of this?" I ask the invisible reporter. "Do you understand what happened in Sidi Bouzid? A young man named Mohamed was selling fruit he had procured on credit. He had a wife and children, and only a simple fruit cart to support them.

"A policewoman. She confiscated his cart on a false charge, and with this one act of corruption made Mohamed and his family destitute. But she did not stop with this. When he pleaded for his cart, she slapped his face and spat upon him. There was no purpose in this, no profit but to see him humiliated. Only to show him that she and President Ben Ali were strong and that he was poor, frail, and weak.

"What was this man, Mohamed, to do? Go home? Accept shame and poverty? Watch his children grow painfully hungry? Was he to strike this policewoman with all his rage and have some measure of violent revenge before they took him to a dungeon without trial? If he had done any of these things, the common people you see here would never have heard of him. They would never have come to this square to stake their lives on this revolution.

"No. He did something far more brave. He fought back not with his strength, but with his frailty. He went to the police station, doused himself in paint thinner, and set his flesh ablaze. He burned himself, right before the policewoman's eyes, to show her just how frail he was.

"And he survived for a time in hospital. The wounds did not take Mohamed until this morning, and in a great mercy from God, he lived long enough to see his countrymen filling these streets because of what he did. Not because we admire his strength, but because we share his weakness and his frailty. We are united by it."

I stop speaking to catch my breath. I feel my friends pressing against my back, cheering even louder than before.

"And I made this decision, too," I continue. "To die in these streets if necessary, though I am not Tunisian. Did I tell you that? Also, I am not Syrian, though my passport says that I am. And I am not Iraqi . . ."

I stop and take a final, deep breath before finishing this thought.

"I am weak. And that is all. But I am not without a home. To be weak? To be scared and frail? This is to have a home. These people behind me are all very weak and all very scared. We are so easy to kill. President Ben Ali has made certain that we are all reminded of this. But to die here? Outside where it is cold? This would be to die at home. And few people are so lucky as to die at home."

Finally, after a long time, I stop talking.

The English journalist, hidden behind his bright lights, speaks. "President Ben Ali claims he will send the army into Tunisia's cities tomorrow if the crowds have not dispersed. Will you stay here even if the army comes?"

"Of course." I laugh. "Where else would I go?"

The crowd shifts again, running from some danger. The cameras disappear from me. There is something more interesting to film now. Perhaps some violence. I see the camera light pushing through the protest camp before I am pulled away by my flatmates. They drag me into a side alley and push me down behind a Dumpster.

We hide through the night, taking turns with the watching and sleeping, wondering if we will all die before we see the sun again.

I fall asleep sometime before the dawn and am awakened by a satellite phone being shoved into my hand.

"Now is the time," a flatmate tells me. "The Army did not come. They refused their orders. Ben Ali is finished. Call your American friend. Read him the letter."

The number has been dialed into the phone for days, waiting for me to gather enough courage. My friends are right. This is the time. I must call.

I press a finger into one ear to muffle the noise of celebration and wait for an answer.

A confused, familiar voice speaks to me. "Hello?"

I swallow my fear. "Lester?"

"No, you've reached Pete. I think you must have the wrong . . . wait. *Who* is this?"

"This is Kateb. I am calling for the Doc. Can you get him?"

There is a long silence.

"I can barely hear you. Say again? Who is this?"

Then I recognize the voice. *"Mulasim."*

"Dodge?" he says into the dirty connection. "Wait. Who is this, really? This isn't someone messing with me, right?"

"Please, *Mulasim*. Please hurry to get a pen and paper. I have something to read. You must write this down."

I pull a wadded page from the front pocket of my jeans, ready to begin.

ACKNOWLEDGMENTS

The characters in this story are fictional, but their battles are real. Among the thousands of Iraqis and Americans who lived through the war in Anbar Province, there are a few to whom I owe an inexpressible debt: Gunnery Sergeants Anderson and Priester, who were mercifully patient with their young lieutenant; Sergeants Bouttavong, McBride, Dixon, and Alviderez, whose gifted leadership humbled me daily; Jack Dietrich, Autumn Swinford, Joslyn Hemler, Rachel Forrest, Steve Ekdahl, John Sorenson, Brad Aughinbaugh, Eric Beckmann, and Ed Donahoo, who have honored me with their friendship; Jaguar, whose real name I never knew, but whose courage defies description; Colonel James Caley, who taught me the imperative of disciplined thinking; and all those Iraqis who risked everything for a chance at a free society, and a life at peace. A generation of Marines will grow old wishing we'd done better for you.

Space permitting, I'd acknowledge dozens more by name. But you know who you are. You're never far from my thoughts.

By dumb luck, I stumbled into a community of writers when I settled in New Orleans. I never would've finished this book without the help and encouragement of early readers such as Nicholas Mainieri, Rush Carskadden, Brock Stoneham, David Hoover, John Van Lue, David Parker, and Cullen Piske.

Rob McQuilkin, thank you for taking a chance on me. Kathy Belden, you protected me, and gave me what I needed to finish this story. I'll always be grateful.

Truly special thanks go to Joseph and Amanda Boyden, who are quietly raising the next generation of New Orleans authors. Amanda, sharing my manuscript was only the most visible of your countless acts of generosity. Joseph, your modesty, fortitude, wit and spirit enrich the lives of all those around you. I treasure our friendship.

I have a remarkable family, with siblings who are my best friends, and parents who indulged our every daft scheme. Mom and Dad, your children built their lives on the unconscious assumption that all things are possible. My older brother, Brian, and my little sister, Julie, growing up wedged between the two of you made me who I am.

Above all, credit goes to my wife, Erin, who is ultimately responsible for whatever good can be found in these pages, and in me. My life orbits twin mysteries: What compelled you to take in the foul, wreck of a man you found, and how, in all the days that remain to me, I could ever repay you. I love you so much.